Advance praise for *Alex Marcoux's*
Back to Salem

"Alex Marcoux has created a metaphysical mystery that informs, entertains, and makes me want to go have a past-life regression. Her work is well crafted, interweaving past and present with flawless detail. You'll find yourself in Salem during the horrific witch-hunts of the 1690s, as well as in the present-day cut-throat film industry. This gender-bending thriller is reminiscent of Kenneth Branagh's *Dead Again*, but with more highly developed characters. Marcoux is an exceptional new talent that definitely should be read in *this* lifetime."

–Paul J. Willis, Executive Director, Lambda Literary Foundation

"Engrossing, imaginative . . . a thought-provoking journey from contemporary Los Angeles to colonial New England as her two heroines–a novelist/screenwriter and a singer/songwriter–explore their connections, the sources of their creativity, karmic disruptions, and mysterious deaths . . . leading up to a nail-biting, thoroughly satisfying finale."

–Suzanne Proulx, author of *Bad Blood; Bad Luck;* and *Bad Medicine*

"Refreshing, full of unexpected twists . . . guaranteed to keep you guessing until the very end. Marcoux peers into the complexities of the human psyche, probing the hidden recesses of the mind, showing how our lives are interwoven in ways we may not be consciously aware of, and how love can last throughout the ages. Filled with intrigue and secret passions."

–Sherry L. Stinson, editor, *www.outlookpress.com*

"A winner! Alex Marcoux has outdone herself as she weaves a tale within a tale of cruel injustices done to two destined lovers. Captivating . . . the insight into the souls of the lost lovers tore at my heart."

–Agatha Tutko, handwriting analyst; author of Instant Insights

"A dramatically written mystery and romance novel . . . suspenseful, captivating, fast paced and heartwarming for all readers of all lifestyles!"

–Sharon Wetter, MBA, business owner, New Jersey

Back to Salem

Alice Street Editions

Judith P. Stelboum
Editor-in-Chief

Back to Salem, by Alex Marcoux

Egret, by Helen Collins

To the Edge, by Cameron Abbott

From Flitch to Ash: A Musing on Trees and Carving,
   by Diane Derrick

Treat, by Angie Vicars

Yin Fire, by Alexandra Grilikhes

*His Hands, His Tools, His Sex, His Dress: Lesbian
   Writers on Their Fathers*, by Catherine Reid
   and Holly K. Iglesias

Weeding at Dawn: A Lesbian Country Life,
   by Hawk Madrone

Façades, by Alex Marcoux

Inside Out, by Juliet Carrera

Past Perfect, by Judith P. Stelboum

Forthcoming

Your Loving Arms, by Gwendolyn Bikis

*A Donor Insemination Guide: Written By and For Lesbian
   Women*, by Marie Mohler, MA, and Lacy Frazer, PsyD

Extraordinary Couples, Ordinary Lives,
   by Lynn Haley-Banez and Joanne Garrett

Foreword

Alice Street Editions provides a voice for established as well as up-coming lesbian writers, reflecting the diversity of lesbian interests, ethnicities, ages and class. This cutting edge series of novels, memoirs, and non-fiction writing welcomes the opportunity to present controversial views, explore multicultural ideas, encourage debate, and inspire creativity from a variety of lesbian perspectives. Through enlightening, illuminating and provocative writing, Alice Street editions can make a significant contribution to the visibility and accessibility of lesbian writing, and bring lesbian-focused writing to a wider audience. Recognizing our own desires and ideas in print is life sustaining, acknowledging the reality of who we are, our place in the world, individually and collectively.

Judith P. Stelboum
Editor-in-Chief
Alice Street Editions

This is a work of fiction. No reference to actual persons, places, or incidents is implied or should be inferred.

Published by

Alice Street Editions, Harrington Park Press®, an imprint of The Haworth Press, Inc., 10 Alice Street, Binghamton, NY 13904-1580 USA (www.HaworthPress.com).

Cover design by Sherry Stinson, The Printed Image

Library of Congress Cataloging-in-Publication Data

Marcoux, Alex.
 Back to Salem / Alex Marcoux.
  p. cm.
 ISBN 1-56023-224-2 (alk. paper)-ISBN 1-56023-225-0 (pbk. : alk. paper)
  1. Women novelists–Fiction. 2. Trials (Witchcraft)–Fiction. 3. Reincarnation–Fiction. 4. Salem (Mass.)–Fiction. 5. Lesbians–Fiction. I. Title.
PS3563.A6365 B34 2001
813'.6-dc21
                        2001041345

Back to Salem

Alex Marcoux

Alice Street Editions

Harrington Park Press
New York • London • Oxford

Acknowledgments

My special thanks to Paula Vaughan for the discussions and friendship; Janet Nelson for rafting the Colorado River with me; Outdoors Unlimited's staff who put up with my questions as we journeyed through the Grand Canyon. I am grateful to the WayShowers, my psychic friends who continue to inspire me; Lynn for planting the seed and Natalie for nurturing it; Liz Goodenough for sharing her experience. Much appreciation goes to Lady Sabrina and her book, *Secrets of Modern Witchcraft Revealed*, and the St. Barnabas congregation members who continue to be supportive. Thanks to everyone at The Haworth Press including Helen Mallon, Julie Ehlers, and Judith Stelboum; a special thanks to my editor, Nancy Deisroth, for her talents and our conversations. Much gratitude goes to my son, Preston, and Susan, for their patience, understanding and love.

Each soul has its own journey,
a trek simply unique.
We all continue searching,
love and respect we seek.

This book is dedicated to all those who strive to be themselves,
but are persecuted because of it.

In Essex County of Massachusetts, 1692, over 150 men and women–along with a four-year-old girl–were arrested. This was the foundation of one of the most hideous chapters in American history, the Salem witch trials. At least four people died in prison, one man was crushed to death, and 19 were executed, all because they were suspected of practicing witchcraft. Witchcraft is one of the oldest religions, surviving centuries of persecution.

AM

Chapter 1

At first, it was so faint, it was barely noticeable, and then the soft whispers intensified. As the noise built, so did the fidgeting. Elbow-to-elbow they sat on the hard wooden pews, waiting calmly, and then they became restless. The pews of the tiny Salem Town courthouse were filled to capacity and the rear walls were lined with men and women waiting for the ruling. The September sun filtered through the windows, elevating the temperature of the courtroom, contributing to their discomfort.

Rebecca Johnson, the accused, sat in front of the room, her eyes fixed on the wooden floor beneath her feet. A white bonnet harnessed her long dark hair. Her blue dress was offset with a white collar and apron, matching the head covering.

A court officer stood silently near Rebecca, pike in hand, guarding his prisoner. Beads of sweat trickled from beneath his armored helmet.

Although Rebecca sat alone, she felt the presence of her beloved husband sitting directly behind her.

The rear door of the meeting room creaked opened, jury members paraded to the front of the courtroom and sat at the vacant benches adjacent to the accused. None of the men looked at Rebecca.

Chief Justice Stoughton entered the courtroom and Daniel Johnson could feel his pulse start to race. Everyone in the room rose to greet the magistrate and Daniel stood taller than most. Beside Daniel was John, his closest friend and comrade. Daniel could feel the palms of his hands sweat and perspiration glistened on his forehead and temples.

How could this be happening to us? Daniel asked himself. He stared at the back of his wife, needing to make eye contact.

As if hearing him, Rebecca turned, her big blue eyes meeting her husband's brown eyes. She smiled at him, reflecting her outward beauty and touching Daniel's soul as she always could. No fear registered in her eyes. Although her full lips were silent, with her mind she spoke to her husband. *"I love you Daniel. It'll be okay. Just remember–I'll always love you."*

Daniel smiled at his wife, but she recognized the concern in his eyes.

A court officer moved to Rebecca and placed his hand on her shoulder, directing her attention away from Daniel to the judge. Stoughton sat at his high bench. A black cauldron sat on the side of the large desk, while a tapestry hung from the front of the furniture, revealing the king's crown.

"Everyone may be seated," the magistrate instructed. As Rebecca sat, Stoughton said, "Not you Goodwife Johnson. Remain standing." Then Stoughton turned toward the jury members. "Has the jury reached a verdict?"

A man from the jury stood. "Yes."

Daniel could feel his heart beat harder and faster as he anxiously awaited the fate bestowed upon their lives.

"We find Goodwife Johnson . . ." The foreman turned to look at Rebecca, but when her innocent eyes returned the stare, he quickly averted his eyes. "Guilty."

"No," Daniel shouted.

The court officer quickly moved to Daniel and attempted to seat him, but Daniel resisted. His friend, John, also had his arms around him trying to control him.

"Goodman Johnson, I will have you removed from the courtroom if you do not sit quietly," Stoughton threatened.

It was Rebecca who finally was able to calm him. She turned and offered him a smile, "Daniel, I'm fine."

Daniel's eyes met his wife's. He could not help but admire her courage and strength. His resistance disappeared and he sat quietly, maintaining his eye connection with his wife.

Immediately the guard moved to Rebecca forcing her to face the judge, breaking her visual connection with her husband.

Stoughton turned to the jury foreman. "Thank you, you may sit."

"Rebecca Johnson," the judge began, "the Court of Oyer and Terminer has heard and determined that you are guilty of witchcraft. This abomination is punishable by death. On September 22–you will be hanged by the neck until dead, and may the Lord have mercy on your soul."

Daniel's temples started to pound and his vision became distorted. Everything seemed to move in slow motion. He was aware that John's arm was around his shoulders and he wondered if it was there for comfort or to control a disruption. Tears formed in Daniel's eyes as he watched the officer slowly move to Rebecca's side, to remove her from the courtroom. Daniel approached her but was stopped by another officer and when he pushed past the man, another officer stopped him. Within seconds, the courtroom was in chaos and Daniel desperately fought to reach his wife. His focus to connect with Rebecca was not broken, even when he took a blow to his head and fell to the floor. Quickly Daniel stood, blood streaming from his forehead, but now he could see Rebecca and she saw him.

John broke into the chaotic circle of confusion. "For the love of God, let them say goodbye," he shouted.

The opposition weakened long enough for Daniel to approach Rebecca and embrace her. Both remained silent as they clung to each other. Then the outsiders pulled them apart, trying to sever their connection. Rebecca's and Daniel's eyes remained fixed on each other, connected, as the sheriff pulled Rebecca to the door.

Although Rebecca's lips did not move, Daniel clearly heard her voice in his head. *"We'll be together, again. Next time. I promise. It'll be the same."*

The door closed between them and Daniel felt his heart race. He screamed, "Rebecca." The courtroom blurred and the light dissipated until there was no more light.

* * *

"Rebecca," Jessie cried out in her sleep. Abruptly she sat up; her heart felt as if it was going to burst from her chest. She could feel the sweat on her palms, on her temples and beneath her long free-flowing hair. *My God. It was just a dream*, she thought. She glanced at Ellen lying beside her, got out of bed and went into the bathroom. At the sink, she studied her reflection in the mirror. A full moon provided her with enough light to notice the glistening sweat on her temples. She ran water over a facecloth, twisted it then raised the cloth to her face. Slowly she washed the sweat away as she studied her face in the mirror.

Three times. The same dream three times in two weeks. What the hell does it mean? Her heart was still beating faster than usual. She lifted her long hair and placed the cool wet cloth on the back of her neck.

Chapter 2

The following morning Jessie and Ellen were awakened by the sound of music from the alarm at 6:00 A.M. "Good Morning LA, rise and shine," the deejay sang. "We're going into a 30-minute music set starting with a new one from one of LA's hometown girls–Taylor Andrews."

Rather than getting out of bed, Jessie lay still trying to recall her dream from hours earlier. Halfway through the song, she found herself drawn to the lyrics. She couldn't understand all the words, but there was one phrase she found interesting. "We'll be together, again. Next time. I promise. It'll be the same."

"Good morning," Jessie spoke softly to Ellen.

"Morning," Ellen groaned. "Why do you get up so early? You work out of your home."

"I like getting up early," Jessie answered. She leaned over and kissed Ellen. "What time do you have to leave?"

"By nine thirty."

"I'll wake you in a couple of hours," Jessie said.

In her kitchen, Jessie made a pot of coffee then turned her attention to Maxwell, her cat, who was rubbing against her legs.

"Good morning Maxwell. How'd you sleep?" She picked up the black cat, who purred at the attention.

When her coffee was finished brewing, she poured herself a cup and moved into her study. Cherry bookshelves, filled nearly to capacity, lined the walls. A large cherry desk centered the room, accompanied by a desk chair and a soft chair. Jessie sat in the desk chair and gazed out the windows that viewed a distant Los Angeles from her elevated location. Even at this hour, traffic lights could be seen overwhelming the highways that approached the city.

Jessie pulled an old journal from the desk drawer and turned the coffee-soiled pages until she found an empty page. She started writing in her journal, but was interrupted.

"Who's Rebecca?" Ellen asked softly. She stood at the entry of the study.

"Who's who?" Jessie's large brown eyes looked up, surprised.

"Rebecca. Who's Rebecca?"

Jessie shook her head; her long sandy brown bangs fell, covering one eye. "I don't know. Come in and take a seat." She tucked her bangs behind an ear then gestured toward the soft chair in the study.

Ellen sat. She fingered her shoulder-length blond hair away from her eyes revealing her pretty face. "Who's Rebecca?"

"Ellen, I don't know a Rebecca."

"You sure did last night."

"Last night?"

"You kept screaming her name in your sleep."

"Really, about what time?"

"It was right before you got up and went to the bathroom."

"Really?" *Rebecca?* Jessie thought. *Yeah . . . that feels right.* She went back to her journal and wrote "*R-E-B-E-C-C-A.*"

"Is there something you want to tell me?"

Jessie looked at her friend and hesitated. "I've been having a recurring dream over the last couple of weeks." She lifted her dream journal.

"How many times?"

"Last night was the third time."

"Always the same?"

"Pretty close. Except they're getting a little longer and more detailed."

"Tell me about it."

"In the dream I'm a man. I'm in a crowded courtroom and either my wife or girlfriend, someone I care very much for, is convicted of witchcraft and sentenced to be executed."

"Witchcraft?"

"Yes, witchcraft."

"What does it mean?"

"I'm not sure. I keep pulling the symbols out of it–but it doesn't make any sense. I remember the floor was wooden with gaps between the boards, like an old floor. Usually floors represent our foundation."

"What other symbols?"

"There was a judge and jury, the costumes and crown . . ."

"Crown?"

"On the judge's desk, there was a cloth that hung in front of the desk and there was a crown on it."

"That sounds like a good thing. What about the costumes?"

"Everyone was dressed in clothing from another time. The court officers carried pikes; you know those long-shafted spears. The women wore bonnets to hold back their hair."

"Did anything from this dream reflect the 20th or 21st century? Or was everything from another period?"

Jessie thought for a minute. "There was a man who sat next to me. I don't know what it is . . . he seemed familiar, but I just can't place him. Other than that–nothing was familiar to me."

"Did you ever consider that you had a past-life dream?" Ellen asked.

"I wondered about that. But I've read that past-life dreams occur when you run into the same problem you've had in another lifetime. What could this relate to?"

"Maybe you haven't run into the problem yet."

"Well, that makes me feel better!" Jessie smiled.

"Could it have anything to do with the novel you're working on?" Ellen asked.

"I can't see how. It's a suspense mystery involving two women in the music business."

"How about some of your other work?"

Jessie thought for a moment, her head turned toward the computer on her desk. Then she studied the shelves that were lined with books she had used to research the twenty novels to her credit. She shook her head. "None of it fits."

Ellen changed the subject. "How's your book coming?"

"Pretty good. I'm in the final editing stage. I'm hoping to finish within a month or so."

"What are you calling it?"

"*Deceptions.*"

"Do you think this has a chance of getting to the big screen like *Beyond Paradise*?"

"Travis Sanders has already asked me for the manuscript. I think the story is good enough to attract a large crossover market. That's what we need."

"What do you mean?"

"*Beyond Paradise* was a more traditional suspense thriller where there's a hero and heroine. But *Deceptions* has a couple of *heroines*, which breaks one of the ten commandments of mystery writing. Before Sanders will agree to make a movie out of it, the story has to be good enough to attract a straight audience, not just a gay and lesbian audience."

Ellen changed the subject. "What are you doing today? Do you want to get together for dinner?"

"I have some errands to run, then I plan on working on *Deceptions* tonight. Want to get together tomorrow for dinner?"

"Sure. Let's go out to Randolph's; I'm in the mood for a steak."

Later that morning, Jessie left in her silver Lexus. She headed away from her neighborhood, which was in the San Gabriel foothills. As she drove down the winding road, she turned on her stereo. A vaguely familiar tune caught her attention and she struggled, trying to place the voice of the singer. Then she remembered. *Oh. This is that new one from Taylor Andrews.* She turned the volume up so she could hear the words a little clearer. Jessie never cared for the artist's music. *I never can understand her lyrics,* she thought as she concentrated. But there was one phrase that got

Jessie's attention, "We'll be together, again. Next time. I promise. It'll be the same."

That's the same phrase that was in my dream last night, Jessie realized. *What a coincidence.*

After going to the post office and the bank, Jessie stopped in at the grocery store to pick up a few things. As Jessie waited in the checkout line, she found herself drawn to the magazines on the rack near the cashier. Within seconds, her eyes fell upon the latest issue of *People* magazine. The cover page caption was *"Divas–The In and the Out."* Pictures of female singers were plastered over the front of the magazine. Jessie was not surprised when her eyes fell upon Taylor Andrews. *Is she in or out?* she wondered. Jessie picked up the magazine and placed it in her basket.

Jessie's home was nestled in an exclusive upper-middle-class neighborhood on the outskirts of Los Angeles County. Although her house was one of the smaller, more modest homes in the neighborhood, her view of the city and ocean was one of the most breathtaking in the area. The contemporary house was going on five years old.

At 38 years of age, Jessica Mercer knew she was lucky to be able to afford such a lifestyle. But it wasn't her twenty novels that had provided her with these comforts, rather, it was the screenplay of *Beyond Paradise* that put her in the big league. When Travis Sanders approached her about doing the screenplay of her novel, she never realized how much her life would change. After the screenplay was written and the movie produced, it earned an Oscar for Best Picture. Now she was not only respected as a novelist, but was also viewed as a talented screenwriter.

When Jessie finally returned home that afternoon she made a fresh pot of coffee to prepare for a long work session. As the coffee brewed, she toured her home looking for Maxwell. She found him asleep on the couch in the great room. "Want some dinner?" she asked.

Maxwell started to purr at the suggestion. The black cat stretched his neck allowing Jessie's long fingers to scratch under his chin. Beside Maxwell was the remote control to the television. Jessie glanced at her watch. *I wonder who's on Oprah today.* She flicked the remote and the television came on, and then she searched for the talk show. Jessie retreated to the kitchen where she poured the cat food and as she lowered Maxwell's dinner to the floor, she heard the familiar tune. She returned to the sunken great room. Taylor Andrews was performing.

This woman really gets around. Jessie sat on a soft chair. As Taylor Andrews performed the song, Jessie struggled to understand the lyrics, catching a word here and there. Taylor sang confidently looking into the eye of the camera. Her clear blue eyes seemed to dance as she sang. The long dark hair fell naturally past her shoulders contrasting with the feminine white suit that complimented her figure. Jessie studied the entertainer's style. The audience was genuinely pleased. After her performance, there was a brief discussion with Oprah. *When have I seen her perform before?* Jessie wondered as she studied the familiar eyes. *I've got to get some work done,* she lectured. She turned off the television.

Around midnight Jessie decided to call it an evening and turned off her computer. She had progressed with her project, and realized she was further along than she had thought. As she climbed into bed, she could not help thinking about *Deceptions,* and her next steps. Soon her thoughts drifted into a dream.

* * *

Daniel Johnson sat alone in the empty courtroom. He was distressed. The tiny room was very warm as the sun filtered through the small windows. But physical discomfort was not what tormented him. His wife was not next to him, and he felt a void in his heart that he could not explain.

Chief Justice Stoughton entered the courtroom and moved to his bench. He sat high above Daniel and appeared not to notice him.

Daniel stood and moved to the judge's bench. "Why?" Daniel asked.

"Why what?"

"Why have you taken away the only thing I care about?"

But the judge seemed to ignore the question, intensifying Daniel's anguish.

"What has she done that is so wrong?" Daniel's voice continued to rise. "When can I see her again?"

Finally, the judge looked at Daniel. "I know it's not clear right now, but you will find the answers to all your questions in this." The judge stretched out his hand. In his palm, there was a tile-size picture. Daniel picked up the small piece of soft wood. The picture vividly portrayed a sun peeking over a mountaintop with a rainbow above the sun. The last color of the rainbow spectrum, purple, was lost in a purple sky. On both ends of the rainbow was an object. The rainbow appeared to be harnessed by a large caldron that sat on a lake in front of the mountain. The vivid colors ran vertically and arched over the sun disappearing in the clouds. The purple between the clouds formed a symbol in the sky, a large T cross with a loop above it.

As Daniel studied the strange picture, the large, rough hands that held the object transformed to smaller, feminine, soft hands. Then Daniel was gone.

"And this will give me my answers?" a softer voice asked.

Stoughton looked into the woman's eyes. "Yes, Jessie. You will find the answers to your questions in this."

* * *

The next morning, Jessie quickly went to work in her dream journal. She used colored pencils to portray the vivid colors of the picture in her dream. *I'll find the answers to my questions in this.* She stared at the picture. *What questions, though?*

As expected, Ellen showed up by seven o'clock that evening, and the women got into Ellen's Mustang to head out to Randolph's for dinner. The June evening was perfect and Ellen had the convertible top down, providing an enjoyable ride through the San Gabriel foothills.

"How was your day?" Jessie asked. She pulled her wind-blown hair away from her face.

"Pretty good. It's only the 12th of the month, and I've made my June quota," Ellen bragged. Ellen was a technical sales representative for Dell Computer.

"Congratulations."

"Thanks." Ellen turned on the stereo. Music filtered through the speakers amplifying the voice of Taylor Andrews' new hit.

What? Is this song following me around? Jessie wondered. Again, Jessie listened intently to the song. As the familiar phrase was sung, "We'll be together, again. Next time. I promise. It'll be the same," Jessie felt warmth in her chest. When the next song came on, Jessie recognized the voice, *It's Taylor Andrews.* "Is this a CD?" Jessie asked.

"Yeah, it's her new one. I got it yesterday."

"Do you have the CD jacket?"

"Check the glove compartment."

Jessie opened the compartment and searched for the CD cover. She found a group of CDs, pulled them out and looked through them. But none of them were by Taylor Andrews. "I don't see it."

Ellen peered over to the glove compartment as she approached a straightaway. "It doesn't look like most CD jackets. It's cardboard, not plastic," she said.

With this insight, Jessie eyed something that was cardboard and appeared to be the correct size. She pulled it from the glove compartment. Jessie felt a rush of warmth, and her heart skipped a beat as she stared at the object in her hand. The voice of the judge from her dream echoed in her head, *"You will find the answers to your questions in this."*

Jessie stared at the same unusual picture she had drawn in her dream journal that morning. *What the hell does this mean?* Every detail she recalled from her dream was perfect, the rainbow, the caldron, the mountain, and the sun rising. *Or maybe it's setting.* Every detail, except the clouds did not form the cross-like symbol. Then she turned the CD jacket over and there it was. The backdrop for the listed songs showed the familiar clouds with the cross-like image.

Ellen noticed that Jessie was quiet and seemed withdrawn. "Are you okay?" she asked, as she pulled the car into a parking spot at the restaurant.

Jessie did not respond.

"Jessie, where are you?" Ellen lightly pulled at Jessie's shirtsleeve.

"Sorry. We're here," Jessie noted. "Can I take this inside?" Jessie held up the CD jacket. "I want to read the lyrics of one of the songs."

"Sure."

By the time they were seated and drinks were ordered, Ellen knew something was different with Jessie. "What's wrong Jessie? You haven't said a word since you got out of the car."

Jessie seemed to look through Ellen. "How long have we known each other?"

"About 15 months."

"Do I strike you as being . . . ," Jessie searched for the word, "flighty?"

"What do you mean?"

"I'm not sure I know. Unusual? Strange? Unbalanced?"

"No. You're probably one of the more balanced and grounded individuals I know. Why are you asking?"

Jessie wondered if she should confide in her friend. "I had a dream last night."

"The recurring one?"

"Same characters, but a different scene. I was in court. It was after the trial. The judge was with me. He said I would find the answers to my questions in something. He handed me a small cardboard picture." Jessie pulled the CD from her purse. "He said I would find the answers to my questions in this."

Ellen smiled.

"You don't believe me."

"No, I do believe you. The judge said you would find your answers in Taylor Andrews' new CD, *Karmic Debt?*"

It was only then that Jessie heard the title of the CD. *Karmic Debt*. "No, he didn't actually say CD but I clearly saw the picture of this CD cover."

"When was the first time you saw the CD jacket?"

"This is the first time. I mean I can't discount the possibility that I may have seen it a couple months ago, somewhere, but I don't remember it."

"It was just released earlier this month. It sounds precognitive."

"What do you mean?"

"Precognition. Seeing something before it actually happens. I've told you many times that you're very psychic, Jessie. Maybe now you'll believe me."

"But what does it mean?"

"I don't know. You're the one that needs to figure it out."

"You don't sound freaked out or even surprised," Jessie mused.

"Jessie, the universe sends us signs everyday. You're just starting to listen to them. Do you have any other connections to Taylor Andrews?"

"No. I don't even like her music. I never can understand the words to her songs, never mind the meanings to them. Except . . ."

"Except what?"

"Over the last couple of days I keep hearing one of the songs on this CD."

"What do you mean?"

"I get in the car and it's playing; I turn on the TV and she's on *Oprah*. I wake up to the radio alarm playing her song."

"And you don't call those connections?"

"I call that coincidence," Jessie answered.

"And you know what I say about coincidence?"

"There's no such thing as a coincidence," the women chorused.

Jessie studied her friend admiringly. Although Ellen was ten years younger than herself, she seemed to have it all together, or certainly was more in control of her life than most.

Ellen continued, "Taylor Andrews' music has always been . . . before her time. Her songs are usually filled with metaphysics. That might be a sign right there."

"Any suggestions? About what I should do?" Jessie asked.

"Have you heard the entire CD?"

Jessie shook her head. "No."

"Then take it and listen to it."

Jessie opened the CD jacket and searched for the lyrics. But the lyrics had not been included with the CD. "The lyrics aren't here," she said disappointingly.

"I guess that means you'll have to listen to it."

Chapter 3

The next morning, Jessie was determined to listen to Taylor Andrews' CD in its entirety. She went to her great room, put the CD in the player and pressed "play." Jessie found that some of the songs were easier to understand, while others were more difficult. After listening to the CD a couple of times she still didn't understand the song that had been following her around.

What is the name of the song, she asked herself. Jessie turned over the CD. Her fingers followed the list of songs on the back of the CD to the number three slot. *"Daniel's Heart." What kind of a title is that?*

Later that afternoon she decided to get online and search for the lyrics to the CD. It didn't take her long before she found many websites that were run by fans as well as one that claimed to be "The Official Website of Taylor Andrews." Here she found the lyrics to *Karmic Debt*, and printed them off. But before she read the lyrics, she stared at a picture of Taylor Andrews on her computer screen. *Who does she remind me of? There's something vaguely familiar about her. What is it?* It didn't take long for her to realize what it was. *It's those eyes.*

She turned off her computer then turned to the paper in her printer bin. But before she removed the lyrics, the phone rang. "Hello, this is Jessie."

"Hi Jessie, this is Travis Sanders."

"Hi, Travis. How are you today?"

"I'm fine. How much longer for *Deceptions*?" he asked. Travis had a habit of getting right to the point.

"I'll finish the manuscript late next week, but it'll be a while before the publisher is finished with the galleys."

"I don't want to wait for the galleys. Can't you send me a manuscript? I know it's not in finished form."

"Yes. I can do that, Travis."

Jessie rested the phone in its cradle then smiled. *I remember a time when I begged movie producers and publishers to look at my work. How did I get so lucky?* She stared at the 400 pages titled *Deceptions* sitting on her desk, then felt a tinge of guilt. *I should be working.* Jessie looked at the paper still resting in the printer bin. *Taylor Andrews will have to wait.* She turned her attention to the manuscript and continued her editing.

Jessie knew that *Deceptions* was special right from its genesis. The story had come to her while meditating. Rather than writing it, however, she nurtured it in her mind for months developing her characters and plots until she had the story complete in her head. Her experience getting it on paper was easier than she had ever imagined. She never had writer's block, and in just four short months, her story was finished. This was her record. Ellen teased her that the book was spiritually inspired, and that she should list the spirits in the book's acknowledgments. Jessie was grateful for whatever helped her conceive and write the story.

She found it amusing that there was so much interest in this book and knew it was because of the success of *Beyond Paradise*. She had not given her agent, publisher, or Travis Sanders, much information on *Deceptions*. Yet, they all waited anxiously for the completion of the story. Jessie promised to deliver a suspense mystery involving the murder of a singer's husband. The singer's lesbian lover is later accused of the murder.

Jessie knew that *Deceptions* was a big step for her, and there were risks. She was finally writing about her own lifestyle, using her own name. Thirteen years earlier, Jessie's first book, a lesbian novel, was published using a pseudonym. After her third novel, she realized that she would never be recognized as a serious novelist and started writing suspense mysteries and thrillers using heterosexual characters rather than gay or lesbian characters. The response was phenomenal. She quickly attracted a serious agent and publisher. When her fourth novel was published, using her real name, reviewers endorsed her as a "fresh new voice."

Deceptions was a test. She knew the story was good, but still wondered if her followers were ready for lesbian heroines. Jessie knew that if she changed the gender of one of the main characters it would become a bestseller. She contemplated doing this on a number of occasions, but opted to stay loyal to her initial vision.

Around eight o'clock that evening Jessie broke from *Deceptions*. She picked up the paper in the printer's tray and brought it to the kitchen. Jessie zapped a TV dinner, sat at her kitchen counter and pulled the lyrics next to her to review them.

She thumbed through the pages until she came to "Daniel's Heart."

I'll never forget the day I lost my heart.
The tears, the pain, the rain.
I said, "We'll be together, again. Next time.
I promise. It will be the same."

Just because you didn't understand me
doesn't excuse the inference.
We're all the same on the inside,
can't you see beyond our difference?

But instead, you choose intolerance,
bigotry and hate.
Eventually, you try,
judge, and eradicate.

Just because you didn't understand me
doesn't justify the pain.
We're all the same on the inside,
I tell you, we're all the same.

Each soul has its own journey,

a trek simply unique.

We all continue searching,

love and respect we seek.

I'll never forget when you were torn from my arms.

It was the day the angels came.

After all this time, I promise,

next time, it won't be the same.

Interesting, she thought. *"Try, judge, and eradicate." The trial? The judgment? It's like my dream. What does this mean?*

Later that evening when Jessie got into bed, her mind could not help reviewing the occurrences about Taylor Andrews. *Her song is following me around. Now her lyrics relate to my dream.* As she lay there, she recalled the *People Magazine* she had purchased at the grocery store a couple days earlier. *Where did I put it?* She remembered, got out of bed, went to the kitchen and pulled the magazine from the junk-mail pile.

Jessie opened the magazine to the article on Divas, her eyes immediately meeting Taylor Andrews' crystal blue eyes. She devoured the article on Ms. Andrews. It highlighted her career and discussed her hobbies and pastimes. Apparently, Taylor Andrews enjoyed skiing, gardening, golf and reading. She admitted a fascination with history and currently was reading *Salem Possessed*, about the Salem witchcraft trials.

The crown on the judge's desk. Jessie recalled. *The clothing. The witch trial. Could that have been Salem?*

As Jessie drove to the post office the following morning to pick up her mail, she listened to *Karmic Debt*. Her mind had been racing since the singer seemed to penetrate her life. Jessie knew she needed to relax, but she couldn't.

She was into the third song of the CD when she noticed a sensation of fullness in her chest. It wasn't objectionable, and it wasn't painful. Jessie realized she was lost in Taylor Andrews' voice. *Don't listen to the words*, she told herself. *Listen to the voice; listen to the person.* With this thought, the fullness increased and warmth formed in her heart area. Jessie could feel her face warm, and the tingling from her own energy surrounding her face. This startled her and she was having difficulty concentrating on her driving. When she saw the park entrance, she drove to the remote parking area and parked away from other cars, under the trees.

Jessie opened the car windows, turned off the ignition but left the CD playing. Her attention to her physical needs had caused the sensation in her chest to stop. She closed her eyes and concentrated on Taylor Andrews' voice. It wasn't long before the fullness and the warmth returned. Then there was a feeling of connection. She couldn't explain it any other way, except, she felt connected to the singer by her heart.

Since Jessie had met Ellen, Ellen had tried to enlighten Jessie with her own metaphysical beliefs. She had dragged Jessie to classes, given her audiotapes and a number of books to read. Now as she experienced this sensation, she could not help but wonder if she was feeling her heart chakra open. She had read about the energy vortexes located throughout the body, and knew one of the major ones was in the heart area. But the question in Jessie's analytical mind was, *Why? What does this mean?*

Back at her house that evening, Jessie worked on editing the final chapters of *Deceptions*. At ten o'clock, she decided to get on the Internet before she went to bed. As she typed in *www.taylorandrews.com*, she thought about the singer and immediately experienced the warmth in her heart. *Now why did that happen?*

Jessie quickly scanned the singer's Website noticing sections titled: "FAQ," "Schedule," "Bibliography," and "Newsworthy Events." She surfed the Website reading each section with interest, trying to understand the connection to the woman. Jessie learned that Taylor grew up on the East Coast, in Connecticut. She was the middle child of a lower-middle-class family; her parents divorced when she was in junior high school. Based on Taylor's graduation date, Jessie placed her about eight years younger than herself. Taylor had been in the Los Angeles area since college graduation. Kurk Warner, the movie star, and Taylor had been seeing each other for five years, with rumors of marriage plans.

It was after midnight and Jessie debated whether to read the last section of the Website, "Newsworthy Events." She hesitated; then double clicked the icon, revealing three articles. The first, "Taylor Changes Management." Jessie clicked the icon and waited patiently for the connection, but wasn't prepared for what she saw.

"Oh my God," Jessie whispered. She looked at a picture of a man escorting Taylor Andrews at some event. Then read aloud the caption below the picture, "Taylor Andrews and her new personal manager, Mark Rutledge, arrive at MTV Music Awards."

As she looked at the picture of Mark, she remembered.

* * *

Mark Rutledge had just finished setting the dinner table in their tiny apartment. He lit the candles then returned to the oven to check on the steak. He was determined to make this evening special.

"Dinner in five minutes," he called into the living area.

Jessie lifted her head from her studies. She pushed her long hair away from her eyes. "What's for dinner?"

"I told you, it's a surprise." Mark grinned revealing his perfect teeth and charming smile. He walked up behind Jessie, his tall and slim frame towering over her. Mark had run track through undergraduate school; his body remained slim yet muscular. Gently, he placed his hands on Jessie's tense shoulders and started to massage them.

"Hmm, forget dinner," she said.

Mark leaned over and gently kissed her neck. "This is a preview of dessert," he whispered. "But you need to have the main course first. Why don't you get ready for dinner?"

Jessie pulled away from her desk and stood in front of Mark. "Okay," she agreed. She gently kissed him on the lips, then turned.

Admiringly, Mark stared at Jessie's attractive figure as she walked away. "Oh, I forgot to tell you, a Julie Redmond called."

Jessie turned. "Really? When?"

"This afternoon. She didn't leave a phone number, do you have it?"

"Yes." Jessie walked away deep in thought.

At 23, Jessie was finishing her graduate degree at Pennsylvania State. She returned to the kitchen and sat at the small dinner table in their eat-in kitchen. Mark quickly served dinner. When Jessie realized they were having steak she spoke up. "Steak. What's the occasion?"

Mark smiled as he served the dinner. "Today is a special day."

"Have you heard from any medical schools?" Jessie asked. Mark had been studying pre-med, had applied to medical schools, and was now anxiously waiting.

"No. Today doesn't mean anything to you? January 28th?

Jessie shook her head. "No. Should it?"

"Three years ago–at the campus center? The two of us ran into each other–"

"And I ruined a perfectly good sweatshirt." Jessie laughed as she remembered their crashing into each other in front of the campus center. Mark's soda had spilled all over the front of Jessie's new sweatshirt, but the two immediately bonded.

"It was destiny," he said.

"It was something," she agreed. Jessie smiled. "This is sweet that you remembered the day we met."

He raised his wine glass and offered a toast. "To us."

As they finished their main course, Mark got serious. "I've been thinking about what will happen at the end of this school year."

"What do you mean?"

"You'll get your masters and move on to finding employment. I'll go to some medical school, someplace.

"Sounds like a plan to me," Jessie said.

"If we follow this path, what are the chances of us staying together?"

"The chances of your finding a med school and my finding employment near each other are not good. But stranger things have happened."

"I think we should manipulate destiny," Mark said.

"What do you mean?"

"Let's get married. Then wherever I go to medical school, I'm sure you could find employment there."

"You're not serious."

"I am. What's stopping us? We love each other. We've been together for going on three years. Why leave it up to medical schools or employment on whether we can stay together?"

"If it's meant to be—it'll be," Jessie said.

"How can you remain so detached from this?"

"What makes you think I'm detached?"

"The thought of losing us is . . . is terrifying. You're not scared of the thought?"

Jessie looked into Mark's eyes. She admired him so for his honesty, which made her feel all the worse. He had always been good to her; now Jessie felt terrible because of what she was feeling. She could no longer look him in the eye.

"Mark, we're still so young to consider marriage."

"We're not that young, Jessie. Tell me, what is your hesitation? Do you still love me?"

"Of course I do." Jessie turned back to him. "Mark, I'm not sure you're going to understand this, but I've been looking forward to graduation and moving on."

"Moving on from us?"

"I think I need time to get to know *me* and sort some things out."

"What's to sort out? We love each other. We don't want to see others, and we're still attracted to each other. Right?"

But Jessie's silence concerned Mark. "Right?" He pressed. "You don't want to see others, right?"

"Mark, something happened last week that I don't understand. I know I'm going to have to sort it out."

"What happened? Jessie, are you seeing someone else?"

She shook her head. "No. But someone did make a pass at me." Jessie studied Mark for his reaction. As she expected, his face reddened, and his jawbone clenched. Jessie placed her hand on Mark's hand.

"Who? What's his name?" Mark asked calmly.

Jessie shook her head. "That's the confusing part, Mark. It's not a he."

Mark stared at Jessie with disbelief. "A woman made a pass at you?"

Jessie nodded. "Yes."

"I see." Mark became quiet. "No, I don't see. What are you telling me, Jessie?"

Jessie looked into Mark's pain-filled eyes.

"Big deal. A woman kissed you. You didn't kiss her back–did you?"

"Yes, I did. Initially I did, then I stopped it."

"What are you telling me? Are you a lesbian?"

"I don't know. I know that whatever happened felt too . . . too real to just ignore it. I think I need some time to do some soul searching. I think we should go our separate ways after graduation. If we're meant to be together, we'll find each other again, and we'll be stronger from our experiences."

* * *

Jessie stared at the picture of her ex-boyfriend and Taylor Andrews on the screen. *What the hell does this mean? What are the chances of this happening?* She stood and walked around her desk. *Am I losing it? Maybe I'm reading too much into this stuff.* Jessie knew the connections to Taylor's life were distracting her from her work and her life. *I need to understand what all this means, but how?*

Chapter 4

When Jessie got up the next morning, she wasted no time. After the sleepless night, she knew she needed to talk with someone about what was happening in her life. While her coffee was brewing, she searched her Rolodex for a business card. A year earlier, she had picked up the card from the instructor of an intuition workshop she attended with Ellen. During part of the workshop, the instructor spoke on past-life issues and karma. *Here it is.* Jessie pulled the business card from the sleeve. "*Carrie Butler, Counselor, Business Consultant, Readings.*"

Later that morning Jessie called Carrie and left a message on her voice mail. Ten minutes later Carrie returned her phone call.

"Hello, this is Carrie Butler; is this Jessie?"

"Yes, it is. Thank you for returning my phone call."

"How can I help you?"

For a moment, Jessie hesitated. "To be honest, I'm not sure. Things are happening in my life that I'm having a hard time understanding. I figured I'd try to speak with a psychic before I saw a psychiatrist or something."

"Is it psychic phenomena?"

"I don't know. Maybe I'm just losing my mind."

Carrie sensed that Jessie was troubled. "I have some time this afternoon around one. Would you like to come in and talk about it in person?"

As Jessie waited for Carrie to come back to the living room, she questioned her intentions. *Why am I here? How would a psychic help me with this?*

Carrie brought in drinks and rested them on the coffee table. "Now Jessie, tell me—what is troubling you?"

Jessie hesitated. "I've been experiencing connections to a person."

"Connections?"

"Yes, connections. That's the best way I can explain it."

"Can you give me some examples?"

Jessie took a deep breath, wondering where to start. "It started with a recurring dream. In the dream, I can remember a very specific conversation. After I had the dream for the third time I woke to a song that has the same phrase as the dialogue in my dream. Then I realized that wherever I went, in the car, in the grocery store, at home, I kept hearing the same song. Or I kept coming across something that had to do with this singer. I had another dream that suggested that I would find answers to my questions in an unusual picture. The next day, I came across the newest CD of the singer I was having connections with. Well . . . the cover of the CD was the picture in my dream."

"And the song that you keep hearing is on the CD with this cover?"

"Yes."

"Interesting," Carrie said.

"I got the lyrics to this song. I'm not quite sure what the song means, except there's a phrase, 'try, judge and eradicate.' In my dream, there was a trial and a verdict."

Carrie smiled and took a sip of her tea.

"I didn't know much about this singer up until this past week. I didn't even like her music. But, because of all this, I've read a lot about her in magazine and Internet articles, and I keep finding connections between her life and my own. I've also found that if I listen to her voice, and concentrate on her voice, not the lyrics, I experience a feeling in my chest."

"What do you mean?"

"I wish I could explain it better. I've noticed a fullness or warmth develop in my heart area. It's like . . . my heart gets filled with something. I don't know how to describe it."

"That's okay. Anything else?"

"Yes, and it's freaked me out. I recently learned that this singer's new personal manager is my ex-boyfriend from college."

"Really? And how did that end?"

"Our relationship?"

"Yes. If you don't mind sharing it with me."

"It ended in our last semester of graduate school. I needed some time away from him to answer some questions about my sexual orientation." Jessie was surprised at her own directness. "He was great during the transition. Very supportive."

"And you got your answers?"

"Yes. I'm gay. We had a great friendship, but he couldn't handle maintaining the friendship. We've been out of touch for close to fifteen years now. We always joked about our relationship being *destiny*, and if we appeared in each other's lives again, it would confirm it."

"So you want to know if the signs are for your ex-boyfriend?"

"I want to know what all this means. Does it mean something? Or is it just a coincidence? I need to get on with my life. I'm finding it difficult to concentrate on my work."

"The universe talks to us all the time with signs that are a lot less obvious than the ones you've described. These signs aren't subtle; they're pretty apparent."

"Well, when the universe gives us . . . signs, what is it telling us?"

"It can be telling us a number of things. Signs can be a confirmation that we're on the right path, or can indicate that we're going in the wrong direction. But your signs are very direct and seem to have urgency about them."

"Could they have anything to do with past-life issues?"

"Oh, yes."

"How can I figure it out?"

"There are a number of ways for us to explore our past lives. Certainly, the obvious is our everyday life experiences. This is where we learn to recognize clues from our everyday life that could relate to our previous lives."

"What do you mean?"

"You can learn a lot about your past lives by cataloging some very basic elements of your present life. For example, what are your fears and phobias? Do you have an attraction to or interest in any historical periods? What type of foods do you enjoy? Do you have any birthmarks? What type of clothing do you feel comfortable in? What are your talents? What climates do you enjoy? There are a number of ways we can find information regarding past lives, without going any further than here and now. But also look to your dreams. Every dream gives us secret messages not only about this life, but also about our past lives."

"It sounds very subjective though."

"It is the slowest and probably most subjective road to past-life recall."

"What else can I do?"

"Past-life readings by a psychic. Here, you get the information very quickly, rather than the first method."

"How do you know if what you're told is accurate?"

"You'll never have proof of its accuracy. The real test is–how does the information feel to you. Try it on for size. Does it feel right? If it does–there's a good chance it's pretty accurate. If it doesn't feel right, wait. If in time it never feels right, then it probably isn't. No psychic is perfect. Everybody has an off day.

"But if you use a psychic, you should look for one that suits you. It's like any professional you use. If you hire an attorney or accountant, you check out their references. If you use a psychic, don't be afraid to check them out. There are a lot of good and accurate psychics as well as a lot of bad ones. Just like any other occupation."

"Is there anything else I can use to recall past lives?"

"Oh yes, your subconscious mind. Think of our subconscious mind as being a reservoir of all past-life memories. The key is trying to access it, and there are a number of ways to do it."

"How?"

"Meditation is the most obvious, but also hypnotic regressions."

"Regressions? How?"

"Hypnotic regressions can be facilitated by psychics as well as psychiatrists. Past-life therapy has become a documented manner in which to treat patients."

"How?"

"By exploring past lives, we can confront past-life issues that manifested fears in our present lives. A patient suffering from claustrophobia may learn that they were buried alive in a previous life. To confront such a fear in a regression can cure them from their condition in this life.

"What do you actually do in a regression?"

"Basically, someone would hypnotize you, and ask you to recall past periods of this life. But they'll take you back past this life into other lives."

"Is it safe?"

"With a trained person, yes. But whoever facilitates the regression should have experience in past-life regressions, not only hypnotherapy."

"Does the person feel like they're actually there? Or do they just see it?"

"Generally, you can completely experience the other lifetime, you can see, hear, taste, feel and sense what is going on."

"Are there any other ways to explore past lives?"

"The only other way, and I don't have a lot of experience with it, is—time travel."

"Time travel? Sounds like something from the movies. I'm not sure I'd buy into that theory."

"Then I won't say much about it, except—there is a belief that all time is coexisting. The past, present and future occur at the same time. Of course, within each there is a past, present and future."

"And there is a safe way to journey to another time period?"

"I have never done it, but I have read about it. Some believe that time is not measured on a two-dimensional scale, but a three-dimensional scale.

Carrie went to a bookshelf and removed a box of stones. She returned and placed a large crystal on the center of the coffee table in front of them. "Think of this crystal as your soul. Like an atom, it's the nucleus of your being." Carrie removed smaller rocks and randomly placed them around the crystal. "Our lifetimes are like the electrons that orbit an atom. All of our lifetimes make up our soul, not just this one, but our past lives and future lives." Carrie pointed to a turquoise rock. "In our life we are experiencing this two-dimensional time, our past, present and future. The theory is that from the soul level, we can travel to other lifetimes. If this is something that would be of interest to you–I could suggest some books to read . . . if you like Einstein."

"I probably wouldn't be interested for my personal experience. But it sounds like a good idea for a book. If you have some recommended books, I'll take their names."

Carrie glanced at the clock on the wall. It was ten minutes to two. "I hate to stop this discussion, but I have a reading at two o'clock. Perhaps you can think about some of the ideas that I have given you."

"I really appreciate your time, Carrie."

Carrie took the notepad from the coffee table and started writing. "I'll write down some books. If you would like to have a past-life reading, I would refer you to someone else. Someone who hasn't heard your story."

"That makes sense."

"If you would want a regression, I have training in that area. I charge $100 a session. Think about it and call if I can help."

Jessie left Carrie and headed for the bookstore. In the new age section, she picked up a number of books on past lives, regressions, and even time travel.

That evening Ellen and Jessie went to a restaurant in Pasadena for dinner. As they were seated at the table, Jessie heard the familiar tune by Taylor Andrews play on the restaurant speakers. She smiled. Moments later she felt the fullness in her chest.

A waitress came to their table and introduced herself. "Hello. My name is Taylor and I will be your server this evening."

Taylor? Jessie mused.

During dinner, Jessie shared with Ellen her meeting with Carrie. Ellen listened to her friend and smiled. "So what do you think? Are you going to have a reading? Or have a regression?"

"I'm not sure. I picked up some books. I'll read them, then make a decision."

"Boy, you've really come a long way."

"What do you mean?" Jessie asked.

"When we first met, you were completely close minded to metaphysics. You used to scoff at the subject of past lives. Now . . . you're visiting with psychics and considering a past-life regression."

After dinner, Ellen and Jessie returned to Jessie's house and were enjoying a glass of wine in the great room.

When Ellen moved closer to Jessie on the couch, she asked, "Can we talk about us?"

"What about us?"

"What are we doing? I mean . . . what are the two of us doing with each other?"

Jessie studied Ellen. "This is going to be one of those serious discussions, right?"

"We've been seeing each other for 15 months, right? Where are we going?"

"I thought we were having a nice relationship," Jessie answered.

"But we've been in the same position for over a year."

"And what position might that be?"

"You know. We date a couple times a week. We sleep together. We both have our own places. We each have other friends, but there really isn't an *us*."

Jessie knew Ellen was right. "Do you need more?"

"Eventually I know I will. I just wonder if there ever would be *more* for the two of us."

"What do you think?"

Ellen shook her head. "No. I don't see this relationship evolving into anything beyond what it is."

"I don't think it'd be fair if either one of us took the relationship farther than what it is. I mean . . . you do know that I love you, Ellen. Don't you?"

Ellen smiled warmly and nodded.

"But I don't believe that either one of us is *in love* with the other." Jessie placed her glass on an end table and took hold of Ellen's hands. "I am content with where we are. But if you need something more, then it wouldn't be fair to continue this."

"I don't want to be *content*," Ellen started. "*Content* is a compromise. I want to be happy. Maybe we should take a break from each other and see other people."

For a moment, Jessie was saddened by the thought of losing Ellen. But she knew Ellen was right. "If you feel that strongly about it, Ellen, I will be supportive."

Ellen rose from the couch. "I think I should go."

"It's almost ten o'clock, you don't want to stay the night?" Jessie smiled, her brown eyes beaming mischievously. "We can spend one last evening together, can't we?"

Ellen laughed out loud, then approached Jessie and took her hands. "Jessie, you know if I stay tonight, I'll end up coming back, and back and back. This will never end. No. I think it'll be better if the two of us get on with our lives." Ellen gently placed her lips on Jessie's, and they kissed goodbye.

Then Ellen backed away and left. Jessie never saw the tears in Ellen's eyes when she got in her car and drove away.

As Jessie watched the tail lights of the Mustang disappear in the darkness, she sensed the loss of Ellen's friendship. Her thoughts were soon interrupted by the sound of her telephone ringing.

She closed the door behind her and answered the phone. "Hello."

"Hi, is Andrew there?" an unfamiliar voice asked.

"I'm sorry, I think you have the wrong number. There's no Andrew here."

"Sorry."

Jessie heard dial tone. *Andrew? Taylor Andrews.*

Jessie went to her study and looked at the stack of papers on her desk. She was close to completing *Deceptions*. She knew she needed something to take her mind off Ellen and decided to work on her manuscript. But as she sat there, she stared at the stack of books she had purchased that afternoon. She picked up the top book and studied the jacket. *I wonder if I'm becoming obsessed with Taylor Andrews.* Jessie knew she was having difficulties concentrating on the simplest things. She had a manuscript that was 95% finished and a movie producer asking for it, but she was having the hardest time focusing to get things accomplished.

I've got to get this behind me, she decided. *I have to figure out what this means. Then I can get on with my life.*

Chapter 5

Jessie spent the next two days devouring the books on regressions and past lives. On the third day she called Carrie and scheduled a past-life regression.

Jessie lay comfortably on a couch in Carrie's office. Carrie had Jessie do breathing and visualization exercises to bring her into a deep state of relaxation and peace. Then Carrie proceeded.

"I'm going to count slowly from ten to one. When I get to one, you'll be in a deeper state of hypnosis. When I get to one, you will be in another time, far back, before you came into your present body. Now, ten, nine . . . with each breath you will enter a deeper state of relaxation. Eight, seven . . . with each breath you become closer to a bridge, a bridge to another dimension, a bridge to another time. Six, five . . . with each breath you are aware of a loving presence, your creator, a presence that will guide you. Four, three . . . with each breath you come closer to another time, a time that will help you understand the signs the universe is showing you. Two, one . . .

"You have arrived at another time, a time–"

"Oh my God . . . it hurts . . . so much pain," Jessie cried.

"Where's the pain coming from?" Carrie asked.

"My chest," Jessie whispered.

"Can you look and see why you're in pain?"

"Blood . . . lot's of blood. I'm wounded . . . I'm weak. It hurts so much."

"Can you tell me who you are? Are you a man or a woman? Where are you? Is anyone with you?"

Perspiration appeared on Jessie's face. She curled into a fetal position, holding her chest. "It's dark . . . I'm a man. Someone is here . . . God, it hurts."

Carrie was concerned that Jessie was in so much pain. "On the count of three, I want you to leave this time. I want you to go to another time, one that is less painful, one that can help you find the answers you are presently seeking. One . . . two . . . three."

With that, Jessie's body no longer wrenched with pain. She straightened from the fetal position and appeared relaxed. A calm replaced her expressions of distress.

"That's better," Carrie took a deep breath. "Can you look at your feet and tell me what you see?"

"I have shoes on . . . they're black. I have black pants on . . . with a jacket. The buttons are high. Three buttons."

"That's great. Where are you? Are you inside or outside? What are you standing on?"

"I'm inside. The floor is wooden . . . It's dark. I'm in a small house or cabin . . . there's a large fireplace and . . ."

"And what?"

"Very old . . ."

"You're very old?"

"No. The furnishings . . . and it's not that they're old but they're from another time."

"Are you a man or a woman? What do you look like?"

"There's a mirror above the dresser."

"Good. Walk to the dresser, look into the mirror and tell me what you see."

A moment passed, then Jessie began. "It's him."

"It's who?"

It's the man from my dream. Jessie looked in the mirror, into Daniel Johnson's brown eyes.

* * *

He picked up the comb and combed his thick brown hair. Daniel stepped away from the mirror to admire his black suit. He tied the scarf-like tie around his neck, then approached the mirror again. A nick on his chin blemished his attractive face. He placed a blood-soiled towel on his chin, and held it in place. Satisfied that the bleeding had stopped, he set the towel down and nervously smiled into the mirror, inspecting his straight teeth.

There was a knock at the solid wooden door and a man entered.

"Aren't you ready yet?" the man asked.

"Yes. I just want everything to be perfect, John." Daniel turned toward his best friend, "How do I look?"

John walked in front of Daniel and inspected his suit. At six-foot-two, Daniel towered over John, almost six-inches shorter. John was also dressed in a suit. He straightened Daniel's scarf. "You look fine. But we must go; we don't want to be late."

The twenty-five-year-old turned and smiled at his reflection in the mirror. His eyes seemed to dance as they reflected the natural light from the window.

"Come, Daniel. We must get you to the church."

The men left the two-room house. Outside, they were greeted with bright sunshine from a perfect May morning. A horse-drawn carriage was waiting in front of Daniel's house. The men climbed into the carriage and John took the reins. Soon the friends were on their way.

"Daniel, are you nervous?" John asked.

"Somewhat."

"If you change your mind, you know it would be my honor to take your place."

"Now, wouldn't you find pleasure in that? Are you still jealous she chose me?"

"Absolutely," John admitted. "Remember, I was to be the priest? I will never forgive myself for trading our costumes."

"I thank the Lord everyday my costume would not fit me," Daniel laughed. He recalled the evening he met his future bride. She went to the costume ball with a vision that she would meet her future husband that night, and he would be dressed as a priest. Originally, John was to be the priest, and Daniel was to be the judge. But the judge's costume did not fit Daniel and at the last minute, the two swapped outfits.

John and Daniel had been friends since grammar school. Their friendship lasted even when John attended Harvard College. Daniel stayed in his hometown of Andover, Massachusetts, and opened a general store for the small farming community. After John graduated, he became a law apprentice in neighboring Salem Town.

As the carriage approached the church, it became apparent that a group had gathered outside. Some people realized that the groom was approaching. Daniel recognized panic in his sister's voice, "Hurry, we must hide her. They mustn't see each other, it would be bad luck."

Daniel smiled as he spotted the back of his fiancée's head. She was hurried to the far side of the small church.

Moments later, Daniel stood beside John at the front of the church, waiting for his bride-to-be at the altar. Daniel's heart raced, and his knees were locked in place contributing to his lightheadedness. But all his anxiety disappeared when his eyes met the crystal blue eyes that always could penetrate his soul. Rebecca smiled, her eyes fixed on Daniel as she walked to him at the altar.

Moments later the minister pronounced the couple man and wife; their lips gently met sealing the promise of being with each other, forever.

Daniel adored Rebecca. He had never met anyone that he instantly bonded with, like he did with her. Likewise, Rebecca understood she had found a life-mate and soul-mate. Rebecca had known they were meant to be together when they first met at the costume ball one year earlier. She had had a precognitive vision the morning before the ball indicating she would meet her future husband that evening, dressed as a priest.

Rebecca knew she was different from most even when she was a young child. She experienced visions, sight beyond natural vision. The clairvoyance increased in her teenage years. Through her visions, she learned that she was precognitive. She was able to see things before they happened. When she was 17, her maternal aunt introduced her to magical arts. Although she was initially cautious of the mysterious rituals, eventually she realized that they were just a different way of praying to the creator for life's needs.

Before Rebecca could marry Daniel, she knew she needed to share with him her spiritual beliefs. One night, she brought him to her sacred place set up in the loft of her parent's barn. An overturned crate with a white cloth covering served as her altar. She lit two candles that sat on either end, between them a chalice and an athame, a double-edged knife.

Daniel picked up the athame to study it. "What do you do with the knife?" he asked.

Rebecca turned to another crate against the wall that was housing many other items. She picked up a rod and moved toward Daniel. "Like my wand, the athame is used to direct personal power. It helps focus energy during a ritual."

"What type of ritual?"

"There are many different types of rituals, Daniel."

Daniel walked around the small table. There was a chill in the air. The creaking from the barn contributed to the uneasiness of the moment. An abrupt slam against the barn's wall caused Daniel's hair to rise on the back of his neck. Seconds later a large black bird appeared in the window of the loft. It sat there, stared at the two then flew away.

"Do you ever hurt or kill animals?" Daniel asked.

Rebecca shook her head, her long dark hair shimmering from the light of the punched-tin lantern and candles. "No. I do not hurt any living thing," she answered calmly.

"We have never talked about religion before, Rebecca. I see you in church on Sundays. Do you believe in God?" He looked around and saw the caldron sitting on the other crate against the wall. "Are you a witch?" he asked calmly. "Do you worship Satan?"

Rebecca put her wand back on the crate then turned to Daniel. She smiled, then removed the knife from Daniel's hands and placed it on the altar. Rebecca took Daniel's hand in her own and pulled him toward the haystack. "Come. Let's sit here and talk."

They sat next to each other. "I do believe in a Creator. I believe there are good forces and there are evil forces. I believe that Satan is a very strong and a real entity, one to be feared and avoided." Rebecca stared into Daniel's eyes, hoping he would understand. "I do not worship Satan.

"I go to your church on Sundays, mostly to protect myself. To give people the impression that I am a Christian."

"But you are not?"

"I respect many of your church's beliefs. But no . . . I am not a Christian." Rebecca knew she was treading on dangerous ground. "You asked me last night to marry you. I cannot marry you unless you know and respect who I really am. That is why I am sharing this with you."

Rebecca remained silent and waited for a response from Daniel.

"I don't understand. I know you are not evil. I know you're a good person; it's obvious the way you live your life and render to others. But I don't understand these things you do."

"May I explain some things to you?"

"Please do."

"When you want something, like prosperity, love, health, you go to church and ask your God in your prayers. Is that correct?"

"Yes."

"Daniel, I do the same. I just do not pray to your God."

"Which god do you pray to?"

"It's actually a goddess, but I don't pray to just one entity. I pray to many forces. What I learned from my aunt is that we can use magical abilities to manifest what we need."

"How so?"

"All around us is energy. In witchcraft we learn how to move this energy around us and within us to manifest powerful thoughts that create positive changes."

"Or negative changes?" Daniel asked.

"Witchcraft is a tool. It is only as good as the person who uses it. Yes, there are those that manifest the negative. But most do concentrate on the positive."

Daniel remained silent, listening to the wind blowing against the side of the barn. "Did you cast a spell on us, or me?" he finally asked.

Rebecca shook her head. "No. I did not need to. I have known since the first time I looked into your eyes that we have been together before, in another life. Actually . . . many lives."

"In another life? That is sacrilege, Rebecca. As Christians, we believe that we have one life on earth, then we go to heaven or hell."

"Christians now believe that. Did you know that up until the fourth century reincarnation was not only believed in, but it was part of the Christian faith?"

"How do you know such things?"

"It is true, Daniel. During the fourth century, the Roman Emperor, Constantine the Great, deleted references of reincarnation from the New Testament. In the sixth century, the Second Council of Constantinople declared that the belief in reincarnation was a heresy. The early church believed it was too difficult for the average man to understand. They also didn't want people to know that we have many lifetimes to seek our salvation. They hoped that by simplifying the religion, the church would grow."

"How do you know these things?" Daniel knew Rebecca had not studied theology and her education was limited to Miss Wilson's Female Academy.

"The same way I know we were together before. Through past-life memories." Rebecca picked up both of Daniel's hands and held them in her own. Daniel felt the warmth from the small hands. With one of her hands, she caressed Daniel's face so that his eyes met her crystal blue eyes. "Can you not admit that we have a connection?"

"I do not understand your question."

"Was it easy to get to know me? At times, have you felt we have talked before we met? When you look into my eyes, can you see beyond this physical body? Can you see my soul?"

Daniel shook his head. "I do not believe in reincarnation, Rebecca. I may have a connection to you, but that is because I am in love with you."

"So, where does that leave us?" Rebecca boldly asked. "Can you accept me as I am? I am not going to change if we marry."

"Could we marry in the church?"

"I am an active member of the church, Daniel. Assuming we do not tell the Reverend Hutchins, I don't see why not."

"Children? How would we raise children?" Daniel asked.

"As I was. I was raised Christian. Then when I was of age, the craft was introduced to me. As an adult, I decided which path to follow. But Daniel, can you accept me as I am? I am not going to change."

Daniel looked around the barn, studying the tools Rebecca used. "Can you safely do this in the privacy of our home?"

Rebecca nodded.

"It would have to remain our secret. Folks do not take kindly to witch-craft. They burn people at the stake for this." Daniel's voice softened. "I love you, Rebecca. I want to be your husband, and I hope you still want to be my wife."

Rebecca smiled. She embraced him, their lips finding each other's.

Rebecca moved into Daniel's house after the wedding, and the bond between them continued to grow. She took over a small shed in the rear of the property where she set up her sanctuary; Daniel never expressed inter-est in seeing it. Both remained active members in the parish church. As the summer passed, Daniel noticed that business had picked up. By fall, he shared their good fortune with his wife.

"I do not know what it is, Rebecca, but we have been blessed. I keep sales records from year-to-year, and sales are up. It seems like every little choice I make at the store is improving business. Last month, I received ten extra bags in my grain delivery. I wrote the supplier and told him about it, so he could bill me. Yesterday I received ten more bags of grain with a note saying 'Thank you for your honesty. Compliments of Porter's Grain.' "

"I'm sure it is because you are very good at what you do," Rebecca said. She turned away, concealing her smile.

Rebecca learned early into the courtship that Daniel and John had a strong friendship. Even after their marriage, the bond did not suffer. John was a fixture around Daniel's house on most weekends and occasionally during weekdays. Rebecca remained supportive of their friendship.

One weekend in October, John and Daniel were sitting at the table enjoying cider and discussing business as usual, which was of little interest to Rebecca. She excused herself, grabbed her cape and a lantern then stepped outside.

The full moon illuminated the worn path that ran to the outhouse. Then thirty feet beyond was her shed. As she opened the wooden panel door, it creaked. The scent of burnt herbs filled the eight-foot square enclosure. Moonlight filtered through a small window, helping to light up her haven.

At a shelf, she removed a black cauldron and placed it in front of her on the floor. Rebecca rummaged through items on her shelves, thoughtfully selecting things and carefully placing them in the pot. From marked jars, she removed dirt from different places, then twigs from various trees. She methodically placed a feather, stone, seashell and a small mirror in the cauldron. Then she selected many different stones. She turned to other jars where she removed a spoonful from each of a half-dozen selected items. Once satisfied with the contents of the pot, she placed it in front of the altar.

Rebecca dressed the altar with a white cloth, then placed the cauldron in the center of the table and selected other items to surround the pot. From the flame of her lantern, she lit a white candle. She carefully placed the candle in the center of the cauldron, on top of the items that lay inside, and then prayed aloud, softly.

"Spirits of the night see my magic flame. Awaken within the womb from where all came. As the moon grows full and shines from above, charge this oracle with truth, power and love."

Rebecca picked up a dish on the side of the cauldron. She lit an object and fragrance filled the room. She blew the smoke from the burning object into the cauldron, filling the pot with smoke and aroma.

"Spirits of the air and this dark hour fill my cauldron with your psychic power. Show me the way the future to foresee. In accordance with your will, so shall it be."

She took some water and salt that sat beside the cauldron. As she sprinkled the two ingredients into the caldron, she continued her prayer. "Spirits of the sea and earth, to my visions now give birth. The future I beckon thee show me that in truth and wisdom I shall grow. Let now the powers come to me, for this is what I need, so mote it be."

Rebecca was so absorbed in preparing her spirit caldron that she never saw the dark face in the window studying her every move, or his mouth open in astonishment when he realized she was practicing witchcraft.

Outside the small shed, John hurried away, heart pounding as he ran past the outhouse only to be abruptly stopped when a large figure stood in his way. John stood momentarily sizing up his opponent, and then bolted around the larger man.

"John, it is me," Daniel yelled. Daniel grabbed hold of his friend's arm. But John continued his struggle, until Daniel had him pinned on the ground. "It's me, John. What in God's name is wrong?"

John looked up into Daniel's face. "Let me up," he demanded.

Daniel released his grip on John and the two men stood facing each other.

"She is a witch? She's a witch, Daniel." John nervously stroked at his mustache, twisting an end to a point.

Daniel remained calm. "Let us go inside and talk about this."

"You knew? You knew she was a witch. No, we can talk right here." John backed away from Daniel.

"John, she's Rebecca. She is still the same sweet woman the two of us met last year. She's the same woman that gives all of herself to anyone that needs her. It's Rebecca."

"She is a witch. She worships the devil."

"That is not true."

"How do you know that?"

"She told me."

"And you believe her? You trust her?"

"With my life, John. She is the same woman we have always known. Yes, she admits to having unconventional spiritual beliefs. But believe me, John, she says she does not worship Satan."

John stood silently trying to digest everything that had transpired after he came outside to use the outhouse. "I wish I never saw that flicker of light in the shed's window," he mumbled.

"John, we have been friends for almost fifteen years. Please trust my judgment. Let us go inside and talk."

As if surrendering, John turned and went back into the house.

It didn't take Daniel long to convince John he had overreacted to the situation. Then when Rebecca returned to the house from her ritual, her charm only confirmed what Daniel had been saying. John promised both of them that their secret would remain with him.

Chapter 6

Fall passed and winter arrived. Business remained good for Daniel, the newlyweds' love never stopped growing, and John continued his friendship. The couple remained active members of the parish church, and formed new friendships with other couples.

One Sunday morning in February, before Sunday service was finished, a couple stood in front of the congregation. Both the husband and wife appeared exhausted, their clothes wrinkled, hair uncombed. Rebecca and Daniel knew Mary and Samuel Osgood. They had a farm about a mile away from their own property and had been living there since their daughter, Ann, was born about one year earlier. Today, Ann was noticeably absent.

The Reverend Hutchins stood between the distressed couple. "I have a disturbing announcement." His arms stretched open to comfort the couple. "Yesterday when Goodman and Goodwife Osgood were at market, their daughter, Ann, was abducted."

Of course, the congregation became involved in the couple's tragedy. The abduction upset the community and the congregation pledged their support to the Osgoods. Later that week, Rebecca made a special basket for the couple, consisting of fresh breads, relishes and jams. While Daniel was at the store, Rebecca took the basket and walked to the Osgood's farm.

Mary Osgood answered the knock at the door, and was surprised by Rebecca's arrival. "Goodie Johnson, please, come in," she said. She smiled then stepped away from the door, permitting Rebecca to enter. The Osgood's house was similar to Rebecca and Daniel's home, a two-room house consisting of a bedchamber and a gathering area.

"Goodie Osgood, I just wanted to bring you this." Rebecca offered the basket.

"Thank you, this is kind of you. May I offer you some tea?"

Rebecca accepted the invitation. Mary Osgood went to the fireplace where stew was simmering in a kettle and water was boiling. She prepared the teapot and the women sat quietly at the table sipping their tea. Rebecca noticed two crates sitting near the bedroom door. Within the chamber she could see a small crib.

"Has there been any news about Ann?" Rebecca asked.

"No. The sheriff was not very hopeful."

"Is Goodman Osgood here?"

"He is out at the barn. Samuel is building a workshop for his furniture. He is very good with his hands, and always wanted to try the furniture business. This time of the year, he could work at it full time." Mary paused. "The work also helps him take his mind off of things."

"It must be hard. Is there anything I can do to help?"

"Continue praying."

Rebecca looked again at the crates. Diapers in one of them told her that Ann's belongings were being packed away. The room was so small Rebecca could almost touch them.

"Is all hope gone?" Rebecca asked quietly.

"Yes. Samuel feels the sooner we get her things out of here, the sooner we can move on with our lives. Would you like more tea? I'll fetch some hot water."

"Yes, thank you."

As Mary turned away to the fireplace, Rebecca moved quickly to snatch a teething ring that lay on top of the nappies. She sat again, noiselessly, and clutching the small object, closed her eyes. Immediately an image of the baby came to her. Ann was smiling. She was playing with a ball inside a house, near a large fireplace. A man and a woman were with her. Both appeared to adore Ann.

"Did you take honey with your tea?"

Mary's voice brought Rebecca back. "Yes, thank you." Rebecca stared at the teething ring in her palm. *Ann is in no harm. I should tell them . . . how would they understand?* Quickly, she pocketed the teething ring. *Maybe I can find out something more helpful.*

Rebecca's heart ached for Mary and Samuel Osgood. The thought of losing a child and not knowing the child's welfare would be devastating. She was determined to find out Ann's whereabouts. Rebecca decided to call upon the goddess Isis for assistance.

Isis was an Egyptian goddess who protected children from the danger of everyday life. Rebecca had called upon her when her youngest brother came down with the fever a couple years earlier. While she was in her sanctuary that evening, Rebecca searched the shelves until she found the box identified "ISIS." Rebecca knew she may never find Ann, but she knew Isis could protect the child.

Rebecca started the preparation for the deity, Isis. She opened the dusty box revealing a statue of the Egyptian goddess, along with an assortment of stones, twigs and animal figures. She set the statue on her altar beside some of the items in the box. Carefully, she dusted the statue. As the cloth caressed the object, Rebecca's eyes noticed the object Isis was carrying in her right hand. She smiled when she saw the ankh the goddess held, then reached deep into her pocket and pulled out her amulet, her own ankh. She had asked a local carpenter to make her the ankh after showing him a picture in a mythology book. Then she psychically energized it to offer her protection. With her fingers, she traced the smooth surface of the maple, starting with the T cross, completing with the loop above the cross.

Rebecca had selected the ankh as her amulet years earlier. She had always been intrigued with Egyptian mythology and almost every god or goddess was pictured holding or carrying an ankh. When she learned the meaning of the cross-like symbol was everlasting life and regeneration, she selected it to become her personal energized object for protection.

The best time to call Isis would be spring and summer. After dusting off the objects, she placed them back in the box except for the statue, which she left on the altar. She lit a candle, then placed a blanket on the dirt floor and sat. Rebecca removed Ann's teething ring from her pocket. She opened her palm displaying the small object then delicately closed one hand over the other so she could feel the energy from the tiny object.

Within seconds, pictures started coming to Rebecca. Again, she saw the baby with the same couple. It was an older man and woman, perhaps in their late thirties or early forties. They appeared to live in great comfort based on their house. It was a two-story, four-room house with imported windows from England. Small diamond borders framed the glass in the windows. There was a magnificent fireplace with large stones harnessing a roaring fire. The couple appeared to adore Ann, as well as each other. *The baby doesn't appear to be in danger.* As soon as Rebecca's intellect started to rationalize the situation, her connection was lost.

The winter weeks passed quickly and most in town seemed to forget the kidnapped baby. Even Mary and Samuel tried to put the situation behind them. During one of Rebecca's many visits to the farm, Rebecca couldn't find any sign of the couple ever having had Ann.

It was a Saturday evening in April when John was enjoying dinner at Rebecca and Daniel's home. John wanted to share some news he had heard with his friends. He nervously twisted the ends of his mustache.

"Have either of you heard what is going on in Salem Village and now Salem Town?" John asked.

Although Daniel had heard some rumors in his store, he knew Rebecca would not know.

"No. What is going on in Salem?" Rebecca asked innocently.

John, twisting his mustache, eyed Daniel before he answered.

Daniel nodded his approval for bringing up the subject at their dinner table.

"There has been an outbreak of witchcraft cases in the village, perhaps a dozen or so. But the examinations have moved to Salem Town. Rebecca . . ." he turned to meet her eyes, "I do not want to see you get hurt. Please be careful."

Rebecca smiled. "That is sweet, John. Please tell me, what did these people do?"

John shook his head. "I don't know. I do know that there are a number of women in jail, along with a child."

"A child?" Daniel asked.

"Yes, a four-year-old, the daughter of Sarah Good. Sarah was one of the first accused. Both mother and child are in a Boston prison."

"What is going to happen to all of them?" Daniel asked.

"It's quite unclear. A new governor is arriving from England some time this spring. Sir William Phips has been appointed and he will establish a new charter when he arrives. To proceed with formal prosecution of the accused witches would be illegal."

"So what happens to these women?" Rebecca asked, even though she already knew the answer.

"The only thing they can do is jail them until a special court is appointed to hear their cases."

"This is not good," Rebecca said. Then she felt Daniel's warm hand slip into her own. She acknowledged his touch by looking into his eyes.

"You will be careful, please?"

Rebecca nodded, then turned to John. "Thank you for letting us know."

"Will you keep us informed?" Daniel asked.

"Yes."

About a month later, Sir William Phips sailed into Boston harbor and quickly formed a six-member advisory council to hear and determine the backlog of witchcraft cases. Phips named his lieutenant governor, William Stoughton, as the Lord Chief Justice of the Court of Oyer and Terminer.

It was a warm mid-June afternoon and Daniel was busy unpacking and displaying new merchandise at the store. Abruptly, John stormed into the storefront. When John realized his entrance was disruptive to one of Daniel's customer's, he quickly apologized.

Daniel, sensing that something was wrong, excused himself from the customer and invited John into the rear stockroom.

"What is wrong?" Daniel whispered.

"The first witches' trial was last Friday."

"And?"

"Her name is Bridget Bishop. She's been imprisoned since April."

"And what, John?"

"She is scheduled to be hanged on Saturday."

"Oh, God."

"But it's not going to stop there, Daniel. They already have five women lined up to be tried at the end of the month. Daniel . . . this witch-hunt is out of control."

"What are you talking about?"

"They have imprisoned over 70 people so far, and they've just begun. Over half of them are from outside of Salem Town and Salem Village. Daniel, last week Martha Carrier was arrested."

"Our neighbor?" Daniel was frightened. "Martha is Rebecca's friend."

"Yes, your neighbor. And let me tell you–it was very easy for me to find out about Rebecca. If I could . . . they will. You must stop her."

Daniel debated all the way home that evening what he would tell Rebecca. *John may be right,* he thought. *The risk is just too great. I will talk with her again.*

But Daniel wasn't prepared for what he found when he arrived at home. As he walked through the door, Rebecca rushed to greet him. She wrapped her arms around his neck, her lips joining his with a passion that hadn't faded since their wedding a little over one year earlier.

Their lips parted from the kiss. Both smiled as they gazed into each other's eyes. "Now what did I do to deserve that reception? Please tell, so I can repeat it every night," Daniel said.

Rebecca laughed. "Oh, I have some exciting news and I just cannot wait to share it with you. Why don't you wash for dinner; it's ready."

"Very well." Daniel went to the basin and washed his hands. He sat at the table and Rebecca immediately served his stew, then she served herself and joined him. Daniel noticed a gleam in her eyes. "Tell me darling, what is on your mind?"

Rebecca smiled, "I found . . . no, we found Ann."

"Ann who?"

"Ann Osgood, Mary and Samuel's baby. Remember? She was abducted in February."

"Really? How? Who are *we?*"

"Me and Isis."

"Who's Isis?"

"She is a goddess that I called upon and asked to help find Ann. I've been working with her for a couple months now. Daniel, Ann's alive and she lives in Boston."

It was obvious to Daniel that Rebecca was excited and under different circumstances, he may have shared in her excitement. "Rebecca, I thought you weren't doing any of your . . . you know–rituals. It's too dangerous–"

"Daniel, I have been very careful. But you can't expect me to completely stop the work I started before the witch-hunt. This is just too important. It's a child's life at stake. Daniel what if it were our child?"

"Rebecca, I'm not scolding. But I have to tell you–we must be careful. This witch-hunt is getting scary. There are over 70 people imprisoned, and they're hanging the first in a couple of days. We can't be careless now."

"This is an innocent child, Daniel. I have information on her whereabouts. Can you just ignore that?"

Daniel remained silent considering their next step. But he knew that if the lead on the baby were correct–it would be just too important to ignore.

"Where is the baby?"

"On Church Road, in Boston."

"Who has her?"

"A couple. I believe their name is Bradberry."

"Bradberry?"

"Yes, Bradberry. That is what she said. The man is very successful, a businessman perhaps. They have a very distinguished home. The woman has jet-black hair with a streak of gray. Daniel you must believe me. Please?"

"I will go to Boston on Saturday and look around. You're staying here."

"You know I cannot do that. You'll never find her if I don't go."

Chapter 7

Daniel was ready to leave for Boston that Saturday morning. He was not surprised when Rebecca boldly climbed into the carriage with him. He knew it would be a waste of time arguing with her, she always had a way with him. Rather than arguing, he took his wife's delicate hand, held it to his lips and gently kissed it. "I love you Rebecca," he whispered. "I just don't want anything to happen to you. Let's be careful."

They traveled all morning before they stopped and ate a picnic lunch that Rebecca had prepared. Then they were back on the road. The afternoon was young when they stopped and asked a man for directions to Church Road. They were delighted to learn that they were close.

"Do you know where the house is?" Daniel asked.

"I'll know it when I see it."

But as Rebecca and Daniel came to the end of Church Road, Rebecca shook her head. "This isn't right."

Daniel reined the horse in a u-turn and stopped, looking down the road they had just traveled.

"It's got to be here, Daniel. How come I can't see it?"

"Let's try it again," Daniel said.

Rebecca was determined to find the house. The street was lined with large trees, pastures, a church, and an occasional homestead. They reached the end of the road, again. "I don't see it, Daniel."

Daniel was patient; he turned the carriage around again. "It's okay, Rebecca. We'll keep trying until you believe it's not here. Okay?"

Rebecca nodded and about halfway down the road, another carriage entered the road from one of the homes. A man approached and smiled at Daniel and Rebecca. Rebecca's hand rested on Daniel's. Somehow, Daniel recognized Rebecca's urge and stopped the carriage. The man from the other carriage saw the subtle plea in Rebecca's eyes and also stopped his carriage so the two buggies were side-by-side.

"Good day," Daniel greeted.

"Good day," the stranger said.

"Sir, do you know where the Bradberrys live?" Rebecca asked.

"You mean the Bradburys?" the man asked.

Bradbury, Rebecca thought. *Yes, that's got to be it.* "Yes, excuse me. The Bradburys."

The man turned around and pointed up the road. "There is a path about 100 yards on the right. The path will take you through the property. The homestead sits away from the road."

"Thank you, sir," Rebecca said. The two carriages parted.

It didn't take them long to find the path. The trail ran through a pasture then into thicket, up a hill and at the crest of the hill, Rebecca recognized the Bradbury's home. She smiled and squeezed Daniel's hand. "This is it."

Daniel stopped the carriage in front of the large house. "Okay. Now what do we do?" Daniel asked. "We certainly cannot just go knocking and asking 'excuse me, did you steal the Osgood's child?' "

"I know," Rebecca said. "We'll just improvise."

"Improvise?"

Rebecca descended from the carriage, boldly walked to the front door, and knocked.

There was a pause, then a woman answered the door. "Good-day. Can I help you?" She smiled warmly.

"Good afternoon. My name is Rebecca Johnson. I'm looking for my aunt. She married a Bradbury from Boston some time ago. I was hoping that she may be here, or perhaps you may know of her."

"Well, my name is Elizabeth Bradbury. What is your Aunt's name?"

"Aunt Veronica."

"And she married a Bradbury? About how long ago?"

"I think it is going on ten years."

The woman appeared thoughtful. Then there was a disruption from be-hind her. She turned away from the door and leaned over to pick up something. "I have her," she called to someone, then turned back to the door, holding a smiling toddler.

Rebecca smiled when she saw the baby. *Right age*, she thought. The toddler squirmed in the woman's arms. She was dressed in clean clothes and appeared healthy. Red hair and freckles stood out on the child. The baby played with the woman's bonnet strings, pulling them out of a neat bow.

"What a beautiful baby," Rebecca said.

"Thank you."

When Daniel heard the baby chatting, he also descended and approached the front entry.

Rebecca noticed Daniel approaching. "Goodwife Bradbury, this is my husband, Daniel Johnson."

"Pleased to meet you; I'm Elizabeth Bradbury," then she turned back to Rebecca. "I don't know a Veronica Bradbury. I've only been a Bradbury a short while, though. My husband should be back anytime, would you like to come in and wait?"

"That would be very gracious of you," Daniel said.

The woman backed away, permitting Rebecca and Daniel into the foyer. A stairwell led to the second floor while a doorway to the right went to the gathering area. "There's a sitting room off to the left here," Elizabeth suggested.

Rebecca was the first to enter. A magnificent stone fireplace dressed the sitting room. *This is it*. Rebecca recognized the room. A varnished board supported by trestles centered the room; chairs were on both sides of it. A soft chair with arms rested against the wall, away from the long table. The walls were whitewashed, the high ceilings were supported with stained beams, while off-white linen curtains lined the diamond-shaped glass windows.

"What a beautiful house," Rebecca said, as she and Daniel sat in chairs on one side of the table, and Elizabeth sat near the head.

"Thank you. Would either of you like some tea?" Elizabeth asked, and she rang a small bell.

Minutes later another woman entered the room with a tea tray and set it on the table. Elizabeth deftly shifted Ann on her lap and served the tea. The baby remained playful, pulling at Elizabeth's white bonnet, exposing long dark locks of hair. Elizabeth remained good-natured and played lovingly with the baby.

"How old is she?" Rebecca asked.

"She's going on 18 months." The baby untied Elizabeth's bonnet strings again. "Do you want my bonnet, Ann?" Elizabeth asked.

Ann? Daniel thought.

Elizabeth took off the bonnet, exposing the long dark hair. The woman gently pulled her hair away from her face. It was Daniel who noticed the distinguished streak of gray.

"So, where are you from?" Elizabeth asked.

"We come from the north, Andover," Daniel answered. Daniel was impressed with his wife's accuracy. *Bradberry. The impressive house. The lady with the dark hair and gray streak. Ann? How did she do it?*

"Mrs. Bradbury, the child must have her father's hair, she certainly did not get yours," Rebecca said.

The woman smiled. "We believe her hair came from her maternal grandmother."

Rebecca and Daniel visited with Elizabeth briefly, then the front door opened and a distinguished-looking man entered from the foyer. He smiled, kissed Elizabeth and Ann, then turned to greet their guests.

"Jacob, this is Daniel and Rebecca Johnson. They are searching for Rebecca's Aunt Veronica who married a Bradbury about ten years ago."

"Yes, and your wife has been most gracious,"

Daniel rose and extended his hand to meet Jacob's outstretched hand.

The man smiled, admiring his wife. "Yes. She always is." Jacob Bradbury methodically went to the cushioned armed chair, picked it up and placed it at the head of the table. He took his seat among the group and as his wife had, he made the strangers feel welcome. "I have a cousin named Veronica Bradbury. But I am not aware of a family member who married a *Veronica*. I would be happy to ask family members. We're having a family reunion next month."

Rebecca and Daniel were asked to share the Bradbury's supper with them. They learned that Elizabeth and Jacob had been married for three years. Before they met and fell in love, both had been previously married and had lost their spouses to smallpox. Jacob had been a lawyer and judge, and was recently appointed by the new Governor as a member in his advisory cabinet. It was apparent that the couple adored the baby. Likewise, Ann appeared to love the couple, was healthy and seemed happy. Both Daniel and Rebecca were touched by the Bradbury's unconditional generosity. As they left the Bradbury's homestead, both felt a touch of guilt about what had brought them there.

"They could not have stolen the baby, Rebecca. They're decent folks," Daniel finally said.

Rebecca knew something was not right. But she was sure that the Bradbury's Ann was also Mary and Samuel's. "I agree. They are good people. But that is the Osgood's baby, Daniel. I'm sure of it."

"What do we do?"

Rebecca and Daniel spoke about the situation all the way home. By the time they arrived, it was dark. They agreed that Daniel would approach Samuel.

The next day there was a church picnic after the service. Rebecca and Daniel placed their blanket and picnic lunch strategically next to the Osgood's blanket. Samuel's furniture workshop had been completed and he had been promoting the furniture, encouraging people to stop by and see some of the pieces he had on display. As the owner of the general store, Daniel knew he could assist marketing Samuel's furniture.

The men discussed the possibilities of marketing the furniture at Daniel's store, and then Daniel changed the subject. "I've been meaning to ask you," Daniel started. "Do you know anyone by the name of Bradbury?"

Rebecca had been watching the men discuss the furniture strategy. She immediately became aware of the subject change by Samuel's altered stance. As if a magnet repelling from a like polarity, the man withdrew; Rebecca could see the energy glow that surrounded him shrink and redden.

"Never heard the name," Samuel finally said. He turned away and approached his blanket.

Daniel didn't let it rest and followed him to within hearing distance of Rebecca and Mary. "Jacob or Elizabeth Bradbury?" he probed.

"I told you–I don't know any Bradbury. Why are you bothering me with this?" The man's personality clearly changed. He was almost hostile.

"They seem to be nice people. We met them yesterday." Daniel knew he was pushing it. "They have a daughter the spitting image of Ann. She's 18 months old. Would you believe their baby's name is also Ann?"

Although Rebecca wanted to keep her eyes fixed to the ongoing conversation, something inside her told her to look within. She closed her eyes and instantly saw the scales of Libra. On one side was a large moneybag in a pan. It outweighed a small object that was teetering in the air. Rebecca couldn't see what was being measured against the money. But clearly, the money outweighed the object. In her imagination, she reached in the pan and picked up the small object. It was Ann's teething ring. When she looked back at the scale, the moneybag had disappeared, and in it's place–a chair. It was Samuel's escalating voice that brought her back.

"You know, I'm tired of you and your wife poking around. This is our life. If I see either of you snooping around my property anymore, I'm telling the authorities."

"Ann wasn't stolen," Rebecca whispered.

The Osgoods overheard the whisper. Daniel turned to Rebecca. "What sweetheart?"

Then Rebecca spoke confidently. "Ann was not abducted. The Bradbury's bought her. The money was used to finance the furniture workshop." There was a part of Rebecca and Daniel that was relieved; they both had liked the Bradbury's and couldn't believe they could have taken Ann.

For a moment, Mary and Samuel were speechless. They just stared at Rebecca. Then a cool tone managed to escape Mary's lips. "How did you know that?"

Daniel didn't give Rebecca a chance to respond. He reached for her hand. "Let's go." The two began packing up their picnic belongings.

"My wife asked you a question," Samuel yelled. "Now answer her."

Rebecca turned and looked into Samuel's cold eyes. *Why couldn't I have seen this before?* Then she saw the same hostility in Mary's eyes. "It's not important how I know this. I'm just sorry that I didn't see it before." Rebecca and Daniel turned to pick up their blanket and basket.

"You have no basis to make such claims," Samuel said. "This is unnatural. This is evil. You're a witch."

With this, Daniel turned to Samuel. "My wife is not evil. You have such audacity, standing here—calling her evil, after you sold your own child." Daniel's temples were throbbing. He turned to Rebecca and took the picnic basket from her. "Let's get out of here."

The two climbed into the carriage. "Rebecca Johnson, you're a witch. You're evil," Samuel screamed.

As the carriage pulled away, Daniel turned back to see other congregation members gather around Mary and Samuel. Their eyes and mouths were opened wide in astonishment.

"I'm sorry," Rebecca whispered.

Daniel took Rebecca's small hand, brought it to his lips, and gently kissed her fingers. "I love you."

Daniel's head throbbed all the way home. He knew he needed to protect Rebecca, but didn't know how to do it. "We must get rid of your things. We need to get them off our property."

"Let's not overreact, Daniel." Rebecca was saddened at the thought of losing her treasured possessions.

"Rebecca, they are hanging witches. There's a major witch-hunt going on. I don't want to take any chances. I'll hide your things in the storage area at the store. I promise Rebecca, I will not throw any of it away."

When they arrived home, they wasted no time and went to the small shed. Rebecca sadly packed all of her ritual belongings. Even Ann's teething ring got tucked in with the Isis bits and pieces. Later that afternoon they went to the store, where Daniel unloaded the crates and hid them in the storeroom.

It was Wednesday afternoon when John arrived at the store. He was visibly stressed and anxiously waited until a customer left the store. Then he wasted no time.

"The Osgoods filed a complaint. They're alleging witchcraft. What the hell happened?"

Daniel took a deep breath. "How bad is it?"

"The complaint has reached the special council. That's how I know about it. They meet in the office next to my own. I fear they may raid your home, to search for evidence." John nervously paced the store, his fingers twisting his mustache.

"I've already moved her things."

"Move them? Just burn them."

"I can't do that. They're Rebecca's belongings. I promised her."

"If they find them—they will hang her."

"I've hidden her things at the store. They are safe."

The following afternoon Daniel was sweeping at the store when he heard a loud bang at the front door. He turned. A group of men entered the store.

"That's him." The local sheriff pointed at Daniel.

Two guards quickly approached Daniel and stood behind him.

"What is the meaning of this?" Daniel asked.

Another man approached Daniel and stood before him. "Goodman Daniel Johnson?"

"Yes," Daniel answered.

"I'm High Sheriff Corwin. I am here on behalf of a council that has been formed to investigate actions involving witchcraft."

"How can I help you?"

"We have had complaints that indicate that you have been practicing sorcery."

Me? But Daniel remained silent.

"We are here to search the premises." With this, two other men went to the storeroom.

"May I ask what type of complaints you have against me?" Daniel asked.

"There has been a complaint from the Osgoods, as well as a letter."

A letter? "May I see the letter?"

"You may see the letter at your examination."

It wasn't long before the two men returned from the storeroom with Rebecca's crates. The evidence was set before High Sheriff Corwin. The sheriff opened one crate revealing the caldron, a double-edged knife, chalice, wand and book.

"This is enough," the sheriff said. He turned to Daniel, "Goodman Johnson I am taking you into custody until the special court has examined the evidence against you."

There was a disruption at the door. Daniel could see John attempting to pass the guards at the entrance. Through the storefront window, Daniel saw a group of people gathering.

"I am John Price, Goodman Johnson's lawyer. Let me through," John demanded.

The sheriff turned to John. "Let him through."

"I want to speak to Goodman Johnson, alone."

John was given five minutes. Two guards remained in the store—one at the front, the other at the stockroom—blocking both exits.

John looked through the evidence that sat before them and then turned to Daniel. "You should have burned the damn things," he said unsympathetically. "What have they said?"

"Just that they believe I'm a sorcerer."

"I heard that there was another complaint. Did they tell you what it was?"

"They said it was a letter." Daniel turned away from a guard and whispered, "They haven't mentioned Rebecca. Do they suspect her?"

John shook his head, "I'm not sure. I don't think so."

"You've got to help me keep it that way."

"Are you mad? They're going to hang you, Daniel."

"So be it. If it means that Rebecca is safe, so be it."

John hesitated. "Are you sure this is how you want it?"

Daniel nodded. "Yes. Can you keep her out of this?"

The front door opened and the sheriff interrupted. "Your five minutes are up."

The guards moved to Daniel and they started removing him from the store. Daniel reached for John's arm. "Can you?"

John finally nodded. "I'll try."

Daniel was escorted from the store. Outside, a large group had formed. He was directed toward a wagon and sat in the rear bed. A group of well-dressed men were talking next to the prisoner's wagon. Daniel was surprised when he saw the familiar face. His distinguished look gave him away. Jacob Bradbury's and Daniel's eyes remained locked on each other until the horse and wagon pulled Daniel out of sight.

Rebecca was surprised when she saw John ride up to the house that afternoon. She greeted him outside as he dismounted from his horse.

"Hello, John. What are you doing out this way today?"

John tied off his horse, avoiding eye contact with her. "We need to talk, Rebecca."

"That sounds serious." When John finally looked into her eyes, her smile disappeared. She knew something was wrong. "Oh my god. It is Daniel. What's wrong?"

John took one of her hands and directed her toward the bench on the side of the house. "There is something wrong. It's terrible."

"What is it?"

"Daniel has been arrested."

"Arrested? For what?"

"Witchcraft."

"Witchcraft? Well, that's ridiculous." She stood, now taking one of his hands. "Let's go. We need to make everything right."

But John remained seated.

"John, I need your help."

"I understand. But Daniel and I have already talked about this. He wants to take the responsibility."

"But you know I would never allow him to do that, don't you?"

"I know you're just as stubborn as he is. Daniel has asked that I protect you from any suspicion. So I certainly cannot take you there, if you're just going to confess."

"Fine. Then I'll just have to do it myself. Where did they take him?"

"I can't tell you."

"You know I will find out."

John sighed. "What if I can arrange a meeting between the two of you? That way you can hear Daniel's position. But you must promise not to disclose any information about . . . you know . . . what you do."

"You don't approve of my spiritual beliefs. You never have."

"Spiritual beliefs? That's a strange way of defining devil worship."

"John, I do not worship Satan. I fear Satan." Rebecca sighed. She knew this was not the time to explain or defend her beliefs. "I do need to see Daniel. Can you arrange it?"

John studied Rebecca but did not respond.

"I promise, I will not say anything about witchcraft."

"I'm going to Salem Town. I'll make arrangements for a visit and try to learn more about the evidence against him. I'll be back tomorrow, mid-morning. "Will you be all right tonight?"

Rebecca nodded, "Yes."

Chapter 8

It was dark. Judging from his perception of time, Daniel thought it would be daytime, but he couldn't tell from the absence of windows. Cool stone walls surrounded him, except for the wooden panel door that was slammed behind him the evening before.

Daniel moved toward the faint light slanting through a grate in the door. He could see only the pierced-tin lantern that hung in the passageway, casting eerie flickering shadows.

Daniel paced the dirt floor of the tiny cell. The stench of human waste penetrated his every breath. A thin blanket lay on the straw-covered bench in the corner; the previous evening it had offered no comfort from the dankness of the cell.

Occasionally Daniel could hear the cries from women in the torture cell across from him. At times, he could hear the scurry of the rats that dwelled within the cell. Most of the time, he could hear his heart beat within him, and, sporadically, he heard the voices. Nobody was there, yet he heard voices. *Am I going mad?* They started when he tried to pray the evening before. In his meditation, he heard the voice of a woman at first, then a man. Then he could have sworn he heard Rebecca. Although he realized it was impossible, he found her voice comforting.

That morning when bread and water were passed through the barred opening, he was told that his lawyer was visiting that afternoon. Based upon the growl from his stomach, Daniel was hoping to see his friend soon.

Finally, he heard someone approach. Instead of passing more bread and water, a guard said, "Back away from the door and stand against the wall."

Daniel obeyed, and the door was jostled opened. A smile came to Daniel's face when he saw John enter, but he ran to Rebecca when she came into the cell. The guard's pike quickly brushed against his chest.

"Against the wall, I said," the guard repeated.

Daniel complied and he stood against the wall, but his eyes remained fixed upon his wife. After John and Rebecca were in the cell, the door abruptly slammed shut, and Rebecca was in Daniel's arms. They kissed.

"We don't have much time," John interrupted.

Out of respect for his friend, Daniel turned to John but did not stop embracing his wife.

"Daniel, the plan is to have an examination of the evidence on Monday. If there is sufficient evidence against you, you will remain imprisoned, here, until you stand trial at a later date. I see you got the blanket." John pointed at the blanket that lay upon the straw.

"Yes," Daniel said.

"I also paid for your bread and water; did they feed you?"

"Yes, John. Thank you."

"I won't allow this to happen, Daniel. I'm the one who should be here. I'm prepared to stay now."

"No. I won't allow it, Rebecca. Please don't do anything foolish," Daniel objected.

"I would have to agree with Daniel on this," John announced. "I've been able to review the evidence against Daniel. Rebecca, I believe if you turn yourself in, both of you would stand trial."

"But Daniel never did anything. I can tell them this, and make it right."

John shook his head. "The problem with it is twofold. First, based upon the Osgood's complaint, they already suspect you, Rebecca. But their complaint is pretty vague. It claims the two of you meddled in their lives and knew things that you could not naturally know. It's only speculative evidence and they're using it against Daniel right now. The decisive argument is this letter. The letter claims Daniel is a wizard and used unnatural means for his personal financial gain. It doesn't implicate you at all, Rebecca. My concern is–if you turn yourself in, they won't release Daniel and both of you will stand trial."

"I can't have you do this, Daniel. I would rather take the chance."

The guard approached the door grate. "Your time is almost up."

Daniel looked at John. "Can I trust you to protect her?"

John nodded.

Daniel turned back to Rebecca. "I don't want to spend this time arguing with you. I love you, Rebecca. It will be all right." He always could find strength while looking into her eyes. "I need to share something with you."

"What, Daniel?"

"I'm hearing voices," he whispered. He didn't want his friend to hear. "Do you think I'm going crazy?"

Rebecca smiled. "You hear the spirits," she said. "Listen to what they tell you."

"I hear your voice, too."

"You're hearing my thoughts, Daniel. You have a gift," Rebecca smiled again.

Daniel did not want John to hear their conversation, so he changed the subject. "Do you know who I saw yesterday, at the store, when they arrested me?"

Rebecca shook her head.

"Jacob Bradbury."

"Jacob?" Rebecca asked.

John overheard. "Bradbury? You know Jacob Bradbury?"

Both Rebecca and Daniel turned to John. "We have met him," Daniel said. "How do you know him?"

But there was a loud bang on the door and the guard instructed Daniel to move against the wall. Rebecca was silent as she walked with Daniel to the wall. The two looked into each other's eyes, Daniel seeing something he had not seen before. *Taylor?* He thought. He saw a familiarity he had not seen before. *Are you Taylor?* He asked in his head.

Then, he clearly heard Rebecca's voice in his head, *"Yes, Jessie. It is I."*

"It's time to leave," the guard said.

She turned to the guard. "One moment, please?"

He was obviously annoyed, but nodded.

Daniel's eyes searched Rebecca's. "What does this mean?" he asked.

"I told you once before that we've been together in other lifetimes," she whispered.

Daniel nodded.

"It's time," the guard interrupted.

Rebecca placed her lips gently on Daniel's and kissed him, then whispered in his ear. "Just remember, all time is one."

Daniel's and Rebecca's eyes remained on each other until the solid wooden door slammed shut between them.

All time is one? What does that mean?

Rebecca and John did not speak very much all the way back to Andover. Rebecca's mind raced, trying to identify ways to get her husband released. Then she remembered Jacob.

"How do you know Jacob Bradbury?" Rebecca asked.

"Jacob is one of the six members of Governor Phips's special advisory council to hear witchcraft cases."

"Really?" *What a coincidence.* "If Daniel went to trial, would Jacob hear the case?"

"He may be part of the trial, but he certainly would be involved in the examination, to determine whether there's sufficient evidence against Daniel. How is it that you and Daniel know Bradbury?"

"Oh, I knew his family," Rebecca lied. "Do you think it would be a good idea to talk with Jacob?"

John shook his head. "I wouldn't. Not while there's a proceeding against Daniel. It would be a conflict of interest for him."

"I guess you're right," Rebecca said. "John, how do you feel about all of this?"

"What do you mean?"

"I know Daniel's your best friend, and I know you don't approve of what I do."

"Daniel and I have been friends a long time. He has always been there for me, I just want to be there for him," John said. "I don't approve of witchcraft. It seems ironic that Daniel has asked that I protect you from yourself."

Rebecca detected a note of bitterness in John's voice. "I know you're hurting. I'm sorry that I'm contributing to it." She placed her hand over John's, and gently squeezed it, "Don't worry, John, we are going to get him out."

"But not at your expense." He softened. "I gave him my word."

When John and Rebecca arrived in Andover, John wished Rebecca good evening, then he said he would be back on Sunday afternoon. They planned to go to Salem Town for Daniel's examination on Monday.

After John left, Rebecca made preparations for her trip the following morning. Rebecca knew she needed more information about her adversary. That evening before she went to bed, she spent hours in meditation, focusing on Jacob Bradbury.

It was still dark that Saturday morning when Rebecca mounted her horse. She was dressed in Daniel's trousers and shirt. The clothing was very baggy on her frame, but she had a long trip ahead of her and knew it would be more comfortable and permit faster travel than a dress.

Rebecca hoped she would remember her way into Boston and the way to the Bradbury's property. Whenever she came to a fork and was not sure which direction to go, she would close her eyes and let the spirits guide her, and they never failed her. Early that morning she arrived at the homestead.

Rebecca took a deep breath before she knocked on the Bradbury's front door. The door opened and Elizabeth peeked out. Elizabeth did not immediately recognize Rebecca dressed in men's clothing, with wind-blown hair, but then she saw Rebecca's crystal blue eyes. The door opened a little more, "Why, is that you, Rebecca?" Elizabeth asked.

"It is indeed, Elizabeth. I'm so sorry to intrude . . . but I was hoping I may talk with your husband."

Elizabeth eyed Rebecca's attire.

"I apologize for the clothing. I'm not with Daniel. It's a long ride from Andover. I wore something that would be more comfortable."

"You're not with Daniel? And you rode all this way by yourself? You must have been out before first light. Please, come in."

As Rebecca was escorted to the familiar sitting area she could hear Jacob from upstairs call down to his wife. "Elizabeth, there's a horse out front. Is someone here?"

"Excuse me," Elizabeth said. She left Rebecca in the sitting room, and in the foyer called upstairs to her husband. "Yes, Jacob. Goodwife Johnson is here to see you."

Rebecca detected a note of tension in Jacob's voice when he called back. "Who?"

"You know. Rebecca Johnson. She and her husband visited last weekend."

There was silence. Then Rebecca heard footsteps and whispering in the foyer. Moments later, Jacob walked into the sitting room. The sparkle in his eyes that Rebecca remembered was now gone, and the color was drained from his face.

"Goodwife Johnson, what can I help you with?" he asked.

"It's about my husband, Daniel."

"I don't think you should be here."

"Jacob." Elizabeth was surprised at her husband's rudeness.

"Goodwife Johnson . . . Rebecca, do you know who I am?"

"I know that you will rule on whether there's sufficient evidence against my husband on Monday."

"Then you should not be here. I must ask you to leave, now." Jacob went to the foyer and opened the door.

Elizabeth just watched, her mouth opened wide in astonishment.

Rebecca looked at Elizabeth, then at Jacob through the doorway. "I know about Ann."

Now Elizabeth could not remain silent. "What about Ann?"

"I know that Samuel and Mary Osgood are Ann's true parents."

"Oh my God," Elizabeth gasped.

"So, is this blackmail?" Jacob asked as he inched back into the room.

Rebecca shook her head. "No, sir. I just want justice. My husband is innocent; I'm the one who is a witch."

Elizabeth stepped away from Rebecca.

"And I am supposed to believe you?" Jacob asked.

"You have an innocent man imprisoned. And it's his love for me that will stop him from telling you the truth."

"How do I know it is not you who is trying to protect the guilty?"

"It is I who found out about Ann and was able to find you last week."

"You weren't looking for your aunt?" Elizabeth was shocked.

"I'm so sorry. I didn't want to lie. The truth is–when the Osgoods claimed that Ann was stolen–"

"Stolen?" chorused Elizabeth and Jacob.

"Yes, stolen. The Osgoods claimed that Ann was stolen and . . . my heart ached for them. I just wanted to help them. I have . . . gifts. I am able to see things, hear things, feel things, sometimes . . . just know things. I know now that I completely misread them. I had asked the spirits to help me find Ann for them, and that is what led me to you. But when Daniel and I met you, we knew something was not right. Daniel asked Samuel Osgood if he knew you and he went mad."

"Look, I don't see how I can help you with any of this."

"Take me–instead of Daniel. He is completely innocent."

"Then talk to a lawyer about this, not me."

"I have. He seems to think that if I turn myself in, they won't drop the charges against Daniel."

"I have seen the evidence against your husband–it is very persuading. The Osgood's complaint is vague; now I have a better idea what the meaning behind it is. But there's another letter that suggests your husband used unnatural methods to help with his financial success, and then they found all these tools used for witchcraft in his store."

"It was I who cast a prosperity spell on his business. He is not even aware of it. And after the confrontation with the Osgoods, Daniel didn't feel comfortable having my possessions at the house and removed them. He hid them at his store."

"I still don't see how I can help you. And I feel this conversation needs to come to an end."

Rebecca was getting desperate. "What are you going to do when the truth comes out about Ann?"

Elizabeth went to her husband's side.

"There's nothing wrong with adopting children," Jacob stated confidently.

"But you didn't adopt Ann. You bought her, but it's not even that simple, is it?"

"What are you talking about?" Jacob asked.

"You made a deal with the Osgoods while Mary was pregnant with Ann. Elizabeth actually pretended to go through a simultaneous pregnancy. But Samuel got greedy and demanded more money after the baby was born. You went through months of negotiating, which put your family into hiding. You didn't have a baby to show off, so you said the baby was ill and could not be around people. You had to let your staff go, until your deal with the Osgoods was final, and Ann was in your possession."

"You seem to think you know everything. Why would we do this?" Jacob asked. "Why wouldn't we just adopt her?"

"That part didn't make any sense to me. Inheritance. Elizabeth's parents' will stipulates that upon their death, the assets are to be divided among blood family only. Elizabeth was very ill right before her first marriage. She got the fever. It was bad; they thought they would lose her. Obviously she recovered, but she became infertile."

Elizabeth went to Rebecca. "How do you know these things?"

"I asked the spirits and they showed me."

"Oh my God, Jacob. What are we going to do?" Elizabeth cried.

"Take me and let my husband go," Rebecca pleaded. "I will plead guilty, you will not need to have the Osgoods testify, and the truth about Ann doesn't need to come out. I promise–I will take your secret to my grave."

Jacob studied Rebecca for a moment then he shook his head. "With the evidence against your husband, I don't think I could eliminate suspicion against him."

"Then the evidence needs to disappear," Rebecca planted the idea.

"I can't do that," Jacob was shocked.

"Without doing it, an innocent man may be hanged . . . and your secret could destroy your career, and disinherit Ann. Is that justice?"

Early Monday morning, John and Rebecca rode together to the home of Jonathan Corwin, one of the members of Phips's advisory council. Here, there would be a preliminary examination of the evidence against Daniel. Daniel remained in Rebecca's thoughts most of the way. When they arrived at the two-story house, they were directed to a room that had been set up for pretrial examinations.

Shortly after, Daniel arrived with chains on his legs and wrists. His clothes were soiled and wrinkled and his hair unkempt. When Rebecca saw Daniel, she immediately went to him but was stopped by two guards. Daniel's and Rebecca's eyes remained fixed on each other, as they were pulled apart. Daniel was brought in front of the room and Rebecca sat behind him.

Some well-dressed men entered and sat in front of the room. Jacob was one of the men.

William Stoughton, the Lord Chief Justice of the council, spoke. "The court of Oyer and Terminer was formed by Governor Phips to specifically hear and determine witchcraft cases in Essex County of Massachusetts. This is not a trial. This is an examination of evidence against . . ." Stoughton looked at some documents, searching for a name. ". . . Goodman Daniel Johnson. Let us begin."

A man brought in three crates containing Rebecca's possessions that were found in Daniel's store. The evidence was presented and reviewed. Then a document was presented to Stoughton. Stoughton reviewed it and passed it on to another member of the council for review.

Stoughton turned to the presenter of evidence. "Where's the other document?"

"We don't know, Sir."

"What do you mean?" Stoughton asked.

"All the evidence was together on Friday. This is all there was this morning."

"What?"

That's my cue. Rebecca thought. *Thank you, Jacob.* Rebecca took a deep breath and stood. "May I approach?"

"Who are you?" Stoughton asked.

"I am Rebecca Johnson. I am the wife of Daniel Johnson."

"No," Daniel objected.

"Rebecca sit," John instructed.

"This is unorthodox," Stoughton said. "What business do you have here?"

"I am here to present testimony." Rebecca did not give Stoughton time to respond. "My husband is no witch. I am. He is innocent. I will plead guilty to your charges in exchange for his freedom."

"No," cried Daniel.

"Objection, your honor," John stood.

"Who are you?" Stoughton asked.

"John Price. I am counsel for the family. I believe Goodwife Johnson is under duress and this is her desperate attempt to free her husband."

"John, you know I speak the truth."

"Order." Stoughton said. "Perhaps *both* Goodman and Goodwife Johnson should stand trial. We can sort this out then."

"Sir, my husband is no witch. He is innocent. Surely you don't want to send an innocent man to trial."

"Goodwife Johnson, there is a complaint by the Osgoods of Andover that does implicate yourself, as well as your husband. All the other evidence suggests that your husband is a witch. We did not bring you in for examination because there is insufficient evidence against you."

"There is no evidence against my husband."

"On the contrary, we found all this in your husband's store." Stoughton pointed to the three crates that sat in front of him. "And we have a letter suggesting that your husband used unnatural means for personal gain."

"These are all my possessions. After the Osgoods threatened me, Daniel took them and hid them. They are mine. Most of the items are even marked with my initials, 'R.M.,' from my maiden name. If you don't believe me, look and see."

It was Jacob who went to the crate and pulled out a black pot.

"Check the bottom of the caldron," Rebecca suggested.

Jacob turned the pot over, nodded to Stoughton, then passed the pot to another member of the council. He then pulled out the double-edged knife.

"Bottom handle of the athame."

Jacob easily found the initials then passed the evidence to another member of the council. He removed the chalice and held it up for Rebecca.

"Actually that was a gift from someone, so my initials are not there, but the initials 'M.C.' are on the bottom." Rebecca repeated accurate details over and over about her belongings.

Jacob removed a box from a crate and held it up. "Goodwife Johnson, I don't want you to tell me, but do you know what is in this box?"

"I do."

Jacob turned to Daniel. "Goodman Johnson, do you know what is in this box?"

Daniel nodded, "Yes."

"Would you tell me then?"

Daniel appeared beat, then guessed. "Stones."

"Is that correct Goodwife Johnson?" Jacob asked.

"That is not correct."

"Could you tell us what is in the box?"

"That box consists of items associated with the goddess Isis. There's a statue of her, some branches, stones, a scepter, cup, and mirror."

"Is that all?" Jacob asked.

"I think so."

"There's something in here that seems out of place. Do you know what I'm talking about?"

Rebecca stared back at Jacob. *What am I missing?* Then she remembered. "You're right. There is an item that would seem out of place. It's a teething ring."

Jacob lifted the teething ring from the box, then turned to Stoughton. "Lord Chief Justice, in view of this woman's testimony, as well as the evidence against Goodman Johnson, I feel Goodwife Johnson should be placed under arrest for practicing witchcraft and Goodman Johnson should be released."

Other members of the council agreed with the recommendation.

"Goodwife Johnson, it would seem that you have your wish. You are under arrest for practicing witchcraft and you will go to trial."

Daniel had a sick feeling in his stomach. *How could this happen?*

Two guards moved to Rebecca and swiftly took her away. It all happened so quickly, Daniel never had a chance to hold her, to kiss her, or to say goodbye. He caught sight of her looking over one of the guard's shoulders as she was taken from the courtroom. Daniel heard Rebecca's voice clearly in his head. "*I love you, Daniel.*"

Daniel tried strenuously to follow, but the chains on his feet tripped him and he fell to the floor. He heard the door slam separating himself and his love. Tired, beaten and hurting, Daniel could not prevent the tears from coming. He lay on the floor, resting his forehead on his arms, hiding his pain from the men that surrounded him.

Chapter 9

Jessie never heard Carrie count down the numbers, bringing her back to the present. But somehow, her subconscious did, and when she came out of the hypnotic trance, she was disoriented. Eventually she became aware that her heart was pounding wildly, and she was perspiring. The light hurt her eyes. She squinted as she looked at her hands. Jessie felt her clammy face and the tears that had fallen to her cheeks.

"Are you okay?" Carrie asked softly.

Jessie could not talk. When she stood, she realized how light-headed she was but managed to find the bathroom. At the sink, she turned on the cold water and splashed it on her face. She studied her eyes in the mirror. *I'm back*, she thought. Jessie continued to look at her reflection, searching for some resemblance of Daniel.

Carrie was outside the bathroom door. "Jessie, are you okay?"

"Yes." Jessie returned to the couch.

"Can you share any of your experience with me?"

When Jessie finally spoke, she was surprised at how foreign her voice sounded. "It was so real."

"Yes, it usually is."

"It was very strange. Initially, I heard your instructions until . . . I saw him."

"You saw who?"

"Me . . . Daniel."

"That's very good. You were able to get your name."

"After I saw that he was the man in my dreams, it became . . . so real. It was like I was actually there. Except . . ."

"Except what, Jessie?"

"The majority of it was as if I was there and experiencing it. Then . . . there were parts of it where I wasn't there and it was like watching a movie."

"What do you mean?"

"There were . . . scenes, for lack of a better word, where I wasn't there. But I was able to see what was going on."

"Now, that's interesting. Perhaps you were able to learn things you didn't know in the last life. You may want to write down your experience. Look at the scenes that you were not in and ask yourself what you learned. See what that little voice inside of you says."

"I recognized her."

"You recognized the person you're having connections with?"

Jessie nodded. "It's so strange. In that life, I recognized Rebecca . . . from a previous life. But from this one."

"What?"

"I didn't initially see her as Taylor Andrews." Jessie stopped. She realized it was the first time she had said Taylor's name to Carrie.

"It's okay, Jessie. Whatever you say remains here. Use me to sort things out."

Jessie took a deep breath. "I was married to a woman who was a witch. Her name was Rebecca. It was during the Salem witch-hunt period. Mistakenly, I got arrested and was imprisoned. Something happened to me in that prison. I started hearing voices, and when I saw Rebecca, I recognized her as Taylor Andrews and she knew me as Jessie Mercer."

"So in your past life, you had past-life recall?"

"But how is that possible? I was recalling the future. It hadn't happened yet. And in this life–I don't even know the woman."

"Yet. You don't know her yet. Remember when we met earlier? I explained that all time is coexisting."

Jessie recalled what Rebecca had told her in the cell. "All time is one."

"That's correct," Carrie said.

"No. That's what Rebecca told me when I recognized her. She said 'all time is one.' "

"This is very unusual. But very exciting," Carrie said. "Tell me. Did it help? Did you get any answers?"

"I guess in some ways, I do have answers–I know I'm not going crazy. But in other ways, it raises many more questions. Like . . . what happened? They took her from me. In my dream, she was tried, convicted and sentenced to be hanged. Did it ever happen?"

"I don't know. Is it important for you to know that?"

For a moment, Jessie feared the worst. "I'm not sure I want to know."

"If you want to know, perhaps you can gather some insight from the history books. You remembered her first name; do you remember the last name?"

"Yes, it's . . . it's on the tip of my tongue . . . Johnson. I was Daniel Johnson and she was Rebecca Johnson."

"There's a lot of documentation on Salem. If you need to know–look it up."

"Maybe I'll do that."

"Was there anyone else in your past life that you recognized from this life?"

"There was one person that seemed familiar. But I can't place him. He was my best friend; his name was John."

Jessie was exhausted when she left Carrie's. Her experience left her totally drained. When she arrived home, she fed Maxwell and went to bed.

The following day Jessie realized she was just as tired. Carrie called around ten o'clock to check on her.

"How are you today, Jessie?"

"I'm exhausted. I came home yesterday afternoon and went right to bed. I slept past my usual wake time, and I'm still exhausted."

"You had a very emotional experience. I guess a little fatigue is expected, but if it continues, you should do something about it. If you need anyone to talk to, just call me. Okay?"

"Thank you, Carrie."

After her phone call, Jessie went to her office. From her Rolodex she pulled a card, picked up her phone and pressed the numbers. The call was answered on the second ring, "Good morning, Powell Library."

"Good morning. Is Sandra there?"

"I'll ring her office."

Moments later a woman picked up the phone. "Hello, this is Sandra."

"Hi, Sandra. This is Jessie Mercer."

"How are you, Jessie?"

"Very good, and you?"

"I'm fine. You doing some research?" Sandra was accustomed to Jessie's calls. Over the years, Jessie had used Sandra to find books on various subject matters for her writing. It had been a while since they had spoken.

"Yes. I need your help. Do you have the time?"

Sandra always made time for Jessie. She always got a kick from seeing her name in the acknowledgement page of Jessie's books.

"I need some information on the Salem witch trials."

"We have a lot of material on that subject. I'll pull it. Stop by and look through it. If none of it helps you, I'll put a request in to the other campus libraries."

"That sounds good. I'll be there around three."

Jessie entered the UCLA library. *Am I ready for this? Do I really need to know what happened to Rebecca?* In the library foyer, she hesitated pressing the elevator button. *What if they hanged her? Will I ever be able to live with that thought?*

"*It happened over 300 years ago, Jessie,*" a voice in Jessie's head said.

Jessie was surprised by the voice. *I should have protected her more. I should have put my foot down when I learned she was seeking Ann. But I didn't.*

"You wouldn't have been able to stop her."

Jessie was still standing next to the elevator in the foyer. The elevator door opened and a young man got in, pressed his floor then held the door open. He looked directly at Jessie and asked, "Are you going up?"

Jessie gazed at the student, noticing his "Salem State College" T-shirt. "I guess so," she uttered. Then she got in the elevator.

When she arrived at Sandra's office, Sandra was nowhere to be found, but there was a note and a pile of books on her desk.

> *Jessie, I'm in a meeting. Look through the books and let me know if they'll do. If not, let me know more specifically what you're looking for. Sandra.*

Sandra had left Jessie eight books. Jessie picked up the pile then searched for a quiet place in the library. She found an unoccupied table in a secluded area, took a seat, and opened her first book. She quickly glanced over the indexes in the books, looking for lists of the accused. She was on her fifth book, *Tituba, Reluctant Witch of Salem*, when she saw the title for Appendix A: "Timetable of Accusations and Confessions, February–November 1692, page 183."

As she read the title, she felt the warmth and fullness in her chest. On page 183, the list of those accused or confessed began. *There are over a hundred names here.* The list showed where each person resided, along with the outcome of the trial, whether they were executed, imprisoned, died in prison, and so on.

Jessie was on the last page of names and she had not found Rebecca Johnson. Then her heart started pounding wildly when she discovered it toward the bottom of the page. With her finger, Jessie followed the information across the page: "Rebecca Johnson, Residence–Andover, Outcome–Unknown."

Unknown? What the hell does that mean? She quickly went through the list again. Although there were some "No Record" outcomes, she could not find another outcome stating "Unknown." *Maybe I'm not meant to find out what happened.*

"Maybe, you're not ready to find out what really happened," the little voice inside her head said.

Since when have I been hearing voices in my head? she asked herself.

"*Since Daniel,*" the voice answered.

Later that evening when Jessie arrived home, she listened to a message on her answering machine from her editor. "Hi, Jessie, it's Catherine. I haven't heard from you in a while. Wanted to see how close you are on your new project. What's the working title? Oh, yes–Deceptions. Give me a call when you can."

After dinner, Jessie went to her office and turned on her computer to check her e-mail. She realized that she had been out of touch with reality for too long when she saw the long list of messages. One of which was a note from Travis Sanders.

> *Jessie,*
>
> *I don't know what it is. I've got a good feeling about this one. When can I see your manuscript?*
>
> *Travis*

As Jessie read the message on her computer screen, she heard a thud. She looked on the floor and saw the pile of unopened mail that had been resting on her desk. *How did that happen?* She sat there staring at the unopened envelopes, trying to come up with a reasonable explanation how the mail fell to the floor. But there was none.

Jessie looked around her office. It was then that she realized how much she had abandoned her own life to explore a past life. *It's time I get on with my life, the here and now. I have some answers.* Jessie picked up an article on Taylor Andrews and looked into her crystal blue eyes. *I don't know what all this means. But I can't lose my own reality. There's a part of me that wants to run to you, Rebecca. But I know I can't . . . I need to let you go. I love you, Rebecca. I need to say goodbye.* Jessie wiped tears from her eyes then closed the magazine.

Jessie knew she was compulsive. She went around her office collecting remnants of Taylor Andrews: articles, notes, CDs, and drawings, and placed them in a box. She labeled the box "T.A." then stored it in the basement crawl space.

When she returned to her office, she picked up the manuscript of *Deceptions*. Somehow, she knew it was her destiny. She glanced at the computer screen, then set the manuscript aside. *There is one last thing I need to do, before I finish this*, Jessie thought. Her fingers settled on the keyboard and she typed in "www.unitedairlines.com."

Chapter 10

TWO YEARS LATER.

Jessie was reviewing the *Los Angeles Times*. *Deceptions* had been in the number-one position for a month. All the reviews for the book were positive.

After Jessie had finished the manuscript for the novel, Travis Sanders had hired her to write the screenplay. The screenplay was now finished, and Travis was in the process of selecting the actors and actresses for the movie. As with *Beyond Paradise*, Jessie's contract had a consult clause for the movie, assuring that Travis would consider her ideas. Although Travis was not obligated to follow any of her suggestions, he made a sincere effort to keep Jessie in the loop, if not because of the contract, because of the friendship and mutual respect that had developed between the two.

For close to two years, Jessie had successfully dismissed the connections to Taylor Andrews. Once she recognized she had become obsessed, she realized how much harm she was bringing to her life, and then she was able to detach herself. Occasionally, she would experience a connection to Taylor. Rather than dwelling on it, Jessie would go inside. *Hi Rebecca. I hope life is treating you well. I miss you.* The thought would put a smile on her face, but she could move on.

Jessie was in her office going through the mail when her phone rang.

"Hello."

"Hi Jessie, it's Travis."

"Hi Travis, how are you?"

"We're meeting on casting the roles and developing a production time-table. Tomorrow at three o'clock. Interested?"

"Sure. I'll be there."

The following day Jessie left her house early to run errands. After the bank, post office and dry cleaners, she met up with Linda Speller for lunch in downtown Los Angeles. Linda had been a friend of Jessie's for years. They met regularly for lunch every couple of months.

"How's the new firm?" Jessie asked.

"Wonderful," Linda answered. "I think this is going to be a good opportunity for me. I should make partner in two years."

"That's great. Are you still specializing in corporate law?"

"Yes. It's one area the firm was weak in." Linda drained her lemonade. "What's new in your life?"

"I'm still working on the movie of *Deceptions*. That seems to be taking up a lot of time right now. What about you? Are you seeing anyone special?"

"Between the new job and the renovation at the cabin, I haven't had time to date."

"What are you doing at the cabin?"

"I'm renovating the kitchen. You should use the cabin sometime. It's a great getaway. Big Pines is not too far, not too close. Why don't you plan on using the cabin after the renovation?"

"Maybe after *Deceptions* is made. Then I'll have more time. Thanks."

Although Jessie knew she would be early for the meeting, she decided to head over to Travis's office. It was about 2:15 when she arrived at TSS Productions. She found Alison, Travis's secretary, swearing at her laptop computer.

"Have you ever tried to sweet talk it?" Jessie asked.

Alison looked up and smiled. Her green eyes seemed to light up at the sight of Jessie. "It doesn't deserve my affection. You're early; Travis is still in a meeting."

"I was downtown for lunch. It didn't make a lot of sense to drive home, just to turn around and come back. What's the problem with the computer?"

"I can't get it to go," Alison said.

"What happens when you turn it on?"

"This is what happens." Alison pointed to a black screen.

"That doesn't look good," Jessie said. She walked behind Alison's desk. "I have a Toshiba laptop, also. Do you mind if I try?"

"Knock yourself out." Alison stood up and offered Jessie her seat.

Jessie sat and pressed the start button on the computer. But again–nothing happened. She could feel Alison's body brush against her shoulder as she studied the computer. Jessie smiled. She enjoyed the flirting she and Alison had been doing over the last year.

Jessie searched for a pen on Alison's desk. She took the point on the pen and pressed lightly in the small hidden hole on the side of the computer. Seconds later the computer started up.

"How did you do that?" Alison asked.

"I told you. Sweet talk. It's amazing the results." Jessie chuckled.

"Cute. But really, how did you do that?"

"When all else fails, try the reset button. They hide it on the Toshiba. It's right here, next to the modem port," she pointed. Jessie watched the screen as the instrument booted up and went into a self-analysis. She heard Travis's door open behind her, then she could hear voices from within the office.

"Excuse me, can we have a pitcher of water please?" a man asked. He coughed to clear his throat.

Jessie concentrated on Alison's computer, while Alison went to the water dispenser and filled up a pitcher. She handed the water to the man in the doorway of Travis's office.

"How about some glasses?" he asked.

To Jessie there was something familiar about the man's voice, but she couldn't place it.

Alison handed him three glasses.

"Thank you," he said.

The familiarity prompted Jessie to turn around and look at the man. Her movement must have caught his attention, because he also turned and looked at Jessie. There was a brief hesitation, enabling each to process what they were seeing.

The man took a step forward. "Jessie?"

Jessie stood. "Mark?"

Both Jessie and Mark smiled. Mark went to Jessie, the desk separating them, until Jessie came out from behind it. He set the pitcher and glasses on the desk and they embraced. Alison just watched, oblivious to what was transpiring. Finally, they parted, but were unable to take their eyes off of each other.

"God, it's good to see you. You look great," he said.

"You do too, Mark."

"I didn't know you two knew each other," Travis yelled from within his office.

"What are you doing here?" Jessie asked.

Mark pulled at Jessie's hand, smiling with a boyish grin that Jessie remembered from their college days. "Come in and visit with us for a few minutes."

Jessie had almost forgotten about Alison and her computer problem. "One minute, Mark." Jessie turned back toward Alison and her computer. The computer had booted up successfully. "Alison, just hit the reset button if it happens again." As Jessie pointed to the small opening, she felt a warming sensation in her heart.

My God, I haven't felt this for almost two years. What does it mean? The voices from Sanders' office were getting closer and disrupting her concentration. *Focus.*

Jessie glanced at Alison.

Alison smiled. "Thank you."

"You're welcome." Jessie turned back toward the doorway, unprepared for what she encountered.

A woman stood at the doorway along with Travis and Mark. She was leaning against the doorframe, her eyes following Jessie's every move. Jessie could feel the warmth in her heart increase and spread throughout her body, especially to her head. Somewhat light-headed, Jessie froze. She closed her eyes to steady herself and when they opened, she confirmed that Taylor Andrews was looking at her.

It was Mark who noticed the subtle hesitation and went to Jessie. "Are you okay?"

Jessie consciously broke her connection with Taylor. "Yes, I'm fine."

Mark took her hand again and directed her toward the doorway. "Jessie, this is Taylor Andrews. Taylor this is Jessica Mercer."

Jessie offered Taylor her hand.

"It's a pleasure to meet you," Taylor said with a slightly husky voice. Her crystal blue eyes seemed to peer into Jessie's soul. "I've been a fan of yours for years. I think I've read all of your books."

Jessie smiled at the compliment. "It's a pleasure to meet you, Taylor. Likewise, I think I own all of your CDs."

"So, how do you guys know each other?" Travis asked.

"It's a long story," Mark said. "A good one for over dinner. Jessie, join us Friday for dinner."

As Mark spoke, Jessie was very aware that Taylor was staring at her.

"What a wonderful idea," Taylor said. "Kurk Warner and I are hosting a small dinner party Friday night, 7:30, at Monique's. It'll be just yourself, Mark and Travis."

"I'm sorry, I have another commitment," Jessie lied.

"*What commitment? Do you have to do your hair?*" that pestering little voice asked.

"One that I'm sure we can change. Right, Jessie?" Travis pressured.

Jessie was surprised by Travis's persistence. "I'm not sure I can change it, Travis. We can talk about it in our meeting."

Mark went back to Alison's desk and poured a glass of water, then drank some. "I hope you can change it, Jessie. It'd be wonderful catching up on old times," Mark said. Then he glanced at his watch. "Please excuse us, but we need to run. We have another meeting across town." He rested his glass on the desk then turned to Travis and shook his hand. "We'll see you Friday." Then he went to Jessie and embraced her. "Let's plan on getting together sometime."

"Sure," Jessie said.

Taylor said her farewells to Travis and then approached Jessie and offered her hand. Jessie shook it but was surprised when Taylor did not release her grip. A smile came to Taylor's lips, enhancing her flawless face. "It was very nice meeting you, Jessie. I hope you can join us on Friday." The women remained facing each other. Taylor still held onto Jessie's hand and seemed to be searching Jessie's eyes.

"No promises, but I'll try." Jessie returned Taylor's stare. *God, I've missed you so, Rebecca.*

Taylor must have seen something. "I'm sorry. I don't mean to be rude, but have we met before?"

Jessie smiled, then nodded.

"I thought so. When?" Taylor asked.

"When you've figured it out . . . let me know."

Taylor smiled. "A mystery. I like that." At last, Taylor released her grip and left with Mark.

"What was that all about?" Travis asked.

"What was *what* all about?"

"You know–what just happened between the two of you."

"I don't know what you're talking about," Jessie lied.

Alison disappeared down the hall to set up the conference room for the next meeting. Travis turned and went back into his office. "So, what's so important this Friday?" he asked.

"Why would I go to this dinner?"

"For one thing–you were invited."

Jessie sensed there was something else. "Give me another reason."

"Taylor is auditioning for the role of Dillon on Monday. You've been to all the other auditions, you should attend this one."

"But I thought we decided to cast Rachel Wiley for that role. She's got more experience. Why the sudden interest in Taylor Andrews?"

"Rachel may have a conflict. Taylor hasn't read for the role, yet. I think it would be a mistake if we didn't give her a shot at it."

"I thought our meeting this afternoon was to approve the final cast."

"It is, Jessie. We're going to select all the roles. We'll pencil in Rachel for Dillon, depending on Taylor's audition. Why don't you try to make it on Friday? It could be a good career move. Kurk Warner has a lot of connections. He could be a good contact for you."

The following day Jessie wasted no time and called Carrie. She hadn't spoken to her in about two years, so Carrie was surprised by the call.

"Jessie, how are you? I have thought of you, often."

"I need to see you Carrie, do you have any time today?"

Carrie made the time to see Jessie that afternoon. "I've watched your success with *Deceptions*. Congratulations," Carrie said, motioning to a chair.

"Thank you, Carrie."

"Now, what is stressing you out?"

"Do you remember the regression I had with you two years ago?"

Carrie nodded. "One of my most memorable."

"After that regression, I had a wake-up call. I realized how badly I was starting to screw up my life, just to understand what happened in my past. I made a commitment after that regression to rid myself of whatever obsession I had."

"Was it obsession or curiosity?"

"Whatever it was–it interfered with my life. So, I did my best . . . and I got on with my life. And it was the best thing that could have happened to me. You see . . . I was able to finish up *Deceptions*, and then the screenplay for the movie. Both of which I consider significant accomplishments."

"They are exceptional accomplishments," Carrie agreed. "Congratulations."

"I'm not here for strokes."

"Then why are you here?"

Jessie hesitated.

"I told you once before–what transpires in any of my sessions is confidential. It won't leave here, I promise."

"Taylor Andrews has come into my life. I'm afraid of this. I don't want to become obsessed and screw things up again."

"Well Jessie, I think you'd be very foolish to think you can stop destiny."

"Destiny?"

"Oh yes, destiny. Isn't she the woman from your past life who recognized you from this life?"

Jessie nodded.

"If that doesn't tell you the two of you are meant to know each other, in some capacity, I don't know what does."

"I think it'd be too hard," Jessie admitted.

"What do you mean?"

"Whatever type of relationship the two of us can have would be insignificant to what the two of us had."

"Being *man and wife*, you mean?"

"Being a significant other. Taylor has got to be one of the most *straight* people I know, so I realize that being with her is not a real possibility."

"So, maybe you're just meant to be friends. Whatever you're supposed to be to her–learn."

"I think I'm learning how my ex-boyfriend felt when we broke up."

"What do you mean?"

"When Mark and I broke up, I wanted to continue with a friendship. But he couldn't, he said; it was too difficult being close to me and not being able to love me. That's part of what I'm feeling with Taylor."

"That's good–you're learning already. Jessie, I know this must be a little scary. You've got to go with it. You can't stop it from happening. This is obviously a karmic situation; you need to be prepared to release any disappointments and learn."

"Disappointments?"

"Yes, disappointments. If you cannot release them, they'll follow you into your next life."

When Jessie got home later that afternoon, there was a message on her answering machine. "Hi Jessie, this is Taylor Andrews. I hope you don't mind that I called you. I got your phone number from Travis. He's so easy. Anyway, there's been a time change for Friday night. Eight o'clock at Monique's. I'm sure I'll see you there. Have a lovely day."

Jessie replayed the message and smiled. "God, Rebecca. How can I do this? How can I be your–whatever I'm suppose to be when . . . I still love you so." *This is probably why we don't remember our past lives. It's too difficult to remember. This is a curse*, she decided.

She went to the bathroom and looked into the mirror. *Monique's. That's a pretty fancy place.* "So, I need to learn from this," she lectured herself in the mirror. "She's not Rebecca, she's Taylor Andrews. She's probably a bitch," Jessie tried to convince herself.

She pulled her long brown hair away from her face revealing her high cheekbones and seductive brown eyes. It had been a long time since she had paid any attention to herself.

Chapter 11

On Thursday afternoon, Jessie walked Rodeo Drive of Beverly Hills searching for the perfect dress, the one that was a cross between professional and seductive. In the absence of the former, she settled for seductive. That Friday afternoon, Jessie spent at the hair salon. After a massage and manicure, she had her hair styled to bring her into the twenty-first century. Jessie couldn't remember the last time she had pampered herself, and decided she needed to do it more often.

It was five minutes after eight when Jessie arrived at Monique's.

The maître d' greeted her. "Good evening, do you have reservations?"

"The Taylor Andrews and Kurk Warner party."

"Of course. The rest of your party has been seated. Come this way."

Monique's was the hottest restaurant in town. Jessie had never been there and had decided earlier that day she was going to enjoy it.

As the host escorted her to the table, Jessie noticed the men's stares. *It's amazing the looks you get when you give your flannel shirt and Levi's a night off.* Jessie smiled at her own humor.

Everyone at the table did a double take when Jessie arrived. Then they all stood to greet her.

Mark went to her and took her hands. "You look wonderful," he said. Then he gently kissed her cheek.

"You do look great," Travis confirmed.

As Taylor approached Jessie, she studied the hairstyle change. "Very flattering. Lovely dress, also." She offered Jessie her hand. "I'm glad you could make it." Taylor gently pulled Jessie toward the table. "Jessie, this is Kurk Warner. Kurk, this is Jessie Mercer.

Kurk smiled as he took Jessie's hand. "I love it, brains and beauty. It's a pleasure to meet you. I love your work." His dark brown eyes flirted. "Have you done any acting or modeling?"

Jessie shook her head, "No. Thank you . . . I think." Kurk seemed shorter in real life, but he was just as attractive as he was in the movies.

"Travis, get this lady in the movies."

"Then who's going to write my Oscar-winning screenplays? No, I think Jessie is better at writing," Travis said as they took their seats. Jessie was surprised when Taylor took a seat next to her and Mark sat on her other side.

Cocktails were served, then it was Taylor who brought up the subject of Mark and Jessie. "So you promised us, Mark; how do you and Jessie know each other?"

Mark looked at Jessie. "Should I tell them or do you want to?"

"After you," Jessie passed.

"Well . . . to make a long story short—Jessie and I knew each other in college, at Penn State. We lived together for three years."

"You lived together . . . as roommates or lovers?" Taylor asked.

"We were lovers. Jessie was the first woman who broke my heart." Mark smiled at Jessie, showing his good nature.

"When was the last time you saw each other?" Travis asked.

"I think a couple months after we broke up." Jessie looked at Mark for confirmation.

"That's correct," Mark said.

"What are the chances of the two of you meeting up again, here in California?" Kurk asked.

"Jessie once told me that if we were meant to be together, we'd find each other again. Does this count, Jessie?"

Travis saved Jessie. "So, did you know then that you would become a successful writer, Jessie?"

"I knew I would write." Jessie turned back to Mark. "What happened to you, Mark? Last thing I heard—you went to Yale Medical School. How did you end up in the music business?"

"Things change, I guess. I switched to law, which eventually got me in the business." Mark's phone beeped. "Would you excuse me? I've been paged. I need to make a call."

Travis and Kurk started discussing trends in the industry. Then Taylor spoke. "So Jessie, tell me, where did we meet before?"

Jessie smiled. "I take it you haven't figured it out."

Taylor shook her head. "I know we've met. But I just can't place it."

"I'm not surprised, it was a long time ago."

"Before I was Taylor?"

Jessie was caught off guard by her question. "What do you mean?"

"Before I went into music my first name was–"

"Darlene," Jessie said.

"That's right."

"Yes. It was before you were Taylor Andrews." *Well, I'm not lying.*

"Where?"

Jessie saw a curiosity in Taylor's eyes that reminded her of Rebecca. "It was at a costume party, many, many years ago."

"Really? What were you dressed as?"

"A priest."

"A priest?"

"Yes."

Taylor appeared to be searching her memories. "What was I dressed as?"

Jessie thought back to the moment that she met Rebecca. She smiled at how appropriate the costume was. "A witch. You were a witch."

"Yes. I've been a witch many times. But I still don't remember you as a priest."

Mark returned, and the waiter took dinner orders. After Kurk gave the waiter his order, Taylor gently poked him. "Don't forget to tell him."

Kurk turned back to the waiter. "No nuts or peanut oil. I'm allergic."

"I'll tell the chef," the waiter said.

"I didn't know you were allergic to nuts," Travis said. "How severe is it?"

"Not bad. I'm used to it. I've been allergic all of my life."

"Not bad? He'll go into anaphylactic shock if he has a sliver of a peanut," Taylor said.

"It must make it tough going to a restaurant. Not knowing how they prepare their food," Jessie said.

"Most restaurants are pretty good," Kurk said.

"And others are very bad," Taylor reminded him. "Remember what happened at Barbados Grill? He went into shock right there at the table."

"Do you carry epinephrine?" Mark asked.

Kurk pulled an EpiPen from his jacket. "I don't leave home without it."

"Yes, they've saved his life, on more than one occasion," Taylor added. "I carry them also."

Dinner was delightful; the food and service were exquisite. Over after-dinner drinks Travis brought up *Deceptions*. "So did the carrier drop off the screenplay this week?"

"Yes. I received it yesterday," answered Taylor.

"Review act 18, the beach scene. That's what we ask everyone to read for the roles of Dillon and Nicole."

"Thanks for the insight," Taylor said.

"I'm not sure if you've heard. We have Jennifer Kendrick for the role of Nicole," Travis said.

"Congratulations," Kurk said. Jennifer Kendrick had been the hottest actress over the past five years. She had been honored with two Oscars. "That must have cost you a pretty penny."

"She's not cheap," Travis acknowledged. "Taylor, she's agreed to read with you on Monday."

"Great, I'm looking forward to meeting her," Taylor said. Then she turned to Jessie. "Will you be there on Monday?"

"Where are you meeting?"

"At my house," Travis said. "We can use the beach for the reading. At two o'clock. You *will* be there, right Jessie?"

Jessie hesitated.

"I would really appreciate the support, Jessie," Taylor said.

Jessie looked into Taylor's eyes. "Sure. I'll be there."

It was ten minutes after two when Jessie arrived that Monday. Travis's property was located just outside of Malibu. From inside the house, Jessie could see the cameras set up in the rear of the property on the private beach. Travis, Mark, Taylor and the crew were talking near the cameras.

Jessie made her way through the back door and down the stairs to the beach.

Mark was the first to greet her, then the others followed. Everyone was there except Jennifer Kendrick, who eventually showed up about forty-minutes late.

Travis took Taylor and Jennifer away from the small group to set the scene for the actresses. Jessie listened to Travis.

"Taylor, you're playing Dillon, a successful singer, a superstar at the peak of her career. Your husband was murdered six months ago and you're still mourning his loss. You're also aware that Nicole, here," Travis pointed to Jennifer, "is the prime murder suspect. Your little secret is–you've fallen in love with Nicole.

"Jennifer, you're playing Nicole. You've been a business associate of Dillon's for a couple of years. You're gay, or lesbian if you prefer. You're out of the closet. You fell in love with Dillon some time ago but you've always hidden your feelings from her. You've always known that she's straight, and she was married up until six months ago. But now . . . you're the murder suspect and if the truth were known that you are in love with her, the police may grab on to it as a motive. And a motive is one of the only things missing in the evidence against you.

"In this scene, Nicole visits Dillon's beach home. Nicole has been calling Dillon for weeks but Dillon won't return her call. Nicole needs Dillon to sign some papers, so she shows up unannounced and finds her walking on the beach." Travis turned to the cameras. "Ladies, we'll be filming the scene. Just relax, Taylor, and have some fun."

Taylor and Jennifer took their places and the women started reading the lines. Even Jessie recognized that their performance was mechanical. It appeared as if both women were just going through the motions. Jessie was surprised that Travis did not cut the scene, rather, he let the woman play it out until it climaxed when Taylor made an unconvincing pass at Jennifer.

"Okay ladies, that wasn't bad for the first try. Let's take it from the beginning again, this time ladies, more feeling."

The performance was repeated with no improvement. Travis gave Taylor some pointers, but still no progress. Jessie was amazed at how patient Travis was. In any other reading, Jessie knew Travis would have stopped the audition. It wasn't just Taylor; Jennifer Kendrick, a seasoned professional, was struggling with her role also.

The group had been at it about an hour when Travis stopped abruptly. "I think we need a break." He pointed at the deck on his house. "Appetizers and refreshments on the deck. Let's take a half hour break and try to loosen up a little."

Loosen up, Travis? Let's just put this group out of our misery and stop for the day. Jessie turned away from the house and walked past Travis. "I'm going for a walk," she called to him over her shoulder. *If I didn't know better, I'd think Taylor is sleeping with Travis. She's not ready for this part; why is he being so patient?*

"Can I join you?" Taylor called to Jessie.

Jessie turned to see Taylor approaching. "Sure."

They walked in silence, and then Taylor finally spoke. "Travis is being such a sweetheart. I know I'm blowing it. I don't know what's wrong." She sighed in frustration.

Jessie remained silent.

"You don't want me to get this part, do you?"

Jessie was surprised at the comment. "Why do you say that?"

"Just a feeling."

"It's not that I don't want you to get the part, I'm a little confused at the whole turn of events. Up until last week, I thought we had Rachel Wiley locked up for the role. I'm just a little set back." Jessie noticed Taylor's disappointment. "You really want this role, don't you?"

"Absolutely."

"Why?"

"I don't know. It just feels right for me. Do you know what I mean?"

"I'm not sure."

"Have you ever felt that you absolutely need to do something, but you're not sure why? It feels like your destiny or fate?"

Jessie finally smiled. "Well then, would you like some insight from the author's perspective?"

"I'd love it, Jessie."

Jessie headed away from the water and sat on the warm sand. Taylor followed and sat next to her. "Travis picked this scene for auditions because . . . it separates the men from the boys. It's probably the most difficult scene in the entire screenplay . . . for a heterosexual woman. But you're not the only one who's struggling. Jennifer is also."

"She's already been cast for the part though, right?"

"Yes, but she's never read for the role. I guess when you get to be at her level, producers evaluate your box office appeal over an audition. She'll be okay; she needs to be coached."

"So what can I do to improve my performance?"

"This is a very intimate scene, not sexual but intimate. What you and Jennifer are lacking is chemistry. It's very difficult to work a scene like this without the chemistry."

"But it's not impossible?"

"No. The first thing you need is to intimately know the character you're playing. Dillon is smart, beautiful, funny and very lonely. She misses her husband, but she's struggling with her feelings for Nicole. If it's difficult for you to understand how a woman can be attracted to another woman, then it's going to be difficult playing the part. This is where you need to get creative. Look into Jennifer's eyes. Then pretend."

"Pretend?"

"Yes. Pretend she is whoever you need her to be to get through the scene. If you need her to be Kurk, pretend. But you've got to be able to look her in the eye and imagine she's someone else. Imagine how you would act if it were Kurk there instead of Jennifer. Otherwise, you're just going to go through the motions."

"Which is what I'm doing."

"Which is what both of you are doing."

Thirty minutes later, the shooting resumed. Even Travis noticed an improvement in Taylor's performance. Jessie watched Taylor carefully. She noticed when Taylor tried to make eye contact with Jennifer, then the subtle diversion of Taylor's eyes. From then on, she wouldn't look Jennifer directly in the eye.

Although there was an improvement in Taylor's performance, Jennifer was still having difficulty with her role. Travis started riding Jennifer on the second take, and by the end of the third take, her patience was noticeably thinning.

Although Jessie was disappointed in Jennifer's performance, she was surprised when words of disapproval were coming out of her mouth. "No, no, no. That isn't how Nicole would act." *What the hell am I doing?* Jessie asked herself. But it was too late, those uncharacteristic words had already left her mouth. All eyes were on Jessie, including Travis's. "I apologize, I didn't mean anything by it."

"Well, it's too late," Jennifer said. "Tell me what's on your mind."

Jessie looked at Travis. "After you," he said.

"Okay." Jessie walked to where the actresses stood, then looked at Jennifer. "Jennifer, you're just not playing Nicole the way I intended when I wrote this."

"You're going to have to do better than that. Give me some constructive advice."

"Okay. Nicole is assertive and aggressive when she needs to be, but not with Dillon. When you're talking to Dillon to find out what's wrong, don't flaunt your body at her. She's shy. She's actually scared to death being here. You've got the lines, but your whole body language is giving a different message."

"I'm sorry. I think you're just going to have to show me what you mean."

"What?"

"Show me what I'm doing wrong. I'm better at mimicking action, than words."

"But I'm not an actress," Jessie turned toward Travis looking for some support. But she got none.

"Actually, I think it's a good idea," Travis said.

"Good idea?"

Travis gestured for Jessie to join him on the sideline, and she did. The two strolled away from the group.

"I'm sorry I opened my mouth, Travis. It'll never happen again. I promise."

"It's okay. If you didn't say something, I might have. And it wouldn't have been that nice." Travis rubbed his neatly trimmed goatee. He seemed to be considering their next step. "Just do it. It can't hurt."

"What?"

Travis gestured for the cameraman to film them. Filming had stopped after the break.

"Why are you going to film it?" Jessie asked.

"If your performance is good, Jennifer can study it and use it as a tool."

Jessie still hesitated.

"Jessie, we need to do something here. Trust me. This isn't working. We need to somehow get Jennifer on board, or she'll take this film down. I promise you. If her performance sucks, I will personally burn the film."

Why did I open my mouth? When have I ever said anything during these sessions? Jessie scolded herself as she stood waiting for her cue.

"Don't worry," Jessie's little voice said. *"Relax."*

I wrote this, just do it the way I saw it in my head. Then it was her cue . . .

Jessie hurried along the beach, and yelled out, "Dillon?" Taylor ignored Jessie's plea and continued her brisk walk. She jogged to catch up with Taylor. "Dillon." Jessie came within a couple feet of her. "Dillon, wait."

Taylor turned, first catching a glimpse of the camera eye, and then turning toward Jessie. "Nicole." Taylor looked directly into Jessie's eyes. "What are you doing here?"

Jessie panted lightly from chasing after her. "Why haven't you returned my phone calls?"

"I've been busy."

"So busy that you couldn't return any one of my five calls?"

"I've been busy." Taylor continued to maintain good eye contact with Jessie. "What do you need?"

"I need your signature." Jessie held up an imaginary attaché case.

"Is it that important that you had to come here?"

Jessie hesitated then shook her head. "No. It's not. But your friendship is."

"What are you talking about?"

"Why haven't you called? And don't tell me you're too busy. Have I done something wrong?"

Taylor remained silent, now avoiding eye contact.

"Not you too," Jessie whispered.

Taylor turned and continued her walk.

But Jessie continued after her, maintaining the same pace about a half step behind her. "You know me better than that. I can't believe they got to you."

Taylor blatantly ignored Jessie and increased her pace.

Jessie gently yet firmly grabbed hold of Taylor's wrist, and swung her around, pulling her to a stop.

Taylor appeared stunned by Jessie's aggressive behavior. She stared at Jessie's hand that remained latched to her wrist.

"Look into my eyes," Jessie whispered.

Taylor ignored the plea.

"Look into my eyes," Jessie repeated.

Taylor's eyes slowly traveled from Jessie's hand, which was still holding onto her wrist, up Jessie's body until they met Jessie's brown eyes.

Jessie released Taylor's wrist. "Are these the eyes of a murderer?"

"What?"

"If you have any doubt, after looking into my eyes," Jessie's voice cracked, "I will turn and leave and never bother you again."

Taylor continued looking into Jessie's eyes until tears formed and ran down her cheeks.

Instinctively, Jessie brushed the tears away with her fingers.

"This has nothing to do with Jeffrey's murder," Taylor whispered. "But you need to go."

Taylor tried to turn, but Jessie quickly took hold of both her wrists and pulled her until the women were inches apart. "If this isn't about the murder, what's this all about?" Jessie asked.

Taylor searched Jessie's eyes.

Jessie noticed that Taylor's lips were approaching her own. She released Taylor's wrists and retreated ever so slightly.

Taylor laced her fingers around Jessie's neck, preventing her escape, guiding Jessie's lips to her own. This time, Jessie did not run.

It was the whistling and clapping that brought Jessie back. She pulled away; Taylor remained staring at her. Jessie knew for a brief moment it was real to her, and it reminded her of when Rebecca had loved her.

Travis stepped between the two women, grinning from ear to ear. He placed his hand in Taylor's. "Congratulations. We've found our Dillon."

Mark was right behind Travis and embraced both women.

Travis gave Jessie a bear hug, then stepped back to look at her. "You might want to consider acting on the side. You're very good."

Even through all the excitement, Jessie could feel Taylor's eyes on her. Occasionally, their eyes would meet, then Jessie would avert her eyes.

While Travis was speaking with Jennifer, Jessie decided she would be on her way. She bid the group good evening and left. She was just getting into her car when she heard a voice from behind her.

"Thank you," Taylor said.

Jessie turned to find Taylor leaning up against a car next to her own. "Congratulations. You did very well."

"Did I?"

"Yes. You were very convincing."

"I didn't need to pretend," Taylor admitted.

"I know."

"How did you know?"

"Because you could look into my eyes. You couldn't do that with Jennifer."

"How will I be able to repeat that performance with Jennifer?"

Jessie smiled and opened her car door. "Study the tape. Then pretend." She got in the car, started the ignition and opened the window. "Give my best to Kurk."

Taylor watched the Lexus disappear around the curve in the road. She was trying to understand what had just happened. "I wasn't acting," she admitted to herself. *I got lost in the role. I lost reality for a minute. It was too easy.*

Jessie hated being rude. But she needed time to process what had just happened. "What the hell am I doing? Why is this happening to me?" *I miss you so much, Rebecca.* It didn't take long before the tears came.

Chapter 12

On Wednesday that week, Travis called Jessie. He had a preliminary schedule for *Deceptions* and invited himself over to review the dates that afternoon. Jessie was surprised when Mark arrived with him.

"Surprise," Mark said, as Jessie answered the door.

"Hi, and it is a surprise." Jessie backed away from the door permitting Travis and Mark to enter.

"I hope you don't mind. Travis asked me to pick up the schedule. Then he slipped that he was coming here. I invited myself," Mark admitted. He smiled with his boyish grin.

"It's fine, Mark." She escorted them through part of the house and past her office. "Let's go into my sitting room. It'd be more comfortable than my office. Would either of you like something to drink? Lemonade, iced tea?"

"Lemonade would be great," Mark said.

"Yes. Lemonade is fine."

"Make yourself comfortable. I'll get the drinks and my calendar."

Jessie left the room, and Mark inspected the pieces of art that were on display in the sitting room. "It would appear that Jessie has done well for herself."

"She's a very talented lady," Travis agreed.

"Do you know if she's seeing anyone right now?" Mark asked.

Travis was surprised by the question. "Mark, you are aware that Jessie is gay, aren't you?"

"Well aware, unfortunately. You've never known her to swing occasionally?"

Travis shook his head. "If she did, Mark–get in line."

Jessie returned with the lemonade and her calendar. She sat down with Travis and compared the tentative filming schedule with her own calendar.

Jessie knew Travis was not obligated to check her schedule, so she appreciated the gesture.

After reviewing the four-month period, Jessie wrote down dates she had conflicts with and passed the note to Travis. "There are only four dates I have conflicts with. Here they are."

A soft beep came from Mark's phone. He removed the phone from his belt and looked at the display, which showed he had a voice message.

"Mark, if you want some privacy, just step into my office," Jessie suggested.

Mark stood.

"It's just right around the corner. You passed it when you came in."

"Thanks. I'll just check on this and be right back."

"You did very well the other day," Travis told Jessie.

Jessie had tried to put the scene with Taylor out of her mind. But somehow, it wouldn't leave her. She smiled weakly, "Thank you."

"I don't usually go out of my way to check the screenwriter's schedule, Jessie. I'm very impressed with how you handled yourself on the set. I want you on the set during the filming of some of the more sensitive scenes."

"Travis, I'm not an actress."

"Jessie, you knew that scene was going no place. Somehow you brought Taylor out of her shell and you've given us a tool to work with Jennifer."

"Acting isn't my forte, and directing certainly isn't. I shouldn't have opened my mouth the other day."

"Under normal circumstances, I may have agreed with you."

Filming for *Deceptions* started within the month. Jessie made an effort to make most of the shootings. Although Jennifer Kendrick was a royal bitch to work with, Jessie recognized that she was a true professional. Jennifer actually studied the tape that had been made of Jessie and Taylor and was able to mimic most of the performance. At times when Jennifer struggled with a scene, she would confide in Jessie at a break and ask for some insight.

After considerable soul searching, Jessie decided to watch the situation unfold with Taylor and Mark. Taylor was always very friendly and seemed to be interested in developing a friendship with her. At times, Jessie would catch Taylor staring at her, but she never asked Taylor about it. Mark was the master of flirtation and seemed to want more than a friendship.

During the filming of one scene at a mall, Mark and Jessie were together on the sidelines. At a break, Mark went to Jessie. "Can I buy you a cup of coffee?" He pointed at Starbuck's Coffee on the other side of the mall. Since most of the people in the mall were watching the movie crew, it was much quieter there.

"Sure."

Jessie and Mark made their way to Starbucks and sat at a table outside the store.

"You've done very well for yourself," Mark complimented Jessie.

"Obviously you have also, Mark."

"Thanks. Things sure have changed over the years. Except . . . you haven't changed much."

"Oh, I've changed plenty," Jessie disagreed.

"Not on the outside. You're just as beautiful as you were in school." Mark's eyes flirted.

"And you're still the charmer you were then."

He smiled. "So what do you think this means? Us meeting up after all this time."

Jessie looked into Mark's eyes. "What a coincidence."

"That's all you have to say? What about–destiny!" Mark said.

Jessie smiled. "Is that what you think?"

"It has entered my mind."

"I think we had a great friendship years ago. But *we* ended so abruptly that we weren't able to continue the friendship, because it was too painful for you. I think I understand that better now. It must be terribly difficult to love someone, be involved in their life and yet not be able to have them." Jessie pondered her feelings for Taylor.

Mark nodded at Jessie's interpretation of their history. "And that's it?"

"After all the years, is it still painful for you to be around me?"

"No."

"Then yes. That's what I think our reconnection means. A second chance at a friendship."

Mark placed a hand over Jessie's. His contact surprised her. "Do you think there could ever be more than friendship?"

Jessie shook her head. "No, Mark. I'm sorry. I'm gay."

Mark pulled his hand away and smiled. "Okay! You can't blame a guy for trying."

After that, Mark seemed fine and his flirtation with Jessie stopped.

It was about one month into the filming, and Jessie arrived a little late one morning on the set. The scene was being filmed at Hansen Dam, a park on the outskirts of Los Angeles County. She parked her car and was getting out when she heard a voice from behind her.

"It's cancelled."

Jessie turned and saw Taylor approach. Other actors, actresses and film crew seemed to be dispersing and leaving.

"What happened?" Jessie asked.

"Travis has had some type of family emergency," Taylor said. "We're meeting tomorrow, same time. Unless somebody calls."

"Is Travis okay?"

"I don't know. He never showed. His assistant took the phone call. I think it had something to do with his wife."

"Well, I hope everything is okay," Jessie added. She opened her car door.

"Have a good day," Taylor said. Then she walked away.

"You too." Jessie got back in her car and started the ignition. Seconds later she heard tapping on the passenger window. Taylor was standing there. Jessie opened the passenger-side window. "You okay?"

"Yeah. I was thinking–I hate to lose a free day."

"A free day?"

"Whenever I'm blessed with an unplanned free day, I try to do something that I've never done before," Taylor said.

"Sounds like a fun custom."

"I've always wanted to go to this artsy community in the San Gabriel Mountains. It's near Phipps Canyon. It's supposed to have great little shops and vendors. It's probably a forty-minute drive from here. It's called Legacy Square. What do you say?"

"What do I say about what?" Jessie asked.

"What are you doing now?"

"Well, I guess I was just going home. Do a little work on a new project."

"Why don't the two of us head over to Legacy? Check out some of the shops, have some lunch. You can start a new tradition for your free days."

Jessie thought about it for a moment. "I guess I could do that."

"Good. Would you like me to drive?" Taylor offered.

"No. Just hop in. I'll bring you back here later for your car."

Taylor got in, and Jessie noticed the manila envelope that Taylor held. As Jessie pulled her car from the curb, she pointed to the envelope.

"Work?"

"Not really. It's fan mail."

"Fan mail?"

"Yes. Mark gives me an envelope every week."

"And you read it all?"

"I can't say I read every word. But I at least open every envelope."

"Really?"

"Yes. It's one of Mark's suggestions. For every touching letter I get, we send out an autographed picture. Mark thinks it's good business. Send them a picture, and earn a lifelong fan."

"That makes sense. Do you ever get some hateful letters?"

"Yes. They're the worst. No. I take that back. The strange ones are the worst."

"Strange?"

"Yes. Strange. You know . . . when you don't know what their motives are . . . or you don't know if they have it all together . . ."

"Do you get a lot of those?"

"Not really. The last month or so I started getting some strange letters from someone with the initials 'I.D.' "

"What's so strange about them?"

"The tone of the letter. He . . . or she I guess, just sounds . . . strange is the best word I can use to describe it." Taylor opened the large envelope and sorted through the smaller envelopes. She looked for one with the initials "I.D." "No. Whoever it is didn't send me . . ." Taylor didn't finish the thought.

"What's wrong?"

Taylor's face paled. "I got a postcard."

"And."

"There's only three words on it."

"They are?"

"I'm your destiny," Taylor looked at Jessie. "Do you think that's *I.D.*?"

"What have the other letters said?"

"Oh, I don't remember except . . . there was something about finding each other someday and the two of us are meant to be together. I don't remember that much; I just gave them to Mark. Come to think of it, this one is addressed to me in care of Mark."

"And the others?"

"They went through World Records."

"Where's it postmarked?"

Taylor studied the stamped card. "It looks like Los Angeles."

"So if it's the same person, they know your record company and personal manager. Both are pretty easy to learn," Jessie said.

Taylor stuffed the postcard back in the envelope and put it on the floor next to her feet.

It was close to eleven o'clock when they arrived at Legacy Square. The quaint community had artsy shops on both sides of a narrow street. The street was closed to traffic and peddler carts were set up in the center. Taylor pulled her sunglasses and scarf from her purse and put them on.

"What are you doing?" Jessie asked.

"I want to enjoy myself, I don't want everyone to recognize me."

"Do you dress up in disguise often?"

"When I'm with Kurk I don't; he loves the attention. But I usually do when I'm by myself."

The women walked the quaint shops for about an hour and a half, and then chose a sunny cafe for lunch. "Do you realize that this is the first time we have had some time alone since we met?" Taylor said.

"I hadn't really thought of it," Jessie lied. In actuality, Jessie had been cautious around Taylor and had intentionally avoided encounters with her. Today, she had surprised herself when she agreed to come with Taylor.

"For a while there, I thought you were avoiding me."

"Avoiding you? Now why would I do that?"

"Just a feeling I had after we worked together on that scene." Taylor's eyes showed a curiosity.

Jessie changed the subject. "How's the filming going?"

"I think okay. I have nothing to compare it to, though. This is my first major role. How do you think it's going?"

"It seems to be going fine."

"How'd you come up with the idea for *Deceptions*?

"It just came to me."

"How long did it take you to write it?"

"It took me four months before I had a manuscript ready for the publisher."

"Four months? That's not very long. I always thought that it took longer to write a book."

"It does, for me anyway. *Deceptions* is my record. The idea came, and then the story took on a life of it's own."

"So, tell me about you and Mark," Taylor said. Her eyes were showing a curiosity again.

"We're old friends from college."

"Old lovers you mean?"

Jessie knew she had built a wall between herself and Taylor. *Why? Jessie asked herself. Why am I trying to stay so unattached?*

"*Lighten up, Jessie,*" that little voice lectured.

"Yes, we were lovers."

"I thought you were a lesbian." Taylor even surprised herself by her own bluntness.

"Yes, I am a lesbian. I was with Mark before I was honest with myself about my own sexuality."

"So, have you only been with women . . . since Mark?"

Jessie found Taylor's uneasiness with the question amusing. "Yes. Actually, Mark was the only man I have ever been with, sexually."

"The two of you broke up and you never saw each other until a few months ago?"

"We broke up, but while we were involved, Mark had always been my best friend. So I wanted to maintain a friendship with him." Jessie looked into Taylor's eyes; she understood now how Mark had felt and smiled. "But it was hard for him to be just a friend. So, he severed the friendship a couple of months after we broke up. He went off to medical school. That was the last I had heard until . . . I learned he was your personal manager."

"Are you happy with the choice of . . . your sexual orientation?"

"I guess I never really thought of it as a choice. It's just who I am."

"How did you know you were gay?"

"Initially, I didn't know. Actually, I didn't even suspect. A woman made a pass at me and then I knew there was a chance I was gay."

"It must have been some pass."

"Oh, it was." Jessie smiled as she remembered. "Up until that point I never thought of being gay as an option for me. Then I quickly realized that I was. All the signs were there. I just never recognized them."

"Excuse me," a stranger interrupted. He was sitting at a table next to them. "You're Taylor Andrews, aren't you?"

"Yes, I am."

The man rose from his table and went to Taylor with a napkin and pen in hand.

"May I have your autograph?" he asked.

Taylor graciously signed the napkin for the man.

When the man left, Jessie changed the subject. "So tell me, what's it like to be a superstar?"

Taylor smiled. "Most of the time it's great. There are other times when it can be a little difficult." Taylor had been staring out the window. Occasionally she seemed preoccupied.

"Is there something wrong?" Jessie asked.

Taylor shook her head. "No. I've just been watching that woman on the sidewalk." She pointed out the window to the back of a woman who sat with a television tray in front of her. Another woman sat next to her; the two appeared deep in conversation. A sign sat next to the table, "Readings $40+."

"You're watching the psychic?" Jessie asked.

"Do you realize that's the third person she's scammed since we've sat here?"

"How do you know she's scamming them?"

"Oh, don't tell me you believe in that hocus pocus," challenged Taylor.

Jessie was taken aback by Taylor's comment and just stared at her.

"What?" Taylor asked.

"You don't believe in metaphysics?"

"No. Not really."

Jessie continued to stare back at her.

"What? Do you believe in that stuff?"

"I think there are some good psychics and there are some bad ones. Just like any vocation. But what surprises me is . . . a lot of your music is filled with metaphysical concepts."

"It's music, Jessie. It doesn't mean I believe in any of the stuff."

"But why would you write music about something that's so unconventional, especially if you don't believe in any of it?"

"It sells."

"No. There's got to be more."

Taylor looked into Jessie's eyes. She wondered why it was so easy and comforting to look into her eyes. "I'm not sure what it is. When I go into my creative shell, which is my way of brainstorming, those songs just come easy."

"Haven't you ever wondered why?"

"No. I don't need to. I just write down the lyrics, the music comes to me and the next thing I know I have a hit."

"Is that how 'Daniel's Heart' came to you?"

"Pretty much."

"So you don't believe in psychics? Or past lives? Or karma?"

Taylor smiled. "No. I don't believe in any of that."

Jessie smiled. She was amazed at how different Taylor was from Rebecca. *But they're the same. How can that be?* "Tell me, have you ever had a reading with a psychic?"

"No."

"Then how do you know it's hocus pocus?"

"Get real. I wouldn't give a scam artist a cent for a reading."

Jessie smiled. "But I will . . . if you're game."

"What are you talking about?"

"After lunch, I'll buy you a reading. If she gives you an accurate reading–you owe me a dinner."

"And if she doesn't?"

"I'll owe you a dinner." Jessie surprised herself by the suggestion.

After lunch, Taylor and Jessie approached the psychic outside the restaurant. Tarot cards sat in front of her on the tray.

"Good afternoon, ladies."

"Good afternoon to you," Jessie said. "My friend would like to have a reading."

The psychic looked at Taylor and smiled. "It would be an honor to do a reading for you Ms. Andrews."

"You already know who I am." Taylor turned toward Jessie. "This won't work. She can say a bunch of things that have been published about me."

"That's true, but that's not how I give a reading." The woman pulled out the chair next to her. "Please sit."

Taylor complied and sat next to her.

"My name is Karen. When I do a reading, I don't spend a lot of time on things that you already know, just to prove my accuracy. For example, I won't tell you that you have a boyfriend with dark hair, you drive a fancy red sports car and you live in a 10,000-square-foot house in Malibu. I don't say these things because frankly–who cares? I try to give the person information that can help them on a soul level. I assure you, Ms. Andrews, *Entertainment Tonight* doesn't give me this information."

"Okay," Taylor said.

Jessie turned to move away from them.

"Where you going?" Taylor asked.

"I'm just giving you some privacy."

"No. I want you to sit in on this."

"Are you sure?" Jessie asked.

"Absolutely."

Jessie sat opposite Taylor and watched.

"Is there any area in particular you want me to focus on?" Karen asked.

Taylor shook her head, "No."

Karen picked up the deck of Tarot cards and appeared to say a prayer. She then handed the deck to Taylor. "I want you to shuffle the cards until you feel like stopping."

Taylor started shuffling the large cards in her tiny hands and a card flew out of her hand.

Karen quickly picked up the card. "The deck is done," she said. She quickly took the rest of the deck from Taylor.

"But I wasn't finished."

"Yes, you are. The cards are done."

Karen laid the card that had jumped out face up on the tray along with a couple other cards. She closed her eyes and appeared to be concentrating. Occasionally she shook her head. "I am having some difficulty with this," she admitted. "What the card tells me does not fit Ms. Andrews. But let me try it anyway." She pointed at the card that had flung itself out; the title was "High Priestess." "This card is a reflection of your past. It indicates that in your past you were very psychic."

Taylor laughed.

"I can tell you're not a believer . . . no there's something else," Karen's eyes shut. She remained quiet for some time and then smiled. She opened her eyes. "That makes more sense."

"That's good. Do you want to enlighten me?" Taylor asked.

"You were very psychic, very metaphysically aware in your past. But it was a past life."

"Right," Taylor said sarcastically.

"This is important. Please hear me out. I'm getting life reading messages from the spirits."

Taylor watched in disbelief.

Karen closed her eyes and then started to speak slowly. "In a past life you were either persecuted or possibly executed because of your awareness, or maybe . . . maybe even a loved one was hurt by this."

Jessie's heart ached. Karen's insight brought back memories and pain she felt after her regression. *I wonder if this is how I'll learn what happened.*

"You have suppressed your gifts because of what happened to you. And this is not the first time you have been here to work on this life's purpose . . . you have been very hurt . . . on the soul level. You feel betrayed. In your previous life, you were a good person and you used some means of psychic awareness to help someone in need . . . but it backfired . . . you have been deeply scarred and you have . . . suppressed so much. And this is why you are here. Your purpose for this lifetime is to awaken these gifts that have been locked away."

Karen opened her eyes and moved to another card, the "Wheel of Fortune." Then she returned to the first card. "You have started."

"I have started what?" Taylor asked.

"The awakening. But it's only baby steps. Your music is a result of this awakening. You have so much farther to go."

"Right," Taylor replied.

Karen momentarily broke away from the cards and stared at Taylor. "Many times I sit with nonbelievers. They come to me, give me money and I give them a reading. I don't understand why they come, maybe to laugh at me . . . but they do come. I don't understand why they don't believe. In your case, Taylor, I understand why it is so hard to believe. You need to keep trying."

Karen returned to the laid-out cards. "This card represents your present," she pointed at the "Wheel of Fortune" card. "There is some type of karmic situation here." She paused. "There is someone from a past life that is involved in some type of karmic debt . . . there is real danger with this person."

When Jessie heard this, she was saddened. *Does she mean me?*

"This person has an enormous amount of love for you. But it's misguided. And there's something . . ."

"There's what?" Taylor asked.

Karen laid out an additional card. Both Jessie and Taylor followed her gaze to the "Death" card.

"Even I know that that card isn't good," Taylor said.

"It's not what you think it means," Karen said. Her fingers wandered back over all the cards. "In your present–fate rules. Something needs to work itself out . . . do your best to release any disappointment. This is a cycle you have fallen into for more than one lifetime."

"I don't understand what you're talking about."

"Souls travel in groups. There is a soul that you have been with before, that is in your life. Their intentions are not healthy and this is what is causing danger. The cycle must be broken, and you must release any disappointment, and learn."

"Do I? Can you see the future? And if so, is the cycle broken?"

Karen gazed at the Death card.

"Is that my future?"

"It is your future as of today. The cards show a future dependent on how you evolve today."

"So . . . I'm going to die?"

"One day you will. We all die, but that is not necessarily what the Death card implies. The card means you are going to go through a dramatic change, a new chapter will begin and the slate will be wiped clean. To me, that implies that the cycle will end."

Karen closed her eyes. "This is a very strong cycle. It is going to be hard, but the rewards are wondrous. When in doubt, Taylor, go with your gut. You are incredibly sensitive and very psychic. Know that your first thought about any given situation is more accurate than if you dwelled upon it. You have taken baby steps. Keep going and don't stop." Karen closed her eyes once more. "Oh, one last thing. You'll find the earring in your purse."

The reading ended, Jessie paid Karen the agreed-upon fee, and Taylor and Jessie stood to leave. Jessie noticed that Karen was looking at her as they departed. After Jessie and Taylor had strolled about ten feet away, Jessie looked back at Karen. She was still staring at her.

The women were silent on their way back to Jessie's car. Jessie's mind kept replaying the reading Taylor had received. *Am I placing Taylor in danger? How could my love for her be misguided?* She glanced at Taylor. Taylor was preoccupied in her own thoughts.

"Are you okay?" Jessie asked.

"Sure," Taylor said. "I was just thinking about where you're going to take me for dinner."

"Dinner? You're that confident she completely misread you?"

"Absolutely."

I hope you're right, Jessie thought. But she knew Karen was at least partially accurate. "What's the deal about the earring?"

"I'm not sure. I have to admit–I do have a missing earring. It's been missing for some time, now. I left my handbag in your car. If the earring is there, I'll admit defeat and buy you dinner."

"Deal."

Taylor pulled the handbag from the car and emptied its contents on the trunk of the Lexus, carefully inspecting each object, assuring the earring was not missed. The earring was no place to be found. "Guess you owe me dinner."

Chapter 13

A week later, Jessie walked onto the set for *Deceptions*. The scene was being shot at the county courthouse and was in progress when Jessie arrived. Jennifer was at the front of the courtroom. Her character, Nicole, was being charged with the murder of her girlfriend's husband. Taylor sat silently behind Jennifer.

Jessie stood quietly in the rear of the courtroom, watching the scene develop. Travis shouted, "Cut." All the action stopped. He directed his frustration at the actor who was portraying the prosecuting attorney.

Jessie noticed that Taylor had turned around and appeared to be searching the courtroom. When Taylor's eyes found Jessie's, the blue eyes softened and a smile came to Taylor's lips. Jessie returned the smile.

Taylor waved, then mouthed the words, "Friday night." But she knew from Jessie's facial expression that Jessie did not understand. Travis was still busy, talking with the actor, and sensing this, Taylor spoke softly out loud to Jessie. "Friday Night. You're buying dinner. Right?"

Jessie nodded.

The back courtroom door opened again, and Kurk walked in. He winked and waved at Taylor. She blew him a kiss and then Kurk went to Travis. Although Travis was busy with the actor, his focus changed and the men started talking. Soon they realized their voices were rising, and they left the room.

Minutes later, Travis returned to the set, his face was redder than usual. Jessie was surprised that Kurk did not return with him. During a break, Jessie approached Travis, but when he uncharacteristically snapped at a crew member, she retreated.

"So is Friday okay?" Taylor came up behind Jessie.

Jessie turned toward Taylor. "You're still convinced you got a bad reading?"

"Yes. Are you going to make good on your word?"

"I always make good on my word. Where do you want to go?"

"I'll make the arrangements. I'll even pick you up," Taylor said.

Friday evening, Taylor arrived at Jessie's, seven o'clock sharp.

"Hi, come in." Jessie backed away from the door permitting Taylor to pass. "I just want to check on Maxwell."

"Maxwell? Who's Maxwell?"

Jessie went to the kitchen. She picked up a bowl from the floor and filled it with some food. "He's my cat. He's probably on the couch in the great room." Jessie pointed, then filled Maxwell's water dish.

Taylor strolled into the room and found the cat asleep on the chair. She stroked the cat's neck and woke him. "Hi, Mr. Maxwell."

Jessie could hear Taylor speak to her cat.

"Nice sound system," she said louder.

Jessie finished with Maxwell's preparations then went to the great room. Taylor was admiring Jessie's B&O system along with her CD collection. "You have a wonderful CD collection," she said. "Except . . ."

"Except what?"

Taylor was searching the shelves of Jessie's collection. Then she turned back toward Jessie. "Except you don't have any of mine."

Jessie remembered that she had stored the CDs away with all the material she had gathered on Taylor more than two years earlier.

"Oh . . . I do. They're around someplace. I must have them in the CD changer in my car." *I better buy her CDs.*

Taylor's eyes returned to Jessie's collection. "You have the new Natalie Merchant CD. How is it?"

"It's pretty good," Jessie said.

"I'd love to hear it. Would you mind if we take it and listen to it in the car?"

"No. Not at all." Jessie removed the CD from her collection and handed it to Taylor. She bid Maxwell farewell and they left through the front door. When Jessie saw the red Porsche parked in her driveway, she smiled. *Hmmm, red sports car.*

Taylor popped the trunk of her car and proceeded to put the CD in the changer, but stopped. "I wondered where this was." She pulled a small hand purse from the trunk, then removed the CD cartridge and put the CD in. "Oh, now I remember. I put it in here after Kurk's last cast party."

"How many purses do you have?" Jessie asked.

"I don't know. Why?"

"Earring . . ."

Taylor opened the small purse. She pulled out the few personal items she had stored away months earlier and found the earring on the bottom of the purse. Taylor picked it up and displayed the tiny treasure to Jessie.

"How did she do that?" Taylor mumbled.

Jessie opened the passenger door. "I hope you brought your credit card."

All the way to the restaurant, Jessie was lost in her own thoughts. There was a big part of her that was saddened to learn Karen was as accurate as she was. *If Karen was right about all these trivial things and about her past life, is she right about the other stuff?* Jessie looked over at Taylor. *How could I be a danger to Taylor? How could my love be misguided?* Jessie gazed out the window, trying to take her mind off the subject. In the rear view mirror, she noticed the front of a dark-blue Ford Mustang and, for a moment, she was reminded of Ellen.

Taylor took Jessie to a small Italian restaurant outside of Pasadena. The host immediately recognized Taylor and quickly escorted them to a private cubbyhole away from others in the restaurant.

"You've been here before?" Jessie asked.

"Yes. The owners are always very protective of me."

"You haven't said much since you found your purse."

Taylor shook her head. "I don't understand how she knew. It must have been such an incredibly lucky guess."

"Have you ever considered that she may be right?"

"I've always made fun of people who believed in this stuff. I feel hypocritical even considering the possibility."

"Why don't you take it one step at a time. Read a book on intuition and see how that feels."

"You believe in this stuff?"

Jessie nodded. "I, too, was once a nonbeliever, then something happened to me and . . . it just changed the way I look at most things."

"If she was right about those things, what about the rest?" Taylor asked.

I wonder if she is reading my mind. Jessie smiled. "How does the rest feel?"

"Not very good."

"Okay. How about the part about your past life?"

"What about it?"

"Does it feel right?"

"I don't know. I keep thinking about my present and future. What karmic situation am I involved in? Who is causing me danger? What is going to change or who is going to die?"

"Taylor, I don't think you should worry about those things. Start reading about metaphysics and see how it feels."

Taylor smiled. "Thanks for listening to me."

"Anytime." She changed the subject. "I saw Kurk at the set on Wednesday. Are Kurk and Travis old buddies?"

"Well, I'm not sure I would call them buddies, but they've known each other for years. Kurk has been Travis's leading man in most of his movies for the last five years. Ever since the two of us started seeing each other, anyway."

"Does Kurk have another project lined up with him?"

"Not that I'm aware of. But the two of them talk about investments all the time."

Throughout dinner, Taylor watched Jessie closely. There was a familiarity about Jessie that Taylor did not understand. She knew, based on earlier discussions, that they had met before, but even now, she couldn't place where. Taylor was surprised at how comfortable she felt with Jessie. She realized that she looked forward to seeing her on the set, and since they had spent the afternoon together, she had looked forward to their dinner together. Taylor never had many close girlfriends so this was a new experience for her. But as she watched Jessie, she started to wonder if she was attracted to her. *That's ridiculous*, she lectured herself. *It's not sexual. It's something else. But . . . what?*

When Taylor arrived at the courtroom to continue shooting, the following Monday morning, Travis approached her. "Here. This came in the mail for you, in care of me." He handed her a cream-colored envelope. Taylor saw the initials I.D. in the upper left-hand corner of the envelope, but there was no return address. "When did this come?"

"Either Thursday or Friday last week. You should discourage any mail coming to me. I'm bad enough keeping on top of my own stuff. I don't need the added responsibility of someone else's mail." Travis hurried away.

Taylor sat on the court bench and opened the envelope. The short note was typed on the same letterhead as the other letters. It was high-quality cream stationery with the initials I.D. professionally printed as letterhead on the paper. There was no address on it. Taylor's hands shook as she read the note.

> *Taylor,*
> *I am your Destiny. It's only a matter of time before the two of us can be together. I have come beyond the reaches of time to be with you, again.*
> *I.D.*

"Are you okay?" It was Mark who drew Taylor back to reality.

Taylor handed Mark the note. He read it. "This is getting serious. How many letters is this?"

"This is the fourth," Taylor answered. "But I also got that postcard, remember?"

"Yes."

"Mark, the first three letters came to me in care of the record company. The postcard came in care of you, now this was mailed to Travis. This person is giving me the creeps."

"I don't blame you, Taylor." Mark sat close to her on the bench and gently took her hands in his own. "I'm going to take the letters to the cops."

"Do you think that's necessary?"

"I don't know. But we don't know what this person's intentions are. I would feel better if we did." Mark gently stroked Taylor's back to comfort her.

"Yes. I guess you're right." Taylor agreed.

"I'll go right now. I'll go back to my office, get the other letters, and then swing by LAPD. You just relax."

By this time the cast was gathering. Travis sensed Taylor's anxiety and approached Mark and Taylor. "Is everything okay?"

"No. There's some nutcase harassing Taylor." He showed Travis the note. "I'm taking the letters to the LAPD, now." Mark whispered to Travis, "Would you keep an eye on her? I'll be back within a few hours."

Jessie arrived on the scene shortly after Mark had left for the police station. The cast was just getting ready to perform. Jessie instantly knew something was wrong when Taylor's eyes met her own.

"What's wrong?" Jessie asked as she approached Taylor.

"I got another letter."

"You did? What did it say?"

"Pretty much the same stuff. You know—we're destiny and meant to be together. Except . . . he wrote something about coming to be with me again."

"Again?"

"Yes. Again."

"Could it be an old boyfriend?"

Taylor shook her head. "No. The way it was worded was strange. The letter said that he was coming beyond the reaches of time, to be with me again. Do you think it could have anything to do with my reading?"

"Reaches of time? You mean implying a past life?"

"It was just a thought."

"Places everyone," Travis shouted.

"I better get to work," Taylor said.

Jessie looked into Taylor's eyes. "Are you okay?"

"Yeah." She moved away from Jessie then abruptly came back, meeting Jessie's familiar brown eyes. "Thank you for dinner the other night. I really enjoyed myself."

"You bought! Thank you."

"Are you sticking around? Do you want to do lunch?"

"Places, now," Travis said. He was speaking to Taylor.

Jessie nodded as Taylor moved to her place.

After the filming started, Taylor settled down. This was the last scene to be filmed in the courtroom, so Travis kept the cast working through lunch, anticipating an early afternoon wrap-up. Mark arrived around 12:30 and approached Jessie.

"Hi, how are you today?" he whispered to Jessie.

"Pretty good. How are you?"

"I just spent the morning at LAPD. Needless to say, I'm much better, now."

"Why were you at the police station?"

"Taylor has been getting some harassing letters. I filed a complaint for her."

"Oh, that's good. She told me about them. What did the police say?"

"Not much. Just to let them know of any other developments. They can't do anything about it now."

Jessie and Mark sat together and watched the scene play out.

A couple hours later Travis yelled, "That's a wrap." The cast quickly left the set.

Taylor approached Mark and Jessie. "Hi Mark, how did it go?"

"It went fine, Taylor. At this point, we just need to keep LAPD informed. So if you receive any other letters, postcards, anything, let me know. Okay?"

Taylor smiled at Mark. "Thanks, Mark." Then she turned to Jessie, "Ready?"

"Sure."

"I took a limo, here. Should I call for a limo or do you have your car?"

"I have my car."

Chapter 14

Security men escorted the cast to a rear exit. As expected, a group of observers had gathered outside the courthouse, anticipating the cast's departure. The majority of the observers followed Jennifer Kendrick as she made her way through the crowd to her limo that waited at the curb. But a smaller group surrounded Taylor and Jessie. Taylor graciously autographed items that were handed to her by swarming fans, until the group reached Jessie's car.

Jessie opened the door for Taylor, and she got in. The group backed away, permitting the car to pass. As Jessie pulled out of the parking lot and onto the main road, she caught a glimpse of blue in her rearview mirror as a car pulled out behind her. *Another blue Mustang. Popular model*, she thought.

"Where do you want to go for lunch?" Jessie asked.

"There's a good place not too far from here. It's called The Moonlight Café. Make your next right, then a left on Broadway."

Jessie obeyed and turned at the intersection. "The letter still has you spooked?"

"No. I'm better," Taylor lied.

As Jessie approached Broadway, she noticed that the blue Mustang was still behind them. She changed lanes to make a left on Broadway and stopped at the light. The Mustang also changed lanes and waited directly behind the Lexus. *I don't like this*, Jessie thought. She couldn't get a good look at the driver of the Mustang because of its dark-tinted windshield. Jessie sat at the intersection waiting for a green arrow while cars still passed on the right side, going straight through the intersection. The traffic signal for the passing cars turned yellow. *This doesn't feel right*. Just as the traffic signal turned red, Jessie abruptly maneuvered the Lexus from the left turn lane into the center lane behind a vehicle that was trying to beat the red light.

"What are you doing?" Taylor was startled as Jessie pulled the car into the intersection. She saw Jessie's eyes fixed on the rearview mirror and turned around in time to see the blue Mustang recklessly peel into the intersection from the turning lane. The Mustang barely missed a passing car which slowed the Mustang, allowing Jessie to put some distance between them.

"The Mustang is following us?" Taylor asked.

Jessie increased speed and made a sharp right-hand turn at the next intersection. When the Mustang also turned, Jessie said, "It sure looks that way." Jessie sped through the streets of downtown Los Angeles. "Where are the cops when you need them? I need to get off this street."

"There's an entrance ramp to the Pasadena Freeway two blocks up," Taylor said.

Jessie's car took the ramp at a high speed, the Mustang following close behind. As she merged onto the highway, Jessie aggressively maneuvered to reach a passing lane. Horns honked and fingers flew in response to Jessie's aggressive driving.

"You really know how to piss them off," Taylor teased. "Who would be following you, anyway?"

It's not me they're after, Jessie thought.

As if reading Jessie's mind, Taylor said, "They're not after you. They're after me, aren't they?"

Jessie's speedometer passed 60, then 70, and was approaching 80 when they came up behind an old man driving below the speed limit. Jessie braked to prevent hitting the old man. Whatever distance she had put between the two cars had been lost. The Mustang again was closing in fast.

Jessie eyed an exit ramp about a quarter of a mile up. Two lanes of cars separated the Lexus from the exit lane. She floored the accelerator, pushing the car to within inches of the car in front of her, then broke across the two lanes of cars. Horns honked as the Lexus peeled in front of a car taking the exit ramp. Tires screeched behind them. Taylor could see the Mustang attempt to repeat Jessie's move, but it missed the exit ramp.

As Jessie continued to put distance between herself and the Mustang, she realized how fast her heart was beating. *Relax.* Jessie looked at Taylor. "Are you okay?"

"They were after me, weren't they?"

Jessie remembered the blue Mustang that was behind Taylor's car the previous Friday evening. *He must have followed her out to my place.*

There was an outburst of sirens and lights behind the car. "Shit," Jessie said.

"Where are the police when you need them?" Taylor said.

A voice was amplified by the police car's PA system, "Pull over and turn off your engine."

Jessie pulled over. She lowered the driver's window and was pulling her insurance card from the glove compartment when an anxious voice shouted into the car, "Hold it right there. Step out of the car and place your hands over your head."

"Great," Jessie said.

She opened the door, stepped out and found two very nervous young men pointing guns at her.

Taylor could see what was going on through the rear windshield. She opened her door and got out. Both police officers' guns were diverted toward the passenger side.

"No, Taylor. Stay inside," Jessie said.

"I will not," Taylor said as she stepped out of the vehicle. "Why do you have guns pointed at us?" she boldly asked the officers.

"Hey, you're Taylor Andrews."

"Yes. Why do you have your guns drawn?"

"A car matching this description was seen driving recklessly on the interstate," the older police officer said. Both officers lowered their weapons. "We just never know what we're going to come up against when we pull someone over."

Taylor and Jessie tried to explain to the officers that a blue Mustang with California plates had chased them. The officers appeared skeptical and suggested that the ladies drive to the nearest precinct, to sort everything out. The police car followed Jessie's Lexus to the police station. By the time they arrived, an eyewitness from the highway had confirmed that the Lexus appeared to be running from a blue Mustang. The officers also confirmed that Mark Rutledge had filed a complaint earlier that day regarding harassment letters.

The women were in and out of the police station within an hour. Jessie knew that having Taylor with her had helped expedite their questioning.

The women returned to the car, and Jessie started the ignition. She pulled out of the parking lot, this time very aware that no one followed her. Taylor took out her cellular phone. "I need to call Kurk. We were supposed to go over to some friend's house for dinner tonight. I'm really not up for it."

"I don't blame you."

Taylor punched in the numbers. "Hi Kurk . . . yeah, I'm sorry. I've been . . . detained." Taylor laughed at the truth to her statement. "No really. I just left the police station. It's been a long day. I don't think I'm up to going out tonight . . . I got another letter and had an incident after I left the set, I'm just on my way home now . . . I'll tell you about it when you get home . . . I know this party is important, I'm sorry, sweetheart. Just go. What time will you be back in town? . . . You haven't even left yet? Just go directly to the party and enjoy yourself. I'll see you when you get home. Love you . . . Bye."

Jessie drove Taylor to her home in Malibu. A security gate stopped the car at the bottom of the driveway. Taylor entered a password and the gate opened. The Lexus drove up the driveway to the stately home that overlooked the ocean.

Taylor had remained quiet most of the way to her home. "Are you going to be okay?" Jessie asked.

"I hate to inconvenience you. But . . . would you want to come in? I know you haven't had lunch yet. You must be famished. I'm sure I can find something for the two of us to eat."

Jessie sensed that Taylor was nervous about being left alone. "Sure, why not?"

Kurk and Taylor's property was beautiful; the contemporary home offered every comfort imaginable and had an incredible view of the ocean.

Taylor immediately went to the fridge and took out some salsa and guacamole, then served them with tortilla chips. She handed Jessie a pamphlet.

"What's this?"

"A menu. There's an Italian restaurant down the street. They deliver. What do you think?"

Jessie dunked a chip in the salsa. "I think that sounds good."

The two munched on the appetizers and sipped on some wine while they waited for their food to arrive.

"Where did you learn to drive like that?" Taylor asked.

"You know how teenagers always hangout someplace. The mall, beach, or something like that."

Taylor nodded.

"I hung out at this race track. Before I had my license, I was racing my brother's GTO." Jessie smiled at the memory. "I wasn't bad either."

"So . . . today you weren't just driving like an asshole. You knew what you were doing?"

Jessie laughed. "Maybe a little of both. I'm sorry if I scared you."

Taylor sipped her wine. "Do you think it was I.D.?"

"The thought has crossed my mind," Jessie admitted. "The other night, when you were driving from my house to the restaurant, there was a blue Mustang behind us."

"There was? So maybe they are after you."

"Or maybe they followed you out to my place."

Taylor cringed at the thought of having someone following her.

"Are you sure it was the same car?"

"No. I'm not sure, but I think it's a good possibility. The car got my attention because my last girlfriend had a blue Mustang."

"Could it be her?"

"Oh, no. Ellen's car would be about three years old, now. This was a newer model. Besides my ex's have no reason to follow me around."

Taylor changed the subject. "So, Ellen was your last lover?"

"Yes."

"What was she like?"

Jessie smiled. "She was fun, intelligent, attractive. Overall she was a nice person."

"Why did it end?"

Jessie thought back to that period. "There was just a lot going on in my life back then. I wasn't able to give her what she deserved."

Jessie and Taylor enjoyed their drinks, then dinner. They spoke for hours, enjoying getting to know each other better. Jessie felt as if she already knew Taylor, and she did. Taylor remained intrigued with the feeling of connection she had with Jessie.

It was close to nine o'clock when Jessie said she needed to get going.

Taylor walked Jessie outside to her car. It was a warm September evening and the ocean breeze felt good. The sound of the waves swelling against the rocks was relaxing.

"Thank you."

"For what?" Jessie asked.

"For being with me today. I'm glad you were with me in . . . all that. And for spending the evening with me."

Jessie smiled. She marveled at how familiar Taylor's eyes were to her. "You're welcome."

Unexpectedly, Taylor hugged Jessie then released her. "Good night." Taylor boldly met Jessie's eyes with an unwavering stare.

"Good night, Rebecca." Jessie opened her car door.

"It's Taylor."

"What?"

"You called me Rebecca."

"I did? I'm sorry." Jessie got into her car.

Taylor went to the car window and leaned over. Jessie opened the window. "So, who's Rebecca?" Taylor asked.

Jessie smiled. "Someone I once knew."

"Was she an ex of yours?"

"Yes. She was."

A curiosity sparkled in Taylor's eyes. "Do I remind you of her?"

Jessie could not help smiling. "I'll see you later." She started the ignition and drove away. Jessie saw Taylor's reflection in the mirror as Taylor watched her drive away.

That evening when Jessie went to bed, she had difficulty sleeping. She tossed and turned hour after hour. Jessie knew she had Taylor on her mind. *I can't believe I called her Rebecca.*

Jessie had tried to keep a safe distance between herself and Taylor. Initially, she didn't want to put herself through the pain of seeing her and not having her. Then after hearing Taylor's reading she didn't want to take any unnecessary chances of being a threat to her. But now, she could feel the wall she had built between them tearing down.

It unnerved her that Taylor was being harassed. Somehow, she wanted to protect her. Thoughts of the blue Mustang and disturbing letters danced in her head. There was a part of Jessie that wanted to set things straight with Taylor. She tossed and turned in bed, knowing that disclosing the truth to Taylor was impossible, and that frustration contributed to her insomnia.

It was just before dawn when Jessie fell into a deep sleep, exhausted from the restless night.

* * *

Jessie's body floated outside her own skin to the ceiling in her bedroom. As her back rubbed against the ceiling, she looked down upon her bed where she could see Maxwell and herself sleeping. "Oh, isn't this interesting. Is this one of those out-of-body experiences?" she wondered. "Maybe it's just a dream."

Jessie's body started floating around the room. *But how will I know if this really happened or if it's just a dream?* With the thought, Jessie's body floated to a wall where a picture hung. She gently removed the original piece of art from the wall. Her body slowly floated to the floor where she leaned the picture against the wall.

I read about these out-of-body experiences. Supposedly, I should be able to go any place I want to go. Where would I like to go?

Before Jessie could complete a thought, brightness engulfed her. She felt as if she were traveling at incredible speeds, and then somehow she landed. Jessie found herself walking on a mountaintop. It was foggy and she felt as if she were actually walking in the clouds. She couldn't see the ground or her feet. There was moisture in the air, but she was not cold.

"Jessie?"

Jessie turned and saw Taylor running to her. Taylor slowed her pace as she came within a couple feet of Jessie. Her eyes seemed to smile at Jessie, the way she remembered Rebecca's eyes.

Taylor studied Jessie's eyes, then her lips, and without warning, Taylor gently placed her lips on Jessie's. Moment's later Taylor backed away.

"Taylor?"

"It's me, Rebecca."

"Rebecca?"

"Yes. I want you to know that I know."

"You know what?"

"About us . . . about everything. Don't get frustrated with me, Jessie. I need time and patience. I need lots of patience. I miss you so. Please be patient."

"Is this real? Or is this just a dream?"

Taylor smiled. "I need your help. We need to break the cycle."

"What cycle?"

* * *

The piercing noise from the alarm jarred Jessie back to reality. She sat up. "Rebecca?" she cried out. But she found only Maxwell curled up against her body. Jessie could feel her heart pound within her chest. She rubbed her eyes. "God. It was just a dream." As she reached for her glass of water on the nightstand, she realized something was not right. Then she saw the painting that had hung on her wall, resting on the floor.

Chapter 15

Jessie became determined to continue the friendship with Taylor, no matter how painful it was at times. Her primary interest was Taylor's safety. After the incident with the Mustang, the letters stopped. Most of the time, Jessie stayed in Taylor's shadows, playing a secondary figure in her life. Occasionally that chasm between the two would shrink, and then Jessie would put up a wall and back away.

Filming for *Deceptions* finished as scheduled, right before Thanksgiving, with a cast wrap-up party the first week of December at the Four Seasons Hotel. The banquet room was set up perfectly for the celebration. A band entertained the guests while an extensive wait-staff mingled, pushing cocktails and appetizers. The cast and crew, along with their spouses, appeared to be enjoying themselves.

When Jessie arrived, Taylor quickly scouted her out. "Hi." Taylor came up behind Jessie. Taylor's eyes naturally combed over Jessie's new dress that accentuated her figure. "Nice dress."

Jessie could feel her face redden as she stared back at Taylor.

"What?"

Jessie shook her head. "You just made me feel like a piece of meat."

Taylor started laughing.

"What's so funny?"

"Remember the first day I read for the role of Dillon?"

"Yes."

"I couldn't look a woman in the eye without blushing. Thanks to you I can even check them out without getting embarrassed."

"I still don't see what's so funny."

"Oh, lighten up. That dress looks very nice on you."

"Thank you," Jessie said.

Kurk came up behind Taylor and surprised her with a kiss to her neck. Then he turned his attention to Jessie. "Why, Jessie, you look beautiful this evening."

"Thank you, Kurk, and I can honestly say . . . you do, too." Kurk was impeccably dressed in a tuxedo with all the trimmings.

Kurk smiled.

Travis and his wife, Dana, joined the small group. "I need to talk with you," Travis said to Kurk.

"Not now. We're here to enjoy ourselves." Kurk smiled at all the people in the group.

"Yes, now," Travis said abrasively.

The men stared at each other before Kurk gave in. "Five minutes. That's all the time you have tonight."

Kurk and Travis left the others and went to an unoccupied bar. Dana excused herself and mingled with other people she knew.

"Hello Ladies," Mark said. "You look spectacular tonight, Taylor." Mark hugged her then turned to Jessie. While he embraced Jessie he whispered, "You look wonderful, also."

"So do you, Mark." Jessie could smell the familiar cologne. After all these years, he hadn't changed from Aramis, but he was wearing it heavier than he used to.

"So are you ladies going to miss working on the set?" Mark asked.

Taylor looked at Jessie then back at Mark. "Yes. I will miss it. Most of it was a lot of fun."

Jessie knew her time with Taylor would be substantially reduced, now that the filming had stopped. She had mixed feelings about this. "I've been putting off a project," Jessie said. "It'll be good to get back to work."

"I'll miss seeing you, Jessie," Mark said.

"This isn't goodbye, Mark. I'm sure we'll be seeing each other."

Travis and Kurk returned to the group. Mark offered his hand to the two men. Travis was quiet, while Kurk appeared to be his regular happy self.

Jennifer Kendrick came by with her husband. Travis was quick to say, "Great job, Jennifer." Then he turned to Taylor. "Taylor, you were a surprise from the beginning. You did very well."

"Thank you."

"I have a good feeling about this film. It's going to do great at the box office," Travis said.

"Of course it's going to do great," Kurk interrupted. "Every man is going to want to see these two ladies kiss." Kurk's comment caught Jessie off guard. Although she knew he said it in fun, there was a demeaning tone in his voice.

After cocktails and appetizers, a bountiful buffet was set up. The group got their dinner and sat at a table away from the band, where it was quieter.

Jessie was sandwiched between Taylor and Mark. Two bottles of wine sat on the table. Mark offered to pour everyone a glass and made his way around the table.

Taylor turned to Jessie. "I'm going to miss seeing you."

Kurk overheard the comment. "The two of you have gotten pretty chummy. If I didn't know you better, Taylor, I would wonder about you two." Kurk's voice seemed to change slightly. He placed his hand over his mouth and coughed, trying to clear his throat.

Taylor smiled at her fiancé, allowing the comment to dissipate. "Are you okay, Kurk?"

Kurk nodded affirmatively, but even Jessie noticed that he was uncomfortable. He rubbed his throat and chest, took a deep breath, then rested his head within his arm on the table.

"Kurk, what's wrong?" Taylor asked.

Kurk looked up at Taylor. He coughed, then gasped for air. His lips were swollen and his eyes were rolling back into his head.

"Oh, God," Taylor cried.

"What's wrong?" Jessie asked.

"I think he's having an allergic reaction," Taylor said. "He needs epinephrine." Instinctively, Taylor searched under the table for her purse. "My purse. I need my purse."

"I'll find it," Jessie said.

"Call for an ambulance," Taylor yelled out.

Mark went to Kurk and helped Taylor lay him down on the floor as Jessie searched for the purse. He opened Kurk's mouth. Kurk's tongue was swollen and appeared to be restricting the airway. Mark pulled his neck up to help facilitate his breathing. Kurk gasped desperately for air.

Jessie found the purse, removed the EpiPen, and gave it to Taylor. Taylor skillfully administered the drug into the subcutaneous muscle, but there was no reaction. Kurk's eyes still were rolling back into his head, his gasps becoming increasingly desperate.

Mark opened Kurk's mouth again. "His tongue is more swollen. It's restricting his air passage." With his fingers, he attempted to depress the enlarged tongue away from the air passage.

"It usually works by now. How come it's not working?" Taylor asked.

Kurk suddenly stopped struggling, and he was still.

"Kurk?" Taylor shouted in his face.

"He's lost consciousness," Mark said. He continued to hold back Kurk's tongue, to facilitate an air passageway.

"Where's the ambulance?" Taylor yelled. Then she started groping his tuxedo jacket.

"What are you looking for?" Jessie asked.

"Another EpiPen. He usually carries one. Mine's a backup. Damn you, Kurk, didn't you bring one?"

Jessie helped Taylor search for another EpiPen, but they didn't find one.

Kurk's breathing was barely noticeable when the paramedics arrived.

"He's in anaphylactic shock," one of the EMT's said.

The other medic administered another dose of epinephrine.

"He's coding," a paramedic said. The two EMT's worked hastily to recover Kurk's pulse and breathing.

Jessie knew the situation was grim. Taylor was still on her knees holding onto Kurk's hand. Jessie put her hands on Taylor's shoulders, leaned over and whispered in her ear, "Taylor, come with me."

Taylor wouldn't budge and shook her head.

"Taylor, we need to let the medics work."

To Taylor, everything seemed to move in slow motion. One paramedic was trying to put a tube down Kurk's throat. Blood now stained his face. The other EMT was compressing his heart. Travis and Mark had cleared most people from the small banquet room. A couple of police officers were now watching what appeared to be futile efforts by the paramedics. Taylor could feel Jessie's hands on her shoulders.

Tears filled Taylor's eyes, distorting the movements of the medics. She could hear the men speak with the doctor on the radio and couldn't understand much of what was being said, until she heard, "Time of death—8:38 P.M."

"No. He can't be dead," Taylor tried to convince the medics. "Please try more."

"I'm sorry, there's nothing more we can do," one of the medics said.

Jessie slid to the floor next to Taylor, her arm around Taylor's shoulders. When their eyes met, Jessie could feel Taylor's pain. *Oh, my love. I'm so sorry.* Jessie pulled Taylor close. "I'm so sorry, Taylor," she whispered.

Jessie realized Taylor was in shock and led her away from Kurk's body. Twenty minutes of chaos followed until a man approached them. "Ms. Andrews?"

Taylor wiped tears from her cheeks. "Yes."

"I'm Detective Bradley from Homicide Special Section. I need to ask you some questions."

"Homicide?" Taylor asked.

"Is this necessary right now?" Jessie asked.

"Yes, it is, Miss?"

"Mercer, Jessica Mercer."

"Were you sitting at the table that Mr. Warner was sitting at?" the detective asked.

"Yes."

"I will need to interview each of you separately. Let me speak with Ms. Andrews first. Why don't you join Detective Roth over there? She's detaining those who sat at the victim's table."

Jessie joined the people from her table. They were instructed not to speak with each other about what had happened.

Taylor remained with the officer. "Ms. Andrews, can you shed any light on what happened?"

"Kurk is . . . was very allergic to nuts, peanuts, actually. He must have had some in his food."

"So you believe it was an allergic reaction?"

Taylor nodded.

"What was your relationship with the victim?"

"He was my fiancé."

"And after you believed he had an allergic reaction, you administered epinephrine?"

"I did."

"Have you given this drug to Mr. Warner before?"

"Yes, twice before. But this time was different."

"How so, Ms. Andrews?"

"The EpiPen had always worked very quickly. This time it didn't give him any relief. He just got worse."

"Do you know anybody that would want to murder Mr. Warner?"

"Murder?" Taylor shook her head in disbelief. "No."

The officer took Taylor's address and phone number. "Ms. Andrews, the team of criminologists is here. They're going to collect evidence and take some pictures."

"But why? I'm sure it must have been his allergy."

"If all the evidence supports that, you'll be the first to know. I know this must be difficult for you. Is there anyone here that can take you home? Or should I have an officer escort you?"

"I know Jessie will take me home," Taylor said.

"Ms. Mercer?"

"Yes."

"Okay, why don't you take a seat, and I'll talk with her next."

While Bradley spoke with Jessie, Taylor watched a man photograph Kurk's body. A group of plain clothes officers taped off where Kurk lay as well as the table where they had sat. Someone also taped off the buffet table. Then two men from the coroner's office removed Kurk's body from the room.

Taylor was numb. She couldn't believe what had happened.

Jessie finally returned with two police officers. "We can leave, Taylor. The valet is pulling up my car." Jessie took hold of Taylor's hand. "Let's get out of here." One officer walked in front of them, while another took the rear.

The lobby was swarming with reporters. Television cameras were shoved in the women's faces. With the help of the officers, Jessie pushed her way through the cameras without letting go of Taylor's hand. At the entry, Jessie could see the Lexus waiting for them at the bottom of the stairs, next to the curb.

Jessie opened the passenger-side door and Taylor got in, then she managed to get around the car. The officers cleared the press from the car and the two sped away.

Taylor and Jessie were silent most of the trip to Malibu. At the security gate a smaller group from the press had gathered.

"Taylor, what's your password?" Jessie asked.

"Ankh," Taylor said.

"Ankh?"

"Yes. A–N–K–H," Taylor spelled the word.

Jessie opened the car window and punched in the password. She ignored the questions the reporters shouted at her. Jessie drove through the gate, then waited while it closed shut, assuring that no one had followed.

When the women finally entered the home, Taylor went to a bar in the living area. She poured scotch into a tumbler. "Would you like some?" she asked.

"No, thanks. I've never known you to drink scotch."

"Occasionally I'll drink it." She took a bottle of spring water from the bar refrigerator. "Want one of these?"

"Sure."

They both sat on the couch. Taylor flicked the remote and the gas fireplace flared to life.

"Are you okay?" Jessie asked.

"Yeah. I'll be okay. I just can't believe all this has happened." She set and took another sip. "I don't believe he was murdered. He couldn't have been. It had to have been an allergic reaction."

Taylor and Jessie sat silently with their drinks. When Taylor finished her scotch, she poured herself another and returned to the couch. She set the glass on the coffee table beside the couch, near a picture of Kurk. Taylor picked up the picture and held it in her lap. With a finger she traced Kurk's delicate features, until tears fell onto the glass of the picture frame. She covered her face with her hands.

Jessie went to Taylor, removed the frame and set it back on the table. Instinctively, she took Taylor in her arms, cradling her as she cried softly.

An hour had passed since Jessie embraced Taylor. Both had remained silent while Taylor sobbed, then she rested her head against Jessie's chest. Taylor didn't understand the comfort she found from listening to the rhythmic beat of Jessie's heart. She closed her eyes and drifted to sleep.

When Taylor woke, she remained lying against Jessie's chest, and wiped her eyes. "I'm sorry," she whispered.

"Don't be."

Taylor sighed, "It did happen, didn't it? It wasn't a nightmare, was it?"

Jessie nodded. "It did happen."

Taylor sat up, her eyes meeting Jessie's. "Would you stay? We have . . . there's a guest room."

Jessie nodded.

In the morning, Jessie found Taylor asleep on the couch in the living room. She spread a blanket over her and went to the kitchen to make coffee.

It was about ten o'clock that morning when the buzzer sounded from the security gate. Taylor answered it, "Who's there?"

"Detective Bradley. May I come up?"

Minutes later, Jessie opened the door, permitting Bradley to enter. He stared at Jessie for a second before he came in. Bradley was a tall man, with distinguished graying sideburns and receding hairline.

"Detective Bradley, good morning. May I offer you some coffee?" Taylor asked.

"No, thank you. May we sit and talk?"

"Yes. Please . . ." Taylor motioned him to a chair in the living room. The three sat. "Do you have any news?"

"Yes. Our preliminary investigation looks like it was an allergic reaction to peanuts."

Taylor wasn't surprised and nodded.

"We found traces of peanut protein on Kurk's tongue. We're unclear where the peanuts came from. Except, we understand that Kurk was at the bar and there was a bowl of mixed snacks there, a combination that included peanuts. Also, although the banquet wasn't serving nuts in any of the dishes, the restaurant at the hotel served almonds in a vegetable medley. We're looking into the possibility that somehow the medley mixed in with the vegetables that were served at the buffet. But we didn't see any evidence of this by the food on his plate.

"Ms. Andrews, I know I asked you this last night, but have you given any more thought to who might have wanted to cause Mr. Warner harm?"

"I thought you said he died from an allergic reaction?" Taylor asked.

"That's what I said, but we haven't dismissed the possibility that it was no accident."

"Oh. No. I can't imagine anyone would have done this."

"Ms. Andrews, who is the beneficiary of Mr. Warner's estate?"

Taylor stared at Detective Bradley before she answered. "I am."

"It was you who administered the EpiPen last night. Correct?"

"Yes."

"You've done it twice before? When?"

"Oh, I don't know exactly. Maybe two and four years ago."

"Mr. Warner relied on you to carry the epinephrine?"

"Usually he would carry one and I would carry another, as a backup."

"And you carried the backup where?"

"In my purse."

"But he didn't carry one last night, did he?"

"I didn't find one on him."

"Do you find that strange? That he didn't have one on him."

"No. He had on a tux. It isn't something he wears everyday."

"I see," Detective Bradley said. "Who was responsible for purchasing and replacing the EpiPens?"

"Well . . . I don't think anyone was *responsible* for it, Detective Bradley. Between the two of us, we just made sure we had backups."

"How long was the EpiPen that you used last night in your purse?"

"Maybe a year."

"And how do you know that?"

"I bought the purse about a year ago. Whenever I get a new bag, I just put one in."

"And where would you get the EpiPen?"

Taylor was starting to show some frustration. "It depends. Sometimes from the pharmacy, sometimes from Kurk, sometimes from another bag. Why all the questions about the EpiPen?"

"Were you aware that EpiPens have a two-year shelf-life, and the one you used had expired by two years?"

Taylor's lips parted, her mouth opened, and she stared back at the detective. "Oh, my God. No, I didn't know that. I only had the purse for a year. That means it had expired even before I put it in. How could that have slipped?" Tears swelled in Taylor's eyes. "What happens when they expire? My God, did I kill him?"

"From what I understand, when the pens expire, they lose potency. Technically, the lower dose of epinephrine wouldn't have killed him, but it wouldn't have given him sufficient epinephrine to reverse anaphylaxis. So you didn't know it had expired?"

"I knew they had a couple year shelf-life." Taylor shook her head, "But I didn't know that it had expired."

"This may have just been a combination of carelessness on Mr. Warner's part. Perhaps he wasn't careful with what he ate last night, and he obviously didn't have his epinephrine with him."

Taylor clearly wasn't interested in discussing theories with Detective Bradley. She withdrew.

"It'll be some time before the toxicology report comes back. When we have more information, Ms. Andrews, we'll call you." The detective excused himself and left.

To Jessie it was clear that Taylor was very upset. "Taylor, what are you thinking?"

"How could I have been so careless? I can't drink milk if it's within a couple days of the *sell by* date. How could this have slipped?"

"Taylor, you can't blame yourself for this. Detective Bradley is right. Kurk didn't have an EpiPen on him, and you certainly didn't shove a peanut down his throat."

But it wouldn't have mattered what Jessie said. Taylor would never forgive herself, and she changed the subject. "Can I ask a favor?"

"What's that?"

"Would you consider helping me with Kurk's arrangements? I've never done this before."

"Of course, I'll help."

"Would you consider . . . staying here, until the service?"

Jessie studied Taylor. The previous evening had been difficult for Jessie. *I wonder how much I can take.*

"Just through the service," Taylor suggested.

"I'll drive home this afternoon, take care of Maxwell, and pick up some clothes."

The next couple of days proved to be a living hell for Taylor. Memories of the dreadful evening, along with the knowledge that, somehow, she was responsible for Kurk's death haunted her. She relied heavily on Jessie to make arrangements for Kurk's body, the memorial service, and an open house to follow the service.

The cinema world was stunned by Kurk's unexpected death and everyone wanted to go back to the house after the service. It was late by the time the last guests left.

Taylor confided in Jessie. "I never knew how much work was involved when someone dies." She sat on her couch in the living room.

Jessie looked around Taylor's living area trying to figure where to start to clean up.

"Don't worry about the mess. I'm having the cleaning service stop in tomorrow."

Jessie wrapped up some perishables, placed them in the refrigerator, and returned to the couch where Taylor was sitting.

"How are you holding up?"

"I'm okay," Taylor said.

"I'm going to be heading home tomorrow. Are you going to be okay?"

"Yeah, I'll be fine." Taylor thought about being alone in her house. "Thank you for everything you've done. I'm not sure what I would have done without you."

"You would have been just fine. But I'm glad I could help."

"What are you going to do now that *Deceptions* is finished?" Taylor intentionally changed the subject.

"I've been wanting to start some research for a new novel. What about you? What are you going to do?"

"I want to finish up another CD. Mark has suggested that I cancel my appearances over the next three months. I think I'll use the time to work on some new music."

Chapter 16

In the days that followed, Taylor tried to adjust to her new life without Kurk. She agreed with Mark and canceled her appearances over the next couple of months. Then she found solace in her new music. Alone, she worked relentlessly on lyrics and music to new tunes. She started to pay more attention to those voices in her head, and she even admitted to herself the results were good. The tunes came quickly and easily. The hours passed, then days and then weeks and she had not left her sanctuary. Occasionally Mark and Travis would visit, both concluding that Taylor was withdrawing.

Initially, Jessie called Taylor every day to see how she was managing. When Jessie realized that Taylor wasn't calling her, she decided to back away, but made a weekly call to see how she was faring. Taylor never sounded depressed, but rather excited about some of her new work.

Over the holidays Jessie visited her brother in New York, and when she returned she called Taylor. It had been about a month since Kurk's death and Jessie asked if Taylor would meet her for lunch sometime. Taylor agreed to meet the following week.

They met at Granita's, a restaurant not far from Taylor's house. Taylor was waiting for Jessie at the table.

"How are you doing?" Jessie asked as she sat.

"I'm doing pretty good," Taylor said. She smiled. "How are you?"

"To be honest, I've been a little worried about you. I know you were alone through the holidays. I wanted to make sure you're okay."

Taylor smiled. Her crystal blue eyes seemed to look right through Jessie. "I'm actually very good, Jessie. I've been using my time to do a lot of thinking and soul searching. I've never had time alone like this before. I needed to come to some peace about Kurk. And . . . that's been hard. But I'm getting there. I'm also working on new material for my next CD. I only have a couple more songs to do."

Jessie was pleased to see that Taylor looked healthy, happy, and somehow at peace. "Well . . . you must be doing something right, you look great."

"It's nice to get out, though. This is the first time I've been out since the funeral. I've been having my groceries delivered."

"Is there anything I can do for you?"

Taylor smiled. "You're sweet. Just have patience with me."

"What?"

"Just have a little patience with me."

Jessie was reminded of the out-of-body experience she had right before Kurk died. As she sat there, she heard Taylor's voice in her head. *"I need time and patience. I need lots of patience. I miss you so. Please be patient."*

Jessie shook the thought and tried to stay focused. "Have you heard anything more from the police?"

"Last I was told–the toxicology report confirmed it was an allergic reaction. I don't think they've given up the notion that it was murder, but they don't have a lot of evidence to support it. I know Bradley is suspicious, but I haven't heard from him in a couple of weeks."

"How long are you planning to stay in seclusion?"

"I have another month off. Then, I know I'll have to get back to work. Mark is being a real sweetheart."

"Yes, that sounds like Mark."

"Jessie, I'm just amazed at how easy the songs are coming to me right now. It's like . . ." Taylor looked around, assuring that no one was listening. "I'm hearing voices," she whispered.

"Voices?"

Taylor nodded. "Yes. Please don't think I'm crazy. I hear voices in my head. I guess I always have, but I usually ignore them. But this time . . . I'm listening to them and writing the words down. It's amazing. Then I start hearing notes . . . musical notes. I put the words and the notes together, the next thing I know–I have a song."

Jessie smiled at Taylor. "You're not crazy. I think you're awakening your gifts, just like the psychic said. What was her name? Karen?"

"I think so."

"This is a good thing," Jessie said.

"I have to admit–I have wondered about what she said. After all, the Death card was pretty accurate."

Jessie was reminded of Karen's other comments, and then she changed the subject. "A friend of mine has offered me the use of her cabin out by Big Pines. I was thinking about driving up there in a couple of weeks, stay three or four days. Would you like to join me?" Jessie asked.

"A couple of weeks? I wonder if I could get everything wrapped up by then. Well . . . does the cabin have running water?"

"Yes. From what I understand it's beautiful, the cabin is right on a lake, and it's supposed to be very comfortable."

Taylor considered Jessie's offer. "I think I'd like that. I just want to make sure I finish the lyrics and music for the new CD."

Taylor returned to her home that afternoon with the objective of getting the music finished before the trip to the mountains. Over the next week, she completed the last two songs of the CD. The following week, she recorded the new music on an audiocassette tape. She sang the vocals accompanied by her synthesizer, and then dropped the tape in an envelope with a note.

> *Dear Mark,*
> *Check it out! I'm going out of town. I'll be back by the 25th.*
> *Listen and let me know what you think.*
> *Best,*
> *Taylor*

On her way out of town the following morning, Taylor dropped the envelope in the mail. She headed east and at eleven o'clock, she arrived at Jessie's house. The Lexus was in her driveway, packed full, ready to go.

When the Porsche pulled into the driveway, Jessie went outside to greet Taylor. "Why don't you pull your car into the garage."

Taylor nodded, then pulled into the three-car garage. She popped her trunk, then pulled a small bag from the Porsche. Jessie took the bag and placed it in the Lexus.

Taylor saw how packed the Lexus was. "I thought you said we were only going away for three or four days."

"We are. From what I understand, there aren't a lot of restaurants or stores up there. I've never been there so I'm not sure what supplies are available. I went shopping yesterday, picked up a bunch of stuff, just in case."

The drive through the heart of the San Gabriel wilderness was beautiful. It didn't take long for the landscape to change to blankets of fresh snow with thriving evergreens covering mountain peaks. They drove for almost two hours, and when they arrived, the women got out of the car and looked around in awe. The cabin sat next to a sparkling blue lake surrounded by majestic snow-covered mountaintops.

"This has got to be one of the most beautiful places I've ever been," Taylor admitted.

"It is beautiful, isn't it?"

They grabbed some luggage and headed into the cabin. Both were pleased that the cabin was furnished with most essentials. The only obvious items that were missing were a telephone and television. Jessie searched for a thermostat to take the chill out of the air. She found one in a hallway leading to the bedrooms. Then the women unpacked the rest of the vehicle. Each found a bedroom and unpacked their personal belongings. When Taylor finished, she returned to the living room where Jessie was building a fire in the fireplace.

"Can I do something to help?" Taylor asked.

"Would you like to open a bottle of wine?"

Taylor found a few bottles of wine in the kitchen. "Red or white?"

"I'll have whatever you're drinking."

Taylor poured two glasses of merlot. When Jessie finished with the fire, she placed a tray of cheese and crackers on the table near the couch. They sat and enjoyed the fire, wine and crackers.

"There's a trail that goes around the lake. It's about five miles. We would need snowshoes for part of it. From what I understand, it's challenging but not impossible. Do you think you're up for a hike tomorrow?" Jessie asked.

"Five miles? Yes, I can do that."

Both enjoyed dinner and the women talked until close to midnight before they retired.

In the morning, Jessie was up at close to her normal wake-up time and found refuge in a book. Taylor was up a couple hours later. By ten, the women were dressed and ready to go. Although it didn't seem very cold, they put extra gloves, scarves and hats in a backpack.

The sun was out; it was a beautiful February day. The temperature was in the low 30s, but both were dressed adequately for the weather. For the first mile, the trail was easy. It was wide, and followed close to the lake with little incline. It gave Taylor and Jessie an opportunity to get used to the snowshoes. Then the path diverted away from the lake and up an incline. Very quickly, the trail became steep. Initially, it was lined with thicket, then the vegetation changed and the women were in the forest with tall evergreens. At times the trail butted up against steep inclines. Deep snow blanketed the forest, sometimes making it more difficult to follow the path. Although Jessie found the hike to be quite enjoyable, it was more challenging than she had been led to believe. Now, she was concerned about whether the trail was more than Taylor could handle.

At one point, Jessie turned to check on Taylor and it was obvious that Taylor was winded. "Are you okay?"

"Sure." But Taylor's huffing and puffing indicated otherwise.

Jessie and Taylor came to a clearing on top of a hill. A rock formation presented the perfect place for them to sit. They had been hiking hard for the last hour and both were tired. They sat on an outcropping, and Jessie removed snacks from the backpack she carried.

"Thanks. I'm hungry." Taylor took the snack and water bottle that Jessie offered. "How far do you think we've come?"

Jessie glanced at her watch. "About two miles. How are you doing?"

"I'm okay."

"This is more challenging than I expected. Are you going to make it?"

"Yes. I'm fine."

Jessie was getting warm; the sun was beating down on them as they sat on the rock. She unzipped her jacket partially, to cool herself.

"You work out, don't you," Taylor asked. Her face was red, showing signs of her fatigue.

"I do. And you?"

"I do work out, but obviously not as much as you."

"Let's rest for a while." Jessie looked in the direction the trail was leading. "What goes up must come down. It should be downhill for a little while."

"Great."

"I take it you finished the music for the new CD."

"I did. I even made a tape for Mark and dropped it in the mail yesterday morning. I'm hoping he has listened to it by the time I get back."

"You sound excited about it."

"I am, and I can't remember the last time I got excited about a new project. I'm intrigued to find out if this stuff is good."

"I bet it is."

"Have you ever . . ." Taylor stopped her question in mid-sentence. "Never mind."

"Have I ever what?"

Taylor hesitated. "Have you ever experienced a déjà vu?" Taylor asked.

"What do you mean?"

Taylor made eye contact with Jessie. "You know—when you experience something for the first time but it seems like it's occurred before?"

"Yes. Occasionally."

"Do you think they relate back to past lives?"

It was becoming obvious that Taylor's interest in metaphysics was increasing. Jessie smiled. "Some people believe déjà vu experiences are past-life memories. Others believe that they're precognitive."

"What do you mean by precognitive?"

"Knowing something before it happens. Somehow, you experience an event through some psychic process or a dream before it happens. Then when you actually experience it, it seems familiar, like you've done it before. Why do you ask?"

Taylor shook her head. "Since yesterday I've had three déjà vu experiences. I can't remember the last time I have felt them so strongly."

"Really? When did you experience them?"

"Once in the car coming out, last night during dinner, and while we were hiking, earlier."

"That's interesting. Over the last month or so, you've been working your creative side very intensely. Perhaps this has helped open up some aspects of your psychic abilities."

"Can't you call it something else? I really don't care for the word psychic."

"Taylor. We're all psychic. We all have different abilities. I've learned the key is to identify what your strengths are and work with them."

Taylor shook her head. "I'm sorry. I am trying, but this is still hard for me."

"I know. It was for me, too. Let's talk about it in everyday terms. Have you ever thought about someone you haven't heard from in a while, then the next day you get a call or a letter from them?"

"Yes. It happens all the time. It's called coincidence."

"The first thing you need to buy into is—there's no such thing as coincidence. Here's another one. The phone rings, and you know who it is before you answer."

"Yes. It's called a lucky guess or deductive reasoning."

Jessie looked into Taylor's eyes and smiled. She was reminded of how different Rebecca was from Taylor.

"*But they're the same,*" that little voice whispered in Jessie's ear.

"Let's put logic aside for a moment," Jessie suggested. "I said earlier that everyone has some type of psychic ability. The key is to determine how the information comes to you. Once you do that you can build on your accuracy."

"Okay. I'll work with you here. What do you mean when you say how the information comes to you?"

"It's how a person processes psychic information. Some people actually see things—they're clairvoyant, while others feel things—they're clairsentient. Sometimes people hear things—and they are clairaudient."

"So, if I hear voices when I work, do you think that's clairaudience?"

"How long have you been hearing voices?"

Taylor looked away as if embarrassed. "I've heard them all my life," she admitted. "I actually shut them out when I was a teenager. Then when I started my singing career, they started to come back. I would hear them occasionally when I was writing music. But nothing like I'm experiencing now."

"Sure sounds like clairaudience, doesn't it?"

"Jessie, you seem very . . . grounded. How did you come to explore this stuff?"

"I was initially introduced to it through my last girlfriend. Then, about . . . three years ago I had a life-altering experience and I was forced to investigate metaphysics, and . . . well, let's just say my life has never been the same."

"Can I ask what happened?" Taylor looked innocently into Jessie's eyes. "What happened that made you consider this stuff?"

Jessie smiled. "Maybe one day I'll be able to share it with you, but right now I think we ought to head back." She pointed at the sky behind Taylor. "It looks like we're going to be getting some weather soon." Dark clouds had penetrated the mountaintops that surrounded them. The sun was minutes away from getting lost behind the clouds.

Chapter 17

The women gathered their things and continued heading down the hill. The trail brought them back into the forest with tall evergreens obscuring the sky. When the clouds obstructed the sun, the trail darkened even more. The climb down was steep and the path occasionally narrowed. The only sound they heard was the rhythmic thud from the snowshoes beating on the deep snow, and trees swaying from wind.

About fifteen minutes down, the trail narrowed. Jessie was concerned that it was too narrow, and it butted up against a steep cliff-like incline. There appeared to be a ten-foot section that was more challenging than Jessie cared for. On the uphill side, the incline seemed just as steep. Jessie stopped and turned around to see Taylor.

"Are you okay?"

Taylor nodded.

"Be careful."

Jessie continued her trek across the narrow path. She heard Taylor following close behind her. Frequently, she would glance back to assure that Taylor was okay. Jessie was within a foot of where the path widened when the snow gave way beneath Taylor's snowshoes.

Jessie heard Taylor scream as Taylor's feet plunged through the falling snow. Jessie turned in time to see Taylor slide down the hill, feet first, attempting to avoid hitting the larger trees, while lunging for branches to grab hold of. About twenty feet down, she collided feet first with a mature evergreen. One of her feet became entangled in a branch and her upper body lunged downhill, face first, until the twisted limb snagged her, abruptly halting her descent.

Taylor winced from her pain, but she knew the twisted limb was the only thing preventing her from continuing the fall.

Jessie scoped out the situation. The snow was unstable for her to step on. She removed her snowshoes and backpack. Jessie knew if she went down, she wasn't climbing back up. Hurriedly, she strapped the snowshoes together, then attached them to the backpack. Aiming carefully, she threw the bundle past the large tree Taylor was caught in. Jessie studied the trees and small saplings that were almost covered with deep snow. Then she started her downward climb. Snatching tree branches and clutching at saplings, she moved carefully, inching her way to Taylor. Jessie was about six feet from the tree when she saw Taylor lying face down on the downhill side of a tall spruce.

A minute later, Jessie was a few feet from Taylor. She could see blood drops surround Taylor's head in the white snow. As Jessie grabbed a branch from a nearby tree, the crack alerted Taylor and her head raised from the snow. Jessie could see the blood was coming from her forehead.

"Are you okay?" Jessie asked. She inched closer, grasping at a bush to prevent her own fall.

"Yeah. My leg hurts though."

"Do you think it's broken?"

"I'm afraid to move it. I think it's what's holding me."

Jessie couldn't see Taylor's lower body. She carefully crept back up the hill and peeled back the lower limbs of the tree. Taylor's right leg was trapped between two branches; her snowshoe prevented her escape. Her other leg was in the tree, but unbound. One of the branches that held Taylor appeared to be severely stressed.

"Your snowshoe is trapped between two branches. One of the branches can break any minute."

"Great."

Jessie inched her way back to Taylor. "I can remove the boot from the snowshoe."

"I'll keep falling, though."

Jessie pushed the snow away from the area around Taylor. She uncovered a small tree near her.

"Taylor, reach for this sapling and pull your upper body up to prepare for your release," Jessie instructed. "When I unbuckle the snowshoe, your legs will fall. Just keep holding on to the branches, don't let go until I get you. We don't have a lot of time before the branch breaks."

Taylor grabbed the tiny tree. "This tree won't hold my weight, though."

"You're right, it won't but it'll give me time to get back to you."

Jessie crawled back up to the tree. She removed the snowshoe from Taylor's unobstructed leg, then carefully threw it down the hill near her backpack. Before she unbuckled the right snowshoe, Jessie planted one of her feet deep in the snow.

"Ready?" Jessie asked.

"Yes."

In one swift motion, Jessie unbuckled the snowshoe. With her right hand, she grabbed hold of a lower downhill limb, and with her left hand, she attempted to reach Taylor. Taylor clung to the branches as her lower body plunged from the tree. Desperately, her legs searched for something to stabilize her.

Taylor's hands slid over the branches, pulling the needles from their twigs. Desperate for something to hold onto, she wrapped the remaining twig around one hand. With her free hand, Taylor reached out for Jessie. But Jessie's grasp remained inches away. A sudden shift of Taylor's body alerted both of them that the sapling was starting to uproot.

"Just hold on," cried Jessie. To give her the extra distance, she lowered her grip on the branch that anchored her. *I hope this holds us.* Her new placement gave her the extra inches she needed. Jessie grabbed onto one of Taylor's hands, just as the sapling was pulled out of the ground.

Jessie clung to Taylor's fingertips while Taylor searched for something to hold onto with her other hand. Jessie could feel the limb that anchored her stressing, but she wouldn't let go of Taylor.

Taylor's feet finally stabilized her enough to grab hold of another tree.

"I'm okay," Taylor said.

"Will you be okay if I let go of you? I don't think this branch is going to last much longer."

Taylor hesitated. "Yeah. I'm fine." She squeezed Jessie's fingers. "You can let me go, now."

Jessie slowly released her grip. She removed the snowshoe that had trapped Taylor and threw it down the incline. Jessie crept to Taylor where she clung to the snow-covered mountainside.

"How's your leg?" Jessie asked.

"It's sore, but it's not broken." Taylor looked up the hill. "Now what?"

Jessie looked down the steep hillside. "It flattens out about 20 feet down. Let's try to get down, and we'll regroup."

Slowly, the women managed to descend the steep incline. On the way down, Jessie recovered her backpack and the snowshoes. When they reached flatter ground, Jessie noticed that Taylor was limping.

"Taylor, sit down and rest." Jessie moved to her side. She lifted Taylor's chin so that she could see her forehead. "You have a nasty scratch on your forehead. But the bleeding has stopped." She removed a Band-Aid from the outside pocket of her backpack and adhered it. "And your leg?"

"My ankle hurts, but I can walk."

The wind had picked up, and the blowing snow sent a chill through both women's bones. Their snow-covered clothes contributed to the coldness. Jessie looked to the sky, wondering if it was snowing or it was just blowing snow.

"We're going to have to make it without the trail. I think we should head down until we reach flatter ground, then head southwest until we reach the lake. The cabin is on the southern corner of the lake."

"Are you sure about the direction of the lake?"

Jessie removed a compass from an outside pocket of the backpack. "Yes."

"Do you happen to have an SOS beacon in there?"

"Sorry. Fresh out of those . . . we're on our own."

Taylor got up. "Well . . . I could use a hot cappuccino right now, let's get back to the cabin."

The women strapped on their snowshoes and put on the dry mittens, scarves and hats that had been stored in the backpack.

The trek to the bottom of the mountain was slow. When they left the wooded section and transitioned into thicket, it was snowing harder. Around each turn, the women were hopeful to catch a view of the lake. Occasionally, Jessie would refer to the compass and confirm that they were moving in the right direction.

Taylor's limping increased, although she didn't complain, and Jessie knew she was in pain.

Jessie moved to Taylor. "Put your arm around my neck," Jessie suggested. "Use me as a crutch."

They pushed on for another half-hour, and Jessie's confidence in her directions was shaken. She had anticipated seeing the lake much sooner. When they finally came out of the thicket and saw the lake, they both shrieked with excitement.

The rest of the trip was easier. They could occasionally see the lake through the snow. By the time they were within sight of the cabin, Taylor was leaning heavily on Jessie. It had become too painful for Taylor to place any pressure on the ankle. Both women were cold and tired and were ready to end this part of their journey.

Chapter 18

Once inside, Jessie turned up the thermostat, removed her jacket and gloves, then turned her attention to Taylor. "Let's get your clothes off." She helped Taylor remove her coat. Jessie placed a chair at the entry for Taylor to sit, and then she carefully removed her boots. Even before the sock was removed, Jessie could see that Taylor's right ankle was swollen. When she saw how discolored the ankle was, her heart sank.

Jessie knew Taylor's jeans were wet and cold, because her own jeans were. "Let's get you to the couch. Did you bring a pair of sweats or something that would be easy to get on you?"

"Yes. I think I put them in the middle drawer."

Jessie picked up the afghan that draped the back of the couch, and placed it within Taylor's reach. "Do you think you can take your jeans off and get under the blanket?"

Taylor started to unbutton and unzip the jeans. "Sure."

Jessie retreated to Taylor's bedroom. In the dresser drawer, she found sweats and dry socks. When Jessie returned to the living area it was obvious that Taylor was struggling to remove her jeans.

Taylor looked at Jessie helplessly. "I think I need your help." She stood in front of the couch trying to balance herself on one foot. The wet jeans had not made it past her hips.

Jessie went to Taylor's side. "Here, lean on me and see if you can get them off," Jessie offered.

Taylor made an effort, but the cold wet jeans would not budge. "This isn't going to work."

Jessie knew Taylor was right. She stood in front of Taylor and placed her hands on both sides of Taylor's hips. Since Jessie was taller than Taylor, she had to lean over her to push the jeans. The tight jeans moved some, but not enough. Taylor sensed that Jessie was uncomfortable.

The two stood face-to-face. Jessie blushed as her eyes met Taylor's. "Excuse me," she said. In one swift motion, Jessie's hands pushed the jeans in a backward motion over Taylor's buttocks. Then Jessie quickly removed her arms from Taylor's waist.

Taylor paused momentarily. *Now why would that feel so familiar?* Taylor pushed the jeans down far enough and then sat on the couch. Jessie kneeled and pulled the jeans off carefully. Both women were quiet, avoiding eye contact. Jessie helped pull the sweats to Taylor's knees, but left them for Taylor to finish.

"Lie down on the couch and raise your leg," Jessie instructed when the sweats were finally on. She handed Taylor a dry sock for her uninjured foot. "Here, I'm going to look for an ace bandage and make an ice pack."

Minutes later, Jessie returned. She picked up the blanket and spread it over Taylor's shivering body, then she turned her attention to the ankle. It was more swollen and had darkened.

Jessie wrapped the injured ankle and shook her head. "I'm so sorry, Taylor. It was thoughtless of me to take you on that trail."

"This isn't you're fault . . . it was an accident."

"I didn't ask the right questions about the trail, and clearly put you in danger." Karen's words echoed in her head. *"There is a soul that you have been with before . . . their intentions are not healthy and this is what is causing danger."*

I should never have asked her here, Jessie lectured herself.

Taylor interrupted her thoughts. "I wouldn't have gotten out of there if it wasn't for you."

"You shouldn't have been there in the first place," Jessie challenged.

"Why are you taking this on?" Taylor asked. "We're both adults. I decided to go with you. You didn't coerce me into going. It was my choice."

Jessie continued wrapping the swollen ankle, ignoring the comment.

Taylor took Jessie's hands in her own, getting Jessie's attention. "This is not your fault, Jessie." Taylor smiled, "Please, believe me."

Jessie tried to smile. She finished wrapping the ankle, then placed an ice pack over it.

"Jessie, why don't you get your wet clothes off?"

"I will. Are you okay for a little while?"

Taylor smiled. "Yes. Go take care of yourself."

Jessie retreated to her own bedroom. As she closed the door behind her, she leaned up against it. *How could I have been so careless? I shouldn't have brought her here.*

Within the hour, Jessie had changed, built a roaring fire, and set out appetizers and wine for Taylor. She had even prepared chicken for dinner and put it in the oven to bake.

"I put dinner in early," Jessie announced.

"Great. I'm starving. Would you join me for appetizers?"

Jessie nodded and poured herself a glass of wine; she took a sip then placed the wineglass on the coffee table in front of the couch. She retreated to the kitchen and a minute later returned with the first-aid kit and a wet face cloth.

"Your forehead should be cleaned." Jessie placed the first-aid kit next to her wine glass and took another sip of wine. She gently pushed Taylor's hair away from her forehead and removed the bloody Band-Aid.

Taylor sat up and moved her injured leg to the floor. She gathered her hair and pulled it away from her face enabling Jessie to inspect the forehead. Jessie awkwardly leaned over her as she washed Taylor's forehead.

Sensing the awkward position, Taylor tapped the couch next to her. "Why don't you sit? I won't bite."

Jessie sat and continued her inspection of Taylor's wound. As she did so, her arm innocently brushed against Taylor's.

"How does it look?"

As Taylor asked, she became aware of how close Jessie was to her, and her feelings puzzled her. There was something familiar about Jessie's touch, but what was confusing was the excitement she felt. Taylor had always been drawn to Jessie, especially her eyes. At times, when their eyes would meet, she often wondered if Jessie felt the same.

Jessie cleaned the dried blood away from Taylor's forehead, revealing the long scratch. She knew that Taylor's eyes were on her.

"It's actually just a scratch. It should be cleaned, though. You don't want it to get infected." Gently she continued to clean the scrape. "How did you get it, anyway?"

"One of the branches of the tree I got stuck in."

Again, Jessie felt guilty about the accident. "You're lucky you weren't killed."

"Lucky? Aren't you the one who said there's no such thing as luck or co-incidence?"

Jessie ignored the comment and concentrated on cleaning the fore-head. She poured some hydrogen peroxide on a cotton ball.

"Jessie, you're just too serious. You've got to relax."

Jessie took the cotton ball to Taylor's forehead. Not anticipating the sting, Taylor jumped and grabbed hold of Jessie's hand, removing the cotton ball from her forehead.

"I'm sorry." Jessie flinched from Taylor's pain. She looked into Taylor's blue eyes. "We really need to get that cleaned, Taylor."

"I know. I was just caught off guard. Go ahead." Taylor released her hold on Jessie's hand but studied Jessie's every move.

Jessie went back to the scrape. White puss oozed from the wound after she applied additional peroxide. Jessie knew it must have stung, but this time, Taylor did not respond to it.

"What's going on here, Jessie?" Taylor asked.

Jessie could not help looking into Taylor's eyes. "What?"

"What's going on here?" Taylor pointed at Jessie's heart, and then her own. "What's going on between us?"

Jessie's gaze reverted to the first-aid kit. She picked up a Band-Aid, opened it and proceeded to adhere it to Taylor's forehead. "I don't know what you're talking about. I just almost killed you and now I'm trying to patch you up."

"Are you saying that there's nothing going on between us?"

Jessie pressed the bandage in place. "Yes. That's what I'm saying; there's nothing here." Jessie avoided eye contact, looked back, and picked up another Band-Aid.

Taylor took the Band-Aid from Jessie. "Jessie, look into my eyes and tell me there is nothing here."

Jessie ignored Taylor's plea and looked away from her.

With one hand, Taylor pulled Jessie's face, forcing eye contact. "Jessie, look me in the eye and tell me there's nothing here."

Jessie looked into Taylor's eyes but remained silent. She couldn't lie but couldn't say anything either.

Taylor's eyes settled on Jessie's lips. She mustered up every ounce of courage she could find, then her lips approached Jessie's. Jessie withdrew slightly, enabling each to reconsider the next move. Taylor found Jessie's neck with her hand, and pulled Jessie to her lips. This time there was no retreat.

Jessie understood the familiarity of their touch and their feelings. It was a reunion that she had waited for, for lifetimes. But Taylor did not understand the intensity and was lost in the moment. Taylor backed away, studying Jessie. She remained silent for some time, then she whispered, "I'm not gay. But . . . how come I've wanted to do that for so long?"

Jessie did not say anything.

"You can't tell me that there is nothing here. I can feel it. How come you don't admit it?"

Jessie sighed and ran her fingers through her hair, pulling the hair from her face. "Taylor, you said it yourself–you're not gay."

"Meaning?"

"Cardinal rule number one of being a lesbian is–never fall in love with a straight woman."

"So, if you have feelings for someone, you just ignore them?"

"If they're straight? Pretty much."

"I don't understand what's going on here. I've never been attracted to women, and then I met you. From the first time I met you, Jessie, I have been drawn to you, and I don't understand why. And yet, I'm not attracted to other women. This is very confusing."

"I can see that. I'm sorry."

"Can I confide in you about something?"

Jessie nodded.

"That day . . . the first day I was to read for the role in *Deceptions* . . ."

"Yes."

"When the two of us played the scene out . . . Jessie, I wasn't acting."

"What do you mean?"

"I remember, I looked into you eyes and . . . I just got lost. I followed your lead. I know when I had to film it with Jennifer later . . . it was hard. It just wasn't natural for me. But what does all this mean?"

"Did our kiss help you find any answers?"

Taylor's eyes returned to Jessie's lips, then back to her eyes. "When we kissed, I wanted . . . more. Tell me, how do you feel about me?"

Jessie smiled shyly, wondering what to tell her. "I've had feelings for you for a long time now. I know they go beyond friendship, Taylor."

"What's next?" Taylor asked boldly.

"As much as I'd love to take you in my arms right now and love you, I can't. My feelings for you run too deep to risk that you may just be curious about being with a woman."

"You think that might be it?"

"I think it's a possibility."

"How will I know?"

"Search your heart. As long as you're honest with yourself, I trust you'll be honest with me."

"What do we do in the meantime?"

Jessie looked into Taylor's blue eyes. She wanted to reach out to her and kiss her again. It had been too long between kisses and embraces. The kiss tonight was a tease of their love for each other. This reminder could be intoxicating and difficult to just discard. Jessie took Taylor's small hands in her own. She leaned over and kissed both hands.

Taylor studied Jessie's move. *Déjà vu?*

"In the meantime, we can be friends."

* * *

The rest of their evening together was awkward. They had an early dinner and decided that they would leave in the morning. Jessie wanted to have a physician look at Taylor's ankle to assure that it was okay. Both were exhausted from the day.

It was just after nine when Taylor announced she was going to bed. Still unable to put pressure on the injured ankle, she hobbled toward the hallway. Jessie went to her, Taylor leaned on her, and they moved toward the bedrooms. At the entry of Taylor's bedroom, Jessie stopped. Taylor turned to Jessie. She smiled and looked into Jessie's eyes, then cocked her head. "Are you sure you don't want to come in?" Taylor asked.

"You are a tease," Jessie said.

Taylor nodded then smiled. "Good night, Jessie." She planted her lips delicately on Jessie's cheek; her eyes remained on Jessie as she closed the door of her bedroom.

Both Jessie and Taylor remained restless that night. It was close to two o'clock when Jessie heard noises in the cabin. Moments later she heard the door to her bedroom creak open. Jessie could see a shadow standing in the hallway.

"Taylor?"

"Yeah. It's me. Are you up?"

Jessie sat. "Is something wrong?"

Taylor hesitated then limped in the doorway. "I just had a terrible dream. Can I come in?"

Jessie pulled the blankets over from the opposite side of the bed, inviting Taylor in. Taylor hobbled cautiously, but hesitated getting in the bed. "I just wanted to see that you were okay."

"Now I promise–I won't bite," Jessie said. "Do you want to talk about it?"

Taylor climbed into bed. "It just seemed too real."

Jessie noticed that Taylor's eyes were wide open. "Tell me about it. Why did you want to see if I was okay?"

"It just seemed so real . . . and you were in it."

"What happened?"

"I was on trial for something and I was found guilty, which really upset you. There was a fight . . . but it wasn't you."

"What do you mean?"

"I'm not sure. You know when you have a dream and things just don't look like they're supposed to? But somehow you just know who or what they are?"

"What were you on trial for?"

"I don't know. When the verdict was announced he . . . you got really upset. Then there was a hill where a bunch of people gathered . . . you got hurt. It just seemed so real. I woke up and wanted to see if you were okay. Do you think I'm a baby?"

"No, Taylor. I don't think you're a baby. Dreams can be pretty intense at times." Jessie lay back down in the bed. "Why don't you lie down and shut your eyes."

Taylor put her head down on the pillow next to Jessie, but her eyes remained open, staring at the ceiling.

"Close your eyes and try to get some sleep," Jessie suggested.

Jessie turned over and closed her eyes. She tried to take her mind off the fact that Taylor was lying so close to her. Her mind wandered, recalling the

events from the previous evening. There was a part of Jessie that was disappointed that she had allowed the situation to develop between them.
Then there was a part of her that was excited that Taylor had expressed interest.

A half-hour had passed and Jessie was still wide-awake. She rolled over
searching for a comfortable spot and realized that Taylor was still wide-
eyed. "Can't sleep?" Jessie whispered.

Taylor shook her head.

Instinctively, Jessie opened an arm, inviting Taylor to her. Taylor took
the invitation and laid her head on Jessie's shoulder. Jessie cradled her.
"Shut your eyes," Jessie whispered and Taylor obeyed. As Jessie held
Taylor, she became aware that Taylor's heartbeat seemed fast. "Relax
Taylor. Try to sleep." Jessie lay there, lost in her thoughts. *God. I had forgotten how good this feels.* Minutes later, she could feel Taylor's breathing
pattern change. *Asleep in my arms, again.* Jessie smiled at the thought.

When Jessie woke in the morning, she was surprised to find Taylor still
lying in her arms. Carefully, she managed to move her without waking her.
She smiled as she closed the door of her room, watching Taylor asleep in
her bed. In the kitchen, she made a pot of coffee, and then she realized it
was going on nine o'clock. *I can't believe how late it is.* She decided to
shower while the coffee was brewing.

After her shower, Jessie noticed that the door to her room was ajar. She
heard the other shower in Taylor's room. There was a part of her that was
saddened that Taylor had left her bed. In the kitchen, she poured a cup of
coffee, then went to the picture window and opened the curtain. Eight
inches of fresh snow lay on the ground, and it was still coming down.

"Good morning." Taylor stood behind her, dressed in sweats.

"Good morning."

Catching a glimpse of the falling snow, Taylor moved slowly, joining
Jessie in front of the window. "It doesn't look like we're going anyplace today."

"I don't give up that easily," Jessie said.

"My leg is better this morning. It doesn't make any sense to leave in these conditions."

Jessie looked outside and knew Taylor was right. "I guess you're right."

"Jessie?"

"Yes?" Jessie turned toward Taylor, but she wasn't prepared for Taylor's assertiveness.

Taylor's lips were planted firmly on Jessie's, her arms wrapped around Jessie's neck. Not anticipating Taylor's unwavering move, Jessie could not help but surrender to her kiss. When Taylor released Jessie from her embrace, she took Jessie's hand and led her down the hallway.

Jessie hesitated at Taylor's bedroom door.

Taylor's eyes met Jessie's. Then Taylor said, "Trust me." And so, Jessie did.

A couple of hours later, Jessie and Taylor lay together in each other's arms, beneath the comforter in Taylor's bedroom. The women were somehow content not speaking. It was Taylor who broke their silence.

"Is lesbian sex always like this?" Taylor asked.

Jessie smiled. "No. This was pretty special."

"That's good."

"Why do you say that?"

"I would hate to think I wasted all my years with men, if it were like this all the time."

Jessie smiled. "How are you feeling?"

Taylor looked into Jessie's eyes and returned the smile. "I feel great."

Jessie needed to know. "What happened? I mean . . . I asked you something yesterday. Did you find your answers?"

"I did. My dream gave me the answers."

"It did? How so?"

"I don't understand most of it. But in my dream, I had genuine feelings for you or this man you kept turning into. I spent a good part of the night thinking about it. I realized my feelings for you were indeed real, whether you're a man or a woman."

"I'm glad you got something good out of the dream. You seemed to be quite uneasy after it."

Taylor moved to her side with her head resting on her hand. Her long dark hair fell naturally over her shoulders. A delicate gold chain draped loosely around her neck, and a small gold pendant caught within her cleavage.

Jessie fingered the gold chain. Teasingly, she traced the path of the chain, starting at Taylor's clavicle, then slowly down her chest to where the pendant was hidden in her breasts. Gently, she tugged at the chain until the small cross-like pendant fell free.

Jessie studied the pendant, and then she realized it was an ankh. "Why the ankh?"

"I like what it symbolizes. Life."

"You used an ankh on the CD cover of *Karmic Debt*.

"I did."

"How did you come up with that design? There was a sunset and mountains and a rainbow, right?"

"You're right. When I was working on 'Daniel's Heart,' I kept getting pictures of strange things popping into my head. I used them to design the jacket."

"It was very subtle, having the ankh in the sky. Some believe the ankh symbolizes more than life. Some believe it means reincarnation." Jessie's eyes searched Taylor's.

"I'm very comfortable with the ankh meaning life."

Jessie smiled. "Still a nonbeliever?"

Taylor looked deep into Jessie's eyes. *Do I know you, Jessie? Is that why I am so drawn to you? Have we known each other before?* Taylor smiled.

"I wouldn't say a complete nonbeliever. Let's just say I'm trying to be open minded, but cautious."

"That's a start."

"Jessie, what do we do now?"

"What do you mean?"

"About us."

"I guess that depends."

"On?"

"Our feelings," Jessie said.

"How do you feel about me?" Taylor asked boldly.

Jessie repositioned her arms to support her head; the two women mirrored each other. "I'm not really sure that my feelings are what's important here."

"Coward," Taylor smiled then inched closer to Jessie.

"Taylor, I admitted yesterday that I've had feelings for you for a long time."

"Annoyance is a feeling, you know."

"Cute." Jessie moved closer to Taylor so they were inches away from each other. She put a finger up to Taylor's lips. "Shh. Look into my eyes, Taylor. Don't say anything." Jessie continued to hold her finger on Taylor's full lips. "When you see my soul, close your eyes and in your mind ask how I feel. You will have your answer."

"Cop out," Taylor whispered.

"Shh, this is far from a cop out. Remember, when you sense you have seen my soul, close your eyes, go inside and see if you can find the answer."

"Okay, I'll play." Taylor had always been drawn to Jessie's eyes, and she didn't understand why. It didn't take long for Taylor to start feeling something. There was warmth in her chest. Initially she thought she was making it up. Then she realized she wasn't. As she stared into Jessie's eyes, the feeling of familiarity grew. *Déjà vu?*

Taylor closed her eyes. The sensation in her chest increased, and the warmth spread to her head. There was a sense of incredible well-being, and the feeling of being blessed for all her gifts. Then she experienced unyielding, unconditional love. Taylor held back the tears; she opened her eyes, finding Jessie's familiar eyes looking at her.

Jessie brought her finger to her own lips. "Shh." She leaned forward and planted her lips on Taylor's. When Jessie backed away she said, "In case you didn't catch that–I love you, Taylor."

"I got it," Taylor whispered.

Chapter 19

Jessie and Taylor lost themselves in the rekindled romance. Although neither one wanted to leave, on the fifth morning they packed up and headed down the mountain.

They had been in the car for a half-hour when Taylor said, "I shouldn't be this happy."

"What are you talking about?"

"I'm feeling guilty."

"Why?"

"Kurk died only two months ago. I don't think I've ever had a happier mini-vacation. I shouldn't be this happy."

"Don't be ridiculous. Kurk loved you. He'd want you to be happy."

"Kurk wasn't that big of a person."

It was close to two o'clock when the Lexus pulled into Jessie's three-car garage. Taylor and Jessie unloaded the car. Jessie stared sadly at Taylor's bag as Taylor placed it in the trunk of the Porsche.

Taylor noticed Jessie's pout. She closed her trunk then went to Jessie. "What's wrong?"

"I'm going to miss you tonight."

Taylor kissed Jessie. "Then why don't you invite me to stay tonight?"

Jessie smiled. "Would you spend the night?"

"Of course."

Jessie had unpacked most of her luggage, started a load of wash, and was giving Maxwell some loving when the Chinese food arrived. The women sat in the kitchen chatting over their dinner. Three white boxes of take-out sat on the table next to an unused set of chopsticks. Maxwell, attention starved, rubbed his neck against Jessie's leg, purring.

"I called Mark. I wanted to see if he listened to my tape."

"And?"

Taylor smiled. "He loved it. He's getting the musicians together. We can start working on the new CD over the next month."

"That's great, Taylor. I can't wait to hear it. You didn't tell him you were with me, did you?"

"No. He still has a thing for you," Taylor pointed at Jessie with her chopsticks. "Doesn't he?"

"I don't think so. We had a chat shortly after filming for *Deceptions* started. He's been fine since then. Besides, I wouldn't be surprised if he has a crush on you."

"Me? Why do you say that?"

"Just little things that I've picked up here and there."

"He's such a nice guy. I'd like to see him meet someone."

Jessie changed the subject. "Taylor, have you given any thought to appearances?"

"What do you mean?"

"I'm openly gay. It's no secret that I'm a lesbian. Have you thought about how it's going to look if you start hanging out with me?"

"It's nobody's business but our own."

"I agree. I just know that rumors could start pretty easily."

"I guess I haven't really given this much thought.

The days passed. It didn't take long for Taylor and Jessie to realize that they were spending every evening and night together. The 70-minute commute between their two houses did not hinder them from being together. At first, it wasn't planned, but they managed to catch up with each other by the end of each day. Then they became wiser and started to plan their evenings together.

The days turned into weeks and although the women became increasingly busy with their careers, they remained committed to being with each other every night. Their relationship thrived. Taylor admitted to herself that she had never been happier. As the months passed, Taylor was surprised that their love and passion continued to flourish.

Early in the relationship, Taylor decided to maintain the secrecy of their courtship. Although it was hard for Jessie, she respected Taylor's decision and was careful whenever they were together.

In the spring, Taylor went on a six-week mini-tour. She traveled from town to town, performing at night and on the road by day. It was the first time Jessie and Taylor were apart for any length of time and it proved to be difficult. In the middle of the tour, Jessie planned to fly to Chicago and join Taylor after a concert there. Taylor had 48 hours until her next appearance, in Madison, Wisconsin. They planned to spend every available moment together.

Jessie took an earlier flight into O'Hare that Friday evening, hoping to surprise Taylor. When Jessie arrived at the Fairmont Hotel, Taylor had not returned from the concert. Jessie retreated to a comfortable corner in the lobby. She admired the polished marble floor and luxurious furnishings, sat, pulled out her cellular phone and called Taylor.

Taylor answered on the third ring. "Hello."

"Hi sweetheart. How was the concert?"

"Hi," Taylor whispered. "Where are you? You should be in the air."

"I'm at the hotel."

"You're here?"

Jessie recognized the excitement in Taylor's voice. "I'm in the lobby. I got an earlier flight."

"That's wonderful. I can't wait to see you. We're getting in the limo now."

"I have some work. I'll just hang out in the lobby. I'll come up to the room after you've come in."

Taylor started speaking cryptically. "Call me when I'm back in my room. I'll be available to chat more in about 45 minutes." Then she whispered, "But call first, okay?"

Jessie could hear other voices on the phone. Then it sounded as if Taylor was in a tunnel. "I'll call you after I see you come in."

"That's great."

Jessie pulled out her laptop and started some work. About fifty minutes later, a group of people entered the hotel lobby. Some reporters and fans swarmed around them. In the center of the group, Mark protectively held Taylor's waist, pulling her through the crowd and into the elevator, leaving the reporters and fans in the lobby. Just as the elevator door closed, Taylor caught sight of Jessie.

Jessie waited patiently before she called Taylor.

When Taylor's cellular phone rang, she knew it was Jessie. "Hi, are you still in the lobby?"

"I am."

"I'm in 3705. But I'm on a secured floor. You need a key to take the elevator to the floor. Meet me on the 36th floor. Okay?"

"Okay."

Jessie got in the elevator and pushed thirty-six. When the door opened, Taylor stood in front of her, smiling.

"Hi," Jessie greeted her.

Taylor raised a finger to her lips, then whispered, "Come with me." She took hold of Jessie's hand and led her to a door that said "Fire Exit." The door opened into a stairwell, and as soon as the door closed behind them Taylor turned to Jessie.

"God, it's good to see you." She kissed Jessie firmly on her lips. The slam from a door on a lower floor startled them both. "Come." Taylor led Jessie up the stairs to another door that had a book wedged in it. She opened the door and picked up the book and the two were on the 37th floor.

Once on the floor, Taylor was determined to get to her room. She hurried down the hallway with Jessie following close behind. Taylor was just reaching the door when they heard a man's voice. "Jessie?"

Both Jessie and Taylor turned to find Mark coming out of a room a couple doors away. He stood staring at them. Jessie knew how it must have looked; she stood at the threshold of Taylor's room, bags in hand. She recognized the pain in his eyes as he stared back at Taylor.

"Hi, Mark," Jessie said.

Mark nodded distantly then turned away.

"Mark?" Taylor called.

He stopped then turned around. "Yes, Taylor?"

Taylor looked at Jessie then back at Mark. "We need to talk."

In the hotel room, Mark sat at the desk, Taylor was in the loveseat while Jessie remained standing. Mark stared at the floor, waiting for someone to speak.

"Mark, I want to tell you about Jessie and me," Taylor started.

"There's no need for that. It's none of my business." Mark would not look either woman in the eye. It was obvious that he didn't want to hear it.

"Well then, Mark, I need to tell you," Taylor started.

"No, you don't. It's plain as day what's going on here."

"Mark," Jessie started. "This is Taylor, not me. Please give her a chance."

Mark looked at both women then softened. "I'm sorry. You have my attention, Taylor."

"Jessie and I have been seeing each other," Taylor started.

"I understand."

"We haven't told anyone, you're the first. And I'm glad you know. I've wanted to share it with you," Taylor confided.

"I've wondered if you were seeing someone, Taylor."

"Why?"

"You've just been . . . different. How long has it been going on?"

"Four months."

"Have you given any thought as to how this could impact your career if the truth gets out?"

Taylor sighed. "Well, I know it wouldn't be a career booster."

"We've been very careful, Mark," Jessie interrupted. "Taylor isn't at a point to let others know."

"But I'm getting tired of being in the closet." Taylor turned to Jessie. "Being without you these last three weeks has been hard. I don't know how much longer I can do it."

"Let's not do anything rash here," Jessie said.

"I agree," Mark said. "To let people know you're having an affair with a woman just carries too many serious consequences."

"It's not an affair." Taylor seemed hurt by the undermining words.

"Whatever it is–I think you need to be careful. If the two of you are seeing each other in a year or so, and you know it's not a phase, then we can talk in a different vein."

"It's not a phase," Taylor said defensively.

"Taylor, Mark is just doing his job."

Taylor was clearly hurt by how Mark had reacted. "Are you going to be okay with this?"

"I'll be fine. May I speak business?"

"Can't it wait?" Taylor did not want her precious weekend to slip away.

"It'll just take a minute."

Taylor nodded.

"There was a note left for you at the front desk. It was from I.D."

Taylor's face paled.

"Someone apparently left it on the desk sometime today." Mark pulled a note from his pocket and displayed it for the women to read. It was written on the Fairmont Hotel stationery; the penmanship appeared to be traced.

> *It's only a matter of time till we're together.*
> *I.D.*

"He's here in Chicago?" Taylor's voice was distant.

"Is this the same person that was harassing you last year?" Jessie asked.

"Yes. We think so, anyway," Mark answered.

"I thought all that stopped," Jessie said.

"I did too," Taylor said. "Mark started getting letters again after Kurk died."

"Not very often, I think there were two, maybe three. I just sent them on to the police. With everything that was going on, I just didn't think I needed to bother Taylor with it."

"But since we've been on the road, every town we've been in, I've either received a call on the hotel phone or my cellular phone. There was a letter mailed from LA County waiting for me in Denver."

"What's being said in the letters and the phone calls?" Jessie asked.

"They both pretty much say the same thing. They say that I'm his destiny and it's only a matter of time before we'll be together."

"What about the voice. What does it sound like? Is it a man's voice?" Jessie asked.

"I think it's a man's voice, but I'm not completely sure, Jessie. The person whispers, there has always been a lot of noise in the background. Most of the time, I have a hard time hearing what he's saying."

Jessie went to Taylor. "How come you didn't tell me this was going on?"

"I didn't want you to worry while I was on the road. Mark has been very careful watching me."

"I'll leave you two to your weekend," Mark said, then he turned to Taylor. "Sunday morning, nine o'clock, the bus leaves."

"I'll be there," Taylor said.

Mark went to the door and Jessie followed close behind. She turned back to Taylor. "I'll be back in a minute." Jessie stepped into the hallway with Mark.

"Are you okay about Taylor and I?" Jessie asked Mark.

"Why wouldn't I be?"

"I know you care for her."

Mark looked at Jessie before he answered. "I do care for Taylor. I care enough to want what's best for her and to want her to be happy. Somehow, you're making her happy. I can see that, Jessie. But, I don't think you're the best thing for her."

"I appreciate your honesty, Mark."

"I have always been honest with you, Jessie."

"I know that. Can I ask you a favor?"

"What's that?"

"I can't be with Taylor while she's traveling, and I don't like the fact that some lunatic is harassing her. Would you keep an eye on her while she's traveling?"

"You don't have to ask me to do that. I always have. It's my job."

"Would you keep in touch with me and let me know how she's doing and what's going on with these letters and phone calls?"

Mark nodded. "Yeah. I'll let you know as things develop."

Chapter 20

Jessie and Taylor spent the major part of the weekend in the hotel suite. That Sunday morning came too quickly for both of them. Taylor went back on the road for another three weeks and Jessie went home to her computer and new project.

Back in California, Jessie found it difficult to concentrate on her work. Taylor was so far away and someone was harassing her; Jessie felt helpless. She hit writer's block on her new book, so she decided to spend most of her time doing research for it. She surfed the Internet for information on prison life.

Jessie longed to hear Taylor's voice. Every morning Jessie would call Taylor, then every night she waited for Taylor to call after she was settled in her hotel room. Mark was good to his word. A couple times each week he would call Jessie and give his perspective about what was going on.

Two days before Taylor was scheduled to return home, Jessie went out to lunch with her old friend, Linda Speller. She thanked her once again for the use of her cabin months earlier in Big Pines. The two always met at a restaurant downtown in Los Angeles, not far from Travis's office, so after lunch Jessie decided to drop in on Travis.

As expected, Jessie found Alison at the receptionist's desk. Alison's face lit up when she saw Jessie approach. "Well, if it isn't Ms. Mercer," Alison flirted. "The famous storyteller."

"Hi, Alison. How are you?"

"Much better now. What's up?"

"I was just in the neighborhood. Thought I'd stop in and say 'hi' to you of course, and Travis, too. Is he in?"

"He is, but not so fast. Have you been busy or something?"

"I have, why do you ask?"

"I remember a time when you used to stop in more often, just to say 'hi.' Are you seeing someone?" There was a spark of curiosity in her eyes.

Jessie nodded, then smiled. "Actually I am."

"What's her name?"

"Alison, I never kiss and tell."

"Well, when it starts to go the other way, give me a ring." Alison pressed the intercom button and announced Jessie's arrival.

Seconds later, Travis's office door opened and he stood in the doorframe. "Jessie, come on in," he bellowed. "You look great. What have you done different?"

Jessie went into his office. "Do I usually look bad?"

"You've never looked bad." He studied her as he walked around his desk. "But . . . there is something different. Whatever it is–it's good. What are you doing here?"

"I was just in the area and thought I'd stop by, and see how you're doing. I heard about you and Dana. Are you okay?"

Travis eyed Jessie. "Yes. I'm fine. She's going to take me to the cleaners, you know."

"I'm sorry, Travis."

"Hey, that's life." He reached into a pile of addressed envelopes, selected one and handed it to Jessie. "Here, save me a stamp."

Jessie looked at the envelope, addressed to her. "What is it?"

"It's an invitation for a special previewing of *Deceptions*. It's scheduled in three weeks, a couple nights before the release. The invitations should have gone out by now, but we just firmed up where the party is going to be catered. It's going to be at L'Orangerie. The entire cast and crew are invited."

"Sounds like quite a party."

"It should be a lot of fun . . . hopefully better than our last get-together. Speaking of which, have you stayed in touch with Taylor Andrews since Kurk died?"

"Why?"

"I haven't seen her since right after the funeral. I know she went into hiding after his death."

"We've occasionally talked. She seemed fine."

"You two always got along. Would you call her and ask if she's coming to the preview? I think it would be good PR if we can get the entire cast together and celebrate."

"Sure. I'll call her next week."

Taylor had not been home a week when Detective Bradley arrived to confer with her. He paused reflectively when he saw Jessie at the house. Then he updated Taylor on the investigation. The police department had categorized Kurk's death as suspicious. Detective Bradley was the only one remaining on the case.

"God. I hate it when that man visits," Taylor told Jessie after Detective Bradley had left. "He always looks at me as if I killed Kurk."

Jessie and Taylor decided that Taylor would go to the preview of *Deceptions* with Mark and they would meet up at the theatre. Both knew that the press would be there with cameras in hand, and it would be better if they arrived and left separately.

When Jessie arrived at the theatre, an attendant took the Lexus keys and handed Jessie a ticket. Reporters and camera-crew members lined the entryway forming a hallway to the theatre doors. None of the reporters were overly excited with her arrival. Inside the theatre, crew members and cast members greeted her.

"Here they are," a man's voice said, drawing everyone's attention back to the entrance.

A white stretch limo was at the curb. The back door opened and Travis Sanders hopped out of the car. He was stylishly dressed with dark sunglasses concealing his eyes. Travis waved for all the cameras; he obviously loved the attention.

Jennifer Kendrick and her husband stepped from the limo next. They both smiled and waved to the cameras as they slowly moved to the theatre doors. Finally, Mark and Taylor came out of the limo. Mark appeared shy before all the cameras, and wanted to move along the human hallway. But Taylor paced herself. She enjoyed working the reporter line, and personally greeted those she knew from past interviews. Before she entered the theatre, Taylor turned around and waved at all the reporters.

Once inside, Travis approached Taylor and Jennifer. "*ET* wants to interview each of you, individually, then together. Taylor, do you want to go first?"

An *Entertainment Tonight* crew member escorted Taylor to an interview location that was set up away from the party's main area. Jessie watched the interview as she mingled and enjoyed some appetizers.

Mark met up with Jessie. "Good evening." His voice drew her attention away from Taylor.

"Hi, Mark. How are you?"

"Fine."

"Mark, thanks for keeping me posted on I.D."

"You're welcome."

To Jessie, the encounter seemed awkward. Mark was uneasy. Travis joined them, and then Mark appeared more relaxed.

"Good evening, Jessie." He kissed her on the cheek. "You look marvelous tonight." Travis shook Mark's hand. "Good evening, Mark."

"Hi, Travis."

"Mark, your rafting trip is coming up, isn't it?"

"Yes, pretty soon. It's in August."

Jessie overheard the men talking. "Where are you going rafting, Mark?"

"The Grand Canyon."

"Oh, he is going to have such a great time. I did the trip last year with Dana. It was one of the best trips I have ever had."

"How many days is it?" Jessie asked. "I understand they're pretty lengthy."

"I'm doing just the upper canyon. It'll take five days."

"Are you going by yourself?" Jessie realized that it was none of her business, and she was embarrassed by her forwardness.

Mark recognized Jessie's awkwardness. "I'm going with a buddy of mine from the east coast."

"It was quite a trip, Mark," Travis said. "It was beautiful and exhilarating; quite an adventure. I'm envious."

Appetizers and drinks were served for about an hour. Jessie was speaking with Travis and Mark when Taylor broke into the discussion. Jessie could not keep from checking out Taylor's black dress, her eyes eventually finding Taylor's.

Taylor smiled at Jessie. "Hi Jessie." She approached Jessie and gave her a hug. "It's so nice to see you, again."

"It's nice to see you, too. You look great," Jessie said honestly.

Mark cleared his throat. Both Jessie and Taylor glanced at him. "Excuse me." Mark smiled then left the small group.

"Actually ladies, if you will excuse me also," Travis said. "I need to check on a few things. I'll see you inside."

Jessie and Taylor were finally alone.

"So, what have you been doing with yourself these days Ms. Andrews?" Jessie teased.

"Oh . . . I've fallen in love."

Jessie smiled. "You've fallen in love? Anybody I know?"

Taylor looked into Jessie's eyes and smiled. "I can't wait to get out of here . . . and take you home."

People started moving to the theatre. "Are you nervous about the movie?" Jessie asked.

"No. Not even a little. Do you think I should be?"

"No. I think you're going to be great."

Fanfare announced that the movie would be starting, and Jessie and Taylor moved into the theatre. Travis quickly seized Taylor's hand and stole her from Jessie. Jessie admired Taylor as she took her place in the center of the theatre, next to Travis. On her other side, Mark took his seat. Travis was sandwiched between Taylor and Jennifer Kendrick.

Jessie watched the movie among the other crew members. Although she had written the book and the screenplay, it was the movie that got her attention. She noticed that certain developments within the story of *Deceptions* had happened to her over the last year. *How interesting. I had never noticed that before.*

As the movie came to the end, whistling and applause erupted from the audience. The lights came on and, as expected, Travis stood and took a bow. Then he turned the attention to the two leading ladies, Taylor and Jennifer. The women stood, and the applause increased. Jessie watched Taylor admiringly, as people congratulated her on her performance.

After the movie, the cast and crew moved out of the theatre and into their cars and limos that awaited them. Jessie ran into Taylor in the lobby briefly. "Congratulations, Taylor. You did very well."

"She did, didn't she?" Travis agreed.

Taylor was rushed off with Travis for a follow-up interview with the *ET* people. Jessie watched the activity, and then decided to get her car. The valet attendant brought the Lexus to Jessie. Rather than rushing off to the party over at L'Orangerie, Jessie decided to wait for Taylor's limo to leave.

She drove her car around the block then swung back, finding a parking spot across the street from the theatre. She pulled up behind a dark green Buick. As she sat waiting for Taylor's limo to leave, she thought about the similarities between events that had occurred in her own life and the subplots of *Deceptions. What coincidences.*

"I thought there was no such thing as a coincidence?" that little voice asked.

The majority of the gang had left for the party. Jessie could see through the windows of the theatre foyer that Taylor, Mark and Travis were the last. Jennifer and her husband apparently caught another ride over to the party. The three came outside and got into the limo, then the limo finally crept into the street.

Jessie started her car, but just as she was about to move, the green Buick that had been parked in front of her pulled out. She pulled out behind the Buick. After the limo made three turns, Jessie realized that the Buick was following the limo also. *Who the hell is that?* Jessie wondered.

Jessie reached for her phone and pushed the speed dial.

In the limo, Mark, Travis and Taylor were celebrating with champagne when Taylor's phone rang. Taylor removed the phone from her purse. "Hello."

"Did I tell you how hot you look tonight?" Jessie asked.

Taylor smiled. "No you hadn't. Is that why you're calling?"

"A-huh. I can't wait for this party to be over."

"I hear you."

"Taylor, could you put Mark on?"

"Mark?"

"Please?"

"See you soon," Taylor said then handed the phone to Mark. "It's for you."

"Hello?"

"Mark, it's Jessie. Please don't get Taylor concerned . . . do you realize you have a tail?"

"A tail?"

"A green Buick has been following the limo since the theatre."

"How do you know this?"

"I'm following the Buick."

Mark glanced out the back window and saw a green car behind them. "It's a coincidence."

"Tell the limo driver to make the next left-hand turn," Jessie said.

"I don't think that's necessary, Jessie."

"Mark, just do it. Please?"

"Travis, would you open the window to the driver so I can talk with him?"

Travis was facing Taylor and Mark; his back was to the driver. Now both Travis and Taylor were curious, and Travis complied.

"Driver, would you make your next left?" Mark asked.

The limo moved to the left lane and turned left at the light. Mark looked out the rear of the limo and saw the green car follow. "You're right, Jessie."

"We're being followed?" Taylor snatched the phone from Mark's hand. "Jessie, where are you?"

"I'm following the car that's following you. Taylor, put Mark back on. Please."

"Be careful," Taylor handed the phone back to Mark.

"I'm here," Mark said.

"Do you have *your* phone with you?"

"Yes."

"Call the police and tell them you're being followed. Keep a line open with them advising your location. Let's get the cops here. This might be the lunatic that's been harassing Taylor. Give this phone to Travis."

Mark complied and handed the phone to Travis.

"Jessie? What's going on?"

"Travis, do you see the green car behind the limo?"

"Yes."

"He's following the limo. Do you know why anyone would be following you?"

"No."

"Travis, I want to get the limo to a safe place where we can bring the police in and get this guy. Do you understand?"

"Yes."

"There's a strip mall on the right-hand side about a mile up. There's a convenience store there. Tell the driver to go into the plaza and go to the convenience store."

"Okay." Travis turned around and talked to the driver. "Driver, what's your name?"

"Jimmy," the young man answered.

"Jimmy, there's a strip mall up here on the right. Get in the turning lane. We're going to a convenience store there."

The driver complied and the green car followed them into the turning lane.

"Travis?" Jessie asked.

"Yeah."

"Do you have paper and a pen?"

Travis grabbed a pen and pad from a pocket. "I do."

"Give this license number to the cops. It a California plate MDR3476. That's mother daughter randy 3476. It's a Buick Century, maybe a year old. Do you know if Mark has talked to the police?"

"I believe he has."

Jessie could hear Travis and Mark speak briefly, then Travis returned to Jessie. "He has them on the line now. They say they should be here any minute."

"Have Mark tell the police our plans." Jessie pulled her car out from behind the Buick and proceeded to pass the car. "The driver of the car has his elbow on the window and his hand is on his head. I can't see his face. He's got dark hair. I think it's a man."

"Why are you passing him?" Travis asked.

Taylor looked out the window and could see Jessie's Lexus coming up on the left hand side of the car.

"I don't want to spook him. There's another entrance down the road. I'm going ahead of you. I'll meet you by the convenience store. Remember, just pull up in front of the store." Jessie looked at the clock. It was after nine. Up until now, there had been sufficient light, but the dark was settling in.

As Jessie passed the limo, she looked into the dark tinted windows but could not see Taylor's face or her hands pressed against the rear window glass.

"Travis?" Jessie said.

"Yeah?"

"I'm going to be out of your sight for a few minutes. Keep telling me everything that happens."

"Okay." Seconds later Travis said, "The limo just turned into the parking lot."

"And the Buick?"

"He hasn't come in yet. Oh, here he comes. We see the convenience store. We're heading over there."

"I'm just getting off the road now." Jessie pulled into the main entrance of a theatre parking lot. The lot was full. She headed back in the direction of the convenience store. Jessie was unnerved that she couldn't see the limo. "How are you guys doing?"

"We're almost at the store. We're pulling right up to the door."

"Great. Do you know where he is?"

"Last I saw he was driving two rows over. But now I can't see him."

Jessie was within sight of the store. She could now see the limo. "Travis, go into the store and buy something. Keep the phone with you. See if you can find out where he went."

Travis complied and opened the car door. He walked around the vehicle and went into the store. Travis stood in front of a magazine rack that sat up against the window. As he pretended to look at the magazines, he searched for the Buick. "Jessie, I still can't see him. There are three rows of cars. I think he was driving in the second row."

Before reaching the convenience store, Jessie turned into the lot, then made a left into the third row. The Buick wasn't there. She turned into the second row and combed the cars. "Travis, I can't see . . . one minute." Jessie put the phone down on her lap. The Buick was parked facing the convenience store. Jessie could see the man's head through the rear window. A parking spot was open across the row, a couple cars down from the suspect's car. Jessie drove past the spot, then backed into the parking space. She cracked the front windows and did not hear the Buick's engine idling.

Jessie picked up the phone. "Do you see me?" she whispered.

"Yeah. You just pulled into a spot in the second row."

"The Buick is right across from me. It looks like he's sitting behind a light-colored sports utility."

"There's a white Grand Cherokee in the front row, about ten feet from the limo," Travis said, and as he did, he could see the flashing lights from the police cars. Two cars entered from the main entrance.

Jessie watched the flashing lights heading toward the convenience store. "Shit. This is going to spook him," Jessie said to Travis. One of the patrol cars pulled up in front of the limo. Travis came from the store and went to the patrol car.

Jessie heard a car engine start, and the Buick abruptly backed out of his spot. Jessie quickly pulled the Lexus forward blocking the Buick from getting by her. When the man saw the Lexus blocking his escape, he put the car in reverse and floored it. But by this time, the other patrol car blocked his getaway.

Jessie took her seat belt off. "I think we got him." From about fifty feet away, she saw two officers approach the Buick from behind, their guns drawn and pointed at the car. The officers shouted something to the driver, but in desperation, the driver floored the accelerator. Jessie heard the wheels squeal and through the passenger-side window, she could see the Buick heading right toward her.

"Shit," Jessie yelled. The Buick rammed into the front section of the Lexus, dragging the car until it came to a standstill. Jessie's head hit the steering wheel hard. She tried to focus her eyes, but the images were distorted, and she started to hear rising voices.

"Get out of the car slowly," a man yelled. "Place your hands over your head."

Is he talking to me? Jessie wondered.

"*No, just relax,*" her little voice comforted her.

Jessie tried to open her eyes, but her vision was still blurry. With her hand, she explored the left side of her head, where her pain originated. She felt the torn tissue on her forehead and blood running down the side of her face.

"Miss, can you hear me?" an unfamiliar voice called to her from outside her window. "Hey, we need an ambulance over here." To Jessie, the voices went away.

Taylor ran to the scene of the accident. The police had removed a young man from the Buick, cuffed him and placed him in a patrol car. Taylor's heart skipped a beat when she saw the crushed front of Jessie's car and a police officer trying to break into it.

"Jessie?" Taylor became frightened at the sight of Jessie. The side of her head was coated with blood. Jessie was motionless, leaning over the steering wheel.

Taylor turned to Mark and Travis, who were watching the scene unfold. "Mark, my purse. Quick. I have keys to the Lexus."

Mark ran to the limo and returned quickly to Taylor, purse in hand.

Taylor quickly removed the keys and clicked the keyless entry twice, enabling all the doors to open. The police officer opened the driver's door while Taylor ran to the passenger's door.

Taylor climbed into the car and pulled Jessie's hair away from her face, exposing the cut on her forehead. "Jessie?" Taylor whispered.

But there was no response.

"Jessie, can you hear me? Babe, you've got to wake up."

"The ambulance should be here any minute," a police officer said.

"Jessie? Please say something?"

Jessie's word was barely discernable. "Headache."

"Jessie, what did you say?"

"I have a headache," she whispered.

A smile came to Taylor's lips. "Honey, are you hurt anyplace else?"

"No." Jessie tried to sit up but quickly returned her head to the steering wheel.

Jessie opened her eyes. Although her vision was blurry, she could make out Taylor. A smile came to Jessie's lips. "Have I told you how hot you look tonight?" she whispered.

"I'm glad to see you haven't lost your sense of humor."

"Taylor, did they get him?"

Taylor nodded. "Yeah. They got him."

"The ambulance is here," a police officer interrupted.

The medics quickly slipped a neck brace on Jessie and lifted her from the crumpled car onto a gurney. Jessie groaned as they moved her, but wanted to know about the car. "How bad is it?" she asked, waving her arm toward her car.

"It's bad enough," said the medic, "but it can be fixed. You just lie still."

"I've always liked this car," Jessie whispered.

Taylor took one of Jessie's hands, "It's just a car, Jessie."

Travis and Mark approached. "Are you okay, Jessie?" Travis asked.

Jessie's eyes focused on the men. "Yeah. I'm fine."

"We'll be the judge of that," said one of the medics. "We're going to transport you to Good Samaritan."

"Is that necessary?" Jessie asked.

"Absolutely," Taylor chorused with the medic.

Jessie was moved into the ambulance.

Taylor went to Travis and Mark. "I'm going to the hospital with Jessie."

"I understand," Travis said.

* * *

While Jessie waited to have her forehead stitched up, the police questioned her about the evening's events. Shortly after, Taylor ran into Mark and Travis outside the examination room.

"What are you guys doing here? I thought you went on to the party."

"We wanted to make sure Jessie is okay," Mark said. He held up a purse. "In all the commotion, this was left in the Lexus."

Taylor took her purse. "Thank you, Mark. I think she's going to be fine. She's already trying to convince the doctors that it's only a scratch and she should be released. Why don't you go in and say 'hi.' "

"I think I'll do that." Mark left Travis and Taylor.

Travis smiled. "Are you okay?"

"Yes. Why do you ask?"

"I guess I couldn't help but notice your genuine concern for Jessie's well being."

"Well, of course I'm concerned."

"Along with . . . the fact that you had Jessie's car keys in your purse." Travis's eyes were inquisitive.

"Travis, if you have something to say . . . just say it."

"Do you want to tell me, Taylor?"

"Not really, Travis. It's nobody's business but our own. But . . . yes, Jessie and I are lovers."

"I knew it. From the first time you read for the role with Jessie, I knew it. Did Kurk know?"

"Travis, sorry to burst your bubble, but we started seeing each other in February, after Kurk passed away. Do you think you can keep this to yourself?"

Travis studied Taylor in silence, and then a smiled curled on his lips. "So . . . you like girls."

"Oh, I give up," Taylor said in frustration.

"Of course I'll keep your little secret, Taylor."

Chapter 21

The following morning, Jessie stared at her reflection in the mirror. The sutures were near the hairline on her forehead, which was black and blue from the impact. With a cool facecloth, she washed her face. Jessie studied her blood-shot eyes. She was tired. Neither she nor Taylor got much sleep when they returned from the hospital; Taylor had wakened her every couple hours.

"Good morning," Taylor said. She walked up behind Jessie and wrapped her arms around Jessie's waist, resting her chin on Jessie's shoulder. They stared at each other in the mirror.

"Good morning, sweetheart."

"How does it look?" Taylor asked.

Jessie lifted the hair away from her forehead, exposing the sutures. Taylor studied the reflection of her forehead, released Jessie's waist and turned her so she could see the injury better. Jessie leaned her head forward.

"It looks sore," Taylor said.

"It's fine."

Taylor placed her lips on Jessie's, and they kissed. "You're lucky you weren't killed. I have breakfast out on the deck."

"Great. I'll be out in a couple minutes."

Jessie always enjoyed her breakfast overlooking the ocean. They sat next to each other chatting about events from the previous evening. "Did you speak with the police about the man that was caught?"

"You mean the *kid* they caught?"

"What do you mean *kid?*"

"The kid from the Buick? I guess you didn't see him. Jessie, he was a kid. Maybe 18, and that's probably pushing it."

"The driver of the Buick was a kid?"

"Yeah."

Jessie stared at Taylor in disbelief. "I can't imagine a kid pulling it off. Now I'm curious if he's the one that's been harassing you."

"The police suggested that we touch base with them today."

"Let's go down to the station this afternoon; I want to find out what happened to my car."

"Okay, then do you want to go to Taggart's for an early dinner?"

"Sure. Sorry that your special occasion was ruined last night."

"It's not your fault."

"I guess we haven't spoken since the preview. I thought you did a wonderful job."

"Thanks. Oh . . . I almost forgot, Travis knows about us."

"Really? How?"

"It doesn't matter. I asked him not to tell anyone. I wish I could trust him more."

"Travis? He's a little rough around the edges, but I think you can trust him."

"I hope you're right."

At the police station, Detective Perry pulled the case file, and then sat with Taylor and Jessie. "Well, Ms. Andrews, I've reviewed the complaint that Mr. Rutledge filed regarding the letters. I also interviewed the suspect." Detective Perry laid a mug shot down on the table for Taylor and Jessie to look at. "I've got to tell you–I don't think this kid is responsible for all the harassment."

As Jessie looked at the photograph of the young man, she sensed the detective was right.

"What's his story?" Jessie asked.

"His name is Brian Cambridge. He's a senior at Central High. He claims that someone hired him to follow Ms. Andrews around and make some harassing phone calls. But that's pretty much it. He says that he was warned not to hurt her in any way, just scare her."

"Who hired him?" Taylor asked.

"That's where his story gets a little fuzzy. He claims that he met the person in a chat room on the Internet."

"In a chat room?" Taylor asked.

"Apparently the kid was in a room discussing violence in schools. Somehow, a dialog started between the boy and someone else. Let's call this someone else–suspect B. Well, suspect B propositioned him. He, or she for that matter, suggested that Brian make harassing phone calls to Ms. Andrews in exchange for cash. The kid agreed. He was provided with a phone number, which I've confirmed is your cellular number, Ms. Andrews."

"How was the money exchanged?"

"The kid got $100 cash in the mail, along with a note suggesting more would come if he did a good job. The kid said he made a few phone calls, then received another $100 cash with a note to go to another chat room at a specified time. And that's how they've communicated each time. He would go into a chat room; suspect B always approached him, then they moved to a private chat room. Brian said that suspect B always had a different screen name."

"So this kid admits that he made some phone calls and followed Taylor around, right?"

"Those are the only things he admitted to."

"Taylor, you said the subject matter of the letters and phone calls was the same, right?" Jessie asked.

"Yeah. Always the same."

"The kid claims that he received instructions about what to say from suspect B while he was in the chat rooms. He wrote it down and repeated a few phrases over and over. The kid was pretty scared. He knew he was in over his head. The Buick Century wasn't even his car. It was his father's company car."

"Did his parents *ever* own a Mustang?" Jessie asked.

"No. I already checked that. Suspect B could have hired someone else last year."

"Did the kid say why he ran into Jessie's car?" Taylor asked.

"Yes. Brian admitted that he got scared and panicked."

Jessie studied the detective. "You believe him, don't you?"

The detective nodded. "I do believe him. I don't think he did it all. I don't think he's a threat to Ms. Andrews now. But . . . there's someone else out there that may be."

A couple hours later, Taylor and Jessie were sitting at Taggart's waiting for their dinner to be served. The hostess had given them a private table away from other customers. Taylor had remained quiet since they left the police station. Underneath the table, Jessie took Taylor's hand in her own, the tablecloth obscuring their affection from view. Taylor smiled at the contact.

"Are you okay?" Jessie asked.

"Much better, now."

"We'll get this guy."

"Yeah. I'm sure we will. I just don't want to see anyone get hurt in the meantime. Especially you."

"I'm not going to get hurt." Jessie removed her hand from Taylor's. She leaned over, opened her purse, and removed something. "I wanted to give you this last night."

Taylor felt Jessie place a long slender box in her hand, beneath the table. She placed it front of her, and grinned as she eyed the brown box.

"What is it?"

"Open it."

Taylor lifted the lid to the box. From beneath a cotton lining she picked up a hand-carved wooden ankh. For a moment, Taylor's world distorted. As she stared at the ankh, Taylor saw her hands change to a younger woman's hands. Taylor ran her fingers over the smooth surface of the aged maple amulet. She turned the ankh over, noticing the initials "*RJ*" carved in the back of the wood. The distortions continued and her hands started to shake.

Jessie took Taylor's hands in her own. "Taylor, what's wrong?"

Taylor closed her eyes and whispered, "I don't know. I . . ." A moment later her eyes opened. "That was strange."

"What happened?"

"I'm not sure. I just started to see things . . . things that aren't here." Taylor looked around the restaurant, and then returned her attention to the wooden object. "Where did you get this?"

"In an antique store, near Salem, Massachusetts."

"Salem? When did you go there?"

"I went back to Salem about three years ago."

"*Back* to Salem? You've been there before, I take it?"

"No. I don't know why I said that," Jessie lied. "I was doing some research on the Salem witch trials. I spent a day in Andover, which is about fourteen miles from Salem. I wandered into an antique store and the ankh was in a display case, marked 'not for sale.' I'm not usually into antiques, but there was something about the ankh that called to me."

"If it was not for sale, how did you get it?"

"Oh . . . everything's for sale for the right price. I started asking the owner questions about it. He said that the ankh belonged to one of the women that went to trial."

"This is interesting. I've always been intrigued with the Salem witch trials . . . as well as outraged," Taylor admitted. "Did you know that 19 people were executed? They arrested over a hundred people. It's outrageous. It was a terrible social injustice, and yet . . . most people aren't aware of what really happened. It would make a good book."

"I take it you've read a lot on the subject."

"I have. Some theorize that mold from the grain that year produced LSD, and that the LSD caused afflictions in some girls. These young women pointed their fingers at people, alleging that they were witches, and that they were the source of their suffering. This is what started the hysteria that led to the witch-hunt."

"Interesting," Jessie said.

"What were you doing research on?"

Jessie hesitated, and then continued. "I was doing some research on my lineage. I learned that a family member was arrested during the trials and I wanted to find out what happened to her."

"Did you?"

Jessie shook her head. "I know she was arrested and sent to trial. I'm not clear on the outcome, though."

"What was her name?"

"Rebecca . . . Rebecca Johnson."

Taylor turned the wooden object over. Her fingers traced the "*RJ*" carved in the ankh. "Was it hers?"

Jessie shrugged her shoulders, "I don't know."

"Jessie, I can't take this."

"I want you to have it, Taylor. Please."

Chapter 22

The following Friday night, Jessie was the keynote speaker during the opening reception for a writer's conference being held in Orange County. Her speech was to be given after a buffet dinner. Taylor had been in New York City most of the week, so Jessie was looking forward to seeing her after the reception.

Taylor arrived at LAX about eight o'clock that evening. She collected her belongings and took a limo to her home. It was about eight thirty when she arrived at the security gate. After punching in her code, the gate opened and the limo drove up to the house.

Taylor could see the lights in the house through the tall trees that landscaped the property. As she entered her house the number of lights that were on surprised her. From upstairs, she could hear music playing. "Jessie," she called upstairs. But there was no response.

It was then she noticed the opened bottle of cabernet on the foyer table at the bottom of the spiral staircase. A single glass stood next to the bottle. *I'll play this game*, Taylor thought. She poured herself a glass, took a sip, and turned to the stairwell. Taylor smiled when she saw the delicate white rose petals on the stairs leading to her bedroom. The flower petals stopped at the top of the stairs, and candles illuminated the rest of her way. *She must have missed me.* The door was ajar and the music was louder now.

Taylor took a sip of wine and pressed open the door. A gentle breeze flowed from the open deck door, candles lit the room, and fresh white roses were spread out on the bed. The music seemed a little loud for the occasion, so she went to the CD player and turned the volume down. Taylor could see the light beneath her bathroom door.

She was about to turn the bathroom doorknob when the phone rang. Taylor went to the telephone. "Hello."

"Hi, sweetheart," Jessie said over the handset. "When did you get in?"

"Jessie? Where are you?"

Jessie detected a note of concern in Taylor's voice. "I'm on my way back from the conference. I should be there in about fifteen minutes. Are you okay?" ·

Taylor turned around. She was staring at the light beneath the bathroom door. "Jessie, when did you do the wine and candles?" The wind had become gusty and some of the candles were blowing out, dimming the room. Taylor could feel the hair on her back rise.

"What do you mean, candles?"

"Oh, God. Someone's in the house." Taylor could feel her pulse start to race.

"Taylor, get the hell out of there. I'll call the police, just get out of there."

A loud noise from inside the bathroom startled Taylor. She dropped the phone and ran out of the room and down the stairwell. From behind her, she could hear a sporadic thud and knock. But she never looked back and kept running, through her kitchen and mudroom to her garage. She quickly flicked the light switch, and went to her Porsche. Inside the car, she automatically pushed the garage door opener but nothing happened. A second attempt confirmed that the door wasn't going to open.

Taylor reached for the keys in the center console, where she always left them, but they weren't there, instead she found a plain white envelope with "Taylor" printed on the outside.

Taylor's heart was pounding so hard it hurt her throat. Mustering up every ounce of strength, she opened the envelope.

> *Taylor,*
> *Now that I have taken care of Kurk, the two of us can be together, for-*
> *ever.*
> *I.D.*

Taylor could feel the tears form in her *eyes*. *Control*, she thought. She dropped the note, got out of the car and ran to the garage door's manual lever. She pulled the handle until her hand hurt, but it wouldn't budge. Then she tried to open the other garage door, but it, too, was jammed. She never saw the crowbars wedged in the tracks, preventing the door from opening.

Taylor felt trapped. She knew the only way to escape was back through the house. Her heart pounded wildly as she climbed the stairs that would lead her back toward the intruder. *I hope I'm doing the right thing*, she thought as she placed her hand on the doorknob and turned it.

* * *

Jessie called the police immediately after she got off the phone with Taylor. The thought that Taylor was in trouble and Jessie was unable to help her overwhelmed Jessie. She raced to Malibu breaking all speed limits, running every stop sign and ignoring every traffic light. Jessie was about a quarter of a mile from the property when she saw the police at the security gate. A patrol car blocked the entrance of the driveway. Jessie honked at the police officers to move, but they did not budge.

"I'm sorry Miss, this is a secured area. We can't let you in," one police officer said.

"I'm the one who called the police. I need to get up there," Jessie yelled.

"We're sorry, Miss. We have our orders," the older man said.

Jessie parked her loaner car, hopped out and proceeded to run past the officers at the driveway entrance. The younger officer quickly blocked her from getting past them. "I guess we didn't make ourselves clear. This is a crime scene. Nobody can go in and nobody can come out."

The words *crime scene* scared Jessie. The overpowering feeling of helplessness consumed her. In desperation Jessie asked, "Is Perry here?"

"Yes. He's at the house," the older officer said. He seemed surprised.

"Call him and tell him Jessica Mercer is on her way up." Jessie passed the officer and continued walking up the driveway. She wondered if they were going to come after her. She heard an officer use the radio.

A couple minutes later the patrol car drove up next to Jessie. "Get in," the older officer said. "Perry wants me to take you to him."

Three patrol cars were parked in front of the house. Jessie got out of the car and ran into the house. "Taylor," she yelled as she crossed the threshold. She immediately heard Perry from the kitchen. Once in the kitchen she saw him in the mudroom and went to him. "Where is she?"

"We don't know. We just got here, too."

"Hey Perry, look at this," a male voice called from the garage.

Jessie went into the garage with Perry. Two officers were looking at the garage doors while one held up a piece of paper for Perry to read. Jessie read the note aloud: 'Now that I have taken care of Kurk, the two of us can be together.' Shit."

"What does this mean? Who's Kurk?" Perry asked.

"It means Kurk Warner *was* murdered," Jessie said. She turned to go back into the house.

"Here's blood," an officer said.

Jessie turned. The officer followed a trail of blood along the concrete and up the stairs. "There's some on the doorknob, too."

Jessie brushed past the police officer and went back to the foyer. Her heart skipped a beat when she saw the open bottle of cabernet at the base of the stairwell. She bolted up the stairs, passing the rose petals, the candles. As she approached the bedroom, she heard voices and music. Abruptly, she rushed into the room only to find two young officers with guns drawn on her.

"Freeze," one of them called out nervously.

From behind, Jessie heard Perry talk. "Roberts! Rodriguez! Relax–she's with me."

The officers lowered their guns.

"She's not here?" Jessie asked.

One of the officers pointed to the bathroom door. "The door's locked. We were just going to break it in."

Perry nodded and the man went to the door, gun in hand. As Jessie stared at the door, she realized how much she feared what could be on the other side. The officer pounded the door and on the third bashing, the door opened. They went in guns drawn.

Jessie followed the officers. The first thing she noticed was marbles spread all over the floor. An overturned silk flower arrangement that had rested on a platform next to the whirlpool tub had fallen to the floor. The curtains on the window next to the platform blew gently in the wind.

"The wind must have knocked the arrangement over," Perry surmised.

"But where is she?" Jessie asked.

Another officer joined the group in the large bathroom. "We've searched the house. There's no sign of her."

"This isn't right." Jessie left the bathroom and looked around the bedroom. Candles were spread around the room. Some were lit while most seemed to have been blown out by the wind through the deck door. The telephone handset lay on the bed amid white roses that were spread on the bed. Music played from the CD player. *Where are you Taylor?* She opened the screen door and wandered out onto the deck that overlooked the beach and ocean. *Where are you?*

As Jessie stood overlooking the beach, the CD player shuffled and started playing "Daniel's Heart." Jessie closed her eyes, and within seconds, she felt the warmth and fullness in her chest. She had grown accustomed to the heart connection with Taylor, at times taking it for granted. But now she at least knew Taylor was alive. A smile came to her lips. *Taylor, help me find you.*

Eyes closed, Jessie prayed for insight to Taylor's whereabouts. At first, the light flashed and then colors came to Jessie's third eye. Her heart started beating wildly. She felt pain in her right hand, and when she raised it to turn the doorknob, she noticed it was bleeding.

Jessie could feel Taylor's terror as Taylor opened the door from the garage and ran through the mudroom, kitchen and out the front door. At first, the darkness swallowed Jessie, but when Taylor's eyes adjusted to the light, Jessie could see the ground Taylor ran on. Jessie recognized the steps that led from the back of the house down to the beach.

As Taylor ran down the steps, she sporadically looked up toward the house. Jessie could feel Taylor's fear that someone was following her. She missed the last step, and fell hard to the beach sand and rocks, skinning her knee. Frantically, Taylor got to her feet and bolted down the beach, eyeing a neighbor's gazebo. Taylor turned and glanced back toward the house to see if someone was following, but Jessie's need to go to Taylor brought Jessie back to reality.

Jessie opened her eyes. Quickly, she looked toward the neighbor's gazebo, but it was too dark to see anything. Without saying a word to the police officers, she bolted through the bedroom, down the stairs and out the front door. Frantically, she retraced the steps that her mind's eye had seen Taylor take. Jessie ran down the steps leading to the beach. Once on the beach, she repeatedly called for her. "Taylor?"

But there was no response.

Jessie continued toward the gazebo, her path illuminated by only moonlight. Shadows engulfed the structure, contributing to the eerie feeling that Jessie sensed. She was about 20 feet from the gazebo when she stopped and yelled out. "Taylor?"

Each passing second of silence added to Jessie's anxiety, then Jessie saw a silhouette standing within the shadows, and slowly emerging from the structure.

"Taylor?" Jessie whispered and then she ran to her. The two silently embraced. Jessie backed away to look at Taylor. "Are you okay?" But before Jessie gave Taylor a chance to respond, she reached for Taylor's right hand; the blood was dry now. Then she looked at her left knee. Her jeans were torn at the knee and blood stained.

"How did you know?" Taylor asked.

"It's a long story." Jessie put her arm around Taylor. "Let's get back to the house."

Taylor stopped. "Are the police there?"

"Yes."

"Jessie, there was a note. Kurk was murdered."

Jessie could see the tears swell in Taylor's eyes. "I know. I saw the note."

"My God. He was killed all because of me. It's just as well I've been in the closet, Jessie. I don't think I could live with myself if something happened to you." Taylor leaned her head against Jessie's shoulder and the two walked back to the house.

Detective Perry expressed relief when Jessie and Taylor walked into the foyer. Both women were surprised to see Detective Bradley there.

"Ms. Andrews, nice to see you again," Detective Bradley said. "I'm sorry it's under such difficult circumstances." Bradley looked at Jessie. "Why Ms. Mercer, you seem to be around a lot."

"It's nice to see you too, Detective Bradley," Jessie said. She went to the kitchen and returned with a wet cloth to clean Taylor's hand and knee.

"Can we sit? I have some questions," Bradley said. He led the women to the living room. "I want to minimize traffic through the house. It's going to take some time to get the criminologists to go through this place. Ms. Andrews, it would be best if you can stay someplace else for a while."

"Taylor, you can stay with me," Jessie said.

Bradley eyed Jessie, "Yeah. I figured that."

Jessie sensed smugness from the detective. "Detective Bradley, what is your problem?"

"My problem is that I have an unsolved murder."

"Other than the note that was found tonight, what makes you think that Kurk was murdered?" Jessie asked.

"It's always been suspicious because the autopsy shows that he had an allergic reaction to peanut protein and yet there was no evidence that he ate peanuts before he died. There were no peanut constituents found in any part of his digestive system. Only in his mouth."

"Could it have been from peanut oil?" Taylor asked.

"No. From what I understand, by the time peanut oil is processed, there's no protein remaining that would cause an allergic reaction. There was no evidence of peanuts anywhere near him when he died, yet he died from contact with peanut protein. Until we understood the protein's source, we would have always categorized it as suspicious. But now . . . it's murder."

"Well, what can we do to help?" Taylor asked.

"I just have a couple questions, then you can leave and we can talk more on Monday. I know it's been a while, but on the night that Kurk had his allergic reaction, you administered epinephrine to him. Is that correct, Ms. Andrews?"

"That's correct."

"We later learned that the EpiPen had expired, correct?"

Taylor remembered. The feeling of being responsible for Kurk's death amplified. She nodded.

"Where did you get the EpiPen?"

"I told you. It was in my purse."

"Did you take it from the purse?"

Taylor thought back to that dreadful night, trying to recall.

"I gave it to her," Jessie admitted.

"*You* gave it to her, Ms. Mercer?"

"That's correct."

"And where did you get it?"

"From Taylor's purse. It was under the table."

"When you took it out of Ms. Andrews' purse, did you notice that it had expired?"

"No."

"Ms. Mercer, what is the nature of your relationship with Ms. Andrews?"

Jessie stared back at Detective Bradley but remained silent.

"What is the relationship between the two of you?" Bradley repeated his question.

"Not that this is any of your business, but we're lovers," Taylor admitted.

"I see. Did Mr. Warner know?"

"We weren't involved when Kurk was alive," Taylor said.

"I see. I want to switch gears to what happened tonight. From what I understand, Ms. Andrews, you were out of town and came back tonight."

"That's correct. I was in New York since Monday, and landed at LAX a little before eight o'clock." Taylor said.

"And how did you get from the airport?"

"I took a limo."

"And the name of the limo company?"

"Herman."

Bradley wrote the name down. "Was there any evidence of a break-in when you arrived?"

Taylor shook her head.

"Perhaps at your security gate?"

"No. The gate was closed."

"Who knows the security password and how often do you change it?"

"I change it usually once a year, around New Year's. I think the only people that know it are Jessie and Doreen Lowell."

"Who's Doreen?"

"She's my cleaning person. I've known her for years. She comes in once a week, usually on Thursdays."

"And she came this week?"

"I believe so."

"What's her number?"

"555-5645."

Bradley made another note on his pad. "Okay, so you get here and find a bottle of wine, some flowers, candles, and music playing. Then what?"

"Initially, I thought Jessie was upstairs waiting for me. I poured myself a glass of wine and went upstairs. There was a light on in the bathroom. I still thought it was Jessie, but then she called."

"So you're in your bedroom on the phone with your lover and you realize that she isn't in the bathroom?"

"That's right. Then there was a noise from the bathroom and I bolted."

"You bolted?"

"Yes. I ran downstairs, went into the garage and into my car. I tried to open the garage door with the opener. It didn't work. Then, I found the note."

"The note about Kurk?"

Taylor nodded. "Yes. I got out of the car and tried to open the garage doors manually, but they wouldn't budge."

Bradley looked at her injured hand. "Is that when you cut yourself?"

"Yes."

"And then what happened?"

"I just bolted and kept running, then Jessie found me."

"Okay. And where were you Ms. Mercer, when you called."

"I was in my car on my way back from a writer's conference."

"What's the name of the conference and where was it?"

"The Western Fiction Writers at the Hyatt Regency in Irvine."

"Are you registered at the conference? Can anyone vouch that you were there?"

Jessie stared back at the detective. "You know, I don't like what you're implying. But yes. About 300 people can vouch that I was there. I was the keynote speaker."

"That's right. You're a big fancy writer. I saw *Deceptions* last weekend. I didn't realize until then that you were the famous novelist and screenwriter." Bradley leaned back in his chair; a scheming smile came to his lips.

"Now how'd you come up with the idea of *Deceptions*? Rock'n Roll singer's husband is murdered. Her lesbian lover is later tried and convicted of his murder . . . I sure hope for both your sakes this plays out differently."

Jessie stood. "Is there anything else?"

"Yes. When was the last time you were here?"

"You really don't think *I* did this, do you?"

"Amuse me."

"I don't stay here when Taylor's out of town."

"So when was the last time you were here?"

"I left Monday morning."

Chapter 23

A police officer drove Jessie and Taylor down the driveway to Jessie's car. It was after midnight and both women were tired as they sped away from Taylor's property. Jessie was quiet. She was actually fuming from Detective Bradley's implications, and Taylor knew it.

"Don't let him bother you, Jessie," Taylor said.

"Yeah. You're right. I shouldn't let him bother me." Jessie reached over to hold Taylor's hand. "How's your other hand?"

Taylor looked at the cut. It had stopped bleeding and was clean. "It's fine."

"We'll get it bandaged as soon as we get home."

"Jessie, how did you know my hand and knee were hurt?"

Jessie thought back to when she had experienced Taylor's flight. "Something happened to me tonight that's never happened before. I don't understand it."

"What?"

"After we searched the house and couldn't find you, I went outside on your bedroom deck."

"You couldn't have seen me from there."

"I closed my eyes, and I experienced your run."

"What?"

"It started with you in the garage. I saw your hand bleeding and I could feel your fear. You ran through house, outside and down the stairs. You missed the bottom step and fell on your knee. I could feel your terror. You thought you were being followed. Somehow, I experienced your flight."

Taylor remained speechless. She knew there was no way of having been seen from the deck, and the flight Jessie described was accurate.

"I'm sorry. I didn't mean to scare you."

"You didn't. I just don't know how to respond to it." Taylor reflected on the events of the evening. "Jessie, I don't think I've ever been that scared before."

Jessie squeezed Taylor's hand. *I don't think I've been that scared before, either.* "Taylor, would you move in with me until this thing is resolved?"

"I don't want to endanger your life. If some wacko wants to be with me and killed Kurk, what's to stop him from hurting you?"

"We're smarter now. I'm not letting you go back to that house alone. We'll keep it quiet, and we'll be careful. Please?"

It had been a hectic week for the two of them. Taylor's Porsche was still in her garage in Malibu, and they shared Jessie's loaner car. The Lexus was not due back from the garage until the end of the week. Jessie and Taylor spent time at the police station, at first together then they were interviewed separately. The police believed that the person who broke in was not in the house when Taylor returned that evening. They believed the noises Taylor heard were caused by the wind. The harassment file that Detective Perry maintained was now combined with Detective Bradley's homicide file.

Taylor went to Mark's office during the week and updated him on the events from the previous Friday evening. He was clearly irate and agreed to increase security measures at all her events until Kurk's murderer and her harasser was found.

"Taylor if there's anything I can do, anything, please don't hesitate to ask me."

"Thanks, Mark."

"I mean it. Use me. Abuse me," he smiled, "I know that Jessie's there for you. But I'm sure she can't be there all the time. Call me if you need anything. Someone to talk to, perhaps."

"That's sweet. You've always been there for me, Mark; thank you."

Mark placed his hand on top of Taylor's and squeezed it slightly. He smiled. Then he withdrew and changed the subject. "I'm going on vacation next month. Your schedule is pretty light while I'm away. I'll have my phone with me if you need me."

"I'll be fine and you have a nice vacation. Where are you going?"

"The Grand Canyon. I'm doing a rafting trip down the Colorado River."

"Are you going camping?"

"Yes. It's a five-day excursion."

"You don't strike me as the camping type, Mark."

"You're right about that. But I've been told that this is the way to go. All the food is provided, gourmet meals, too. I've got to get out to the sporting goods store soon. I still need to pick up some camping stuff."

"You know, I think Jessie has a lot of camping equipment. I'm sure she'd be happy to lend it to you rather than buying some stuff that you'll never use again."

"That would be great. I don't need a lot. They provide the tent and sleeping bag, but I know I need rain gear, a solar shower, daypack and general camping accessories."

"Let me check with Jessie and I'll let you know what she has."

Previously, Jessie had noticed the coincidences between her story of *Deceptions*, and her own life. But now that they knew Kurk had been murdered, she became more concerned. She spent more time meditating that week, trying to understand the meaning. Then she called Carrie and arranged a meeting with her.

Jessie reviewed the coincidences between her life and the story of *Deceptions* with Carrie. "Do you think *Deceptions* was precognitive?" Jessie asked.

Carrie was careful not to conclude about the meaning. "How was the story conceived?"

"It was very different from anything else I've written. The story just came to me."

"How? Was it visual?"

"Not visual like moving pictures, but visual like in my imagination. I would just imagine a set of circumstances and the next thing I knew it took off on me. The plots and even subplots developed in my head easier than usual. Getting the words on paper was easier than ever before."

"Perhaps you're just using your creativity differently, and things are happening easier."

"Or perhaps I'm going to be accused and convicted of Kurk Warner's murder."

"I don't think you can jump to those conclusions, Jessie."

"What concerns me is I've started the sequel to *Deceptions*. As I'm writing, I'm wondering if these things will happen to me."

"What's that story about?"

"In *Deceptions*, Nicole is convicted and sent to prison for the murder of Dillon's husband. The sequel is about Nicole's struggle to prove her innocence from within the walls of the prison."

A week had passed since the scare at Taylor's house, and Taylor agreed that she would move in with Jessie until Kurk's murder was solved. The two drove out to Taylor's property the following Saturday. They were told that the criminologist had finished with the house. Doreen had agreed to go there that Saturday morning and start cleaning up. The candles, flowers and wine bottle had been removed by the police officers, and Doreen had cleaned the bedroom and bathroom by the time Taylor and Jessie arrived.

Within a couple of hours, Taylor and Jessie had packed Taylor's belongings and removed them to the Porsche and Lexus. Doreen had finished, Taylor paid her for the services and explained that she was going on an extended trip and would not need her for a while.

They closed up the house, and, on their way out, Taylor changed the security code at the gate.

"I don't want to know your new password," Jessie said.

Taylor and Jessie settled into their life together. Taylor didn't seem to be bothered that she was missing some of the comforts of her home. Jessie knew that having a *live in* was a big step for her. It had been years since she lived full-time with a lover. She was pleased that she enjoyed having Taylor around.

Jessie and Taylor maintained the secrecy that Taylor was with her. Only the police and Mark knew. Jessie took extra precautions around the house. She beefed up her security system and had motion lights installed around the property. Taylor did not go out very much, and when she did, most of the time Jessie went with her.

Detective Bradley continued questioning the couple, especially Jessie. Like clockwork, once a week he would call, set up a time to visit and drive out to Jessie's house. There had been no incidents or threats against Taylor in a month, and yet each week Bradley would interrogate the couple. Often, he would inquire about matters that had already been dwelled upon, over and over.

During a recent visit with Taylor, Bradley asked about Kurk's financial matters.

"Were you aware that during the last five years of Mr. Warner's life he deposited pretty substantial amounts of cash into a savings account?" Bradley asked.

"No. How often? How much?" Taylor asked.

"Every month, for almost five years. The deposits averaged over four thousand dollars each month. The total exceeded a quarter of a million in the five years."

"I had no idea."

"Do you know where he would get the cash?" Bradley asked.

Taylor shook her head. "No. I would talk with his accountant, Justin Brenner. He handled all Kurk's finances."

"We've already spoken with Mr. Brenner. He claimed that the money was gambling winnings and was reported on his tax returns."

"Gambling?"

Later that evening Taylor shared the information with Jessie. "Jessie, the strange thing is—I never knew Kurk gambled."

Chapter 24

It was a Wednesday morning when Jessie kissed Taylor goodbye and left for a weekly visit to the library. Jessie had continued work on her new story. She found the work harder than her previous novel; she questioned every idea relating to the story. Because of this, her sequel kept changing.

Each week when Jessie went off to the UCLA library, Taylor stayed at the house and worked on her music. Today was no different than any other Wednesday, until the phone rang.

"Hello," Taylor answered.

"Hi, Taylor."

"Hi, Mark. How are you today?"

"Great. I'm getting ready for my trip. Did you happen to ask Jessie about the camping gear? I'm going shopping tonight for the things I need and I'm just trying to finalize my list."

"Yes. I did speak with her. I'm sorry I didn't let you know; it slipped my mind."

"Don't worry about it. I know you're under a lot of stress."

"Actually I haven't been. Being at Jessie's has been very good for both of us. But anyway, she said she has a bunch of stuff, including a solar shower and a daypack. Would you like me to find it and perhaps you can swing by and look through it?"

"That would be great."

"Let me find the stuff, then I'll call you back and we can make further arrangements."

"That's fine."

Taylor went back to work on a new song. When she was finished, she decided to look for Jessie's camping equipment. She looked in the obvious places, the garage and workroom in the basement. When she didn't find the equipment in the workroom, she opened the door to the crawl space. The room was dark and Taylor searched for a light switch along the side of the door, but found none.

She retrieved a flashlight on the workbench, turned it on and pointed it into the room. A lighting fixture hung from the low ceiling in the middle of the room. Taylor stepped down to the dirt surface that was lined with tarp and walked to the light, leaning over so she didn't hit her head on the low beams. A heavy musty smell filled the room.

Taylor pulled the string and the light came on in the dank storage area. She looked around the small room. Boxes were neatly lined along the walls, each labeled with its contents. There were many boxes labeled as tax records with years. Then boxes were labeled with titles of Jessie's novels. A corner of the room had sporting equipment. It was here Taylor saw a tent rolled up. Next to it, there was a garbage bag labeled on the outside "Sleeping Bag." Beside the sleeping bag, there was a box labeled "Camping Accessories."

Carefully, she picked up the box and brought it toward the workroom, leaving it near the crawl space entrance. *Where's her daypack?* Taylor turned to search for the missing bag. She didn't find it, but she was curious about an unlabeled box that sat next to the box labeled *"Deceptions."* She looked closer and found the initials "T.A." on top of the box.

"T.A.?"

Taylor opened the box, but the light was too poor to see its contents. She clumsily picked up the box, and carried it directly below the light. She opened the box and saw what was inside.

"What the hell . . ." she whispered, when she saw a set of her own CDs. Then she found magazine articles, pictures, downloaded Web articles, notes, lyrics, drawings and a journal. Everything related directly to Taylor. Taylor could feel her pulse race and her face heat with anger.

"What the hell is she doing collecting these things? Was she obsessed or something?"

Taylor turned back to the wall and searched the titles of the boxes starting with *"Deceptions."* She recognized most of the titles of her books, with the exception of the first three boxes. Then she felt her heart pound wildly when she saw the initials "I.D." below the title on the three boxes.

"It can't be," Taylor told herself. But she picked up one of the boxes and placed it beside the other box, beneath the light. Inside she found notes clearly written by Jessie, and a manuscript titled *In Her Way*. The title page of the manuscript said, "A Novel by Ivy Deverell."

"Ivy Deverell? Who the hell is she?"

Taylor dug through the box searching for clues. She pulled a folder and opened it. Taylor's world started to spin when she recognized the stationery with the initials "I.D." on top. The letter was signed by Jessie. "Oh my God." She skimmed the content of the letter. It was only then that she realized that Ivy Deverell was Jessie's pen name.

Taylor could feel her anger grow. Vicious thoughts spun in her head. The feelings of betrayal, deception and misjudgment plagued her.

Then, she clearly heard whispering. *"There is someone from a past life that is involved in some type of karmic debt."*

The whisper startled Taylor. She spun around looking for its source.

"There is real danger with this person," the voice became louder.

It was then that Taylor recognized the words from Karen, the psychic, from her reading the previous year.

"This person has an enormous amount of love for you. But it's misguided."

Taylor covered her ears with her hands to stop the words. But they kept coming.

"Their intentions are not healthy and this is what is causing danger. The cycle must be broken . . ."

Taylor's hands started to shake. "I've got to get out of here." Carefully, she folded the letter with the "I.D." letterhead and stuffed it in her jeans back pocket. She pulled the string of the light fixture and bolted out of the crawl space, leaving the boxes displaced and the camping gear by the door.

She ran upstairs to the bedroom, pulled a small duffle bag from the closet and started throwing her clothes into it. Taylor hesitated when she saw the wooden ankh lying on the nightstand next to the bed, then picked it up and placed it in the bag. She glanced at her watch. Taylor knew she had thirty to forty minutes before Jessie returned. "I hope this is one day she doesn't come home early."

Within fifteen minutes, Taylor had a bag packed and in the trunk of the Porsche. She got in the car, opened the garage door, and started the ignition. As she backed out of the driveway and into street, she could see the Lexus heading toward her.

"Shit." Taylor resisted every temptation to bolt, because she knew Jessie would follow. Taylor lowered her window and inched her car past the driveway, waiting at the curb.

Jessie's car pulled alongside of Taylor's car. She also opened her window. "Where are you off to?" Jessie asked.

"We need some stuff at the grocery store."

"Do you want me to go with you?"

It was hard, but Taylor smiled. "No. I'm fine. I've got to start getting out eventually. I'll be back in an hour or so."

"Okay. Be careful," Jessie smiled.

Taylor waved, then drove away. In the rearview mirror, Taylor watched Jessie pull into the driveway.

Once inside the house, Jessie went to her office. She removed a file folder labeled "Hopkins" from her attaché and placed it in the filing cabinet, right in front of a file labeled "Peanut Allergies."

When Taylor reached the San Gabriel River Freeway, she started to feel better. *Where do I go? This doesn't make any sense. I need time to sort this out. But where do I go?* She discarded going to the police right away. Then she picked up her phone and punched in the numbers.

The phone was answered on the second ring. "Rutledge Management."

"Hi, Theresa. Is Mark in?"

"Sure, Taylor. Hold on."

A couple minutes later Mark picked up the phone. "Hi, Taylor. So what do you have for me?"

"I need to see you right away."

Mark detected a note of unease in Taylor's voice. "Where are you?"

"I'm about a half-hour outside of LA."

"Are you okay?"

Taylor wasn't sure how to answer that question. "No. I'm not okay."

"Can you make it to the Harrison's Bar and Grill? It's across the street from my office."

When Taylor arrived at the bar, Mark was waiting for her. He quickly claimed her at the door and took her to a private table. A beer rested where Mark sat and within seconds, a bartender asked Taylor what she wanted. Taylor ordered scotch.

Mark knew that Taylor was upset. "What's wrong, Taylor?"

Taylor saw sincere concern in Mark's eyes. She reached into her back pocket, pulled out the folded letter, and then handed it to Mark.

He opened the document, and reviewed it. Mark was visibly shocked. "Jessie is I.D.?"

"That's what it looks like."

"I don't believe it. I'm sorry Taylor, I just can't buy into this."

"I don't know what to do. I don't know what to think. I'm so confused."

"Where did you get this?"

"In her crawl space. I went looking for her camping gear, and I found this box filled with stuff about me."

"What are you talking about?"

"Mark, it was scary. There were pictures of me, articles, drawings, a collection of my music. The entire contents of this box related to me."

"Really?"

"And then I found this." Taylor pointed to the letter.

"Well, I have to admit the stationery sure looks like what your harasser used . . . but I just find this too difficult to believe."

"Tell me about it. All the way here, I've been questioning myself. There's got to be some logical explanation. But . . . what the hell is it?"

"I agree with you there. There has to be a logical explanation. Did you talk with her about it?"

"No. I just bolted. I saw her on the way out and told her I was going to the grocery store. She's probably expecting me back any minute, now. You didn't tell anyone you were meeting me, did you?"

"No. But I left the office shortly after I spoke with you, and Theresa knew I was speaking with you." Mark appeared thoughtful. "Let me call Theresa and tell her not to say anything if Jessie calls."

While Mark spoke with Theresa on his cellular phone, Taylor withdrew. The events of the afternoon kept replaying in her head. Then she heard the voice again. *"There is real danger with this person . . . their love is misguided . . . the cycle must be broken."*

"Go away," Taylor said holding onto her ears.

Mark hung up the phone. "You want me to leave, Taylor?"

"No. I'm sorry. I was thinking aloud."

"I just spoke with Theresa. Everything is fine. Taylor, I think you should bring the letter to the police station and have them check it out."

"I don't know. I need to sleep on it. It's the strangest thing, Mark."

"What's that?"

"I became so angry when I saw the box of stuff relating to me, but . . . I'm still in love with her. I'm afraid of her, but damn it . . . I'm still in love with her."

"Taylor, it's possible that all this is just a misunderstanding."

"God, I hope you're right." Taylor hesitated and then changed the subject. "Mark, do you believe in reincarnation?"

"Wow. Now there's a change in direction."

"No. Not really. There are so many things about Jessie that I just don't understand."

"Like what?"

"For one, my attraction to her. I know I'm not gay, yet here I am in this same-sex relationship. Up until this afternoon, I've never been happier in a relationship. Yet, I'm not attracted to other women, just her. And I still find men attractive."

"Maybe it's a phase, Taylor."

Taylor shook her head. "No. I know it's not a phase. There's something about her. You know what déjà vu is, right?"

Mark nodded.

"I have déjà vu all the time when I'm with her. And there's something about her eyes. I had this psychic reading . . . she said that somebody from a past life would cause me danger and I should break a cycle." Taylor realized how senseless she must have sounded to Mark. "I'm sorry, Mark. You must think I'm crazy. Just forget this conversation."

"I don't think you're crazy at all. I very much believe in past lives, and that we're here to learn certain lessons."

"I need to call her," Taylor said abruptly.

"What?" Mark saw the spell Jessie had cast on Taylor.

"I should have been back by now. She's going to start getting worried."

"Taylor, think about how you're sounding. You have evidence that implicates Jessie as being Kurk's murderer, and yet you're concerned that she's going to be worried?"

Taylor looked at Mark. "You're right," she admitted. Then she pulled out her cellular phone and punched in Jessie's number. "Shh. Don't say anything, okay?"

"Hello," Jessie answered.

"Hi, Jessie."

"Oh, Taylor. I'm glad you called. I was getting worried. Where are you?"

Taylor tried to focus. "Jessie, I'm calling because I need some time away from us right now."

"What? What are you talking about?"

"Please, let me finish. This is hard enough."

"Okay," Jessie whispered.

"I don't know if I can do this gay thing much longer. I hate living in the closet and yet I realize the other choice is too much of a sacrifice to my career. I need time away from you. Being with you is clouding my judgment."

"Okay, Taylor. The last thing I want to do is hurt you."

"I've got to go. I'll call you when I'm ready to talk." Taylor disconnected the phone ending the conversation.

"Do you think she believed you?" Mark asked.

"I just need to buy a little time to figure out my next move, right?"

"Where are you going tonight?"

"Back to my house."

"Do you think that's safe? I mean after everything that happened last time."

"Yeah. I think I'll be okay. I changed the security password and she doesn't know it. I'll be fine."

Mark hesitated. "Look, I don't want you to think this is inappropriate, but I have a guest room that you are welcome to use. Actually, I would prefer it if you did. I don't think you should go back to your home until this thing blows over."

Taylor smiled then laughed.

"What's so funny?"

"That's what Jessie told me."

Chapter 25

Both Jessie and Taylor had a sleepless night. Jessie lay in bed wondering what went wrong, and Taylor pondered her next move. The following morning, Taylor was up before dawn. She had made her decision–she would go to the police.

At eight o'clock, Taylor phoned Detective Bradley and told him she was on her way in. Mark went with her to the police station. Taylor struggled with whether she was doing the right thing as she handed the letter to the detective.

"I found this in Jessie Mercer's crawl space." Taylor waited while the detective read the letter.

"So you believe that Ms. Mercer is Kurk's murderer."

"I didn't say that. I was hoping you could compare this stationery with the notes that were sent to me."

Bradley picked up his phone. "Reynolds, I'm sending something down. Compare this document against those sent to Ms. Andrews, in the Kurk Warner case." Bradley flagged down another detective. He handed the letter to the woman. "Get this to Reynolds, now. He's expecting it."

"Did you find anything else?" Bradley asked.

"I found a box in her crawl space. It's full of stuff relating to me: pictures, articles, lyrics, audio cassettes, CDs. You name it."

"Where's the box, now?"

"It's still in her crawl space."

Bradley took notes. "Is that it?"

Taylor nodded. "Yeah. That's it."

"Okay, we'll call you and let you know what we find out."

"No. I'm not leaving until I know about the letter. I have my whole life on hold. I'm not leaving," Taylor said defiantly.

"It might take a while before we have an answer."

"I'm not leaving."

"Suit yourself," Bradley said.

"You don't seem surprised by all this, Detective Bradley."

Bradley hesitated. "Ms. Mercer is one of our suspects in the Warner murder. We already have some evidence that implicates her."

"She is? How come you never said anything?" Taylor's voice rose.

"Motive."

"What?"

Bradley looked at Taylor. "We don't understand Ms. Mercer's motive. After all, you're the one that inherited the Warner estate."

Taylor stared back at the detective. "I'm a suspect also?"

Mark knew this was upsetting Taylor and moved to her side. "Don't worry Taylor, this is going to get cleared up soon."

Taylor and Mark waited in an interrogation room for forensics to report on the stationery. An hour passed. They spoke little during this time; occasionally Mark would offer some words of comfort.

"I can't believe they suspect me."

"Don't be insulted, Taylor. I think the spouse or partner is always suspected. Statistically, the incidence is high that they did it."

Bradley walked into the room. "The preliminary report is finished. First, the letter you brought in is a copy. It is very possible that the original was on the same stationery that was used by your harasser.

"It's possible, not definite?"

"No, we can't be 100% certain without the original. We're contacting the publishing company now to see if they have the original letter."

"Now what?" Taylor asked.

After her sleepless night, Jessie sat at the kitchen table nursing a cup of coffee. She could not take her mind off Taylor. She had tried to work on her new project earlier that morning but could not concentrate. Jessie knew she needed to do something to take her mind off Taylor. She decided to do some yard work. *I need to do something mindless.*

In her garage, she collected an assortment of gardening tools then went to the basement workroom to fetch other items. Jessie took pruning sheers and a branch saw from the wall behind the workbench. She was about to leave when she noticed the displaced flashlight sitting on the bench. When she picked up the flashlight, she realized the light was on. The batteries were almost dead, the stream of light barely noticeable. *I haven't used this in six months. I know I didn't leave it here.* As Jessie stood in the workroom, she could feel that something was terrifyingly wrong. *Why would Taylor have used the flashlight?* With that thought, she turned and stared at the door of the crawl space.

With each step closer to the door, Jessie could feel her pulse race. Before she opened the door, she whispered, "God, please no." Jessie squeezed the doorknob and turned it. There wasn't adequate light to see much inside. She knew where the light was and proceeded toward it, but after three steps she stumbled upon something and fell to the damp tarp. *What the hell?* With her hands, she felt the box that she had tripped over. She dragged the box closer to the crawl space doorway to see what it was. *I know I didn't leave a box at the door.* Then she saw the camping gear.

"Shit." Now Jessie was certain that Taylor had been here. Jessie stood, arched over and proceeded toward the center of the room. Her hands groped, searching for the string of the lighting fixture. One of her feet hit an object on the floor. She knew something else was displaced, and then she found the string, quickly pulled it, illuminating the storage room.

Her heart sank when she saw the corrugated box opened before her. *Oh, God.* Her eyes combed the personal items she had collected years earlier regarding Taylor. She turned to another box that sat next to it. It was a heavier box and she turned it so she could read the outside label, "*In her Way* by I.D."

Shit. She found out, Jessie thought sadly.

"*It's begun,*" that little voice echoed in her head.

Jessie quickly picked up the box containing the personal information on Taylor, turned the light switch off and went through the workroom. She knew she had to work fast. Jessie could feel her adrenaline rush as she ran upstairs to her office. She immediately turned on her paper shredder and proceeded to destroy the contents of the box. Quickly, she fed the paper cutter. The downloaded articles, lyrics, drawings, magazines easily went. Then she picked up her journal and started tearing the pages from it, destroying the evidence. Finally, she was left with the CDs. She went to her entertainment center in her living room and randomly dispersed the CDs in the vast collection of music.

Jessie went back to her office. She broke down the corrugated box into smaller pieces and threw it in a trash bag along with the shredded papers. Jessie removed the trash bag to the garage. *I've got to find that receipt from Rollins.* In her kitchen, she pulled a shoebox from a cabinet and placed it on the counter. Frantically, she scanned the receipts. About a third of the way through the box, she found it.

She recalled the afternoon she went into Rollins Florist and purchased the white roses. The owner's wife, Betty, had helped her that day. Jessie remembered driving over to Taylor's house before the conference and staging the seduction scene. Jessie tore the receipt repeatedly, and then put the tiny pieces down the garbage disposal. She could feel her quickened pulse start to slow down. *What else? What am I forgetting?*

Later that afternoon, Jessie was online in a chat room when she heard the doorbell ring. "*I've got to go.*" She sent the message then detached herself from the conversation. She exited the program, breaking the phone connection. Jessie wasn't surprised when she opened the door and found Detective Bradley among a small group of men at her front entrance.

Bradley held up a piece of paper to Jessie. "Ms. Mercer, we have a warrant to search your property." Immediately the other men infiltrated the house.

Jessie watched and did not interfere as the men searched the premises. At some point, she decided to leave the house. She went outside and sat at a bench in the rear of her property, beneath the tall trees.

Well, now I know why Taylor left so abruptly. I need to set her straight. She pulled out her cellular phone and called Taylor's house. There was no answer, but Jessie left a message on her answering machine. "Hi Taylor. It's me. We need to talk. Please call when you get this message." She left a similar message when she called Taylor's cellular phone.

Jessie called Mark's office and Theresa answered the phone.

"Hi Theresa. This is Jessie Mercer. Is Mark in?"

"Not right now. He's out shopping for his rafting trip. He leaves tomorrow."

"Oh, that's right. I'll call him on his cellular. Thanks." Jessie ended the conversation and started pressing the buttons again.

"Mark Rutledge," he answered.

"Hi Mark, this is Jessie."

"Oh . . . hi Jessie." Mark's hesitation confirmed that Taylor had spoken with him.

"Mark I need to speak with Taylor. It's important."

"Well . . . why don't you call her?"

Jessie took a chance. "Because I know she's with you."

There was silence on the other end, then dial tone. Mark had disconnected.

It was close to five o'clock when the police officers were loading the van and getting ready to leave. Jessie caught a glimpse of the back of the van before the doors were shut. She noticed they had packed up her research boxes on three of her novels, by her pseudonym Ivy Deverell. There was also an unidentified box and garbage bag that sat next to the three larger boxes.

"We'd like you to stop by the police station tomorrow. Ten o'clock. We have some questions regarding the murder of Kurk Warner," Bradley said.

"You want me to come by the police station?" Jessie knew that only serious suspects were interrogated at the police station. Yet, she also knew that the suspects were generally escorted to the station. *He doesn't have enough on me*, Jessie concluded.

"Having counsel available wouldn't hurt."

The following morning Jessie met her long-time friend, Linda Speller, at a coffee shop across from the police station. Jessie had asked for the meeting.

"I need your help. I'm in trouble," Jessie confided. "I'm a suspect in the Kurk Warner murder and I'm scheduled for an interrogation in an hour."

"Murder? I thought Warner had an accidental allergic reaction."

"We don't have a lot of time. Would you stay through my interrogation? Make sure I don't make any fatal errors?"

"Of course, but you need to tell me why you're a suspect."

"I think the only thing they have on me is that the initials of the person that has been harassing Taylor is I.D. I believe that Taylor came across some of my work on my first novels. I used a pen name, Ivy Deverell."

"What's the connection between the harasser and the murderer?"

"The last letter implied that the harasser took care of Kurk to be with Taylor."

"I see," Linda said. "You know I'm a corporate lawyer, Jessie."

"I know. I just need someone that is going to make sure I don't do something stupid."

"Are you and Taylor still involved?"

Jessie shook her head. "She left two days ago saying she needed time. She hasn't returned any of my phone calls. It doesn't look good, Linda."

Linda and Jessie walked into the police station at ten o'clock sharp. The two were escorted to a second-floor interrogation room. It was a simple room. There were no windows and nothing lining the walls. A wooden table with four wooden chairs centered the room. Bradley and a female officer, Detective Roth, joined the women in the small room. Bradley didn't seem surprised when Jessie introduced Linda as her attorney.

The four sat around the table, then Detective Bradley started asking Jessie questions. Roth just took notes, and Linda observed.

"Ms. Mercer, how many books did you write under the pen name Ivy Deverell?"

"Three."

"What years were they written?"

"They were my first three novels. The first was published about fourteen years ago."

"And the last?"

"Back then I wrote a book a year, so about eleven . . . maybe twelve years ago."

"There are a number of correspondences in your files that use a special letterhead with the initials 'I.D.' on them. We found some of this in your office." Bradley placed a sheet of the unused stationery in front of Jessie.

"And your question is, Detective Bradley?" Linda asked.

"When was the last time you went by the initials 'I.D.'?"

"I guess about eleven years ago."

"When was the last time you used this stationery?"

"About eleven years ago."

"Then why do you still have it around?"

"I don't know. Maybe one day I'll return to writing by the pseudonym Ivy Deverell."

"You are aware that Taylor Andrews has been harassed by an individual with the initials 'I.D.' "

"I am."

"Have you seen any of the letters from the perpetrator?"

"I've seen some."

"Are you the perpetrator, Ms. Mercer?"

"No."

"July 10th was the day someone broke into Ms. Andrews' Malibu home. On the afternoon of the 10th, a white Oldsmobile 88 was seen at the security gate of her house. The witness says the car was driven by a woman." Bradley referred to his notes. "He said she stopped at the security gate, punched in a password, the gate opened and the car drove through the gate. The witness said this happened around four that afternoon."

"And your question, Detective Bradley?" Linda asked.

The detective laid down a group of papers on the table. Jessie recognized the documents; inside her heartbeat hastened, outside she remained cool. "This is paperwork regarding the repair on your Lexus. It appears that you rented a loaner while your Lexus was being repaired." The detective pointed to the rental document. "You rented an Olds 88. It was white, also. Why did you lie when you were questioned earlier about being at the property that afternoon?"

Jessie remained silent.

"Contrary to what you told us earlier, Ms. Mercer, you did go to Ms. Andrews' property that afternoon, didn't you?"

"I would like to confer with my attorney before I answer that," Jessie said.

One of Bradley's eyebrows rose. "Let me ask you a couple other questions, then I'll leave you with your attorney." Bradley placed a merchant copy of a credit card imprint on the table. Jessie recognized the receipt for the flowers she bought Taylor that afternoon.

"This is a credit card receipt for flowers you purchased at Rollins Florist at 3:39 the same afternoon. Although the receipt doesn't say what kind of flowers you purchased, Betty Rollins was quite certain they were white roses. She says that's what you always purchased."

Linda didn't understand the implication of the white roses, but recognized Jessie's subtle sign of irritation; her jaw tightened. "Ms. Mercer is going to confer with me on that before she responds, Detective Bradley. Is there anything else?"

Bradley sighed and held up a document. "This is one of the letters from the perpetrator, 'I.D.,' that was sent to Taylor Andrews." He laid it next to the stationery from Jessie's office. It was clear that the letter was written on Jessie's stationery.

Jessie's heart beat wildly when she saw the evidence. She closed her eyes. *It's happening*, she thought sadly.

"Is there anything else, Detective?" Linda asked.

The detective placed a file folder on the desk. Jessie recognized her handwriting on the label, "Peanut Allergies." "We found this folder on peanut allergies in your office. Can you explain your interest in this area?"

Jessie remained silent.

"Ms. Mercer, we have sufficient evidence that supports that you are Taylor Andrews' harasser. We can put you at the house the afternoon of the incident. We have evidence showing you purchased the white roses that were used to vandalize the property. We have numerous harassment letters written on your stationery. But what we're not clear on is how and why?"

"How and why what, Detective?" Linda asked.

"Why did you murder Kurk Warner? Was it jealousy?"

"Time out," Linda said. "I missed something. How did you go from harassment letters to murder?"

Bradley laid the last letter on the table. "Ms. Speller, this note was left at the house the night of the incident."

Linda read the letter. "Is my client under arrest?"

"That depends on how she responds to all the unanswered questions."

"Is that all you have?"

"For now." Bradley stood and Roth followed. "How much time do you need with your client, counselor?"

"I'll let you know when she's prepared to address these issues."

It was close to three o'clock when Linda told Detective Bradley and Roth that they were prepared. Jessie and Linda had spent close to four hours locked in the small room preparing a statement.

"My client is ready. Please let her make her statement without interruption," Linda instructed.

Roth and Bradley took their seats. Jessie sat with notes laid out on the table in front of her.

"I did go to Taylor's house the afternoon in question," Jessie admitted. "I also brought with me white roses, because they're Taylor's favorite. We hadn't seen each other in four days and I wanted to make her homecoming special. I put the roses in a vase on the dresser in the bedroom. It was about 4:20 when I left, and everything at the house seemed normal. I lied that night, because I was scared. When I saw the flower petals spread over the stairs and then the flowers tossed on the bed, I realized that they were the flowers I had bought.

"The note that was found at the house implied that Kurk was murdered so that the harasser could be with Taylor. I became scared because I had Taylor. Somehow, I knew then that I would be a prime suspect.

"I can't explain how my stationery was used for the harassment notes. Only . . . give me some credit. If I did this, do you think I'd be that stupid?

"Finally, I started doing research on peanut allergies after Kurk was murdered. I was trying to understand peanut allergies and anaphylaxis."

Both Linda and Jessie waited for a response from Bradley.

"And that's it?" Bradley asked.

"I believe we have addressed all your questions," Linda stated flatly.

"You spent four hours locked in this room and that's the best you can do?"

"Detective Bradley, this afternoon we have been in telephone conference with an associate of mine, perhaps you have heard of him, Lyle Fallon. Lyle specializes in criminal defense. I do not practice in this area, but, as a favor to Ms. Mercer, I sat in on her interrogation. Mr. Fallon will be taking over Ms. Mercer's representation. Much of our time this afternoon was needed to bring Mr. Fallon up to speed on this complicated case. Both Lyle and I agree that you have insufficient evidence to arrest Ms. Mercer. We have spent way too much time here and I ask you now to either read Ms. Mercer her Miranda rights or terminate this interview."

Bradley stared intently at Linda. "I have one final question."

"And then Ms. Mercer and I are leaving," Linda said.

"Maybe. It depends on how she answers the question. Ms. Mercer, did you kill Kurk Warner?"

Jessie hesitated before she answered. She looked at both detectives then Linda. "No. I did not kill Kurk Warner." Jessie saw relief in Linda's eyes.

Linda stood and pulled her notes together, not giving Bradley time to object. Just as Linda and Jessie were ready to leave, Detective Bradley said, "Ms. Mercer, don't plan on doing any traveling."

Once outside, Jessie felt better. The women walked to their cars, and as they reached Jessie's Lexus, Linda stopped. She handed Jessie a business card. "Here's Lyle's card. Your appointment is at eight o'clock, Monday morning. Don't miss it, Jessie."

"Thanks, Linda, for everything," Jessie hugged her friend.

"Can I offer you some words of advice?"

Jessie nodded.

"I know you, Jessie. I know you're not telling me everything. There's a cloud of suspicion that surrounds you. You're going to keep drawing attention to yourself if you don't dispel this cloud. You need to think of yourself right now. Don't miss your meeting with Fallon."

Chapter 26

Once in her Lexus, Jessie pulled out her phone. Her desperation to speak with Taylor had amplified. She called Taylor's house and cellular, but there was no answer. Then she called Mark's cellular and his voice mail answered. At Mark's office, Theresa answered the phone. "Rutledge Management."

"Hi, Theresa, is Mark in?"

"No, he's left for his vacation, Jessie."

"Well, maybe you can help me. I'm trying to reach Taylor and there's no answer at her house or on her cellular phone."

Theresa hesitated. "Jessie, I've been asked not to tell you where they went."

"They're together? Mark took Taylor on the rafting trip?"

"Yes, Jessie and I'll have to ask you not to call again."

"Thank you, Theresa." Jessie heard dial tone in her ear.

"Rafting?" Jessie mumbled. "Taylor went rafting with Mark?" Jessie knew that Mark planned the rafting trip at Travis's recommendation. She was ten blocks from Travis's office. *Maybe Travis can tell me the name of the rafting company.* She started her car and pulled out of the parking lot.

It was a little after five when Jessie arrived at Travis's office. Alison was just leaving the office suite and was locking the door when Jessie got off the elevator. "Hi, Alison. I need to talk with Travis. Is he here?"

Alison smiled when she saw Jessie. "Hi, Jessie. No. Travis is out of town." Alison studied Jessie. She knew something was wrong. "Are you okay?"

"It's really important that I speak with him. Do you know where he is?"

"Yeah." Alison just stared back at Jessie, smiling.

"Would you share that with me?"

"I'm heading over to Station's for happy hour. You look like you need a drink. Join me and I'll tell you."

* * *

Jessie was in no mood to go to the gay bar, but admitted, *I could use a drink.* On her way over to the bar, she noticed a car following her. *I've got a tail. I'm sure it's the police.* Jessie found a parking spot a block from the bar. She noticed the car that had followed her had parallel parked across the street.

When Jessie entered the bar, she immediately saw Alison waving to her from a corner table. Jessie quickly moved to the table and joined her. Alison had already placed an assortment of appetizers in front of them. Two beers sat on the table.

"I hope you don't mind. I took the liberty of ordering you a beer."

"This is fine. Thanks." Jessie took a bite of a tortilla chip and was reminded of how hungry she was. Being at the police station all day, she did not have lunch. "So, where's Travis?"

"Well, that's a fine how do you do," Alison said.

"I'm sorry, Alison. I've just had an incredibly tough day. I'm actually looking for Taylor. I was told that she went with Mark Rutledge on a rafting trip. I know that Mark got the information on this trip from Travis. Where is he?"

Alison stared back at Jessie before she answered. "So you're trying to find out where they went?"

"Yes."

"So you can go after Taylor?" Alison pried.

"It's important that I speak with her."

"You guys break up?"

Jessie wasn't surprised that Alison was aware of their relationship. The rumors were obviously manifesting. "There's been a misunderstanding. It's important that I clear it up as quickly as I can. How can I reach Travis?"

"Jessie, Travis is on the rafting trip with them."

Jessie felt a sick feeling in her stomach. "Travis went on the rafting trip, also?"

"Yeah. Yesterday Travis asked me to call the rafting company to see if another person could be added. I didn't know I was adding Taylor."

"Do you remember the name of the rafting company?"

"Yeah. It's Grand Canyon White Water. Their phone number is real easy, too: 1-800-RAFTING."

Jessie wrote the information on a napkin. "Alison, how long have you been working with Travis?"

"Almost ten years."

"Do you remember an actress by the name of Stacy Hopkins? From what I understand, she worked with Travis on the movie *Aces*.

"How could I forget her? She was the blond that had a drug overdose and died about six years ago."

"What do you remember about all that?"

"Why?"

"Just curious."

"She was a young thing. *Aces* was her first big project. She just loved Travis. She used to follow him around like a puppy dog."

"Really? Were they ever involved?"

"Oh, probably. I don't know how Dana put up with him all those years. If you ask me, she really got the short end of the stick."

"What do you mean?"

"She got nothing in the divorce."

"How?"

"I guess Travis is pretty close to broke."

"Broke?"

"He has a gambling problem."

"Really?"

"Yeah. But I have to give him credit. He seems to be trying."

"How so?"

"He used to take some pretty hefty cash withdrawals against every check. Then he just stopped, cold turkey, at the end of last year. He said it was his New Year's resolution.

"Did he tell you he had a gambling problem?"

"No. He told Dana during a divorce proceeding when she realized how broke he was. She was devastated. She's been married to him for twenty years, she gave up her career when they married, now she finds out he's totally broke and she has to start over." Alison took a sip of her beer. "Why all the interest in this?"

"No reason," Jessie lied. She casually took a sip of her beer. "Kurk Warner was in *Aces*, with Stacy Hopkins, wasn't he?"

"Yeah. Actually, I think that was the first time Travis and Kurk worked together. Since then, Kurk has been Travis's leading man in most of his movies."

"They must have worked well together."

"Not really. But Travis knew Kurk Warner could get people to the movies. Why are you asking all this?"

Jessie looked at Alison. *I wonder if I can trust her.* Then she remembered the police car that had followed her to the bar.

"*Do you have a choice?*" Her little voice asked.

Jessie sighed. "I'm in trouble, Alison. The police suspect me of murdering Kurk Warner and now Taylor does, too, but she's in Arizona. There's an unmarked police car outside; I know I'm being followed. I need to go to her. Would you help me?"

"You really love her, don't you?"

Jessie nodded. "I love her very much."

Jessie waited patiently as Alison analyzed the situation. "I'll help you, Jessie, with one condition."

"What's that?"

"When all this is worked out, if you and Taylor don't reconcile . . . have dinner with me."

Jessie smiled.

Hours later, when it was dark, she left the bar and walked along the sidewalk. From the corner of her eye she could see the dark unmarked car sitting across from the Lexus. She could see a silhouette of one man sitting behind the wheel. With the keyless entry, she opened the doors of the Lexus, and got in. She turned the ignition and pulled out of the parking spot. In the rearview mirror, she could see the dark car pull out behind her.

Alison whispered to herself, "It worked." She smiled as she drove by the bar entrance where Jessie waited in the shadows.

When Jessie saw the car tailing her Lexus, she started to search for Alison's Honda Civic. Jessie and Alison had exchanged clothing and keys. Jessie quickly found Alison's car, beginning a new journey.

Jessie knew she needed to get out of the metro area before the police realized they were tailing the wrong person. Before she got on the Santa Monica Freeway, she stopped at an ATM for cash. With about $700 and Alison's credit card, she set out for the Grand Canyon.

Based on the information from Alison, she knew that the rafting trip started on Sunday morning in Marble Canyon, Arizona. Almost 600 miles separated Jessie from Taylor, and Jessie knew she had to get to the Grand Canyon before the rafting trip.

About ninety minutes later, Jessie's cellular phone rang.

"Hello."

"Hi, it's me," Alison said. "I'm at your house. Everything is fine. The cops followed me all the way back. They're parked down the street watching the house."

"Make yourself at home. Maxwell's food is in the kitchen pantry."

"Yes. I've already taken care of him. I'll plan on hanging out here until Monday morning, Jessie. Then I'll have to get to work."

"That should give me enough time to get there and talk with Taylor. I owe you Alison."

"Yes. Dinner . . . if it doesn't work out with Taylor."

"Thanks. I'll only use your credit card if necessary. I got some cash. I just don't want to leave a trail. You are being very trusting, Alison. I can't thank you enough."

"Travel safely . . . and good luck."

"Thanks."

* * *

Hours later, Jessie was having a hard time keeping her eyes open. The lights from the passing cars had a mesmerizing effect on her. She stopped at a rest area and purchased coffee and snacks. The coffee helped bring her back to reality. Back on the road, her mind reviewed the events of the past few days. So much had changed. Her racing mind brought up a conversation with Linda Speller that afternoon, after the detectives had left them to talk.

* * *

Detective Roth and Bradley had just left the interrogation room. Jessie looked over at Linda; her head was in her hands. Silence penetrated the room for what seemed an eternity to Jessie. Linda's head finally lifted. "We have a lot of work to do."

Linda paced the small room while Jessie remained seated. She ran her fingers through her short blond hair. "This is over my head, Jessie. I'm not a criminal attorney."

"You think I'm a criminal?"

"I didn't say that." She rolled up her sleeves and sat in front of Jessie. "I don't think they have enough to arrest you or they already would have. Jessie, you've got to level with me. What's going on?"

Jessie remained silent.

"You're not going to tell me?"

Jessie shook her head. "I don't know what to tell you, Linda." Jessie sat staring at the table.

"Jessie, you have to give me something to work with. I know you. You're not a murderer–but that's not your defense. You have to level with me. For starters, why did you lie when you were questioned about the break-in at Taylor's house?"

Jessie was pensive. With her fingers, she delicately rolled a pencil on the table in front of her until Linda could no longer stand it and slammed her hand on top of the pencil. Jessie jumped, and her eyes met Linda's.

"Is this just between us?" Jessie asked.

"Yes."

Jessie sighed and leaned backwards in her chair. "I don't know where to start Linda."

"How about at the beginning?"

"That's just it–I don't know where the beginning is."

"Talk to me."

"Have you read my novel *Deceptions*?"

"I saw the movie last weekend."

"Does anything strike you as odd about *Deceptions* and what's going on in my life?"

Linda's eyebrows scrunched together. "In the movie, Nicole is framed, sent to trial and convicted of murdering her girlfriend's husband." Linda paused momentarily. "Do you think you're being framed?"

"Linda, there have been a number of things that have happened to the characters in my story that have happened to both Taylor and me over the last year."

"What are you saying?"

"I'm not sure. What would you think if you wrote a story and years later it seemed to become your reality?"

"That's not going to help your defense, Jessie."

"I'm starting to wonder if my story was somehow precognitive insight into my future. And . . . if it is, I'm being framed for the murder of Kurk Warner."

"How long have you been wondering this?"

"I've had it in the back of my mind since I saw the preview of *Deceptions*."

"Why did you lie to Bradley about not going to the house that afternoon?"

"It was stupid. I know. I just got scared, Linda. When I got there, I saw the note that pretty much implicated me, then the rose petals on the stairs and all over the bed . . . I got scared."

"What about the peanut allergy file they found in your desk?"

"When I started seeing the connections between my own life and *Deceptions*, I started investigating Kurk's death. One of the things I looked at was peanut allergies. I was just trying to theorize how Kurk came in contact with peanut protein."

"You need a criminal attorney. Let's set up a conference with Lyle Fallon. He's the best criminal attorney at our firm. But before we do, is there anything else you want to tell me?"

Jessie shook her head.

"I don't understand this precognitive stuff. But if it's indeed becoming your reality, aren't you a little concerned? After all . . . wouldn't that make Taylor the murderer?"

Jessie stared back at Linda, then nodded. "In the movie, Dillon murders her husband and frames her lover for the murder."

* * *

The blast of an air horn from a semi startled Jessie back to reality. Shaking, she pulled over and drank the rest of her coffee.

Chapter 27

That Friday afternoon, Taylor, Mark, and Travis flew from Los Angeles to Las Vegas, then they caught a commuter shuttle to Marble Canyon. As they stepped off the airplane, a blast of hot desert air welcomed them to Arizona.

"Oh, my God. It's so hot!" Taylor said.

"Yes," the pilot agreed. "It's actually 112 degrees."

The group looked around the dry desert. High mesas and the Vermillion Cliffs surrounded the area. Across the street from the landing strip was the Marble Canyon Lodge. "That's our stop," Travis said.

They checked into the quaint lodge, had dinner, then enjoyed a stroll to the canyon rim. Here, they walked over the pedestrians' Navajo Bridge. A new bridge ran parallel to the original bridge allowing transportation over the canyon and the Colorado River from 467 feet above. Even at nightfall, the view of the canyon was impressive.

Mark knew that Taylor was not all that enthusiastic about the rafting trip. He also knew that she was preoccupied. As they walked back to the lodge from the rim, he tried to cheer her up. "Taylor this is going to be fun. I'm glad you decided to come."

"And you're lucky, too, Taylor," Travis added. "These trips get booked up so fast. What are the chances that there'd be a last-minute cancellation?"

"It isn't luck," Mark added. "Taylor was meant to come."

"How long have you guys been planning this trip?" Taylor asked.

"I made reservations at the beginning of the year," Mark said. "I was originally coming with a buddy of mine from law school. But he was having a trial this week."

"So I substituted for him," Travis said. "I loved the trip last time."

Taylor just smiled and walked along in silence.

"Taylor, I called LAPD earlier today," Mark announced. "They brought Jessie in for questioning this morning."

"Have you heard how the search went yesterday?" Taylor asked.

"Bradley didn't tell me a lot, except they had sufficient evidence to bring her in for questioning. From what I understand, she brought an attorney with her to the interrogation."

"Do you know if they found the box of stuff about me in the crawl space?"

Mark shook his head, "I don't think so. I heard they found her stationery and a file on peanut allergies."

"Peanut allergies?" Travis interrupted. "My God, do you think she really did it?"

Mark shook his head. "I have a hard time with this. I can't believe Jessie is capable of killing someone." Mark raised his hand to Taylor's back and rubbed it affectionately. "But I'm glad you're here with us, Taylor. Try to enjoy yourself this week. Hopefully by the time this trip is over, everything will have sorted itself out."

As they arrived back at the lodge, Mark took a seat on a bench outside. Taylor joined him.

"I think I'm going to head in," Travis said. "I'll see you in the morning."

"Good night."

Mark and Taylor sat silently in the summer heat. Although it had cooled off some, it was still in the 90s. The moon was almost full, providing enough light to see the magnificent Vermillion Cliffs behind the lodge and trimming the canyon rim.

Taylor stood. "I think I'm going to head in, also."

Mark knew that Taylor was preoccupied. He stood next to her. "It's going to work out, Taylor. Don't worry."

Taylor looked at Mark. There was a sparkle in his eyes that Taylor had never noticed before, and yet it seemed familiar. She smiled. "You're sweet, Mark. Thank you for everything." She looked away then returned to

Mark's eyes. "What would I have done without you?" Taylor approached Mark and placed her lips on his cheek, but she wasn't prepared when he turned his face and their lips met.

The contact caught Taylor off guard and she instinctively backed away. "I'm sorry Mark, I can't."

"No. I'm sorry," he said obviously embarrassed. "I was out of line. I apologize."

"Good night, Mark." Taylor smiled slightly, then turned and walked to her room. As she placed the key in the doorknob of her room, she closed her eyes momentarily. "How come things just seem to get more complicated?" she whispered.

The following morning, Taylor joined Mark and Travis in the Marble Canyon Lodge's restaurant for breakfast.

"Good morning," Taylor said as she sat at the table.

"Good morning," the men chorused.

"So what's on the agenda today?" Taylor asked.

"We need to do a little shopping, and then we have the orientation tonight. Other than that, we can drive out to the Glen Canyon Dam and Lake Powell."

"Shopping? What do you need?" Travis asked.

"Taylor needs just about everything on our 'what to pack list.' "

Taylor shook her head. "I still can't believe I dropped everything and I'm going camping in the Grand Canyon."

"Trust me, Taylor. I'm not a camper either. But this is certainly the way to go," Travis said. "We don't have to worry about food. The rafting company's staff prepares the meals. Eventually, you get used to the lack of running water."

"What are you talking about?" Taylor asked naively.

The men just stared back at her.

"Are you telling me that there will be no restrooms for the next five days?"

"The rafting company sets up portable toilets at the campsites each night," Travis said.

"What about washing up?"

"You use the water from the river," Travis said. "Eventually the 48 degree water is bearable."

"Oh, God. What have I gotten myself into? No shower for five days?"

The trio spent the morning shopping at the Trading Post and picked up Taylor's essentials. Then they rented a car from the lodge's manager and drove up to the dam and Lake Powell. That evening they met the group of people that would accompany them on their five-day excursion. There were 23 people at the orientation, excluding the rafting company's six staff members. Four paddle rafts were to be launched, each holding six passengers and led by a trained guide. Two oar boats, run by staff members, would take the luggage, food, and sleeping gear throughout the journey.

When the group realized that a celebrity was among them, Taylor became the center of attention. Eventually they all settled down when the staff asked everyone to introduce himself or herself. At the end of the meeting, the staff handed out small river bags for everyone to repack their gear. The entire crowd was excited when they broke up, each looking forward to starting their new adventure.

Jessie arrived early at the parking lot of the Marble Canyon Lodge the following morning. The staff was busy tending to last-minute details and waiting for the arrival of the vacationers. Jessie approached a staff member who seemed to be in charge.

"Hi, I'm Alison Townsend," Jessie said. "I missed the orientation last night. Pat, from your office, suggested that I meet up with Ted."

"That's me." The man gave Jessie a warm smile, revealing his white teeth against his bronze skin. "We covered a lot of material last night. It's too bad you missed it. Have you ever done any rafting?"

"I've taken a few trips down the Arkansas River."

"In Colorado? Through the Gorge?"

"Yes," Jessie answered.

"You'll be fine. You're pretty lucky to get on the trip this late. There was a last-minute cancellation. A couple out of Detroit had a death in their family, so there were two last-minute openings. But now we're full. Did you get your river bag?"

"No. Pat suggested I get one from you."

"Okay." Ted went to a van, pulled out a rubberized bag, and handed it to Jessie. "Everyone else was given this last night. Use this to pack your personal items. When we reach camp tonight, you'll be given another bag just like this, which will include a sleeping bag, foam pad and a ground cloth." Ted looked around for Jessie's bag. "Where's your bag?"

"I have it in my car."

"The rest of the group will be here in about 30 minutes. Why don't you go pack your bag and then I'll introduce you to the rest of the crew, including your guide. Just remember, you're not going to have access to your bag until we reach the campsite. Set aside any personal items you want along with you during the day, like a camera, sunscreen, and extra clothes. Each raft has three river bags you can keep those things in.

"Have you made arrangements about your car? You'll be hiking out at the south rim, down by Phantom Ranch."

"Yes. I hired the shuttle service. Someone is driving the car down to the top of the Bright Angel Trail."

The man pulled out a sheet of paper. "What's your last name again?"

"Townsend. Here, let me help." But as Jessie scanned the roster, she searched for Taylor's name. She learned that Taylor, Travis and Mark were in Ted's raft with three others.

"Oh, here it is. You're with Justine." Ted pointed at a woman who was loading the van.

"Great. I'll go pull my stuff together and meet up with Justine in a little while. Thanks for the help, Ted."

Back at the car, Jessie opened the back hatch. There was an assortment of shopping bags she needed to pull together. After leaving California unexpectedly, Jessie had spent the previous day shopping for everything from clothing to camping accessories. She made a substantial dent in her cash, leaving her with less than two hundred dollars.

Quickly, Jessie packed the clothes and accessories in her river bag. She tidied up Alison's car, leaving her personal items hidden in the rear of the car. Jessie glanced at her watch. She realized she had a couple of minutes to spare and pulled out her cellular phone to call her house, but "No Service" was prominently displayed on the phone.

Jessie closed up the vehicle, picked up the packed river bag and empty backpack, and set out for the pay phone outside the lodge. She quickly punched in the numbers.

"Hello," Alison answered.

"Hi, it's me."

"How's it going?"

"I was able to get on the rafting trip. I only have a minute. I used your credit card to pay for the trip. I wanted to make sure you knew. It's costing about $1,300. I promise I'll take care of you when I get back."

"Have you seen Taylor?"

"Not yet. I'm kind of hoping she doesn't see me until we're on the river. I don't need any problems right now."

A familiar laugh brought Jessie's attention to a small group that was passing the lodge. When she saw Travis, Mark and Taylor walking in her direction she quickly hid her face. Calmly, she placed the river hat on her head then followed with sunglasses. *Please don't see me.*

The three carried river bags and backpacks. Travis continued his belly laugh as he came within a couple of feet of Jessie. None of them saw her.

After they had passed, Jessie whispered, "They're here. There's no cellular reception in the canyon. So, I don't know when I'll speak with you again. But thanks for everything, Alison."

"Good luck, Jessie."

Jessie waited until other passengers arrived at the gathering area before she made her way back over to the van. Most of the people seemed to flock together in one area and Jessie quickly surmised that Taylor was at the center. Jessie approached Justine and introduced herself.

"Hi, Justine, I'm Alison. I understand I'm in your group."

Justine turned and studied Jessie, then shook her hand. She wore a long-sleeve white nylon shirt concealing her muscular frame and screening her upper body from the sun.

"Hi, Alison. I understand you didn't make it last night. You didn't miss too much. Everyone introduced themselves and river bags were handed out. I see you have yours." Justine reached for Jessie's bag. "Here, let me show you how to seal the bag so it's watertight." Justine quickly pressed the bag, expelling the air and creating a vacuum. She then rolled up the bag and tied it off.

"Got it?" Justine asked.

"Got it."

Justine continued to study Jessie. "I'm sorry, Alison. I don't mean to be rude. It's just that you look a lot like one of my favorite authors. Has anyone ever told you that you look like Jessica Mercer?"

"Yes. Actually I have heard that before."

The river bags and daypacks were packed in the van, then Ted announced that they were ready to go to the launch site. Jessie watched people disperse to either the parking lot to get their vehicles or board the van. She waited on the sideline as Travis, Mark and Taylor boarded the van, then she went to Alison's car. It was a quick drive to the fourteen-day parking lot across from the launch site. Here she was instructed to leave her car and conceal the keys in a "hide a key."

A short walk brought her to Lee's Ferry, where six rafts were neatly lined up. The rubber rafts were yellow with gray accents. Four were smaller, with seven paddles, while the equipment rafts were larger and had a set of oars. A rope was tied around the outside of each raft, and two nylon-netted bags were secured to the rope in the front of each raft.

Justine made an announcement to review safety protocol. She discussed safety procedures in the event someone fell out of the raft. Then she asked everyone to take a lifejacket, note the number displayed on the front of the jacket, and securely fit it.

Jessie picked up jacket number 201 and put it on. To avoid Taylor, she quickly walked away from the group.

It was Justine who followed her away from the crowd. "Has a guide checked your jacket yet?"

"No," Jessie admitted.

Justine took hold of one of the four straps. Her eyes met Jessie's. "These need to be tightened more." She quickly tightened the straps. "Remember your number. You'll save a lot of time not having to fit these each day. But they loosen up, so tighten the straps every day, okay?"

Justine was friendly enough, and it didn't take Jessie very long to figure that she was gay.

Jessie and the other members boarded the raft. Jessie was surprised at how firm the raft was. She easily walked along the outside of the tube to the rear of the raft, where she sat, then stored her personal day items and a fanny pack in one of the waterproof bags that was secured to the raft. Her water bottles were placed in the nylon-netted bag that would eventually be dropped into the river, to keep the drinking water cool.

Within a short time, all the rafts were packed and smaller groups had formed around their guides. Jessie carefully kept track of Taylor, Mark and Travis's whereabouts. Ted's raft was the first on the river. Justine's group was second.

Once in the water, the guides assessed how the crew was able to paddle together. Jessie sat in the rear of the raft; Justine sat behind her. A couple from Miami and a family of three from Cleveland completed the crew. A lead person in the front was selected for the crew to follow. Justine reviewed instructions for forward commands and turns. The teams worked together practicing turning for the first seven miles, then the river changed and the rafts hit Badger Creek Rapids. The rafts hit the white water, offering an exciting ride, before they broke for lunch.

As the raft reached the tiny beach, Justine said, "In case you're wondering where to go tinkle, as a guideline we generally use skirts up–pants down. So ladies go up river, and men go down."

Once on shore, the staff quickly set up a wash bucket near the rafts and a table in the limited shade. Two guides busied themselves laying out sandwich makings.

Others from Jessie's raft went off together. Jessie knew she was being antisocial. She found it interesting that even after rafting with her group that morning, she couldn't describe her raft-mates. The majority of her focus had been to keep an eye on Taylor and stay out of sight from the three.

When the opportunity presented itself, Jessie made a sandwich, took her water bottle and moved away, finding a quiet part of the beach, while Taylor stayed with the rest of the group.

For most, the afternoon offered plenty of excitement and fun. For Jessie, her focus never changed. It was five-thirty when the rafts stopped at a sandy beach. The group was asked to hang tight and form human chains to facilitate unloading of the rafts. Jessie watched from afar as people passed bags from person-to-person until the luggage had been neatly unloaded and placed on a large tarp.

Then Ted demonstrated how to put up and take down a tent. He cautioned, "If you choose to use a tent, just remember, they're extremely hot; I don't recommend them unless it's raining."

It was Taylor who pointed to the sky and asked, "Ted what's flying overhead?"

The group looked up to see the tiny birdlike creatures circling above.

"They're bats."

It was Taylor who took the first tent. Jessie overheard Mark offer to help Taylor put it up.

"One last word before we set up dinner. Do not remove your sleeping bags from the river bags until you're ready to use them. Snakes and scorpions love unoccupied sleeping bags. Also, don't leave any of your bags opened. Close everything up after each use, and always shake out your clothing before you put it on."

The group finally dispersed and people sought their own private area on the beach to lay out their tarp. Jessie waited for everyone to claim their bags and sleeping area and then found an area on the opposite side of the beach from Taylor.

Taylor was exhausted. The day had proven to be fun, yet she had a hard time taking her mind off Jessie. Both Mark and Travis had been good to her and showed concern in their own ways. She was glad that Mark hadn't brought up the kiss from the evening before. It was one thing she didn't want to deal with. Taylor had been the center of attention the first day and hoped that the group would settle down soon and give her some space. She had been introduced to the majority of the people on the trip. Occasionally, she caught sight of a woman she hadn't met, yet, who reminded her of Jessie. Taylor never saw her face, but it was the way the woman stood.

Taylor wondered how it had gotten as bad as it was. A week earlier, her life had seemed perfect. *How could I have been so wrong? How did I fall in love with her? How can I fall out of love with her?*

The staff was working on setting up appetizers and dinner. Taylor decided she would take the opportunity to find a private area along the river to wash up. Mark offered to escort Taylor for her walk. She held up her toiletry bag; Mark blushed then smiled.

As Taylor walked away from the camp, she realized it was the first time she had been alone since the evening before. She enjoyed the peace and quiet. She walked along the riverbank until she found an area that offered some privacy by rocks and vegetation.

Taylor splashed the cold water over her face. She gasped at the initial contact, removed her soap and proceeded to wash up, then brushed her teeth. Once finished bathing, she moved away from the river and headed back, but the quiet was soothing. Taylor found a rock overlooking the river and sat, enjoying the peace and quiet. She was there for a minute before she realized that she wasn't alone.

In her peripheral vision, she saw a figure standing on her right side. Startled, she looked to see who it was, but she wasn't prepared.

At first, Taylor didn't recognize Jessie under the river hat and sunglasses. When she did, Taylor stood and backed away.

"Please don't run," Jessie said calmly. "I'm not going to hurt you."

But Taylor continued to back away. "What are you doing here?"

"I need to talk with you," Jessie walked to her. She removed the sunglasses, allowing them to hang freely from her neck.

"I have nothing to say to you."

When Jessie saw that Taylor kept backing away from her, she stopped. "Taylor, I'm not going to hurt you."

"You shouldn't be here."

"I didn't do it, Taylor. I didn't kill Kurk."

"Tell that to the police."

"You're what's important to me, Taylor. I need you to believe me."

Taylor just shook her head. "Please go."

"I can't. Not until you believe me."

"Jessie, what am I supposed to believe? I saw the box. The box in the crawl space."

Jessie sighed. She removed her hat and her long brown hair fell past her shoulders. "I know what that must have looked like. I'm sorry. I should have been honest with you about it." Jessie moved to the rock that Taylor had been sitting on, and sat. "I'll tell you everything, if you give me a chance."

Taylor remained standing.

"Why don't you sit?" Jessie pointed to the large rock that she was sitting on.

"I'm comfortable. Tell me–why did you collect that stuff about me?"

Jessie looked into Taylor's eyes. She could see Taylor's doubt and fear and it pained her. Jessie wondered if the truth would help. *Or will it make things worse?*

"You've come this far, Jessie. Tell her," the little voice pestered.

"A little over three years ago, I started noticing connections between you and me," Jessie started.

"Connections?"

"That's the only way I can explain it, Taylor, connections. They started with dreams, then I started noticing that everywhere I went, you were there."

"How?"

"I would get in the car and hear one of your songs playing on the radio. I'd go to a restaurant or a store and one of your songs would come on; I'd wake up to my alarm and one of your songs would be playing. I would turn on a television and you'd be on it. I'd pick up a magazine, and you'd be there."

"Coincidence."

"Taylor, I had a dream, and in my dream I was given a picture. And the person who gave me the picture said that I would find the answers to my questions in this picture."

"And it was a picture of me?"

"No. It was a picture of the CD cover to *Karmic Debt*. The strange thing was, I hadn't seen the jacket before. So, the next day when I came across the jacket . . . it just blew my mind. I've got to admit, Taylor, I hadn't been one of your fans. I wasn't very familiar with your music so I needed to sort out why I was having these . . . connections to you."

"So you collected this obsessive box of items about me?"

"I guess that's when I started collecting things. But you see, every time I found something about you, an article, your lyrics, anything . . . I seemed to be even more connected." Jessie shook her head, "I know this has got to sound crazy."

"Yes, it does."

"At the time, I was in the process of writing *Deceptions*, and I realized that I was becoming distracted and I couldn't concentrate on finishing the novel. I spoke with an intuitive about what the connections could mean."

"An intuitive?"

"A psychic." Jessie sensed that her credibility was slipping. "Taylor, I was hypnotized and had a past-life regression."

Taylor stared back at Jessie. Karen's words raced through her head. *"There is someone from a past life that is involved in some type of karmic debt. There is real danger with this person. Their intentions are not healthy and this is what is causing danger. The cycle must be broken . . ."*

"And we were together in a previous life," Taylor said.

"Yes. We were." Jessie was surprised at how calmly Taylor said it.

"Tell me about it."

"We knew each other during the Salem witch trials."

"Salem?" Taylor said. *I was there.*

Jessie was surprised at how detached Taylor seemed. "I was your husband."

"Was I a witch?" Taylor asked, even though she knew the answer.

"Yes."

"You told me once that you went back to Salem to do some research on an ancestor."

Jessie nodded.

"Was that really me you did research on?"

"Yes."

"Was I executed?"

Jessie got off the rock and took a step toward Taylor, so she could better see Taylor's eyes. "I don't know. From the records I found, I was able to determine that my regression was accurate, but my regression ended when you were being sent to trial."

"Do you know what my name was?"

"You were Rebecca Johnson. I was Daniel."

Daniel's Heart? Taylor pondered.

"We lived in Andover, and you were brought to trial in September of 1692."

"My name wasn't among those listed as executed?"

"For some reason, Taylor, your name is listed among those accused, but the outcome of your indictment is unknown."

Taylor stared back at Jessie.

"You don't believe me?" Jessie asked.

Taylor sighed. "It's not that I don't believe you. It actually fits. I have wondered about a past-life connection between the two of us. It would explain my attraction to you. And I've always had some pretty strong feelings about the injustices from the Salem witch trials. But it's irrelevant whether we were together before, anyway."

"What?"

"What's important is the here and now."

"I agree. That's why I did the regression."

"I don't understand."

"Before the regression these connections to you were driving me crazy. I was having a hard time focusing on my life. My work was slipping, and I ruined a good relationship. After the regression, I had a strong need to know what happened to you. By going back to Salem, I exhausted every effort to find out what happened. When I didn't find out, I figured I was just not meant to know. But after that–I was able to get on with my life. I packed all the items I had collected about you in a box, and stored it in my crawl space.

"After I packed everything up I was able to get on with my life. I was able to get on with the here and now. I finished *Deceptions* then I wrote the screenplay. A couple years after that, *you* expressed interest in playing a part in *Deceptions*. It was *you* who claimed *Deceptions* was your destiny."

"Our past is still irrelevant."

"How can you say that?" Jessie inched closer and looked deep into Taylor's eyes. She could see her pain. "You still think I killed Kurk."

"God. I want to believe you Jessie. But . . . I understand you bought the flowers and went to my house the afternoon it was broken into. I understand that the police found a huge file on peanut allergies at your house . . ." Taylor's voice cracked as she finished.

Jessie cautiously approached Taylor. She stopped in front of her. "Taylor, you know me. Not just from now, but from many other lifetimes. Look into my eyes and tell me–do you see a killer?"

Taylor looked deep into Jessie's familiar eyes.

"If you have any doubts, Taylor, I'll walk out of your life and I'll never bother you, again." As Jessie finished her statement she thought, *déjà vu?* Then she mumbled, "It happened again."

"What?" Taylor asked.

"It happened again," Jessie said louder.

"What are you talking about?"

"I just felt like we did a scene in *Deceptions*."

"Yes, I see a similarity," Taylor acknowledged.

"Taylor, I did buy you flowers the afternoon your house was broken into. And I did go to your house. But I left the flowers in a vase next to the bed. I swear."

"Why did you lie to the police that night about not going there? And what about the file on peanut allergies?"

Jessie hesitated. "Have you noticed any similarities between some of the subplots of *Deceptions*, and what's happening?"

Taylor remained silent.

"I lied to the police that night because I saw my roses used to vandalize your house and I was very aware that the note you found implicated me. I got scared, Taylor. *Deceptions* is becoming our reality."

"What?"

"Take a look at the subplots of the story. Many of them had already happened. I think that *Deceptions* was somehow precognitive, a vision of my future. And now it's becoming our reality. I've been watching this for some time. That's why I was doing research on peanut allergies."

"I don't understand."

"The research was done after Kurk died. When we started seeing each other, I started seeing coincidences between what was happening with our lives and the plots of *Deceptions*. I started my own little investigation. In *Deceptions*, Nicole is convicted of murdering her lover's husband."

"Yes. I know. But in *Deceptions*, my character was the actual murderer."

Jessie stared back into Taylor's eyes. "Yes. I know."

"You think *I* murdered Kurk?"

Jessie's eyes met Taylor's and the women studied each other. Then Jessie shook her head. "I know you didn't do it, Taylor."

"But doesn't that defeat your precognition theory?"

"Taylor, are you okay?" Mark's cry startled both Taylor and Jessie. He moved to Taylor, placing his body between the women.

"You shouldn't be here," he said to Jessie.

"It's nice to see you, too, Mark," Jessie said.

"Are you okay?" Mark asked Taylor.

"Yes. I'm fine." Taylor started to back away from Jessie.

"Taylor, I think we need to talk more," Jessie said.

"No. I think we've talked enough for one night. I need time to sort this out."

"I understand." Jessie watched Mark escort Taylor away from her, back to the camp.

When Mark and Taylor were out of listening range from Jessie, Mark spoke. "I'm calling LAPD as soon as we're back to the camp."

"No. Please don't, Mark. I want to sort this out first," Taylor said.

Chapter 28

The following morning, everyone packed their river bags and was getting ready for a new day on the river. It was going to be another hot day. At only seven o'clock, Jessie could feel the sweat soil the back of her sleeveless tee shirt. As she carried her river bags back to the community area, she heard a familiar voice from behind her.

"Good morning," Travis said.

But Jessie knew from the tone of his voice that he was not pleased to see her. Jessie returned the cool greeting, "Morning, Travis."

Travis moved closer to Jessie then whispered, "You've got a lot of nerve coming here."

Jessie stared back into his dark eyes. "I guess that makes two of us."

"What is that supposed to mean?"

"I've got your number, Travis."

"Meaning?" He leaned over her.

"I know about Stacy."

"Stacy who?"

There was a trace of nervousness in his voice. Jessie smiled at his unease, turned and continued her trek toward the rafts.

"Don't you turn and walk away from me." Travis's voice escalated.

Jessie dropped the river bags to the ground, then walked back to Travis. "Travis, you're going to draw attention to yourself with that temper of yours." Jessie looked into his eyes and without flinching said, "Hopkins, Stacy Hopkins. I know about Stacy . . . and about Kurk."

Travis glared back at Jessie. He removed a kerchief from a pants pocket, and nervously wiped perspiration from his goatee. "You're going to regret the day you came on this trip, Jessie." Travis turned and walked away.

Wow. I was going for a single and I think I got a home run.

* * *

The morning went by fast. Jessie couldn't take her mind off Travis as she maneuvered the river with her crew. Now, she was determined to prove that Travis was Kurk's killer. It unnerved her that Taylor was in the same raft as Travis.

In the morning, the group hiked up 19-Mile Canyon. The afternoon offered plenty of white-water excitement through the Roaring 20s, then the group set up camp at Mile Marker 41 for another evening. Jessie continued to watch Taylor from a distance; occasionally the two would make eye contact, yet Taylor would divert her eyes and continue her business. Both Travis and Mark remained protective of Taylor and helped her avoid Jessie.

It was the third day of the rafting trip, and the group broke for a hike up Saddle Canyon. The majority of the group had left for the hike, but Jessie remained at the beach where Justine and another guide started to set up the lunch table for when the group returned. Jessie took a granola bar from her fanny pack and found a shaded area near the rafts. Justine sat next to Jessie.

"Are you having a good trip, Alison?"

Jessie was unaware of Justine.

"Alison?" she repeated.

"I'm sorry Justine, did you say something?"

"Yeah. I was just wondering if you were having a good trip"

"It's fine, Justine. I'm sorry. I just have a lot on my mind."

"I understand."

Justine was aware that Jessie had not bonded with other members of the trip. She knew how unusual this was.

About twenty minutes later, Ron, another guide who was running an equipment raft, returned to the beach. "Justine, there's been an accident."

Justine immediately stood. "What happened?"

"Someone fell from the trail. He hurt his leg."

Justine quickly went to her raft and removed a first-aid kit from a community bag. Ron showed Justine the way and Jessie followed them up the steep trail. After a brisk climb, Ron finally stopped on the narrow trail and pointed down. About twenty feet below, a man was on the ground. Two other people stood next to him.

Justine quickly took control of the situation. "Ron, continue up the trail and get Ted." Justine and Jessie scouted the easiest route to get to the injured man and started their descent. Within minutes, they reached him.

Jessie recognized him; he was a member of Taylor's crew. His leg was badly twisted with bone protruding and blood oozing all over the leg. His wife and teenage son were with him and very upset.

"What happened Henry?" Justine asked calmly.

He pointed up the incline to the trail. "I was walking on the trail, twisted my ankle and fell down here."

"Now, that doesn't sound like fun," Justine smiled at him. "Henry, we're going to clean and dress your leg then splint it, okay?" Justine pointed at the first-aid kit by Jessie. "Would you help, Alison? I need some gauze and antiseptic."

Jessie removed the ointment and gauze and handed the antiseptic to Justine. Justine carefully applied the medicine then took the gauze from Jessie. As she dressed the wound, she spoke candidly with the couple. "Well, isn't this enough to ruin a vacation," Justine said.

The man tried to smile. "I'm sorry, sweetheart," he said to his wife.

As Justine and Jessie finished splinting the man's leg, Ted came from the trail above. With him came Travis and Taylor. The three of them carefully descended the steep incline. When Taylor saw the man on the ground she went to his side. "Henry, what happened?"

The man smiled at Taylor. "Oh, I just have a little scrape."

Ted went to Justine. "How bad is it?"

"Compound fracture. He's going to need an airlift," Justine said. "The radio is in my raft. You have the satellite phone, right?"

"Yeah. It's in my raft," Ted answered. "I'll make my way down there and try to establish communications with the outside."

"Do you need a satellite phone?" Taylor asked.

"We have one in the raft," Ted said.

"I have one right here," Mark called from the trail above. He had over-heard part of the conversation and was studying Henry Clements lying on the rock in pain. "What's going on?"

"We need an emergency air evacuation." Ted said. "You have a phone with you? Can we use it?"

"Yes." Mark carefully made his way off the trail to the small group and turned his fanny pack around so that it rested on his stomach. He opened the bag. From inside the neatly packed bag he pulled out a plastic bag con-taining allergy medications, then his phone.

Ted took the phone and dialed his office phone number. He walked away from the growing group that had gathered around the Clements. Mark followed Ted. "The reception is not good enough," Ted said.

"What?"

"These satellite phones work about 90 percent of the time in the can-yon. We just need to keep trying. Let's make our way down to the river, in case we don't get a signal. Then we'll at least have the radio."

The men climbed up to the trail, then Ted attempted to call out, but there was still no reception. They continued their descent and were about fifty yards downhill when Ted stopped. "I have a signal." He punched in the familiar number then waited. "Hi, Pat. It's Ted . . . yeah. We have an emergency, Pat. We need an air evacuation. It's for Henry Clements. He's in his mid-to-late fifties. He has a compound fracture of the tibia. His leg is splinted, but he'll need a lift. We're at the Saddle Canyon Trail, Mile Marker 47. We're about a mile up the trail."

Ted finished his phone call then handed the phone back to Mark. "Thanks, Mark. That just saved us quite a bit of time."

"You're welcome." Mark turned the phone back on. "I'm going to call my office." He turned, then continued his hike down the trail.

Minutes later, Mark was on the phone with Detective Bradley of the LAPD.

"Hi, Detective Bradley. This is Mark Rutledge, Taylor Andrews' personal manager."

"Hi, Mr. Rutledge. How can I help you?"

"Well, I was wondering if you happened to know where Jessica Mercer was."

"Why are you asking?"

"Well, I know she's a suspect in the Kurk Warner murder. Just wondering how good the LAPD was doing keeping tabs on her."

"How come I sense you know more than you're telling me, Mr. Rutledge?"

Mark hesitated. "I'm on a five-day rafting trip in the Grand Canyon with Taylor Andrews and Travis Sanders, and Jessie Mercer is with us."

"She's with you? Along with Travis Sanders?"

"That's correct. Are you going to come and get her?"

"Has she threatened anyone there?"

"No. She's talked with Taylor. From what I understand, she maintains that she's innocent."

"And she may very well be, Mr. Rutledge. Jessie Mercer is a pretty sharp lady. I have a hard time believing, if she were the harasser, that she would use her own stationery to write the harassment notes."

"So she's not a suspect anymore?"

"No, I didn't say that. It certainly doesn't look good that she's skipped town. We learned she was missing yesterday morning, but we weren't sure where she was. What's the name of the rafting company you're with?"

"It's Grand Canyon White Water."

"Thank you for the call, Mr. Rutledge."

"Is that it?"

"Mr. Rutledge, it's embarrassing that she's slipped through our fingers. It's going to be hard to justify the expense of going to Arizona to pick her up. I'll alert the local authorities to what's going on. Call me if she appears to become a threat to anyone there."

As Bradley rested the phone in the cradle, Detective Roth entered his office. "What's up?" he asked.

"I just got the autopsy report on Stacey Hopkins," she said. "You may want to see this."

Ted knew that it would be some time before a helicopter would evacuate Henry Clements. As the senior guide, he decided to split up the group. After lunch was served, Ted and Justine's group would remain with the Clements until they were safely evacuated. The other two groups, along with the oar rafts, would get back on the river without delay. The groups planned to meet up at the campsite later that evening.

About an hour after the first set of rafts left, the helicopter arrived. The evacuation took about forty-five minutes. Finally, all three Clements left the area, prematurely ending their vacation.

On the way back to the rafts, Ted approached Justine. "I'm three people short. Can you get a volunteer from your group to finish the trip with me? Tomorrow, I'll ask for another volunteer from one of the other rafts."

"Yeah. I'll ask Alison. She's solo; the others are part of a group," Justine said.

Jessie was one of the first to make it back to the river after waiting in the hot afternoon sun. It was over 110 degrees and she needed to cool off. Once she reached the beach, she climbed into a raft, walked to the rear and stood on top of the outside tube overlooking the cold deep water. A quick bend to her knees provided her with enough spring to plunge head first into the Colorado River. Jessie gasped when she came to the surface, shocked by the sixty-degree drop in temperature.

Others watched as Jessie swam back to the beach. When they saw that she survived the cold water, many followed her lead and jumped into the water.

Jessie climbed onto the beach, then found a rock in the shade to sit on while others enjoyed the water.

"Hi, Alison. Feel better?" Justine asked.

"Yes. The heat was starting to get to me."

"We have a favor to ask. Would you mind riding the rest of the way in Ted's raft?"

"You want me to ride with Ted?"

"Without the Clements, they're three people short. We need to do a little shifting. I thought I'd ask you, since you're solo."

"That's fine Justine. Wherever you need me." *This is strange how it's worked out.*

When Justine and Jessie returned to the rafts, everyone was getting ready to go. Jessie retrieved her lifejacket, put it on, then went to Ted.

"Hi, Alison. Are you going to be joining us?"

Jessie could feel Taylor, Mark and Travis staring at her. "If that's where you need me."

Ted turned to the three remaining crew members. "Alison is going to join our group for the rest of the trip. Does everyone know each other?"

Jessie's eyes scanned Mark, Travis, then Taylor. "Yes. We know each other," Jessie said.

Ted reassigned positions in the raft. "Mark and Travis, you guys stay in front where you've been. Taylor and Alison take the middle section, and I'll take the rear."

There was little conversation among the group that afternoon, and it was after six o'clock when the two rafts arrived at the campsite.

After the long day in the hot sun, Jessie wanted to find a quiet area of the river and wash up. While everyone else had dinner, Jessie set out with clean clothes, a towel, shampoo and a bar of soap. It didn't take long for her to pick a spot. Quickly, she removed her clothes except for her Tevas. Wasting no time, she walked out into the cold water and bathed.

Taylor stood by a large rock that contributed to the privacy of the area. When she saw Jessie in the water, she could not help but watch her. Taylor admired Jessie as she strolled to the shore and reached for the towel on the beach.

As Jessie dried herself, she saw something move in her peripheral vision. It was then that Jessie noticed Taylor staring at her. Taylor was carrying a toiletry bag, clothes and a towel.

Jessie continued to dry herself, then dropped her towel and put on her clothes. Once dressed, she strolled to where Taylor stood watching her. The women's eyes met momentarily, but both remained silent.

Jessie started to walk away, then turned back. "You *are* going to let me know when you're ready to talk. Right?"

Taylor nodded. "I will. I promise."

Back at the campsite, Justine handed Jessie a dinner plate. "Here, I know you said you were skipping dinner for a bath, but I thought you'd be hungry later."

"Thanks, Justine. That was sweet."

"You're welcome. Well, I've got to get back to cleaning up."

Later that night, Jessie didn't think she'd have problems sleeping because she was exhausted. But as she lay alone under the stars, her mind would not rest. She was glad that she had changed rafts; she could keep a better eye on Taylor. The comment from Travis still blew her away. *I can't believe he threatened me like he did.*

Jessie continued to toss and turn on top of her sleeping bag. She stared at the moon that illuminated the sky. Occasionally she would see the silhouettes of the tiny bats that remained restless into the night. The roar from the river only feet away from her seemed louder than usual. Then the wind picked up, blasting the sand all around her. As quickly as the sandstorm started, it ended.

It was close to midnight when Jessie gave up on sleep. She sat up, shaking the sand from her face and hair. Then she crawled to the bottom of the sleeping bag searching for her sandals. Jessie could feel her biceps ache from the three days of paddling, and as she sat, she could feel the boater's rash on her extremity. A beam of light from the community tarp area caught her attention. *I guess I'm not the only one that can't sleep.* Jessie reached for her flashlight, stood, and went to the gathering area. When she realized it was Mark that was still up, she hesitated, and then strolled to the area.

Mark looked up at Jessie. He didn't seem surprised to see her.

"May I sit?" Jessie asked.

Mark was coughing, but he nodded yes.

"Are you getting a cold?" Jessie asked, as she sat on the sandy tarp.

Mark shook his head. "Just my allergies," he said.

She rested her back against a pile of lifejackets until she caught wind of the body odor seeping from the jackets. Then she moved and rested her back against some river bags.

"That's better," she said.

Mark remained silent, and after a couple minutes, Jessie broke down. "I didn't do it, Mark. I didn't kill Kurk."

Mark looked at Jessie. "I believe you."

"You do?"

Mark nodded. "Yes. You're no killer."

The silence thickened before Jessie spoke again. "You're in love with her, aren't you? And my presence here is pissing you off."

Mark laughed. "That's what I've always loved about you, Jessie. You say it the way you see it." He paused. "I do care for Taylor, more so than I should. But . . . I know she's still in love with you."

"She is? Has she said so?" For a moment, Jessie realized how childish she must have sounded. But she didn't care.

"No. It's just what I sense."

"I hope we can get through this."

"If it's meant to be, Jessie, it'll work out."

Jessie smiled. "I hope we can still be friends, Mark."

"Of course we can still be friends." Then he laughed.

"What's so funny?"

"I keep wondering why I fall in love with women who love women."

Jessie laughed, too. She could see the sparkle of the moonlight in Mark's eyes. "You really are a good sport, Mark."

He smiled showing his perfect teeth and charming grin. Then he picked up a box of wine that sat beside him and refilled a plastic cup. "It's cabernet. Would you like some?"

"Do you have an extra cup?"

"Of course. I'm always ready for meeting pretty ladies that can't sleep." Mark poured another cup of wine and handed the cup to Jessie.

"Cheers," she said as she raised her cup.

"Cheers."

Jessie took a sip of her wine. "Mark, can I run something by you?"

"Sure."

"It's about Travis."

"What about him?"

Jessie hesitated.

"What about him, Jessie?"

"Have you ever heard the name Stacy Hopkins?"

"No. It doesn't ring a bell, who is she?"

"She was a young actress who worked on the movie *Aces* about six years back."

"Oh, is she the one who had a drug overdose?"

"That's her."

"What about her?"

"Well, I understand she was very taken with Travis."

"That wouldn't surprise me. From what I understand, there are a number of young ladies who have been taken with him."

"*Aces* was the first film that Kurk Warner worked on with Travis."

"Okay."

"What would you think if, shortly after Stacy died, Travis started taking significant cash withdrawals against his paychecks?"

"I don't know. It could mean a number of things."

"Like gambling?"

"Sure."

"What would you think if you learned that Kurk Warner made some pretty substantial cash *deposits* after Stacy died?"

Mark stared back at Jessie. "Is this fact or fiction?"

"Fact."

"It's getting more interesting," Mark said.

"Did you know that Kurk Warner played the leading man in every one of Travis's pictures after Stacy died?"

"It's no secret that Travis made Kurk Warner," Mark agreed.

"It's also no secret that the two didn't like each other, either. What would you think if Travis stopped making these cash withdrawals after Kurk Warner died?"

"You think Kurk Warner was blackmailing Travis?"

"Is that what you would conclude?"

Mark leaned forward looking intently into Jessie's eyes. "Yeah. But why?"

"I don't know. Stacy was under age; could that have been it?"

"Maybe he was being blackmailed regarding the circumstances of her death."

"Maybe. I guess it's just speculation," Jessie admitted. "You know, come to think about it–the night Kurk died, Travis pulled Kurk away from the party for a few minutes. Travis wanted to talk with Kurk. And Kurk said he would only give him five minutes of his time."

"My God, Jessie, do you think he did it? Do you think *Travis* killed Kurk?" whispered Mark.

"I don't know, Mark. When I saw him Monday morning I said something to him to feel him out."

"What did you say?"

"I told him that I knew about Stacy and Kurk."

"And what did he say?"

"He told me I was going to regret the day I came on this trip."

"That sounds like a threat, Jessie. You better be careful."

"I am. Would you do me a favor, Mark?"

"What's that?"

"Would you help me keep an *eye* on Taylor? I don't trust him, and I have a bad feeling about this trip."

Mark drained the last of the wine from his glass. Then he turned to Jessie and hugged her. "Thank you for sharing everything with me, Jessie." Gently, he kissed Jessie's forehead. "Don't worry."

Chapter 29

The following morning, Jessie waited patiently outside of Taylor's tent. When she heard Taylor's familiar stir she went to the coffee decanter, poured a fresh cup of coffee, and prepared it the way Taylor liked it. Then she returned to Taylor's tent.

"Knock, knock," Jessie said.

There was a pause, then a stir and the tent canvas opened. Taylor's eyes squinted from the brightness. Her long dark hair enveloped her face. "Jessie?" Her voice was huskier than usual.

"Yeah. It's me. I just brought you a cup of coffee. I know you don't like breathing in the morning without coffee."

Taylor reached for the cup. "Thank you."

"You're welcome." Jessie stood and walked away.

That morning Ted found another volunteer to fill one of the vacant seats in his raft. Bill was single, in his mid-thirties, and jumped at the opportunity to be in the same raft as Taylor. The day started off with mild rapids, and then the group took a break where the Little Colorado River merged with the Colorado River.

Taylor was amazed at how beautiful the Little Colorado was. The contrast between the blue water, pink eroded rocks and beach sand, with erupting red canyon walls was breathtaking. The smaller river was warmer than the primary river and the pinkish-white sand on the bottom reflected the blue sky, creating a distinct turquoise river.

With the exception of Jessie, everyone removed their lifejackets and put them on upside down, with legs through the arm slots. The diaper-fitted lifejackets offered protection from the rocks while body surfing the smaller rapids.

Jessie removed her lifejacket and sat in the only shaded area, up against a rock face. She watched everyone play like children in the water, and she observed Taylor laughing and enjoying herself. Feet first, Taylor rode the rapids downstream a couple hundred feet, and then got out and walked back upstream. Jessie could feel her pulse race when she watched Travis and Taylor join together, form a train, and ride the rapids. The thought of Travis attached to Taylor unsettled Jessie.

After a few rides, Taylor retreated to the shaded area where she had left her fanny pack and water bottle. She was only a few feet away from where Jessie sat. Taylor picked up her water bottle and took a drink. "You should take a ride. It's fun," Taylor said to Jessie. She removed her lifejacket and placed it near Jessie's. Then she removed a brush from her fanny pack and started to stroke her hair.

"It looks like fun," Jessie admitted. Jessie was amazed at how awkward she felt talking to Taylor. She kept hoping that Taylor would talk to her about the issues. But she did not.

The group broke for lunch at a small rocky beach. They frequently heard rattling from snakes, which discouraged most from exploring the area. Jessie had wandered down the river not more than fifty feet when she found a cluster of small quartz stones on the ground. She followed the trail of stones until she reached the quartz vein. Movement from the corner of her eye caught her attention. At first, she thought the yellow-backed lizard was a snake and it startled her.

"You scared me," she admitted to the lizard. The reptile stood still, more startled than Jessie. She watched the lizard, perched on a larger crystal jutting from the mother vein. Even when Jessie inched closer to view the large lizard, it remained still, waiting patiently for Jessie to move away. Eventually the lizard bolted, leaving its crystal throne. Jessie reached for the long crystal that protruded from the vein. But as she felt the stone, she was surprised at how loose it was, and with little effort, the crystalline piece separated from the vein.

Jessie stared at the large crystal in her hand. It must have been four inches long with a defined pointed end. "It's beautiful," Jessie whispered. Jessie felt guilty that such a beautiful piece had separated from its home. She could feel the energy from the crystal in her hand. Jessie debated on whether she should leave the stone at the vein, then decided to take it when she realized that if she didn't–someone else would. She placed the prized possession in her shorts pocket. *What a wonderful souvenir.*

After lunch was served, Ted gave a safety talk. The pace of the rapids would change dramatically after lunch and Ted wanted to make sure everyone was prepared. Up until this point of the trip, none of the rapids delivered the power and punch that Hance or Sockdolager was capable of.

"I want to spend a little time discussing the rapids we're going to hit this afternoon. The temper of the river changes from here on. So, I know you've heard this before, but if anyone is ejected and you're separated from the raft, keep your legs up and point them downstream. And remember, if someone falls out of the raft, pull them out of the river by picking up the lifejacket shoulders." Ted illustrated the proper way to pull someone out of the river.

"And everyone tighten your lifejackets. They've probably loosened up along the way. Take some extra time and really tighten them up."

"Is it that difficult?" Mark asked.

"Once we get into the inner gorge, we're going to hit some 9s and 10s and even some no-name rapids that will give us a challenging ride. They're not impossible. It's just important that each raft works as a team. Up until this point, we've been playing, and practicing, now we're going to be tested."

After lunch, the groups returned to their rafts, eager to master Hance and Sockdolager.

"So do you really think it's going to be that bad?" Taylor asked Mark and Travis as she grabbed her lifejacket.

"No. It's going to be fine," Mark said.

Travis helped Taylor tighten her jacket. Jessie noticed the smirk on Travis's face as Jessie put on her lifejacket.

Soon all the rafts were heading downstream. Almost immediately, the river changed. Ted's raft tailed, and his group watched the other rafts leave the safety of the calmer water and delve into the rapids of Unkar. Violent waves quickly swallowed the rafts. The rapid ran alongside the tall canyon walls, which contributed to its fierceness. The other groups maneuvered the rapids for almost a half-mile. Then the canyon walls abruptly turned and funneled the water toward another series of rapids. With the success of the other groups, the crew's confidence grew.

"We're up," Ted said. "Relax everyone, this is going to be fun."

The small raft followed the other rafts into Unkar. With the first sight of big white water, the group was anxious, and forgot how to perform as a team. The paddlers responded to the surge of adrenaline by randomly paddling and forgetting their lead person. With lots of luck, the raft managed to escape the huge waves of Unkar, unscathed.

"What the hell was that?" Ted yelled after they were safely past Unkar. "You've been paddling for four days, you should be working as a team." Ted was visibly upset. "We have to work together or we won't make it through Hance."

All the crew members felt like children being scolded for doing something wrong. It was Taylor who spoke on their behalf. "Well, why don't we analyze what went wrong, and let's practice before we get to the next rapid."

The group practiced their turns over the next mile, rebuilding shattered confidence. Then they took Nevills, Hance, Son of Hance and Sockdolager without a flaw. Although the waves were huge, the group stayed together and, after conquering each rapid, the crew ceremoniously raised their paddles, clapping them high above their heads.

The thrill of their victory was contagious. Jessie's and Taylor's eyes met following the paddle clap after Sockdolager, and they could not help smiling at each other. It was Taylor who finally averted her eyes.

"Was that it?" Bill asked Ted. "Was that the last of the big rapids?"

"We still have some good-size rapids coming up," Ted said. "They won't have the punch that those had, though."

It had been a long day. It was close to four o'clock, eleven hours after their morning coffee. Ted knew everyone was tired and drained, but they had another forty-five minutes on the river before they would reach the campsite.

As the small raft made its way down the river, Ted studied the upcoming rapid. He watched all the other rafts in front of him ride the waves. The rapids appeared larger than they usually did in this section. "Forward, please."

The crew acknowledged Ted's command; everyone followed Travis's lead. The raft maneuvered to the right side of the river, close to the canyon wall. An intense current pulled the raft downstream, toward a huge breaking wave.

"Forward hard," Ted yelled.

The crew responded, increasing their effort to hit the first wave head on. As the nose of the raft rose, the wave broke, and white water covered Travis and Mark.

"Left back," Ted yelled. His voice was hard to hear over the roar of the river. Travis, Jessie and Ted on the right side of the raft provided forward strokes while Mark, Taylor and Bill backstroked.

The raft responded nicely, correcting its position. "Stop," Ted yelled. "Forward hard." Again, the crew headed toward another huge wave that was breaking above their heads. The crew members' adrenaline rushed. Jessie placed her left foot securely beneath the tube in front of her, enabling her to lean over the side of the raft to paddle. Her foot had become raw over the four days from the continued abrasion, but now in survival mode, she did not notice the pain. White water surrounded the crew as the wave broke over them. The raft twisted violently and thrashed in the mighty current. As expected, the force put a spin on the raft as it was sucked downstream toward another wave.

"Stop." To counter the spin, Ted yelled, "Right back."

Those on the left side paddled forward while Travis, Jessie and Ted backstroked.

The spinning of the raft slowed. "Stop," Ted yelled. He studied the position of the raft and its spin, estimating the raft would hit the rapid on the left side. "Right back," Ted called. But either Ted's voice was drowned in the roar of the rapids or there was too much confusion, as Travis paddled forward.

The raft didn't turn enough. "Right back, hard," Ted screamed. It was too late.

The raft hit the rapids on the left side and Bill, Taylor and Mark were swallowed. When the raft struggled to the surface Mark and Ted remained, but Taylor was gone. Ted assessed the raft's position. "Left back." But Jessie left her station to search for Taylor.

Raging white water surrounded them. The raft bounced uncontrollably. Jessie's adrenaline rushed as she searched for signs of Taylor. At first, she didn't see Taylor's hand clutching the rope on the side of the raft. Taylor continued to be sucked down, her head hidden in the white water.

Catching a glimpse of Taylor's hand, Jessie grabbed it. She found the lifejacket shoulders. With one foot planted firmly, she pulled the lifejacket with all her strength. As Jessie lifted Taylor one of the shoulder seams crumbled. Taylor plunged back into the river, but Jessie held firmly onto the other shoulder.

Jessie didn't understand how, but the lifejacket was being torn from Taylor's back. She grabbed Taylor's hand and pulled. Jessie would never forget the fear she saw in Taylor's eyes when Taylor's body jerked harshly. And then the lifejacket was gone.

"Alison, let her go. We need you at your station," Ted yelled. The raft was out of control.

"She doesn't have a lifejacket," Jessie screamed.

"Shit. High side," Ted ordered.

The raft started to rise on Jessie's side. Jessie gripped Taylor's hand firmly. As the men climbed to the *high side* of the raft, Jessie felt a sharp pain on her arm.

Even with the additional weight from the *high side* command, it was too late. The raft lifted up and capsized, but Jessie would not let Taylor go. She fell into the water beside Taylor.

Jessie tried to latch onto Taylor, but the raging water continued to pull Taylor under. She struggled to pull Taylor to her, until finally, Taylor's back was up against Jessie's breast. Taylor gasped as Jessie kept Taylor's head above water. With the one lifejacket between them, they were barely able to stay afloat, but continued downstream, feet first. Jessie prayed that they wouldn't hit a hole. It would have made their escape impossible.

Taylor could see a calm eddy ahead on the left side and a keeper hole on the right. Mark and Travis were standing waist deep in the eddy waiting for them. But there was no sign of Ted or Bill.

Taylor turned her face. "There's a calm on . . . the left side," she yelled between mouthfuls of water. "There's a hole to the right." The current took the women toward the calm water, and Mark and Travis pulled them to safety.

Mark took Taylor and helped her to the beach. Taylor was shaken. She coughed all the way to the rocky shore.

Jessie turned to Travis. "Where are Ted and Bill?" She could hear riffles ten feet from them.

Travis pointed up stream. Ted and Bill were guiding the capsized raft down the rapids. "They're going to need help getting that raft off the river before it gets stuck in the hole."

"You're right," Jessie agreed.

Travis and Jessie swam as far as they could without getting taken by the current. They knew they had only seconds to get the raft off the river before the current would take it out of their reach. When the raft met the calm water, they all worked quickly and calmly. The capsized raft was pushed and pulled to the rocky shore where Mark and Taylor stood.

"I want to flip it," Ted said.

Mark, Bill and Travis helped Ted flip the raft. Everyone sighed when they saw the community river bags still strapped in place.

"Shit," Ted said. "I was hoping some of the paddles stayed with the raft." Ted walked away from the raft and sat on a rock.

The others followed his lead, removed their lifejackets, and sat. As Jessie removed her jacket, she tried to look at the back of her sore arm. Taylor had been watching Jessie, without saying a word; she walked behind her to see her arm.

"When did this happen?" Taylor asked. "You've got a nasty cut." Her eyes easily met Jessie's for the first time during the trip.

"In the raft, before it capsized. It must have been from a paddle." Jessie tried to see it but it was at a bad angle. "How bad is it?"

"You need stitches."

"I'd settle for a Band-Aid."

Taylor went to the raft and opened the rear common bag. She searched among the contents for the first-aid kit. As she removed the kit, she noticed the raft walls on one side were not as firm as they usually were.

"Who's hurt?" Ted noticed the first-aid kit in Taylor's hands.

"Jessie's arm is cut pretty bad," Taylor said.

"Who's Jessie?" Ted asked.

"I'm sorry. Alison's arm is cut." Taylor didn't want to explain.

Mark and Travis watched as Taylor returned to Jessie, who was now sitting up against a granite wall. Taylor sat next to Jessie and opened the first-aid box. She removed a tube and applied ointment to the wound.

"Does it hurt?"

"Not too bad."

Taylor placed three large gauze pads on the wound; blood quickly soaked through the first two. "Thank you," Taylor whispered softly. "I owe you my life."

Jessie shook her head. "No, you don't owe me anything, Taylor."

Taylor finished dressing Jessie's wound then returned the first-aid kit to the raft. Now, one section of the raft wall was clearly less firm than another section. "Ted, the raft seems to be softening. I think we have a leak."

Ted went to the raft and inspected it. "Yeah. Looks like a slow leak." Ted took his frustration out on Taylor. "Why the hell weren't you wearing your lifejacket?"

"I had it on. It just fell apart around me when I was in the water."

Ted looked at Taylor. "That's impossible."

"That's actually what happened," Jessie attested.

"Must be a manufacturer defect," Travis said.

"Or maybe you just didn't have it buckled. I guess it doesn't do us any good to bitch about it now. Okay, we've got to make some decisions." Ted looked around at the surrounding area. It was small and there were lots of large boulders and shrubs. "We can't go anyplace without paddles. And we need to isolate where the leak is, patch it and blow it up. We have a patch kit and a hand pump."

"How are we going to get paddles?" Bill asked.

"Most likely they are downstream, right?" Mark said.

"You're right. And hopefully the other groups have a couple of them and are waiting for us." Ted looked down the river. They could see just shy of a mile, but the other rafts were nowhere in site.

"Do you think they're waiting for us?" Travis asked.

"There's a good chance the other rafts are just around the corner." Ted glanced at his watch; it was going on 4:30. "I suggest that we split up. One group hikes down the river and is prepared to hike back with some essentials, like food and sleeping bags and hopefully some paddles. The other group stays here and works on the raft. There's a small camp area that's right above Grapevine Rapids, that's where we spilled. It's not even a half-mile up. After the raft is fixed, the three bags and water bottles should be taken up to the camp area. We need to be prepared to stay the night, and we certainly can't do it here. Does anyone have any questions? Objections? Perhaps, better ideas?"

"Is there any way to call the other groups, to guarantee that they're not miles down the river?" Travis asked. "Mark has a satellite phone."

"I do, too," Ted said. "But none of the other groups do. They have a radio. Ted pointed to the tall granite walls that lined the canyon. "But now that we're in the inner gorge, the radio is pretty useless."

"What are the chances of patching the raft, getting some paddles and still making it to the camp with the rest of the group?" Taylor asked.

"Not very good. If the other rafts are right around the corner, we're going to need a minimum of two to three hours to get there and get back. It'll be too late; at eight o'clock, the canyon is dark."

"Well then, we better get moving, we're wasting time," Travis said.

"So, let's split up. Let's have two stay and three others come with me."

Mark and Taylor agreed to stay at the raft and move the bags to the camp area, while Travis, Bill, Jessie and Ted headed down the river.

Ted's group followed the riverbank downstream. Travel was slow. The shoulders of the river were narrow with large boulders, making the hike challenging. At times the group needed to hop in and out of the river to make their way downstream. Then the shoulder disappeared and they were unable to follow the river.

"We're going to have to go up," Ted said as he headed into an inner canyon.

The group hiked up a steep inner canyon. Tall granite walls lined the trail, until the trail reached a plateau. Rather than continuing up the trail, Ted directed everyone to the right, so they followed the river from three hundred feet above. Everyone paused momentarily, admiring the canyon view. To their right was a steep precipice, falling to the river below. To the left, the tall canyon walls rose behind an abyss. For the most part, the plateau was flat with occasional irregularities, either jutting rock formations that restricted their view or cliffs that fell to chasms below.

They weren't on top very long when they heard voices ahead of them. From around a rock came Justine and a couple of others.

Ted smiled at his coworker. "It's nice to see you. We had a bad spill. But everyone is okay."

Justine immediately noticed the bloody gauze on Jessie's upper arm. "How bad is it?" she asked Jessie.

"It's okay."

"No one else is hurt?" Justine asked.

"A few bumps and bruises but we're fine. But we've lost all our paddles," Ted said. "And we have a leak. Mark and Taylor are trying to patch it now."

"We found three paddles."

"Well, that's a start."

"Let's get back to my group. We'll give you what you need to get you down the river," Justine said.

At the raft, Taylor and Mark had found the leak and patched it. As Mark pumped additional air into the raft, Taylor rummaged through the common bags. From each common bag, she removed a waterproof dry bag. There were also fanny packs, a first-aid kit and articles of clothing that were not in the dry bags.

Once she had everything lined-up on the rocks, Taylor repacked the dry bags. She was having difficulty closing the last of the three dry bags. An object was restricting her from sealing the bag. She opened the bag to rearrange the contents. It was a box that prevented the bag from sealing. Taylor repositioned a box marked "Flare" to lie on top.

She pulled the large nylon net bag, containing water bottles, from the water into the raft. She unclamped the bag from the raft and removed the heavy bag to the shore.

* * *

Ted's group hiked a half-mile then went into another inner canyon, where they descended three hundred feet to reach the other rafts.

Justine glanced at her watch. "The only campsite downstream from here is four miles away. You're not going to be able to make it to the campsite tonight."

"Yeah, I know. I'm going to need some essentials to get through the night. We're planning on camping above Grapevine. There's a small camp area there. I'll plan on meeting you at Phantom Ranch in the morning."

"If you're going to Grapevine, when you hike back on the plateau, stay on it until you reach the second inner canyon. That'll take you along Grapevine Creek and bottom out at the campsite," Justine suggested.

Ted and his group loaded up. Food, essentials and bedding bags were packed among four daypacks. The extra bedding bags and paddles were divided up among the four to hand carry.

Before they left, Justine pulled Ted aside. "I have something I want to show you."

"What's that?"

"I found two other items on the river." Justine pulled two sections of what appeared to be a lifejacket. "Can you explain this?"

Ted examined the two pieces of the lifejacket. The outside appeared normal, but inside there was discoloration along the jacket seams. "My God. She wasn't lying."

"Who?"

"Taylor Andrews. She went over before the raft capsized. She said her jacket fell apart around her. I didn't believe her. I thought she was careless and didn't have it strapped."

"My God, Ted, she's lucky she's alive," Justine said. "Look at the seams. The thread is gone, and the material around the seams is discolored, like it was burned. This was obviously tampered with."

"You're right. Let me take these back to the camp. I want to ask the group about it."

"You better be careful."

"You too. You may want to do a lifejacket inspection before you get on the river."

Jessie noticed that Ted was quieter than usual on the way back. She didn't want Travis at her back so she kept to the rear of the line. The hike down to Grapevine Creek went smoothly, and as Justine had said, it brought them right into the small camp area. It was 6:45 when they arrived. Taylor and Mark had brought up the dry bags from the river and placed them together on the beach. The roar of Grapevine Rapids could be heard just downstream of the campsite.

"How's the raft?" Ted asked Mark.

"It's fine. We found the leak and patched it."

All the backpacks were placed near the dry bags. Ted opened a bag and pulled out some food. "We have some sandwich makings. Everyone help yourself. I'm going down to the raft before it gets dark."

"Do you want some company?" Bill asked.

Ted looked briefly at Bill. "Sure."

At the raft, Ted found a small patch by one of the seams. The section was still not as firm as the others. Ted opened the common bag in the rear of the raft. As expected, most of the possessions had been removed. Three lifejackets, used by Henry Clements and his family, remained. Ted was reminded of Henry's broken leg and his evacuation. He removed one of the lifejackets, then closed the bag. The other lifejackets were strapped together on the front of the raft. Ted unclamped the strap then started to remove them.

"What are you doing?" Bill asked.

Ted handed Bill a couple of lifejackets; he took the rest. "I just want the jackets closer to camp."

By the time Ted and Bill returned, a small tarp had been spread and everyone was sitting around eating sandwiches. Bill and Ted joined them. Daylight was quickly slipping away.

"Before we lose the light, let's find a sleeping spot," Ted suggested. "We have enough sleeping bags for everyone. It would have been too disruptive to the equipment raft to find all the sleeping bags we have been using. Some of your bags were right on top of the pile, so we grabbed them." Ted went to the pile of dry bags. All of them had names on them. "So, if you're one of those that does not have *your* bag, use the sleeping bag, but just ignore any personal possessions in the bag."

Bags marked "Taylor Andrews," "Mark Rutledge" and "Travis Sanders" were found, while everyone else took another bag. The sleeping bags and possessions from the raft were distributed.

"I want to have a meeting before we completely lose the light." Ted checked his watch. "Let's meet back here at 7:30."

Jessie took her fanny pack and a sleeping bag, and found a small area that provided privacy by large rocks and shrubs. She opened up the dry bag, pulled out a tarp and spread it on the sand. Jessie neatly placed the rest of her items on the tarp, and then went to the river to wash up.

When Jessie made it back to the community tarp, everyone was exchanging war stories about their day. Jessie sat quietly among the group. Occasionally her eyes met Taylor's, but Taylor would quickly avert hers.

Ted excused himself for a minute. When he returned he had a daypack and a bunch of lifejackets. He dropped the jackets where he had been sitting.

"What's up, Ted?" Travis asked.

"Justine pulled something from the water this afternoon that I found quite disturbing," Ted said.

"What did she find?" Taylor asked.

Ted pulled the two pieces of lifejacket from the daypack. "She found these. They're sections of Taylor's lifejacket. When Taylor said her jacket fell apart, I didn't believe her. I'm sorry, Taylor."

"That's okay, Ted. But how could something like that happen?"

Ted turned the lifejacket sections over for the others to see. "There's no thread holding the jacket sections in place and there's discoloration at the seams. I don't know how this could have happened, perhaps some type of acid. But I know it wasn't natural; this was sabotaged. Taylor, do you know why anyone on this trip would want to harm you?"

Taylor remained silent.

"Perhaps it was your secret admirer," Travis stated. "I.D. Isn't that the name, Jessie?"

Jessie glared back at Travis but remained silent.

"Why do they keep calling you Jessie? Isn't your name Alison?"

"No. I'm sorry, Ted. My name is Jessie Mercer."

"Why did you introduce yourself as Alison Townsend?"

"Go ahead, Jessie, tell him. I want to see you squirm out of this one," Travis teased.

"I used a friend's name so that I wouldn't bring attention to myself. You see . . . I'm a suspect in the murder of Kurk Warner. And I needed to come here to talk with Taylor."

"Kurk Warner . . . the movie star?" Ted asked.

"Yes."

"If I remember correctly, Kurk was Taylor's fiancé," Ted stated. "And everyone here knows you?"

"Except for Bill. Yes."

"How do you know everyone?"

"I don't think that's important," Jessie said.

"Fine," Ted said. "Taylor, do you know why anyone would want to harm you?"

"No. I really don't."

"Well, I brought up all of our jackets, including one of the extras, and I want each of us to look at the inside seams to make sure they're okay. Let's do this before it gets much darker."

Ted called out the numbers marked on the jackets, then handed them to the appropriate person. He had three jackets remaining in front of him. "This one's mine," Ted said. He picked up another, "This one is 209 and was used by one of the Clements." He handed the jacket to Taylor, "Why don't you plan on using this the rest of the trip."

Taylor took the lifejacket.

"And the last jacket is number 208," Ted said.

"Two-oh-eight?" Taylor and Jessie chorused.

"Yeah, 208."

Taylor and Jessie looked at each other.

"What's the problem?" Ted asked.

Taylor spoke. "Number 208 is my jacket."

The group looked around to see who did not have a jacket in front of them.

"And the plot thickens," Mark said when he saw that Jessie was the one that was missing a lifejacket.

"I must have grabbed your jacket by mistake at lunch break," Taylor said to Jessie.

It took a minute for Ted to understand the significance. "How about you, Jessie. Do you know anyone that would want to hurt you?"

Instinctively Jessie's eyes met Travis's. But she didn't say a word.

Travis's cold, dark eyes stared back at Jessie, his fingers casually tracing his goatee.

"Jessie, didn't Travis threaten you Monday?" Mark asked.

"Yes."

"What did he say?" Ted asked.

"He said I would regret the day I came on this trip." Jessie maintained eye contact with Travis.

"That sounds like a threat. Travis, why did you say that?" Ted asked.

But Travis remained silent, his eyes still on Jessie.

"Jessie, what's going on?" Ted asked.

"I told Travis Monday morning that I knew about Stacy Hopkins and Kurk Warner. And that's when he threatened me."

"What about Stacy Hopkins and Kurk?" Taylor asked.

"Kurk had been blackmailing Travis about Stacy's death," Mark said.

Jessie was surprised by Mark's aggression, but knew from Travis's reaction that Mark was correct. Travis didn't flinch.

"Kurk was blackmailing you, Travis?" Taylor asked.

Travis finally spoke. "I think we've all had enough entertainment at my expense." Small beads of perspiration broke out on his face.

"You did kill Stacy, didn't you?" Mark said.

"It was an accident. She overdosed."

"She was drinking and taking prescription drugs; phenobarbital for epilepsy. But you didn't know about the epilepsy or the phenobarbital, right Travis?" Jessie said.

Travis would not look at anyone.

"And you gave her methadone, which caused a fatal reaction with the alcohol and phenobarb. Did you know she was taking the phenobarb?" Jessie asked.

"It was Kurk's idea," Travis admitted. "We went to her place, the three of us agreed to have . . . a little fun."

"What do you mean by a little fun?" Taylor asked.

Travis looked up at Taylor. "You know the kind of group fun Kurk liked to have. But when we got there, she was nervous, so I gave her something to relax. The three of us started . . . and she started getting sick and seizing and . . ." Travis seemed to have trouble breathing. He pulled out a handkerchief and wiped sweat from his forehead and neck.

"So she died, and Kurk blackmailed you because you gave her the drugs," Jessie surmised.

"And because . . . she was underage," Travis admitted. "So for almost five years, that asshole bled me dry." Travis's voice rose. "I almost went bankrupt because of him. Every movie I worked on, he had to be the leading man. Except *Deceptions*. Since there was no leading man, he demanded that Taylor get the role. I was sick of having him in my face."

"Was that what you argued about the night Kurk was murdered?" Mark asked.

"I told him I had nothing more to give him. I was going broke and I couldn't work with him anymore." Travis started to rub his arm.

"So you murdered him," Mark said.

"Everybody is better off without that—" Travis clutched at his chest and grimaced. His eyes rolled back in his head and he slumped over.

"Oh my God. He's having a heart attack," Jessie said.

Ted went to him and felt his pulse. "It's weak."

Taylor knelt next to Travis. "What are we going to do?"

"We need to get help." Ted initiated CPR on Travis.

"How?" Jessie asked.

"Let me try my phone." Mark pulled his satellite phone from his fanny pack and called 911, but the signal was too low. "I can't get a signal."

"Walk away from the campsite, and keep trying till you get a signal," Ted said as he compressed Travis's chest.

"That's a good idea. Ted, you have a satellite phone, too, don't you?" Jessie asked.

"It's in my bag, over there," Ted nodded his head.

"I'll get yours and head in a different direction." Jessie went to Ted's bag and removed his phone. She watched Mark head up toward Grapevine creek, and then she turned toward the river, into the darkness.

Bill sat next to Ted. "What can I do to help?"

"We can rotate. Here, watch my hands and the pace I'm doing. Why don't you take over for five minutes." The men switched.

Taylor stood feeling helpless. "What can I do?"

Ted thought briefly. "Why don't you try to collect driftwood? If there's any chance of having an evacuation, we may need a visual aid. We have only one flare. A fire would be a good backup."

"Okay." Taylor went off into the darkness, down near the water. After stumbling a couple of times, she realized she needed a flashlight. *My flashlight is with my sleeping bag.*

Taylor dumped the first load of driftwood near where Bill and Ted were working on Travis.

Where's my bag? Taylor looked around the campsite. An hour earlier, when there was daylight, the camp looked different. Now, she felt displaced.

Then she recognized the unique boulder. *I put it over there.* She found the dry bag on the backside of the boulder, and sat, resting her back up against the rock. The boulder temporarily shielded her from the situation. The only light source was from the moon. Taylor opened her dry bag and reached in, groping for the slim flashlight she knew she had left in the bag that morning.

Taylor could feel something slim, tangled within the sheet. *Here it is.* She pulled the linen from the bag, and the object fell from the cloth onto her lap.

Taylor's heart skipped a beat when she picked up the wooden ankh. She traced the wood grain with her fingers, recalling the day Jessie had given her the precious piece. She turned it over and continued to follow the natural course of the wood until she found the irregular indentations in the back. With a finger, she unconsciously traced the grooves over and over until she realized how familiar the pattern was. It felt so natural to her. *What is it?*

Taylor held the ankh up to the sky so the moonlight fell upon it. She could see the pattern she had traced so naturally with her finger. Her heart fluttered when Taylor recognized the initials "*RJ*" freshly carved in the back of the ankh. Stunned, Taylor closed her eyes then opened them again, but this time the initials were noticeably aged.

Calmly, Taylor closed her eyes and retraced the initials on the back of the ankh until the pattern was no longer smooth. She could feel the freshly cut maple in her hand and a sharp-edged rock in the other hand. There was a stench and a chill in the air. When Taylor finally opened her eyes, she could see the flicker of light coming through a grate adjacent to her. She held up the ankh so she could see the newly carved initials in the lantern's light. As she blew the sawdust away from the amulet she realized, *My God. I'm back in Salem.*

Chapter 30

I can't believe I'm back here. I wonder how it happened. . . . I wonder why it happened. Rebecca's back rested against the hard stone wall. She dropped the small stone she had been carving with, pocketed the ankh, then stood away from the straw-lined bench she had been sitting on. Rebecca couldn't see around the room very well, her vision was limited to where the lantern's light fell within the cell. At the walls, she felt the cool, damp stones, then a solid wooden door blocked her freedom. The door grate looked onto a hallway where a lantern flickered. Down the hall, she could see similar barred openings and from within the dungeon cells she could hear the cries from other prisoners.

The stench became overwhelming, and Taylor thought she was going to get sick. Just then, she realized how weak and hungry she was, and needed to sit. She was ill. Her hand felt her forehead, confirming she was feverish. It was then she realized that she was the source of the foul odor. *I wonder how long I'm going to be here.*

Why am I here? Maybe I'm here to find out what cycle needs to be broken. I need to remember what happened to me here. But—how?

Rebecca closed her eyes. *I need to remember. . . .* Within minutes, memories started flooding back. She recalled her marriage to Daniel, and the Osgoods alleging their child had been abducted, and then finding the Bradburys. She remembered that Daniel had been arrested in her place, and she had made an arrangement with Jacob Bradbury to exchange her freedom for Daniel's. She was arrested, and spent weeks here, waiting for a trial. But it wasn't much of a trial. She had admitted that she was a witch and was sentenced to be hanged . . . this morning.

I'm supposed to be hanged this morning. How come I can't remember anything that happened to me after this?

Suddenly, there was pounding at the door. "Stand back against the wall," a man's voice yelled.

Rebecca complied and backed against the wall while the large wooden door opened. When Daniel entered, she immediately recognized him and he ran to her taking her in his arms. *God, it's good to see you again, Daniel.* But when she looked up into his tired and worried eyes she realized, *Jessie, it is you.* There was no physical resemblance between Jessie and Daniel except their eyes. There was something in the eyes she could not explain. She had heard the expression once that the eyes were the windows to the soul. Now, she knew it to be true.

"I've missed you, so," Rebecca said as they embraced.

"God, I've missed you too, Rebecca."

"We don't have much time," John interrupted.

"Hi, John," Rebecca greeted.

John looked inquisitively over his head. "High?"

"I mean . . . good day, John."

"Good day, Rebecca. Let's quickly go over this," John instructed.

"Over what?" Rebecca asked.

"We're going to get you out of here," Daniel whispered.

"How?"

"I will return shortly. I'm going to take a hostage and swap him for your freedom," Daniel said.

"No," Rebecca objected. "It's too dangerous. I don't want to see anyone get hurt."

"I'm not going to hurt anyone, I promise," Daniel said.

"I don't want to see you get hurt."

Daniel smiled. "I'll be fine. You just be ready to move; do you understand?"

John had been standing near the door, listening for the approaching guard. "He is coming."

Seconds later there was a bang on the door, and the guard looked through the door grate. "Goodwife Johnson, stand against the wall."

Before she complied, she asked Daniel. "When is the execution scheduled?"

"High noon."

"How far off is that?"

"It's now just after sunrise."

Rebecca placed her hands on Daniel's chest, then kissed him goodbye. "In case I don't see you again–I love you, Daniel."

"You'll see me, again," he whispered in her ear. "I love you, too."

The door closed, separating Daniel and Rebecca. Rebecca could sense something dreadful was to happen. *My execution must be my destiny.*

Some time later, Rebecca could hear shouting outside the doorway. The voices were drawing closer. As instructed, she stood against the wall, waiting. The door opened and two guards walked in.

Rebecca could hear Daniel's voice from outside the doorway. "On the ground. Now," he barked. They got to their knees, then lay on the ground. "Rebecca, come out," Daniel said.

Rebecca looked outside the doorway and walked out. Daniel was holding a dagger to Jacob Bradbury's throat. As Rebecca walked through the door, Jacob's and Rebecca's eyes met, and she realized, *My God . . . it's Travis. Jacob is Travis.* Once Rebecca was safely outside, Daniel pushed Jacob into the cell. The solid door was quickly closed and locked.

Daniel picked up Rebecca in his arms and bolted. Cries for help from the men as well as other prisoners echoed in the hall as Daniel and Rebecca fled the dungeon. Out front, a horse was waiting. Daniel helped Rebecca climb on, then he mounted and they headed out of town. The horse trotted at a steady pace, not to draw attention to them. Rebecca glanced back at witches' hill, the execution site. She could see the gallows and the locust tree on top of the hill.

Once outside the town limits Daniel increased the pace. The horse ran hard for over an hour before the couple stopped at a pond to water the horse. Daniel quickly dismounted and helped Rebecca from the horse. As the horse drank, the couple embraced for the first time since their escape.

"Where are we going?" Rebecca asked weakly.

"We're going to meet John. He's waiting for us." Daniel pulled out some dried meat from a pouch and handed it to Rebecca.

"Thank you, Daniel." Rebecca hungrily gnawed at the meat.

They were back on their horse in no time. Two hours later, they arrived at a cottage set deep in the forest. No other cottages were in sight from this location. There was a clearing behind the cottage, and soon Rebecca realized that the house was near a lake. A covered wagon and horse stood in front of the small house, and John was waiting on the porch.

Rebecca had been feeling weaker by the minute. Daniel dismounted, and as he helped her off the horse, she collapsed in his arms.

He carried her quickly toward the house.

"What's wrong?" John asked.

"She's feverish. She's starved," Daniel carried her into the cabin.

A fire was going in the hearth, above it kettles of water steamed along with a kettle of stew. Daniel laid Rebecca on a bed in the corner of the room. A tub was next to the bed.

Rebecca's eyes opened. "I'm sorry . . ."

"Shh, don't be sorry. Can you eat? We have some stew."

Rebecca nodded. "I'll try." Slowly, she sat up and Daniel propped her with pillows. Then Daniel fed her.

After Rebecca ate she felt stronger, and she then expressed interest in a bath. Daniel and John poured the kettles of boiling water into the half-full tub. John left the cabin, and Daniel helped Rebecca remove her clothes and get into the tub.

After her bath, Daniel helped Rebecca into some clean clothes, then returned her to the bed. "Why don't you try to sleep for a little while," he suggested. Gently, Daniel kissed her lips.

* * *

When she awakened, she saw John sitting alone at the table. "Where's Daniel?" Rebecca asked. She sat up.

"He's fetching water for the horses. Should I get him?"

She shook her head. "No."

"How are you feeling?"

Rebecca stood. The dizziness that had been plaguing her was almost gone. "I feel like a new person." She sat at the table with John.

"That's a strange expression . . . feel like a new person."

Rebecca realized there was a language barrier between colonial New England and the twenty-first century. She smiled. "It just seemed right. Thank you for all your help, John." She looked around the one-room cabin. "Where are we?"

"This is Jacob Bradbury's summer cottage."

"Jacob Bradbury? He knows we're here?" Rebecca asked.

John nodded.

"Why would Bradbury help?"

"I don't understand either," John admitted. "If you ask me, he's risking much to help you."

"I guess you are, too." Rebecca smiled. "Thank you."

Daniel must have heard Rebecca's voice from outside because he abruptly entered the cabin. "Rebecca, how are you feeling?" He rushed to her side. He felt her forehead, then kissed it. "Your fever is down."

"I'm better." Rebecca's eyes met her husband's. She marveled at how similar they were to Jessie's. "Daniel, why would Jacob help?"

"I'm not sure," Daniel admitted. "After the trial, he approached me. He was very grateful that you didn't disclose the information about Ann. The hostage scenario was his idea. He said we could use his cottage, to get you better before we travel. Both John and I have been working the last three days getting a wagon ready. I think he's a good person. That's all."

He is a good person. Rebecca recalled the time she went to Jacob and proposed to swap herself for her husband's freedom. *What happened to Travis? How can people be so different from incarnation to incarnation?*

"We left Travis–I mean . . . Jacob in the dungeon. When will he be freed?"

"I'm sure he's free, now," John said.

"How do you know?" Rebecca asked.

"At high noon, nine people, including yourself, were to be executed," John stated. "I'm sure when they retrieved the prisoners, the guards and Jacob were freed."

"Nine people executed?" Rebecca's heart sank. *How could it have gotten so out of control?*

"Eight now," John corrected.

"What's the date, Daniel?"

"It is the 22nd day of September. Why?" Daniel asked.

The last executions were in September. "How long have I been imprisoned?"

"Over two months."

"Two months? Where are we going, now?"

"We're heading to a town called Framingham. I've heard that a woman named Sarah Clayes escaped from jail and fled to Framingham. Many others that are running from this witch-hunt are fleeing there. If it's not safe, we'll keep heading west. We can stay here for the evening then leave in the morning at first light."

"I'll leave in the morning also, and head back to Salem," John said.

Daniel was reminded that he would be leaving his friend and did not know when he'd see him again.

Daniel took Rebecca's hand and led her back toward the bed. "Rebecca, why don't you rest? You'll need your strength for traveling."

Rebecca knew Daniel was right; she was very tired. She climbed onto the straw mattress and lay down.

"John and I will be right outside. We have some more work to do on the wagon." Daniel held her hands and his lips met them. "I love you."

"I love you," Rebecca said.

John and Daniel left the cabin and Rebecca became lost in her thoughts. *Why am I here? What do I need to learn?* She thought of her life as Rebecca and wondered what impact her past had had on her life as Taylor. The lyrics from "Daniel's Heart," came to mind.

. . .

Just because you didn't understand me
doesn't excuse the inference.
We're all the same on the inside,
can't you see beyond our difference?

But instead, you choose intolerance,
bigotry and hate.
Eventually, you try,
judge, and eradicate.

Just because you didn't understand me
doesn't justify the pain.
We're all the same on the inside,
I tell you, we're all the same.

. . .

I knew "Daniel's Heart" was about respecting individual differences. But I never would have guessed its genesis was from being persecuted, because I was a witch. But . . . why am I here?

Rebecca fell into a deep sleep and was later awakened by a knocking sound. She opened her eyes and looked around the cabin. *I'm still here.* Judging by the light of the room, she thought it was close to sunset. She sat up too fast and became dizzy. "Daniel?" she called out. There was another knock on the door, and it opened.

When Rebecca's eyes adjusted from her lightheadedness, she saw Jacob Bradbury standing quietly next to the door, staring at her.

Rebecca felt a lump in her throat. She didn't quite understand why, and then she remembered. *This is Travis.* "Jacob, what are you doing here?" She stood.

"How are you, Rebecca?"

Rebecca nodded. "I'm well. Are you alone?"

"Yes."

There was an uncomfortable pause. "Why are you here?" Rebecca asked.

Jacob ignored her question. "I'm glad to see that you're safe."

"Jacob, I can't help but wonder—why did you help us? I mean . . . you have so much to lose if someone finds out."

"I do have much to lose," Jacob agreed. Then he changed the subject. "I came because I need to see your husband. It's important."

"He's outside. I'm surprised you didn't see him." As Rebecca said it, pictures flashed through her head of Daniel and John at the waterfront. Daniel seemed to be tense. *That was strange.* "Maybe he's down by the water."

"I'll wait. If you don't mind."

"Jacob, this is your house. May I ask what is so important that you rode out all this way to see him?"

Jacob hesitated then he shrugged his shoulders. "There was an anonymous letter written that implicated Daniel in witchcraft."

"Oh, I remember, the letter that disappeared the morning of Daniel's hearing. I didn't realize it was anonymous."

"I have the letter." He pulled it from his pocket. "I wanted to give it to him."

"Why don't you just burn it?"

"There's something about the letter that is bothersome."

"What is it?"

"One of the reasons the letter had so much bearing on the case against your husband is that it was written on special stationery."

"What do you mean by special stationery?"

"It was written on stationery used by Governor Phips's office only."

"Really?"

"So the belief among the judges was that the accusation was coming from someone within the Governor's office."

"Which is why it was regarded so highly."

"Yes."

"May I have the letter please?"

Jacob hesitated.

"I don't need to read it." She held out her hand. "I just need to feel it."

Jacob placed the letter in Rebecca's tiny hand. She covered the letter with her other hand and closed her eyes. In her mind's eye pictures came to her. She saw the back of a man sitting at a desk. There was a lantern on the desk. Rebecca could see the man's well-manicured hand writing the letter. He methodically dipped the ink at the end of each line. After he closed the letter anonymously, his fingers moved to his whiskers and twisted the ends of his mustache. And then she saw him. Intently, Rebecca looked into his eyes, and finally saw what she had been missing. *It's Mark.*

"Oh my God. It's John. John Price wrote the letter," Rebecca said in disbelief.

"That's what I feared. I keep stationery like this in my temporary office in Salem Town. While I was in the dungeon, I remembered that your lawyer works in the office next to mine. Then I knew I needed to tell Daniel before you left."

The images of John and Daniel came back to Rebecca. She grabbed Jacob's arm to steady herself.

"What's wrong?" Jacob asked.

"They're together. I can see them."

"John is here?"

"Yes. They're at the waterfront." Fear overwhelmed her. "Something is wrong." She could see that John had something in his arms. Then she realized what it was. "Oh my God, John has a musket."

Both Jacob and Rebecca bolted for the door. Once outside, Jacob ran to his horse and removed a musket while Rebecca ran to the back toward the water. Jacob quickly caught up with her. A late afternoon shower had started, making the ground slippery. They ran down the embankment, which had a modest grade and led them toward the water. Jacob, being familiar with the terrain, passed Rebecca and maneuvered effectively between the trees and down the hill. It was just before sundown, and the shadows from the trees contributed to the eerie feeling in the woods.

They must have been about forty feet from the water when Jacob stopped behind a tree. He pulled Rebecca next to him. Jacob placed a finger on his lips. "Shh," he whispered.

Rebecca's heart was beating so hard it hurt in her throat. They strained their ears and could hear muffled voices in the distance. Jacob rested the heavy weapon on the ground and inspected it, assuring that the weapon was properly loaded. Then he picked up the musket, took Rebecca's hand, and the two inched their way through the trees until Daniel and John were in their sight. They got as close as twenty feet from them and still remained camouflaged by the dense trees.

The men were standing by the water. Daniel was about seven feet from John with a musket pointed at his chest.

"Sorry it has to be this way, friend," John said. "It wasn't supposed to be like this. You were supposed to be hanged, remember?"

Daniel stared at John. His voice was calm. "What are you talking about?"

"I knew you would protect Rebecca and take the blame. I just didn't expect that she would be so stubborn and turn herself in."

"Did you . . . you did. You're the one that sent that letter claiming I was a wizard."

John laughed.

"Why? We've known each other all our lives. Why John?"

"I want her."

"You want who?"

"Rebecca, of course."

"What makes you think she wants you?"

"She will. When she learns you've abruptly run off, who else will take care of her and flee the area with her? Now you would save me much trouble if you can walk with me to find a gravesite."

"I will not." But as Daniel said it, he saw something move in his peripheral vision. His focus was taken off the barrel of John's musket for just a second, but long enough to see Rebecca.

Daniel's heart started beating wildly when he realized Rebecca was within danger. He never saw Jacob advancing to get a better shot at John. The sound of breaking twigs from beneath Jacob's boots got John's attention.

"Who's out there?" John yelled.

John turned and Daniel lunged for the barrel of the gun and the two men struggled for control. Daniel stood between Jacob and John, obstructing Jacob's shot. As Daniel and John struggled with the musket between them, Daniel searched John's eyes. He saw something that he had not seen before. It startled him; it was evil. When the gun went off, Daniel could feel the tissue shred from his chest.

As Daniel sank to his knees, he heard another shot. A bullet pierced John in the heart and John toppled near him.

"Oh God," Rebecca cried, and she ran to Daniel.

Blood soiled Daniel's chest; Rebecca opened his shirt to view the wound. When she saw the open chest she knew it was too late. She cradled Daniel in her arms and gently rocked him, her tears camouflaged by the pouring rain.

Daniel's eyes met Jacob's as Jacob knelt next to Daniel. "Take care of her," Daniel whispered.

"I will," Jacob promised. Then he gave Rebecca some privacy.

The pain in Daniel's chest subsided. He could feel life seep from his body. He gazed into Rebecca's eyes, "I love you," he said weakly.

Rebecca's eyes closed, shedding her tears. "I love you too, Daniel."

"I'll wait . . ." His last words were cut short. Although his eyes remained staring at Rebecca, she knew he was no longer there.

The sun burst through a break between the clouds just above the mountaintop across from the lake. Daniel's face lit up as the rain poured. Rebecca looked up at the sun setting over the mountain across the lake. A brilliant rainbow formed, stretching from the lake to the sky above the mountain. The vivid landscape would forever remain engraved in Rebecca's mind.

As Rebecca cradled Daniel's body in her arms, the familiar words came to her over and over. *"The cycle must end. The cycle must end."* Now she knew exactly what needed to end as other past-life memories flooded back to her. Each past-life memory showed her relationship with Daniel tragically ending at the hand of John. And then, she thought of Jessie.

I need to end the cycle. As she thought it, she realized she was sitting under the moonlight in the desert with her treasured ankh in her hand.

* * *

Chapter 31

As Jessie walked the dark beach, she pressed the numbers on the satellite phone. She was careful to avoid occasional rocks in her path, along with the cactuses and shrubs. Each time she pressed 911, she hoped to make a connection. And each time she tried, she knew she was heading further downstream, toward Grapevine Rapid.

The roar from the rapids was getting louder, and most of the soft sand had been replaced with larger rocks. Jessie pressed redial and listened intently over Grapevine's growl, only to hear nothing, over and over until . . . there was a ring. But as soon as she heard it, it was gone.

Jessie tried it again. It rang, and then, "This is 911. What's the nature of the emergency?"

"Oh, thank God." But Jessie could tell the reception was bad. "I'm not sure how long this signal is going to last," she shouted. "We need a helicopter evacuation immediately."

"Your location?"

"We're in the Grand Canyon. We're on a rafting trip with Grand Canyon White Water. We're around mile 81, just upstream of Grapevine Rapid, on the south side. A man is having a heart attack."

Jessie heard static coming from the other end.

"Can you hear me? We need help."

". . . can . . . hear . . . insurance . . . name?"

"I don't know if you can hear me. I'm catching every couple of your words. We need an immediate air evacuation. We have a man down with what appears to be a heart attack. We're in the Grand Canyon, in the inner gorge, just upstream of Grapevine Rapid. Can you hear me?"

"Yes, we got that. What's your name?"

"This is Jessie Mercer," Jessie said without thinking. *Shit. I gave her my name.*

"Will you be able to signal the helicopter?"

"I think we have a flare gun." But Jessie did not get a response after that. "Hello? Do you hear me? Hello?" Her connection had been broken. *Well, at least I got through.*

Jessie turned back in the direction she had come from and quickened her pace. Preoccupied with thoughts of the evening, she stumbled over a rock on the riverbank and fell to her knees. "God. I'm so clumsy." Jessie stood, then leaned to brush the sand from her knees. When she straightened, a man stood directly in her path. Jessie's heart beat wildly at the sight of the figure in front of her. Then she recognized Mark. "Mark. You scared the shit out of me," she said.

Mark offered no apology. "It is dangerous out here." There was chill in his tone that surprised Jessie.

"Yes. Let's get back to the camp."

"Did you reach 911?"

"Yes. I did."

"Good."

The canyon was different in the dark, somehow creepy. At this hour, the moon had not quite cleared the canyon walls.

As Jessie walked past Mark, she could feel him turn with her and follow close behind. Jessie sensed something was wrong, but she didn't know what. Before she could do anything, Mark had seized her throat. It took Jessie a few seconds before she realized that Mark's forearm and upper arm were crushing her windpipe. He dragged her to the river. Jessie tried to pull his arm from around her throat, but the more she resisted the harder Mark's grip became around her neck.

The cold water crept to Jessie's ankles, then knees, then waist. The roar of the rushing rapids was getting louder. Jessie could feel herself weaken with each passing moment. In desperation, she reached into her pockets for anything that could help. She removed the crystal she had found at the quartz vein earlier that day, and plunged the pointed rock into Mark's forearm. Mark flinched from the pain, releasing some pressure off Jessie's trachea, giving her an opportunity to fight back. Gasping for air, she thrust the crystal further into his arm and pried herself free. But when Jessie turned, she wasn't prepared for the handgun Mark bashed against her cheek, causing her to fall back into the rushing water.

In moments, the current took Jessie's limp body into the raging rapids of Grapevine. Mark watched as she was swept into the uncontrollable white water. She quickly disappeared into the night.

The current sucked Jessie under. It took all her strength to keep her head above water, but Grapevine's force was too powerful; she was failing. Her chest hurt from the lack of air. She thought her lungs were going to explode and then her body thrashed against an obstacle. Jessie gasped and cried out in pain, as she clung to the boulder she had collided with. Intense pain suggested she had broken a rib. The violent water crashed against her, attempting to carry her downstream.

The moonlight had cleared the canyon wall and Jessie could see that she was about twenty feet from the river's edge. About twenty-five feet downstream the current changed from white water to running water. Jessie knew she couldn't hold onto the boulder much longer, and with that thought, she was swept downstream.

Jessie fought to keep her head above water. The current sucked her under and pulled her downstream. She knew the water's rage would subside, but she didn't know when. Her lungs felt like they were going to burst, and she didn't think she could last any longer.

"You can do it, Jessie. Don't give up," the voice in her head lectured. *"Just a little longer."*

I don't think I can. But then, the rage of the water weakened. Jessie found herself struggling to reach the surface. Her lungs hurt. She feared she would pass out. Just when she thought she could not hold on any longer, she surfaced. She gasped for air. Jessie knew she still wasn't safe. The current was swift, and it wouldn't be long before hypothermia set in.

With *every* ounce of strength, Jessie moved to the shore. It was a slow and painful journey. The current continued to carry her downstream, past the rafts and then some. By the time she reached the shore, she was unable to move. She lay motionless on the riverbank, her body beaten.

I've got to warn Taylor. With the thought, she tried to sit. *God, I'm sore.* The laceration on Jessie's arm was bleeding again, and Jessie could now feel the tear on her cheek from where Mark's gun had struck her.

As Jessie tried to rise, she felt a sharp pain in her ribs. Then she heard footsteps coming from upstream, taking her mind off her pain. *My God. He's looking for me.*

Jessie turned and moved downstream. She knew she didn't have far to go before she reached the trail that led up the inner canyon. But as she entered the inner canyon, the darkness swallowed her. The high canyon walls prevented the moon's light from reaching the trail.

I can't hike this in the dark. It was hard enough during daylight. Jessie moved back toward the river, only to see Mark combing the area. She quickly ducked back inside the inner canyon. *I've been through here before. I would have an advantage over him.*

Jessie quickly moved up the trail. With her arms in front of her, she groped forward, trying to recall the path from earlier that day. The first fifty feet were very treacherous. It was a steep rocky trail, then the canyon widened, enabling some light to filter into the inner canyon.

About halfway up the trail, Jessie thought she heard something. Quietly, she found a dark area along the canyon wall and listened. The noise repeated, and then she saw him. The figure moved into sight. As Jessie squatted behind a boulder, Mark moved to within fifteen feet of her then he stood still.

Jessie held her breath. She was afraid that her breathing might draw attention to herself. Her heart pounded wildly within her chest, and the throbbing from the injured rib made her position uncomfortable.

To Jessie, it seemed that Mark stood there forever. Then, he turned and walked slowly down the trail. Jessie resisted the temptation to run. Just when Mark was out of sight, that little voice warned, *"Jessie, stay put."*

Seconds later, Mark appeared down the trail. He looked up the inner canyon, and then he finally disappeared around an outcropping. *He knows I'm here.* Jessie squatted patiently behind the boulder, in the dark. Occasionally, the thought of rattlesnakes and scorpions popped into her head. She wondered if she was running from one predator, while others waited for her in the shadows.

Once satisfied that Mark had left, Jessie stood, then turned uphill. She continued her ascent, but stayed within the shadows along the walls. Occasionally she stopped, listened, and she thought she heard footsteps following. But most of the time, she heard only her heavy breathing that aggravated her injured rib.

Jessie knew she was getting close to the top by the disappearing canyon wall. Up until this point, she chose to climb within the shadows, fearing that Mark lurked down the trail. But now, fifty feet from the summit, the full moon illuminated the rest of the way. Before she plunged into the moonlight, she stopped and listened. Once satisfied that she didn't hear Mark, she stepped from the shadows, but quickened her pace, fearing that she was too exposed. About ten feet from the top, Jessie stepped on a loose rock; the rock fell, bouncing steadily down the trail. To Jessie, the noise was terrifyingly loud. Her heart pounded. Impulsively she ran up the last of the trail. As she reached the summit, she turned and looked down the path. Mark emerged from the shadows and was making his way up the trail.

Jessie turned and ran along the plateau, back in the direction of the camp. Most of the terrain was flat. To her left was a slight incline that followed to the cliff where the Colorado River ran three hundred feet below. To her right, she could see the rise of another wall, another four hundred feet above. But since Jessie had been here only hours earlier, she remembered that an abyss lay between the plateau and the rising canyon wall. Shadows spread from the canyon wall to the plateau, concealing where the plateau ended and the abyss began. Jessie felt trapped. There was no place to hide, except among the shadows.

In desperation, she retreated to the dark. She stepped a couple of feet out of the moonlight and into the shadows, and once again, the eerie feeling returned. At a steady pace, she moved in the direction of the camp. She tripped over a rock and fell on her hands, scraping her palms. She brushed her raw hands together, shaking the tiny pebbles away from the torn skin. As Jessie squatted, she sensed danger but didn't know what it was from. She searched the ground until she found a pebble. Jessie picked it up, closed her eyes.

"*Right side.*" That little voice warned her.

Instinctively she tossed the small stone to her right about three feet away. She never heard the rock collide with the stone floor, fifty feet below.

Holy shit. When she opened her eyes, she realized the moon was peeking over the high walls, revealing where she was. To her right she could now see that she had been walking parallel to a cliff and about six feet in front of her the precipice shifted directly in her path and ran to the left of her. *My God. If I didn't fall, I would have run right off the cliff. Thank you. I guess it wasn't my time.*

Jessie stood and turned to back out of the area, but then she saw him. The moonlight exposed the barrel of the gun that pointed in her face. *This just seems too familiar*, she thought. *Déjà vu? When?* "It was you all along."

Mark laughed.

"How did you kill Kurk?"

"It was a pretty good murder, wasn't it?"

"How did you do it?"

"Patience. That's how I did it. I had patience. Over a six-month period I swapped expired EpiPens in every handbag that Taylor owned."

"So when Kurk really needed it, it wouldn't work."

"Right."

"But there was no evidence that Kurk digested peanuts. How did the protein get in his mouth?"

"Now that is the beauty of the crime," Mark bragged. "Before I saw Kurk that night, I had some peanuts at the bar. After that, I just simply shook his hand."

"He had an allergic reaction just by touching you?"

"Yes."

"Your cologne was very strong that night. I remember now. Was that to hide the peanut smell?"

"It was great, think about it. Kurk goes into shock about an hour after I shook his hand, you hand Taylor an expired EpiPen, and then, since I was the only one in the group with any medical experience, it only seemed right that I helped Taylor."

"Kurk's tongue was swollen. He couldn't breath so you used your fingers to open his air passageway."

"Yes."

"That's what killed him. The protein on your fingers was transferred to his mouth. Why? Why did you do it?"

"The same reason I'm going to kill you."

Jessie realized just how vulnerable she was. She was alone in the desert with a madman pointing a gun at her head. The cliffs surrounded her, with her only safe passage blocked by Mark. "You wrote the letters, too."

"Guilty."

"How did you get my stationery?"

"That day Travis and I visited your home before filming began. I had a phone call and went to your office for privacy. After snooping around, I found the stationery. It was perfect."

"What about the lifejacket?"

"Guilty."

"How?"

"Potassium hydroxide. It's caustic and corrodes thread, not synthetics. I just applied some to your jacket threads and straps. So in the rage of a rapid, the seams just disintegrated. You were supposed to have the jacket on, not Taylor."

"That's why the lifejackets reeked the other night. I thought it was from the body odor. And that's why you were coughing; it had nothing to do with allergies. But . . . why? Why on earth would you carry potassium hydroxide?"

"I learned about it in my pre-med days, and I always found this chemical intriguing. It's a poison, an irritant, and corrosive." A sinister smile came to Mark's lips, "You never know when you can use a chemical of such diverse properties."

The sound of a helicopter was approaching. It was a Blackhawk, a military helicopter with night vision. Mark and Jessie could see the bird come closer, hover over the camp area and then disappear as it landed below.

"And you were going to let Travis be the scapegoat."

"Not initially. You were going to be it, but Travis just walked into it. So, poor Travis will die from a heart attack and you'll walk off a cliff in the dark. Now, turn around," Mark ordered.

Jessie did not move; she searched for an escape route. "And then you'll have Taylor. That's what this is all about. Isn't it?"

"We're meant to be together. She just can't see it when others are around."

"So, you're going to kill me. How do you propose to do it? You've been too careful this far to put a bullet in me. And you know I'm not going to walk off a cliff or let you push me off."

Jessie could see the boyish grin she used to love. "Well, I could make it relatively painless for you. I'll knock you on the head and throw you over a cliff."

"Now you know me better than that, Mark."

"Yes, I do. Or . . . you can run but I'll get you and make it all that much more painful for you. Eventually I'll win and splatter your brains against the canyon rock walls."

Jessie smiled. "And what do you think my odds are?" But Jessie didn't give Mark a chance to answer. She bolted to her right, directly toward the precipice that she almost ran off. At the ledge, she jumped, barely clearing the four-foot wide chasm.

"So, you choose the pain." Mark yelled and chased after her.

Jessie ran. She could hear Mark follow close behind. He was fast and Jessie was no match for him with her injured rib. Mark tackled her to the ground; the two landed together on the hard surface; Jessie's body cushioned his fall.

Mark's arms curled around Jessie from behind, restricting the use of her arms. Roughly, he picked her up and dragged her to the cliff. Jessie dug her heels deeply into the rocky soil, desperately fighting to save her life. When she kicked his lower leg, he groaned in pain, and then slammed her body to the hard surface, which momentarily stunned her.

"I gave you a choice," he said sternly. "The easy road or this." Mark slapped Jessie's face, then he picked up her injured body and dragged her to the cliff. Although Jessie continued to fight back, Mark was much stronger. He was within a couple feet of the cliff when he heard a voice.

"Let her go, Mark."

Mark could see Taylor's silhouette about fifteen feet away.

"Taylor?"

The sound from the helicopter grew louder as it lifted and swung overhead, carrying Travis's body away.

"Yes, it's me, Mark. Let Jessie go."

"I can't."

"Mark, killing Jessie is not going to make it so that I'll be with you."

"Yes. It will. I know you can't see it yet, but we're meant to be together. It's our destiny."

"Why do you believe this is so?"

"I know it's right. We just need to eliminate all your other influences."

"And that's what you've been doing for how many lifetimes?"

Mark looked at Taylor. "You remember?"

"I remember that you have killed my partners in many lifetimes, all to be with me. But each lifetime has ended tragically and I have never been with you." Taylor inched closer. "Mark, this time is going to be different."

"It is, isn't it?"

"Yes. Something needs to be done so that this pattern won't repeat itself next lifetime."

"And what do you propose?"

Taylor walked closer. "Let her go, we need to talk."

"No." He repositioned Jessie so that she stood in front of him now, with his arm pinned around her neck. "We're all family, talk."

Taylor moved to within a couple feet of Mark. "If you don't kill Jessie, and I stay with you, the cycle would be broken."

If you stay with him, he won't have to kill me, Jessie thought; *I'll kill my-self.*

My God, I heard that, Taylor thought. *Is that you, Jessie?*

Jessie's eyes met Taylor's. *Yes.*

"So, if I don't kill Jessie, you'll be with me?" Mark asked.

"That would seem to be one way to end the cycle," Taylor admitted. Taylor walked even closer to Mark. She could see how close they were to the edge of a cliff.

"That's far enough," Mark said.

"I need to talk with you, Mark. I don't want Jessie to hear this," Taylor said.

Mark repositioned Jessie's body to his right side, lending his left ear.

Taylor approached so that she was within inches of both Jessie and Mark. She leaned forward to his ear and whispered. "There's only one other way I know to break this cycle and guarantee it'll never happen again."

"What makes you think I don't want it to happen again?"

"I believe you do want this to happen again," Taylor whispered. "But I don't." Taylor's voice got louder. "I don't love you, Mark. I never will." Taylor's movements were swift. Her right arm came from behind her back. "And I'll never be with you. So this is the only way I know to end this–"

Taylor pulled the trigger on the flare pistol and the flare exploded into Mark's chest. His eyes opened wide with shock and his clothes quickly burst into flames. Taylor fell back, horrified, but only a moment. She reached out to Jessie, but Mark's arm remained latched around Jessie's neck as he fell back toward the rim of the precipice. The flames started to engulf Mark's body. Jessie freed herself from his rigid arm just as her body hit the edge of the precipice, crushing her already injured rib cage. Mark went over the cliff, colliding with the cliff walls and falling to his death.

Jessie clutched at the stone, grasping for something to cling to as her body slid from the rock face. Just as she was about to plunge over the cliff, Taylor grabbed hold of Jessie's hand and stopped her from falling. Slowly, Taylor managed to pull Jessie's body away from the edge, to safety.

Jessie painfully crawled to the ledge to see Mark's body still ablaze on the floor of the abyss. She returned to Taylor and sat next to her.

"I don't think he'll want to repeat that any time soon," Jessie said. "Thank you, Taylor."

"I'm sorry, Jessie. I should never have doubted you." Taylor brushed Jessie's hair away from her face, exposing the dry blood on her cheek. Gently she embraced Jessie's beaten body, grateful that she was safe in her arms. When they finally parted, Taylor's eyes met Jessie's, then they strayed to her lips. Taylor found Jessie's lips and they kissed, sealing their promise to be together, forever, once again.

Chapter 32

"How did you know about Mark being in your past lives?" Jessie asked.

Taylor couldn't take her eyes off of Jessie's. She felt closer to her than she had before. "Remember my reading?"

Jessie nodded.

"Karen said that I needed to break a pattern or a cycle."

"Yes. I remember," Jessie said. "She said someone from a past life was bringing you danger. And this person's love for you was misguided."

"I feared that person was you," Taylor admitted. "But it was Mark."

"But how did you find out?"

"The strangest thing happened to me, Jessie. After you and Mark went off to call 911, I went to get my flashlight from my bag. I came across the ankh you gave me. Jessie, it was mine . . . in Salem."

"It was?"

"I went . . . back to Salem. I don't understand how, but I did it. I was there. I went to the time when I carved the initials 'RJ' in the ankh. I was in a jail cell, and it was the morning I was to be executed."

"Oh God, you didn't go through an execution. Did you?" Jessie was horrified.

Taylor's blue eyes lit up and she shook her head. "I was never executed."

Jessie smiled with relief. "You were never executed?"

"No. Jessie I recognized you; it wasn't that Daniel looked anything like you do. I could see you in Daniel's eyes. I also recognized Travis and Mark."

"They were there?"

"Yes."

"Who were they?"

"Travis was Jacob Bradbury, and Mark was John Price."

"John? My best friend?"

"Yes."

"Tell me what happened. Please?"

"You broke me out of jail and we escaped. We met up with John at Jacob's cottage. Jacob suspected that John was the one that framed you. You and John were at the lake and Jacob and I went to find you. But . . ."

"But what?"

"John ended up killing you and then Jacob killed John."

Jessie stared off into the darkness. "It was a chest wound, right?"

"Yes. Do you remember?"

"When I had my past-life regression, the first place I went to I was severely injured and distressed, so Carrie brought me someplace else . . . our wedding day." Jessie moved slightly and a sharp pain came to her rib cage. The pain showed on her face.

"Are you okay, Jessie?" Now that the two were sitting next to each other, Taylor could see how badly Jessie's body was bruised and cut.

"Yeah. I'll be fine."

"The psychic, Karen, was right about a lot of things."

"She was," Jessie agreed.

"Remember she told me that I was suppressing my belief in the metaphysical because I was either persecuted or executed in a past life?"

"Yes."

"When I was there, Jessie, I could hear things and see things, or just know things. I know now that I didn't believe in it because of what happened to you in Salem. I could never forgive myself for putting our family in jeopardy, and then for losing you."

"And that's why you suppressed your intuitiveness, even though you've really been using it all along."

"You're right. I used it to find you here tonight. When I came back from Salem, I knew I needed to find you. If I had followed my logic, I would have gone to the river. But I listened to the voices."

A noise from behind Taylor and Jessie startled them. They turned and saw a figure approaching. Both were surprised when they recognized Detective Bradley.

"Detective Bradley?" Taylor asked.

The man had been standing behind them for some time. He walked to the women, pistol in hand, then put the pistol in his holster. He studied the women. "Where's Mark Rutledge?"

"What are you doing here?" Jessie asked.

"I got a call from Mark Rutledge. He said he was on the rafting trip with Travis Sanders and Ms. Andrews, and you crashed the party." Bradley pointed at Jessie. "Although he was concerned about you, I was more concerned about Travis Sanders. We've connected Travis to Stacey Hopkins's death. We've also learned that Kurk Warner was blackmailing Sanders, giving Sanders a motive for Kurk's murder.

"I just happened to arrive at the Grand Canyon Airport when the emergency call came in and the helicopter was being dispatched. When I heard that Jessie Mercer made the 911 call, I pulled a few strings to take a ride. Now, where is Mark Rutledge?"

Taylor and Jessie pointed over the ledge. The detective leaned over and viewed something aglow on the cliff floor. "What the hell happened?"

"Mark was Kurk's murderer and Taylor's harasser," Jessie said.

"Mark?" Bradley eyed the women skeptically.

"How is Travis?" Taylor asked.

"He was stable when the copter left."

"Great," Jessie said.

Taylor saw the distrust in the detective's eyes. "Detective Bradley, Mark murdered Kurk."

The detective continued to study the women, then turned to Jessie. "Tell me about *Deceptions.*"

"What about it?" Jessie asked.

"Was it precognitive?"

"You've been following that theory?" Jessie asked.

The detective nodded. "There are a lot of coincidences between the two of your lives and your story."

"So, you didn't really suspect me then?"

"You were a suspect, but no I didn't really suspect you. So, was it? Was it precognitive?"

Jessie and Taylor looked at each other. Jessie nodded. "Yes, it was."

"But wouldn't that make Taylor the murderer? How do I know the two of you didn't kill Mark Rutledge because he found out about it?"

"Detective Bradley, I knew all along that Taylor didn't do it, because I wrote the novel before the screenplay."

"The novel?"

"In the novel, Nicole's best friend framed her," Taylor said.

"Travis thought the end of the story would have more commercial appeal if the lover framed Nicole."

"And I saw the movie three times," Bradley said.

"Should have read the book," Jessie said.

Bradley offered Taylor a hand. As he pulled her up, Taylor's eyes met the detective's. There was familiarity that she had not seen before. As Bradley helped Jessie up, a picture flashed in Taylor's head. She saw a judge's desk, dressed with a tapestry illustrating the king's crown.

Stoughton? Taylor wondered. The detective turned back to Taylor. She looked into his eyes again. *It is Stoughton.*

"Detective?" Taylor asked.

"Yes?"

"How do you feel about colonial New England?" *This is going to be fun.*

About the Author

Alex Marcoux, author of *Façades,* was born in Leominster, Massachusetts. In 1981, she graduated with a degree in Food Science from the University of Massachusetts, at Amherst. In recognition for *Façades,* Alex was presented a Rocky Mountain Fiction Writers' Pen Award. *Back to Salem* is her second novel.

Alex resides in the foothills of Colorado with her partner and son. She is currently working on the sequel to *Back to Salem,* another paranormal mystery featuring Jessie Mercer. For more information about Alex and her work, visit her Website at *www.alexmarcoux.com.*